"Habere, non haberi."

PENGUIN CLASSICS

PLEASURE

GABRIELE D'ANNUNZIO (1863–1938) was the most influential and controversial Italian author of the twentieth century and a prominent figure in European Decadent literature. Born in Pescara, Abruzzo, to a wealthy bourgeois family, he was a brilliant student who acquired a solid humanistic cultural base—Latin, Greek, ancient literature, Italian, French, German, and English. He published his first book, a collection of poems, at the age of sixteen, and over the course of his life he wrote several novels, collections of poetry, and plays.

During his long public career, D'Annunzio played a central role in many of the major historical events of his day, working not only as a writer but also as a journalist, a fighter pilot, and a politician. His nationalistic rhetoric and charismatic leadership of the Italian Regency of Carnaro helped set the stage for Mussolini's fascism. D'Annunzio died in Gardone Riviera, at his estate on Lake Garda, having greatly influenced the literature and politics of his time.

LARA GOCHIN RAFFAELLI is an honorary research associate at the University of Cape Town in South Africa.

ALEXANDER STILLE is a frequent contributor on Italy to *The New York Review of Books, The New York* [illegible] *The New Yorker* and the author of [illegible] *Sack of Rome.* He lives in N[illegible]

GABRIELE
D'ANNUNZIO

Pleasure

Translated with a Foreword and Notes by
LARA GOCHIN RAFFAELLI

Introduction by ALEXANDER STILLE

PENGUIN BOOKS

PENGUIN BOOKS

Published by the Penguin Group
Penguin Group (USA) Inc., 375 Hudson Street,
New York, New York 10014, USA

USA / Canada / UK / Ireland / Australia / New Zealand / India / South Africa / China
Penguin Books Ltd, Registered Offices: 80 Strand, London WC2R 0RL, England
For more information about the Penguin Group visit penguin.com

This translation first published in Penguin Books 2013

Questo libro è stato tradotto grazie a un contributo alla traduzione assegnato dal Ministero degli Affari Esteri italiano.
This book has been translated thanks to a contribution to the translation awarded by the Italian Ministry of Foreign Affairs.

LIBRARY OF CONGRESS CATALOGING-IN-PUBLICATION DATA
D'Annunzio, Gabriele, 1863–1938.
[Piacere. English]
Pleasure / Gabriele D'Annunzio ; Translated with a Foreword and Notes by Lara Gochin Raffaelli ;
Introduction by Alexander Stille.
pages cm.—(Penguin classics)
Includes bibliographical references.
ISBN 978-0-14-310674-6
I. Title.
PQ4803.P513 2013
853'.912—dc23 2013006549

Printed in the United States of America
3 5 7 9 10 8 6 4 2

Dedicated with love, appreciation, and respect to the memory of Professor Nelia (Cornelia) Cacace Saxby, who taught, mentored, and unceasingly inspired me from 1986 to 2010 and died far too young, long before I could learn a fraction of what she knew

Contents

Foreword

This translation project began in April 2009,[1] when I decided to teach Gabriele D'Annunzio's novel *Il piacere* in translation, for a module of the "Aspects of Eros from Sappho to Cyber" course offered by the Classics section of the School of Languages and Literatures at the University of Cape Town, South Africa.

Set mainly in Rome, *Il piacere* was published in 1889 and found great success with the Roman public, despite the publisher's initial alarm at the many scandalous passages in the book.[2] It is considered the first Italian Decadent novel and to this day is regarded as a classic of Italian literature.

It was translated into English in 1898 with the title *The Child of Pleasure* by Georgina Harding, who followed the example of the French translation, *L'enfant de volupté,* carried out by Georges Hérelle under D'Annunzio's supervision and published the year before.

With only a few days left to the beginning of lectures, I discovered that the English version had been heavily bowdlerized by Miss Harding, who cut out any allusions of a sexual nature or indeed of any nature that could offend Victorian sensibilities. It was clear that I could not teach, in a course commonly referred to as "Sex," a book with no sex in it. I had no alternative but to begin translating all the "sexy bits" from the original Italian, and to give these to my students on a separate document to integrate into Harding's version. At the end of the course, since I had compiled a substantial mass of translated text, and because of the interest students had shown in the book, I thought it would be a good idea to republish the book with my sexy bits added. At that stage, my idea was simply to take Harding's text and reintegrate my translated sections where they were missing.

In translating *Il piacere* into English, Georgina Harding was advised by Arthur Symons to follow the structure of the French translation. This radically changed the structure of the original novel in Italian. Symons wrote the introduction to the translation and also translated all the sonnets into English. But, John Woodhouse notes, it was Harding who made all the decisions to excise aspects of the text on her own. Woodhouse and George Schoolfield have dedicated much attention to the extensive changes Harding made in her translation. Schoolfield counts twenty-five major omissions[3] and writes, "The English translation omits a great many passages that would have shocked a late Victorian reader's sensibilities; on the flyleaf of the copy in Yale's Sterling Library, an unknown hand has written: "Beware of translations by Victorian ladies."[4] Woodhouse points out that it was understandable that "the sanitized version offered to the Victorian reading public would omit voyeuristic descriptions of the naked Elena being seduced by the libidinous Andrea; also understandably excised was any characterization of the sadistic and perverted tastes in literature and art of the noble Englishman, Heathfield."[5] Woodhouse ascribes some of the cuts to the translator's "usual modesty";[6] others he sees as being amusing examples of the "bourgeois manner" with which she renders the Italian. But beyond the sensibilities of the Victorian mentality, why would it be so important for Georgina Harding to make these cuts? There are numerous articles that discuss the strength of the censor's office in Britain (and the United States) in the nineteenth and early twentieth centuries, which prevented many literary and theatrical works from being published or performed.[7] Without the cuts Harding made, the novel would not have met with the approval of the British censor, and hence would not have been permitted to be published.[8]

So what did the book look like without the sex? And how was it perceived in Britain and the United States in the form to which Harding reduced it? While removing any reference to anything lubricious, Harding also removed much or most of the analytical and philosophical contemplation of poetry, art, and other intellectual notions from the novel. Woodhouse observes that *The Child of Pleasure*, "heavily bowdlerized," "omits any kind of serious reflection on serious subjects" and hence reduces the novel to the level of "sentimental fiction."[9] While this brought D'Annunzio's work into line with the "literary fashions favoured by the majority at the time,"[10] it inevitably conditioned the way it was rated by literary critics of the era.

One critic, G. B. Rose, who was able to read *Il piacere* in Italian, underscores the attitude that prevailed toward foreign authors such as Zola and Balzac, as well as indigenous ones such as Bernard Shaw, who were subject to the same degree of censorship. That Rose read D'Annunzio in Italian is significant; it allowed him to fully appreciate the beauty of D'Annunzio's style. Having read the complete, unexpurgated version of the novels, however, he is well aware of the dynamics among the literary establishment in the English-speaking world:

> By reason of his immodesty as well as because the graces of his style cannot be reproduced in another language, he can be understood and appreciated only in his own tongue. Imagination fails to depict the indignation of Mr. Comstock[11] should one of these books fall into his hands. Some of d'Annunzio's novels have been translated into English, but the reader need not imagine that he gets in them the brilliant colors, the graceful forms or the subtle perfume of these poisonous flowers.[12]

Of *Il piacere,* Rose observes: "That he had no superior among his fellows became apparent upon the publication when a very young man of his 'Piacere' (Pleasure)."[13]

The republication by so many publishing houses of Miss Harding's original text during the 1990s and after has not been met with approval by the literary establishment. John Woodhouse, one of the foremost Anglophone scholars of D'Annunzio, said: "His merits as a creative writer were being judged by critics and littérateurs in Britain only from what they were able to read of him in translation. Very few could read him in Italian. That problem has continued until the present day, compounded most recently by the unscrupulous actions of the publishing house Daedalus,"[14] which reissued *The Child of Pleasure* unchanged as soon as its copyright expired in 1988. At least three other publishing houses currently reproduce and republish Harding's excised version.

The decision I finally made regarding the translation was a result of reflection on *The Child of Pleasure* in its present form. Given how much D'Annunzio's novel had been changed by Miss Harding, simply reintegrating my translations would not contribute in any effective way to scholars without Italian who might wish to read *Il piacere* in English. *The Child of Pleasure* is not simply *Il piacere* in English with bits missing. Harding's changes altered the character, the content, and the significance of the original novel, so that it could no longer be seen as an exemplar of psychological introspection and analysis, representing a dichotomy between art and sexuality, salvation and perdition. It is D'Annunzio's urtext that is of value, not Georgina Harding's sanitized and purged version. If Italians have the privilege of being able to read *Il piacere* in its original form, why should those who do not speak Italian be deprived of this possibility? For this reason, I decided to produce a new translation of *Il piacere* that faithfully followed the original in every detail. I chose the title *Pleasure,* which is a direct and accurate translation of the title, succinctly expressing the essence of the novel, which is centered entirely on the quest to experience ever greater and more transcendent forms of pleasure, whether as an aesthetic principle or a physical sensation. It is this pursuit of pleasure, of attempting to move beyond pleasure, that ultimately leads to ruin, exemplifying the Decadent theme of ultimate moral dissolution.

I also decided to make this translation an annotated critical edition, which explains the abundance of endnotes. There are several scholarly critical editions of *Il piacere* in Italian, but these are inaccessible to readers who do not know the language. In my translation, I have retained text in Latin, Greek, French, Spanish, German, and so on in the original language and provided translations thereof in endnotes. Where text that is originally Latin, Greek, French, or another foreign language has been translated into English within the body of the work, that is because D'Annunzio himself translated it into Italian. I have attempted to remain true to D'Annunzio's rendering of names, such as where he Italianized first names. Where there are misinterpretations of the text or of meaning, I take full responsibility. I did not annotate every cryptic term or classical allusion; I felt

I should leave some homework to those wishing to explore the abundant classical and mythological, cultural and literary background from which D'Annunzio drew so heavily.

Readers will note that there is an abundance of words beginning with capital letters in this translation (such as "Soul," "Spirit," "Good," "Autumn," and "Talisman"), which may seem superfluous to the modern eye. I have attempted to follow D'Annunzio's original text closely and therefore have retained the majority of his capitalizations, because they generally indicate lofty ideals, personifications, words expressed in ode or with irony, or deeply symbolic words denoting layers of meaning.

In 1897, not long after the beginning of D'Annunzio's literary career, G. B. Rose wrote of him:

> The harmony of his verse has continually gained in richness, while its meaning has become clearer as he has won a fuller mastery over the instrument that makes his music. His prose has gained in strength, in flexibility, in warmth and brilliancy of coloring . . . Whether he is to be merely a baleful comet or a fixed star in the literary heavens cannot yet be determined; but if he continues his progress toward higher ideals and perfection of form his position must soon be established.[15]

D'Annunzio's unflagging popularity and influence in the twenty-first century, as his novels are taught in universities around the world, are a testament to his skill as a poet and a novelist. *Pleasure,* the first of his novels, remains to this day the object of debate, study, and discussion among scholars, students, and critics. A translation is never the equal of the original, but it is hoped that this new one will be of value to English-speaking followers and lovers of D'Annunzio, that it affords pleasure in the reading, that it allows understanding and insight into this seminal Decadent work, and that it in some small way permits readers an intimation of the literary and poetic skill of this great writer.

LARA GOCHIN RAFFAELLI

Introduction

Gabriele D'Annunzio was among the first authors to consciously fashion himself into a media celebrity. When he published his first book of poems, at the age of sixteen, in 1879, he sent in a false account of his own death to a local newspaper in order to generate publicity and create the image of tragic youth.

The creation of his persona was D'Annunzio's principal vocation in life and art. He regarded life itself as a work of art, a credo he shared with some of his late-nineteeth-century contemporaries. "Life imitates Art far more than Art imitates Life," wrote Oscar Wilde, with whom D'Annunzio had much in common. In his first novel, *Pleasure,* published in 1889 when D'Annunzio was only twenty-six, he created an exceptionally complex game of life and art imitating each other in infinite regression, like a pair of opposing mirrors in which it is impossible to distinguish the object from the reflection.

While still a teenager, D'Annunzio moved from a Tuscan boarding school to Rome and set about taking the new capital of Italy by storm. He was eager to assert himself as a brilliant young poet, to win a place of renown among the wealthy noble families of Rome, to seduce its most beautiful women and scandalize its public. The protagonist of *Pleasure,* Andrea Sperelli, is an alter ego of the young D'Annunzio: a poet and refined aesthete, a dandy, a seducer, a slave to beauty and pleasure, utterly immoral and yet curiously appealing. And in the wake of *Pleasure*'s spectacular and scandalous success, Sperelli became for an entire generation a type that many chose to imitate—as Goethe's Werther was for readers of the Romantic era, or Jay Gatsby for the Jazz Age. Modeled on the real D'Annunzio, Sperelli in turn became a model for others as well as for D'Annunzio himself, since others saw D'Annunzio through the lens of his fictional creation, who conferred stature and erotic allure on the young writer.

Having imbibed some Nietzsche, D'Annunzio saw himself as a kind of superman and was not content with mere literary fame. Observing the growth of modern democracy (which began in Italy with unification in 1870) and mass politics, he saw politics as a natural theater for the projection of his personality and the expression of his greatness. "The world . . . must be persuaded that I am capable of anything," he wrote during his first electoral campaign in 1897, in which he presented himself as "the candidate of beauty." D'Annunzio later played a crucial role in whipping up public support for Italy's intervention in World War I, haranguing crowds in Rome and urging them to storm the palaces of the cowardly politicians who were hesitating to commit Italy to the path of war and greatness. During the war effort, D'Annunzio, although now well into middle age, participated actively in combat, specializing in spectacular acts of derring-do, including flying over the enemy capital of Vienna to drop leaflets from a small propeller plane. In another mission, he lost an eye and was nearly killed. These exploits were accompanied by the simultaneous chronicle of countless love affairs—tragic stories of countesses and princesses leaving their husbands and children only to be abandoned by D'Annunzio when he tired of them, of women risking and losing everything, and attempting suicide for the great poet.

D'Annunzio published his last novel in 1910 and issued relatively little in the remaining twenty-eight years of his life, having become consumed increasingly by his role as a public figure and national hero. He emerged from World War I a major leader of Italian nationalism. Referring to Italy's "Mutilated Victory," he led public opposition to the Treaty of Versailles, which awarded Italy less territory than many had hoped. In 1919 he led several thousand veterans on an illegal military mission to occupy the port of Fiume, a city on the Dalmatian coast that had been part of Austria-Hungary but was designated an independent city because of its multicultural and multilingual population. The occupation of Fiume, in defiance of international treaties, represents the first breach in the peace that was supposed to have followed the war to end all wars. D'Annunzio's legionaries were a mix of nationalists, patriotic-minded socialists, syndicalists—the same unstable mix of left and right that filled the ranks of the early fascist movement, which was starting at about the same time. In fact, during the Fiume occupation, which lasted about a year, D'Annunzio invented a lot of the pageantry and rituals that later became part of fascism. Some have referred to D'Annunzio as the John the Baptist of fascism, paving the way for Mussolini. He had a genius for political rhetoric and theater but none of Mussolini's tactical abilities. Mussolini appears to have feared D'Annunzio, recognizing him as one of the few figures charismatic enough to challenge his leadership. As a result, Mussolini helped support his extravagant lifestyle in his princely villa on Lake Garda. D'Annunzio was simultaneously honored as a kind of unofficial poet laureate of fascism and spied upon. He lived out his declining years still pursuing his erotic fantasies, but now with the help of drugs and prostitutes.

D'Annunzio became so closely associated with exasperated nationalism and fascism that his very real status as one of Italy's major writers of the late nineteenth and early twentieth centuries has become obscured. The Italian writer Alberto Arbasino wrote that D'Annunzio is "the proverbial body hidden in the basement, one of the most cumbersome of all literature, of all countries, vilified, trampled, neglected." D'Annunzio's place in the pantheon of great Italian poets is widely acknowledged, but it is easy to forget that such major twentieth-century authors as James Joyce and Marcel Proust were great admirers of D'Annunzio's novels. It is thus extremely valuable to return to D'Annunzio's literary contributions, starting with his extraordinary first novel, *Pleasure*.

Lara Gochin Raffaelli has performed a real service by restoring *Pleasure* to an English-speaking public, or rather giving it to us, in effect, for the first time. The frank eroticism of *Pleasure* was so shocking at the time of its publication, especially in the prudish English-speaking world, that the novel was butchered almost beyond recognition to pass muster with British censors when it appeared as *The Child of Pleasure* in Georgina Harding's translation of 1898. The Victorian Harding had managed, in effect, to take the sex out of a novel in which sex is a central, if not the central, preoccupation. "Today, tomorrow, until death," D'Annunzio wrote, "the work of the flesh is in me the work of the spirit, and both harmonize to achieve one sole, unique beauty. The most fertile creatrix of beauty in the world is sensuality enlightened by apotheosis." Harding, for example, removes in its entirety the first chapter of the book, in which Sperelli awaits his former lover Elena, and relives their passionate affair in his mind. Elena has the "slightly cruel habit" of tearing the petals off the flowers that Sperelli has carefully arranged for their trysts and scattering them across the rug where the two of them evidently make love. D'Annunzio provides a memorable description of the nude Elena's feline body becoming increasingly excited as she stokes the fire in Sperelli's Roman palace, and of her imperious habit of making Sperelli tie her shoes after they make love: "Nothing could compare with the grace of the posture that she would assume every time, lifting her skirt slightly and putting forward first one foot and then the other, so that her lover, kneeling, could tie the laces of her shoe, which were still unfastened."

One of the many striking things about reading *Pleasure* is its obsessive interest in things, in the buying and possessing of beautiful objects, of furniture and décor, drapes, bowls, bric-a-brac. Sperelli is obsessed with surrounding himself with beautiful things and is always careful to compose the room with objects as he conducts his love affairs. The objects themselves bear a kind of erotic charge that becomes bound up with the erotic bond between the two lovers.

> For him, all those objects among which he had so many times loved and taken pleasure and suffered had taken on something of his sensitivity. Not only were they witness to his loves, his pleasures, his moments of sadness, but they had participated in them . . . And because he sought out these things with skill, like an aesthete, he naturally drew from the world of objects a great part of his exhilaration. This delicate actor could not comprehend the comedy of love without the backdrops.

In one of the many extraordinary scenes in *Pleasure,* Sperelli in effect wins over Elena at a public auction in which they are both bidding on beautiful objects being sold off from some venerable Italian collection. When Elena turns to him and says, "I advise you to buy this timepiece," Sperelli senses that something has changed between them. "Is she advising me to buy it *for us*?" he wonders. As they hand the objects they have purchased back and forth, an erotic charge passes between them.

> In Elena's aristocratic hands, those precious materials seemed to acquire value . . . It seemed that a particle of the amorous charm of that woman passed into them, the way some of the qualities of a magnet pass into a piece of iron. It was truly a magnetic sensation of pleasure, one of those intense and profound sensations that one feels almost only at the beginning of a love affair.

This scene is, frankly, much more interesting than the famous seduction scene in *Madame Bovary* in which Flaubert has Emma grant her favors to Rodolphe while we hear a cattle auction outside the window.

The world that D'Annunzio describes is the Rome of the nineteenth century, only recently the capital of Italy, with one foot in the old papal Rome, a sleepy, provincial, but extravagantly beautiful city dominated by the old aristocracy, and a newer world of lawyers, politicians, and a rising bourgeoisie. D'Annunzio—the lover of beauty—sides clearly with the first over the second.

Sperelli is a member of that dying breed of Italian aristocracy, which still has a feeling for refinement and beauty. And yet D'Annunzio, although from a family of minor nobility, was one of the thousands of provincials who descended on the new capital to make his fortune. In fact, D'Annunzio helped support himself in his first years in Rome in a quintessentially new profession, journalism, contributing hundreds of pieces to various lively, gossipy illustrated magazines that were part of a new mass culture made possible by high-speed printing presses. D'Annunzio wrote, among other things, about fashion and high society, which helps explain the novel's extremely fresh, minute descriptions of Roman life. He helped chronicle the aristocratic world he was anxious to be a part of, but in writing about it he participated in a process in which the nobles and their precious possessions became objects of consumption.

D'Annunzio describes an amazing scene in which the princesses and countesses of the Roman nobility contribute to a charitable fund-raising event by offering for sale objects they have touched. Some sell cigarettes they have lit in their own mouths, one sells glasses of champagne from which she has sipped, others sell pieces of fruit they have bitten sensuously into—which men purchase for the pleasure of placing their lips on something that has been in a beautiful woman's mouth. One princess even performs the stunt of selling cigars she has placed under her armpit: "—Every act of charity is blessed, the marchioness decreed. —I, with all my biting of fruit, managed to gather about two hundred *luigi*."

Of course, the objects that Sperelli is most interested in possessing are women. *Pleasure* is a fascinating psychological novel about the mind of a seducer, with D'Annunzio clearly using himself as subject. One of the things that makes *Pleasure* so interesting is that D'Annunzio is pitilessly frank in his analysis of his alter ego, Sperelli: "The basis of his power lay in this: that in the art of love, he had no repugnance for any pretense, for any falseness, for any lie. A great part of his strength lay in his hypocrisy."

Part of Sperelli's charm for women is his ability to make each one feel, in spite of much contrary evidence, that she is the only woman he has truly loved and will ever love: "He spoke to her in a low voice, kneeling, so close that it seemed he wanted to drink in her breath. His ardor was sincere, while his words sometimes lied." D'Annunzio understands that eroticism is very much an affair of the mind and a matter of perception. He describes the way in which his conquest of Elena suddenly raises his status in the eyes of other women in the Roman aristocracy:

> The contagion of desire is a very frequent phenomenon in modern societies. A man who has been loved by a woman of singular esteem excites the imagination in other women; and each one burns with desire to possess him, out of vanity and curiosity, competing

> with the others. The appeal of Don Giovanni is more in his fame than in his person.

At one point, when he is courting another woman, Maria, while also trying to win back Elena, Sperelli attends a concert with Maria and then notices Elena looking at them both, a gaze that is not lost on Maria either. Sperelli senses that a little jealousy may push the reluctant Elena back into his arms, while having a similar effect on Maria. "He was therefore on his way toward a double conquest," D'Annunzio writes. As Sperelli imagines this "double conquest," the two women become melded in his mind and transformed into a third:

> How strange, Elena's tones in Donna Maria's voice! A crazy thought flashed into his head. That voice could be, for him, the element of an imaginative work: by virtue of such an affinity, he could fuse the two beauties in order to possess a third, imaginary one, more complex, more perfect, more *real* because she was ideal . . .

For D'Annunzio the erotic life and the life of the literary imagination are one and the same, and imaginary reality is the most real.

Although only twenty-six at the time of the novel's publication, D'Annunzio firmly resisted any attempts on his publisher's part to cut or soften *Pleasure*. Curiously, the passage that his publisher was most worried about was not an erotic one but a brief cryptic allusion to a painful contemporary political event: the slaughter of Italian troops at the hands of Ethiopian soldiers at Dogali, an inglorious moment in Italy's inglorious effort at African colonization. Politics hardly figures at all in *Pleasure*, and we experience the defeat at Dogali (which occurred just before D'Annunzio wrote the novel) in the form of a noisy rabble that slows down Sperelli's carriage. Sperelli dismisses the event by saying, "All for four hundred brutes, who died brutally!"

When his publisher suggested the line would offend patriotic sentiment, D'Annunzio reacted with apparent outrage: "That phrase is spoken by Andrea Sperelli and not by Gabriele D'Annunzio, and it fits well in the mouth of that monster."

Sperelli was thus a perfect foil for D'Annunzio, a character he could both inhabit and disown as needed, hero and monster.

Perhaps with D'Annunzio in mind, Luigi Pirandello, a writer of a very different kind, wrote, "Life: either you live it or you write it. I have never lived it except by writing." This was a division D'Annunzio did not accept: he lived writing and wrote living, a dynamic and explosive combination that lasted for about twenty years, until his public life crowded out his writing.

ALEXANDER STILLE

Pleasure

To Francesco Paolo Michetti

This book, composed in your house as a welcome guest, comes to you as an offering of thanks, as an *ex-voto*.[1]

In the tiredness of the long and heavy exertion, your presence was as fortifying and consoling to me as the sea. In the disgust that follows the painful and captious contrivance of style, the limpid simplicity of your reasoning was an example and a correction for me. In the doubts that followed the effort of analysis, not infrequently was your profound judgment a source of light to me.

To you who study all the forms and all the mutations of the spirit as you study all the forms and all the mutations of things, to you who understand the laws that govern the internal life of man, the way you understand the laws of design and color, to you who are as much an acute connoisseur of souls as you are a great creator of paintings, I owe the exercise and the development of the noblest among the faculties of intellect: I owe the habit of observation, and I owe, especially, the method. I am now, like you, convinced that there is one sole object of study for us: Life.

We are, in truth, very far from the time in which, while you were in the Sciarra Gallery intent on penetrating the secrets of da Vinci and Titian, I was extending a salutation to you of nostalgic rhymes

> to the Ideal that has no sunsets,
> to Beauty which knows no pain!

However, an oath taken in that period was indeed fulfilled. We returned together to our sweet fatherland, to your "vast house." There are no Medicean tapestries hanging on the walls, nor women assembled at our Decameronian gatherings; nor Paolo Veronese's[2] cupbearers or greyhounds strolling around the tables, nor supernatural fruits filling the crockery that Galeazzo Maria Sforza ordered from Maffeo di Clivate. Our desire is less presumptuous: and our lifestyle more primitive, perhaps also more Homeric and more heroic, if one may count the meals, worthy of Ajax,[3] taken alongside the resounding sea, interrupting the fasts of one's labors.

I smile when I think that this book where I examine, not without sadness, so much corruption and so much depravity and so much vain insidiousness and falseness and cruelty, has been written amid the simple, serene peace of your house, between the last starlings of the harvest and the first pastorals[4] of the snow, while my pages grew together with the precious life of your small son.

Certainly, if there is any human compassion and any goodness in my book, I render thanks to your son. Nothing inspires tenderness and uplifts one as much as the sight of life unfolding. Even the vision of dawn cedes its place to that wonder.

Here, then, is the volume. If, while reading it, your eye skips on ahead and you see Giorgio holding out his hands to you and smiling at you with his rounded face, as in Catullus's divine strophe, *semihiante labello*,[5] you must interrupt your reading. And may the small rosy heels before you press down on the pages where all the misery of Pleasure is represented; and may that careless pressure be a symbol and an augur.

Hail, Giorgio. Friend and teacher, great thanks.

FROM THE CONVENT: JANUARY 9, 1889.[6]

FIRST BOOK

CHAPTER I

The year was ebbing away, very gently. The New Year's Eve sun radiated almost imperceptible veiled warmth, infinitely soft, golden, almost vernal, in the sky above Rome. All the roads were crowded, as on Sundays in May. On Piazza Barberini, on Piazza di Spagna, a multitude of carriages were rushing back and forth; and from the two squares the mingled and constant noise, rising up Trinità de' Monti to Via Sistina, reached the rooms of Palazzo Zuccari somewhat dulled.

The rooms were slowly filling with the scent emanating from fresh flowers in vases. Thick, fat roses were immersed in certain crystal goblets that rose, slender, from a sort of gilded stem, widening into the shape of a diamond lily, similar to those that appear behind the Virgin in the tondo by Sandro Botticelli at the Galleria Borghese. No other form of goblet equals in elegance such a form: the flowers in that diaphanous prison seem almost to become spiritual, resembling rather a religious or loving offering.

Andrea Sperelli was awaiting a lover in his rooms. Everything around him revealed special loving care. Juniper wood burned in the fireplace and the small tea table was ready, set with majolica cups and saucers from Castel Durante decorated with mythological scenes by Luzio Dolci, ancient forms of inimitable grace, with Ovidian hexameters written in blue-black cobalt[1] italic script below the figures. Light entered the room softened by curtains of red brocade with pomegranates, leaves, and mottos embossed in spun silver. As the afternoon sun struck the windowpanes, the flowered design of the lace curtains cast its shadow on the carpet.

The clock of Trinità de' Monti sounded three thirty. There was still half an hour to wait. Andrea Sperelli rose from the couch on which he had been lying and went to open one of the windows; then he walked around the apartment; then he opened a book, read a few lines, closed it again; then he looked around for something with a dubious expression. The anxiety of the wait stabbed him so acutely that he needed to move about, to engage in some activity, to distract his internal suffering with physical action. He bent toward the fireplace, took the tongs to revive the fire, and placed a new piece of juniper atop the burning pile. The pile collapsed; the coals rolled, scintillating, down to the metal plate that protected the carpet; the flames split into many small bluish tongues that vanished and reappeared; the embers emitted smoke.

Then a memory arose in the waiting man's mind. In front of that very fireplace Elena had once loved to bask before dressing, after an hour of intimacy. She possessed much skill in heaping great pieces of wood on the andirons. She would take the heavy tongs with both hands and lean her head back slightly, to avoid the sparks. Her body on the carpet, in this slightly difficult task, in the movements of her muscles and the flickering of the shadows, seemed to radiate beauty from every joint, every fold, every hollow, suffused with an amber pallor that brought to mind Correggio's *Danäe*. And indeed her limbs were somewhat Correggian, her hands and feet small and supple, almost, one could say, arboreal, as depicted in statues of Daphne at the very beginning of her fabled metamorphosis.

As soon as she had completed her task the wood would flame up and emit an immediate radiant glow. In the room, that warm russet light and the frozen dusk entering through the windows would vie with each other for a while. The aroma of the burnt juniper made one slightly dizzy. Elena seemed to be overcome by a sort of childish frenzy at the sight of the blaze. She had the slightly cruel habit of scattering the petals of all the flowers in the vases onto the carpet at the end of every tryst. When she returned to the room after having dressed, pulling on her gloves or closing her fan, she would smile in the midst of that devastation; and nothing could compare with the grace of the posture that she would assume every time, lifting her skirt slightly and putting forward first one foot and then the other, so that her lover, kneeling, could tie the laces of her shoe, which were still unfastened.

The place was almost completely unchanged. From every object that Elena had looked at or touched, flocks of memories arose, and the images of that distant time came tumultuously to life. After almost two years, Elena was about to cross that threshold again. Within half an hour, certainly, she would come, she would sit in that armchair, lifting her veil from her face, panting slightly, as she had once done; and she would talk. All those objects would once again hear her voice, maybe even her laugh, after an absence of two years.

The day of the great parting was precisely March 25, 1885, outside Porta Pia, in a carriage. The date had remained indelible in Andrea's memory. Now, waiting, he could evoke all the events of that day with infallible lucidity. The vision of the Nomentano landscape unfolded itself now before him in an ideal light, like one of those dreamscapes in which things seem to be visible from afar by virtue of a radiance that emanates from their shapes.

The closed carriage rolled along with a steady sound, the horses moving at a trot: the walls of the ancient patrician villas passed before the windows, glowing white, almost oscillating with a constant and gentle movement. Now and then a great iron gate would appear, through which one could see a driveway flanked with high box hedges or a clump of greenery inhabited by Latinate statues or a long portico covered in foliage, through which the rays of sun glinted palely here and there.

Elena was silent, wrapped in her full otter-skin mantle, with a veil over her face and her hands enclosed in suede. He inhaled with delight the subtle odor of heliotrope that arose from her costly fur coat, feeling against his arm the shape of hers. Both believed themselves to be far from others, alone; but suddenly the black carriage of a prelate would pass by; or a herdsman on horseback, or a throng of purplish clerics, or a herd of cattle.

Half a kilometer from the bridge she said:

—Let us get out.

In the countryside the cold and clear air seemed like springwater; and as the trees were undulating in the wind it appeared, as with an optical illusion, that the undulation transmitted itself to all things.

She said, embracing him and stumbling on the harsh terrain:

—I am leaving this evening. This is the last time . . .

Then she remained quiet; then she spoke again, haltingly, about the necessity for her departure, about the need for the breakup, with a tone full of sadness. The furious wind tore the words from her lips. She carried on talking. He interrupted her, taking her hand and seeking with his fingers the flesh of her wrist through her buttons:

—No more! No more!

They walked on, struggling against the insistent gusts of wind. And he, near the woman, in that profound and grave solitude, suddenly felt enter into his soul, like the proud sentiment of a freer life, an excess of strength.

—Don't leave! Don't leave! I still want you, always!

He bared her wrist and pushed his fingers into her sleeve, tormenting her skin with an agitated movement that harbored the desire for greater possession.

She turned upon him one of those looks that inebriated him like glasses of wine. The bridge was nearby, red-hued, in the light of the sun. The river seemed immobile and metallic along its entire sinuous length. The rushes curved over on the banks, and the waters bumped up gently against several poles stuck into the clay, perhaps to hold fishing lines.

Then he began to goad her with memories. He spoke to her of their early days, of the ball at Palazzo Farnese, of the hunt in the countryside of Divine Love, of their morning trysts in Piazza di Spagna along the shopwindows of the goldsmiths or along Via Sistina, peaceful and elegant, when she came out of Palazzo Barberini followed by peasant women offering her roses from their baskets.

—Do you remember? Do you remember?

—Yes.

—And that evening, with the flowers, in the beginning; when I came with all those flowers . . . You were alone, near the window: you were reading. Do you remember?

—Yes, yes.

—I came in. You barely turned around; you greeted me with

harshness. What was wrong with you? I don't know. I placed the bouquet on the little table and I waited. You started talking about futile things, unwillingly and without pleasure. I thought, disheartened: *Already she doesn't love me anymore!* But the scent was strong: the whole room was already full of it. I can still see you, when you grabbed the bouquet with both hands and buried your whole face in it, inhaling. Your face, when you lifted it again, was bloodless, and your eyes seemed strange as if from a kind of intoxication . . .

—Carry on, carry on! said Elena, with a faint voice, leaning over the parapet, spellbound by the fascination of the rushing waters.

—Then, on the couch: Do you remember? I covered your chest, your arms, your face with the flowers, oppressing you. You kept on coming up through them, offering me your mouth, your throat, your closed eyelids. Between your skin and my lips I felt the cold and damp petals. If I kissed your neck, you shivered throughout your body, and held out your hands to keep me away. Oh, then . . . You had your head pressed back in the cushions, your chest hidden by roses, your arms bare to the elbows; and nothing was more loving or sweeter than the slight tremor of your pale hands on my temples . . . Do you remember?

—Yes. Carry on!

He continued, his tenderness growing. Drunk on his own words, he almost lost consciousness of what he was saying. Elena, with her back to the light, was leaning toward her lover. Both could feel through their clothes the indecisive contact of their bodies. Beneath them, the waters of the river moved, slow and cold to the eye; the great slender rushes, like thatches of hair, curved themselves into it at every gust and floated with ample movements.

Then they spoke no more; but, looking at each other, they heard a constant sound that persisted indefinitely, taking with it a part of their being, as if something sonorous was escaping from the intimate recesses of their brains and expanding to fill all the surrounding countryside.

Elena, straightening up, said:

—Let's go. I'm thirsty. Where can one ask for some water?

They headed then toward the Romanesque inn on the other

side of the bridge. Some carters were unfastening their pack-horses, swearing loudly. The light of the setting sun struck the human and equine group with intense force.

The entry of the two aroused no sign of wonder among the people in the inn. Three or four feverish men, taciturn and yellowish, stood around a square brazier. A ruddy-skinned cowherd slumbered in a corner, still gripping his extinguished pipe between his teeth. Two scrawny and squinting youths played cards, glaring at each other during the intervals with an expression of brutal fervor. And the innkeeper, a plump woman, held a baby in her arms, rocking it ponderously.

While Elena drank the water in the glass, the woman showed her the baby, lamenting.

—Look, my lady! Look, my lady!

All the limbs of the poor creature were miserably thin; its purplish lips were covered in whitish spots; the inside of its mouth was covered with what seemed to be milky clots. It seemed almost as if life were already fleeing from that small body, leaving some matter upon which mold now grew.

—Feel, my lady, how cold his hands are. He can't drink anymore; he can't swallow; he can't sleep anymore . . .

The woman sobbed. The feverish men looked on with eyes full of immense exhaustion. At the sound of her sobs the two youths made a gesture of impatience.

—Come, come! Andrea said to Elena, taking her arm after having left a coin on the table. And he drew her outside.

Together they returned toward the bridge. The Aniene River flowed on, lit now by the fiery sunset. A scintillating line passed through the arch; and in the distance the waters took on a brown but glossier color, as if slicks of oil or tar were floating on its surface. The rugged countryside, like an immense ruin, was tinted all with violet. Near the Eternal City the sky grew increasingly red.

—Poor creature! murmured Elena with a profound tone of compassion, hugging herself tightly to Andrea's arm.

The wind grew enraged. A flock of crows flew past high up in the enflamed air, cawing.

Then, suddenly, a kind of sentimental exaltation filled the souls of the couple, in the presence of solitude. It was as if something tragic and heroic entered their passion. The highest point of their sentiment blazed under the influence of the tumultuous sunset. Elena stopped.

—I can't go on anymore, she said, panting.

The carriage was still far off, immobile, where they had left it.

—Just a little farther, Elena! A little farther! Do you want me to carry you?

Andrea, taken by an unstoppable lyrical impetus, abandoned himself to words.

"Why did she want to leave? Why did she want to break the enchantment? Weren't their *destinies* bound together, by now, forever? He needed her in order to live, her eyes, her voice, her thoughts . . . He was completely penetrated by that love; all his blood was adulterated as if by poison, with no remedy. Why did she want to flee? He would wind himself around her, he would first suffocate her against his chest. No, it could not be. Never! Never!"

Elena listened, her head bent, struggling against the wind, without answering. After a while, she lifted her arm to make a sign to the coachman to approach. The horses pawed the ground.

—Stop at Porta Pia, the lady cried, mounting the carriage together with her lover.

And with a sudden movement she offered herself to his desire. He kissed her mouth, her forehead, her hair, her eyes, her throat, avidly, rapidly, without breathing any longer.

—Elena! Elena!

A fiery scarlet glow entered the carriage, reflected by the brick-colored houses. The trotting sound of many horses came closer.

Elena, leaning on the shoulder of her lover with immensely sweet submission, said:

—Farewell, love! Farewell! Farewell!

As she straightened up, to the left and to the right ten or twelve scarlet-clothed horsemen passed at a rapid trot, returning from foxhunting. One of them, the Duke of Beffi, passing very close by, arched up to see inside the carriage window.

Andrea did not speak anymore. He now felt his entire being becoming faint, falling into an infinite depression. The puerile weakness of his nature, the initial upliftment having ebbed away, now brought him to the need for tears. He would have liked to bow down before her, humble himself, arouse the woman's pity with his tears. He had a confused, dull sensation of dizziness; and a sharp chill assaulted the nape of his neck and penetrated the roots of his hair.

—Farewell, Elena repeated.

The carriage was stopping under the archway of Porta Pia so that he could alight.

In this way, hence, while waiting, Andrea saw that far-off day once more in his mind's eye; he once more saw all the gestures, heard all the words. What had he done as soon as Elena's carriage had disappeared in the direction of the Four Fountains? Nothing extraordinary, in truth. Even then, as always, as soon as the immediate object from which his spirit drew that type of fatuous exaltation distanced itself, he had almost immediately regained his tranquillity, his everyday consciousness, his equilibrium. He had mounted a public carriage to return home; there he had put on a black suit, as usual, not omitting any elegant detail; and he had gone to lunch at his cousin's, as on every other Wednesday, at Palazzo Roccagiovine. Everything in his external existence exerted upon him a great power of oblivion, kept him occupied, aroused him to the swift enjoyment of worldly pleasures.

That evening, in fact, contemplation had come to him quite late, namely, when returning to his home he saw shining on a table the small tortoiseshell comb forgotten there by Elena two days before. Then, in compensation, he had suffered all night and with many tricks of the mind he had intensified his pain.

But the moment was nearing. The clock of Trinità de' Monti sounded three forty-five. He thought, with profound trepidation: *In a few minutes Elena will be here. What shall I do when receiving her? What words shall I say to her?*

The anxiety in him was real, and love for that woman had truly reawoken in him; but the verbal and plastic expression of feelings in him was, as always, so artificial and so far from simplicity and sincerity that he resorted, by habit, to rehearsing even the most profound emotions of the soul.

He tried to imagine the scene; he composed some sentences;

he looked around to choose the most propitious place for their talk. Then he even got up to see in a mirror if his face was pale; if it was appropriate to the circumstance. And his gaze in the mirror lingered at his temples, at his hairline, where Elena used to place a delicate kiss *then*. He opened his mouth to admire the perfect shine of his teeth and the freshness of his gums, remembering that once, Elena had liked in him, above all, his mouth. His vanity, which was that of a spoiled and effeminate youth, never neglected any effect of grace or form in a love affair. He knew, in the practice of love, how to draw from his beauty the greatest possible enjoyment. This felicitous aptitude of body and this keen search for pleasure indeed won him the hearts of women. He had in him aspects of Don Juan and of a cherub: he knew how to be both the man of a Herculean night and the shy, ingenuous, almost virginal lover. The basis of his power lay in this: that in the art of love, he had no repugnance for any pretense, for any falseness, for any lie. A great part of his strength lay in his hypocrisy.

What shall I do when I receive her? What words shall I say to her? He became confused as the minutes fled past. He did not yet know in what kind of mood Elena would come to him.

He had encountered her the previous morning along Via de' Condotti, while she was looking at shopwindows. He had returned to Rome a few days earlier, after a long, obscure absence. The sudden encounter had provoked in both an intense emotion; but as they were out in public they were forced to be courteously reserved, ceremonial, almost cold. He had said to her, with a serious, slightly sad air, looking her in the eyes: —I have so many things to tell you, Elena. Will you come to me, tomorrow? Nothing has changed in the *buen retiro*.[2] She had answered simply: —Fine, I will come. You can expect me at about four. I also have something to tell you. Now leave me.

She had accepted the invitation immediately, with no hesitation whatsoever, without placing any conditions, without seeming to give any importance to the matter. Such readiness had at first aroused in Andrea a vague worry. Would she come as a friend or as a lover? Would she come to renew their love or to shatter every hope? In those two years, whatever had passed through her soul? Andrea did not know; but he still felt the sensation caused by her gaze, in the street, when he had bowed to greet her. It was still the same gaze as always, so sweet, so profound, so flattering, from beneath her infinitely long eyelashes.

There were still two or three minutes to go until the appointed hour. The anxiety of the waiting man grew to such a pitch that he thought he would suffocate. He went to the window again and looked toward the steps of the Trinità. Once, Elena used to climb those stairs to their assignations. Placing her foot on the last step, she would hesitate for a moment; then she would rapidly cross that section of the square in front of the Casteldelfino house. One would hear her slightly undulating footsteps resonate on the paving, if the square was silent.

The clock struck four. The sound of carriages could be heard from Piazza di Spagna and from the Pincian Hill.[3] Many people were walking beneath the trees in front of Villa Medici. Two women sat on the stone bench before the church, watching over some small children who were running around the obelisk. The obelisk was entirely crimson, struck by the setting sun, and it cast a long, oblique, slightly turquoise shadow. The air was growing icy cold, the more sunset approached. The city below was tinged with gold against a pale sky on which the Monte Mario cypresses were already traced in black.

Andrea gave a start of surprise. He saw a shadow appear at the top of the small flight of stairs that runs alongside the Casteldelfino house and descends to Piazzetta Mignanelli. It was not Elena, but a woman who turned into Via Gregoriana, walking slowly.

What if she doesn't come? he mused doubtfully, drawing back from the window. And drawing back from the cold air, he felt that the tepid warmth of the room was softer, the aroma of the juniper and the roses more intense, the shadow of the drapes and the door curtains more mysterious. It seemed that in that moment the room was completely ready to welcome the desired woman. He thought about the sensation that Elena would feel upon entering. Certainly she would be won over by that sweetness, so full of memories; she would immediately lose every notion of reality, of time; she would believe herself to be back in one of their habitual trysts, never to have interrupted that sensual affair, still to be the Elena she had once been. If the theater of love was unchanged, why should love have changed? Certainly she would feel the profound seduction of the things that had once been beloved.

Now a new torture commenced in the waiting man. The senses, heightened by the habit of contemplative fantasy and of poetic dreaming, invest objects with a sensitive and changeable soul, like the human soul; and they perceive in everything, in shapes, in colors, in sounds, in perfumes, a transparent symbol, the emblem of a sentiment or a thought; and in every phenomenon, in every combination of phenomena, they believe they can conjecture a psychic state, a moral significance. Sometimes the vision is so clear that it produces a sense of anguish in those spirits: they feel they are suffocating from the fullness of life revealed to them, and they are alarmed by their own phantasms. Andrea saw his own anxiety reflected in the appearance of the things around him; and as his desire dispersed uselessly in the wait and his nerves became weaker, so it appeared to him that the almost erotic essence of those things also vaporized and dissipated into futility. For him, all those objects among which he had so many times loved and taken pleasure and suffered had taken on something of his sensitivity. Not only were they witness to his loves, his pleasures, his moments of sadness, but they had participated in them. In his memory, every shape and every color harmonized with a feminine image, was a note in a chord of beauty, an element in an ecstasy of passion. By nature of his taste, he sought out multiple aspects of enjoyment in his love affairs: the complex delight of all the senses, intense intellectual emotion, abandons of sentiment, impulses of brutality. And because he sought out these things with skill, like an aesthete, he naturally drew from the world of objects a great part of his exhilaration. This delicate actor could not comprehend the comedy of love without the backdrops.

Therefore his house was the most perfect theater; and he was an extremely skillful set designer. But he almost always invested all of himself in this artifice; he lavishly spent in it the richness of his spirit; he would sink so far into oblivion within it, that not infrequently he would be deceived by his own insidiousness, wounded by his own weapons, like an enchanter trapped within the circle of his own spell.

Everything around him had taken on for him that inexpressible appearance of life that is acquired, for example, by sacred implements, the insignia of a religion, the instruments of a cult, every figure on which human meditation is accumulated, or from which human imagination rises toward some ideal height. Just as a vial still emits after many years the scent of the essence that was once contained in it, so, too, did certain objects still preserve even just an indistinct part of the love with which that fantasizing lover had illuminated and penetrated them. And such a strong stimulation came to him from these objects that he was disturbed by it at times, as by the presence of a supernatural power.

It truly seemed that he knew the latent aphrodisiacal potentiality of each of those objects, and that he felt it at certain times bursting forth and developing and palpitating around him. Then, if he was in the arms of his beloved, it gave his and her body and soul one of those supreme feasts, the memory of which alone is sufficient to illuminate an entire life. But if he was on his own, a deep anguish pressed down upon him, an inexpressible regret at the thought that that great and rare apparatus of love was going uselessly to waste.

Uselessly! In the tall Florentine goblets the roses, also waiting, exhaled all their intimate sweetness. On the couch, on the wall, the silvery verses dedicated to the glory of women and wine, which blended so harmoniously with the indefinable silken colors in the sixteenth-century Persian carpet, scintillated as they were struck by the light of the setting sun in a bare corner framed by the window, which rendered the nearby shadows more diaphanous and spread their glow to the cushions beneath. The shadow all around was diaphanous and rich, almost animated by the vague luminous palpitation found in dark sanctuaries that hold some occult treasure. The fire in the fireplace crackled; and each of its flames was, as in Percy Shelley's imagery, like a precious stone dissolved in ever-moving light.[4] It seemed to the lover that every shape, every color, every scent offered up the most delicate flower of its essence, in that moment. And *she* was not coming! And *she* was not coming!

Then there arose in his mind, for the first time, the thought of her husband.

Elena was no longer free. She had renounced the merry freedom of her widowhood, entering into a second marriage with an English gentleman, a certain Lord Humphrey Heathfield, some months after her sudden departure from Rome. Andrea indeed remembered having seen the announcement of the marriage in a social column, in October 1885; and having heard an infinite number of comments about the new Lady Helen Heathfield throughout all the holiday resorts in that Roman autumn. He also remembered having encountered that Lord Humphrey about ten times during the preceding winter at Princess Giustiniani-Bandini's home on Saturdays, and at public auctions. He was a man of forty, with ash-blond hair, bald at the temples, deadly pale; with light-colored sharp eyes and a great protruding forehead crisscrossed by veins. His name, Heathfield, was indeed that of the lieutenant general who had been the hero of the famous defense of Gibraltar (1779–83), also immortalized by Joshua Reynolds's paintbrush.

What part did that man play in Elena's life? By what ties, beyond those of marriage, was Elena bound to him? What transformations had the material and spiritual contact of her husband exerted upon her?

Enigmas arose all of a sudden in Andrea's mind, tumultuously. Amid this tumult, the image of the physical union of those two appeared to him, clear and precise; and the pain was so unbearable that he bounded up with the instinctive reflex of a man who has suddenly been wounded in a vital limb. He crossed the room, went out into the entrance hall, and listened at the door that he had left slightly open. It was almost a quarter to five.

After a while he heard footsteps coming up the stairs, a rustle of skirts, someone breathing heavily. Certainly, a woman was coming up. All his blood then surged with such vehemence that, unnerved by the long wait, he thought he would lose all his strength and collapse. But still he heard the sound of the feminine foot on the last steps, a longer breath being drawn, her tread on the landing, on the threshold. Elena entered.

—Oh, Elena! Finally.

In those words the expression of his protracted anguish was so profound that an indefinable smile appeared on the woman's lips, of compassion mixed with pleasure. He took her right hand, ungloved, pulling her toward the room. She was still panting; but a faint glow lit her entire face beneath the black veil.

—Forgive me, Andrea. But I couldn't get away until now. So many visits . . . so many calling cards to return . . . The days are tiring. I can't take it anymore. How hot it is here! What a scent!

She was still standing in the middle of the room; slightly hesitant and troubled, although she was talking rapidly and lightly. A mantle of Carmelite fabric[5] with sleeves in the imperial style cut with wide puffs at the top, flattened and buttoned at the wrist, an immense collar of blue fox fur its only embellishment, covered her entire body without diminishing the grace of her slimness. She was looking at Andrea, her eyes full of a tremulous smile that veiled their acute examination. She said:

—You are somewhat changed. I could not say how. Your mouth, for example, has something bitter about it that I don't recall seeing before.

She said these words with a tone of affectionate familiarity. Her voice resounding in the room gave Andrea such intense delight that he exclaimed:

—Speak, Elena; speak again!

She laughed. And asked:

—Why?

He answered, taking her hand:

—You know why.

She withdrew her hand; and looked the young man deeply in the eyes.

—I don't know anything anymore.

—You've changed, then?

—Changed very much.

Already the "sentiment" was drawing both of them. Elena's answer clarified the problem all at once. Andrea understood; and rapidly but with precision, by some phenomenon of intuition that is not rare in certain spirits well exercised in the analysis of their internal being, glimpsed the moral disposition of the visitor and the unfolding of the scene that had to follow. He was, however, already completely invaded by the sorcery of that woman, the way he had once been. Also, his curiosity was pricking him strongly. He said:

—Won't you sit down?

—Yes, for a moment.

—There, on the armchair.

Oh, my *armchair!* she was about to say with a spontaneous impulse, because she had recognized it; but she stopped herself.

It was a wide, deep chair, covered with an antique leather skin scattered with pale embossed Chimeras,[6] in the same style as one that covers the walls of a room in Palazzo Chigi. The leather had acquired that warm and opulent patina that recalls certain backgrounds of Venetian portraits, or a beautiful bronze that still retains a trace of gilding, or a fine tortoiseshell through which gold leaf glints. A large cushion cut from a dalmatic of a rather faded color, the color that Florentine silk weavers call saffron pink, softened the headrest.

Elena sat down. She placed her right glove on the edge of the tea table, as well as her calling-card case, which was a slender case of smooth silver with two linked garters engraved on it, bearing a motto. Then she took off her veil, lifting her arms to untie the knot behind her head; and the elegant act caused a shining ripple to run through the velvet: at her armpits, along her sleeves, along her bust. As the heat of the fireplace was so strong, she shielded herself with her bare hand, which lit up like rose alabaster: her rings glittered with the gesture. She said:

—Cover the fire; please. It's burning too strongly.

—Don't you like the flames anymore? And you were once a salamander! This fireplace remembers . . .

—Don't stir up memories, she interrupted. Just cover the fire and light a lamp. I'll make the tea.

—Don't you want to take off your mantle?

—No, because I must leave soon. It's already late.

—But you will suffocate.

She rose with a small sign of impatience.

—Help me, then.

As Andrea took off her mantle, he caught a whiff of her scent. It was not the same as the one she had once worn; but it was so exquisite that it reached his innermost fibers.

—You're wearing a new perfume, he said, with a strange tone.

She answered, simply:

—Yes. Do you like it?

Andrea, still holding the mantle in his hands, buried his face in the fur that decorated the collar and that was therefore more scented from the contact with her skin and her hair. Then he asked:

—What is it called?

—It has no name.

She sat down again on the armchair and was illuminated by the flames. She was wearing a black dress made all of lace, amid which innumerable beads sparkled, black and steel.

The twilight was fading against the windowpanes. Andrea lit some twisted candles of an intense orange shade, on the wrought-iron candlesticks. Then he drew the fire screen in front of the fireplace.

Both, in that interval of silence, felt perplexity within their souls. Elena did not have an exact consciousness of the moment, nor self-confidence; even if she attempted to do so, she could not grasp her sense of purpose or ascertain her intentions or find her willpower once more. In the presence of that man to whom she had once been bound by such a great passion, in that place where she had experienced the most ardent moments of her life, little by little she felt all her thoughts vacillate, dissolve, disappear. By now her spirit was about to enter that delicious state, almost, one could say, of sentimental fluidity, in which it perceives every movement, every disposition, every form of external events like ethereal vapors caused by mutations of the atmosphere. She hesitated before abandoning herself to it.

Andrea said, softly, almost humbly:

—Is that all right?

She smiled at him without answering, because those words had given her an indefinable pleasure, almost a tremor of sweetness at the summit of her breast. She began her delicate work. She lit the lamp below the pot of water; she opened the lacquer box in which the tea was kept, and put into the porcelain pot a measured quantity of the flavor; then she prepared two cups. Her gestures were slow and slightly irresolute, as occurs with someone working with the mind turned to some other object; her white and pure hands had, in their movement, a lightness almost of butterflies, not appearing to touch things, but rather barely brushing against them; from her gestures, from her hands, from every light undulation of her body wafted some faint emanation of pleasure that soothed the senses of her lover.

Andrea, sitting nearby, watched her with eyes slightly closed, drinking in through his pupils the voluptuous allure that radiated from her. It was as if every act became ideally tangible for him. What lover has not felt this inexpressible delight, in which it almost seems as if the sensitive power of touch becomes so refined as to be able to experience sensation without the immediate materiality of contact?

Both were silent. Elena had leaned back on the cushions: she was waiting for the water to boil. Watching the blue flame of the lamp, she was removing her rings from her fingers and putting them on again, lost in an apparent dream. It was not a dream, but a kind of vague, wavering, confused, fleeting remembrance. All the memories of the past love affair were rising again in her mind, but without clarity: and they gave her an uncertain impression that she could not identify as pleasure or pain. It was similar to when many flowers have wilted and each has lost its particular color and scent, and a common exhalation arises from them, in which it is not possible to recognize the different elements. It appeared as if she were bearing within her the last breath of already vanished memories, the last traces of joy that has already passed, the last aftereffects of already dead happiness, something similar to a dubious vapor from which nameless, shapeless, interrupted images emerge. She could not tell if it was pain or pleasure; but slowly that mysterious agitation and that indefinable disquiet were growing and swelling her heart with sweetness and bitterness. The obscure forebodings, the dark perturbations, the secret regrets, the superstitious fears, the vanquished aspirations, the stifled pains, the embattled dreams, the unrealized wishes, all those turbid elements that constituted her inner life now roiled within her and assailed her.

She was silent, absorbed within herself. While her heart was nearly overflowing, it pleased her to increase its commotion even more with silence. By speaking, she would disperse it.

The water in the pot started slowly to come to a boil.

Andrea, seated on the low chair, with his elbow supported on his knee and his chin on the palm of his hand, now gazed at the beautiful being with such intensity that she, even not turning toward him, could feel that persistence on her person and it gave her almost a vague physical unease. Andrea, watching her, thought: *I once possessed this woman.* He repeated this affirmation to himself, to convince himself; and made, to convince himself, a mental effort to recall to his memory some pose of hers during the act of pleasure, attempting to see her again in his arms. The certainty of possession was escaping him. Elena seemed to him to be a new woman, never enjoyed, never embraced.

She was, in truth, even more desirable than she had once been. The almost plastic enigma of her beauty was even more obscure and alluring. Her head with its narrow forehead, straight nose, arched eyebrows, of such a pure design, so firm, so classic, that it seemed to have emerged from a Syracusan medal, had about the eyes and mouth a singular contrast in its expression: that passionate, intense, ambiguous, superhuman expression that only some modern spirit, impregnated with all the profound corruption of art, has been able to infuse into types of immortal women such as the *Mona Lisa* or Nelly O'Brien.[7]

Others possess her now, Andrea thought, watching her. *Other hands touch her; other lips kiss her.* And, while he could not manage to form in his imagination the image of his union with her, he saw once again with implacable precision the other image. And an acute frenzy invaded him, to know, to discover, to interrogate.

Elena had leaned over the table because steam was now escaping through the joint of the lid from the boiling pot. She poured a small amount of water onto the tea; she put two cubes of sugar into one cup; she poured some more water onto the tea; then she extinguished the blue flame. She did all this with almost tender care, but without ever turning toward Andrea. Her internal tumult was now becoming such a soft tenderness that she felt her throat close up and her eyes moisten; and she could not resist it. So many contrary thoughts, so many contrary anguishes and alterations of her soul gathered now together into a tear.

With a movement of her hand she knocked over her silver cardholder, which fell onto the carpet. Andrea picked it up and looked at the two linked garters. Each bore a sentimental motto: *From Dreamland—A stranger hither.*[8]

When he lifted his eyes to her, Elena offered him the steaming cup with a smile slightly veiled by tears.

He saw that veil; and at that unexpected sign of tenderness was invaded by such an impetus of love and gratefulness that he put down his cup, knelt, took Elena's hand, and placed his mouth on it.

—Elena! Elena!

He spoke to her in a low voice, kneeling, so close that it seemed he wanted to drink in her breath. His ardor was sincere, while his words sometimes lied. "He loved her, he had always loved her, he had never ever ever been able to forget her! He had felt, meeting her again, all his passion rising up with such violence that he had almost been terrified of it: a type of anxious terror, as if he had glimpsed, in a flash, the overturning of his entire life."

—Hush! Hush! Elena said, with her face drawn in pain, extremely pale.

Andrea went on speaking, still kneeling, becoming more impassioned in the imagination of his sentiment. "He had felt the greatest and best part of himself dragged away by her in that sudden flight. Afterward, he could not tell her about all the misery of his days, the anguish of his sorrow, the assiduous implacable devouring internal suffering. His sadness grew, breaking every dam. He was overcome by it. Sadness was at the base of everything, for him. The passage of time was an unbearable torment. He did not miss so much the happy days as much as he mourned the days that now passed uselessly, deprived of happiness. The former at least had left a memory for him: the latter left him a profound grief, almost remorse . . . His life was consuming itself, drawing into itself the inextinguishable flame of one desire alone, the incurable disgust for every other pleasure. Sometimes he was assailed by impulses of almost enraged lust, by a desperate fury for gratification; and it was like the violent rebellion of a heart not sated, like the flaring up of hope that cannot resign itself to die. Sometimes it also seemed to him that he had been reduced to nothing; and he shivered in the face of the great empty abyss of his being: and of the great flame of his youth nothing remained to him but a fistful of ashes. Sometimes, too, as in one of those dreams that vanish at dawn, his entire past, his entire present dissolved; they detached themselves from his consciousness and fell, like a fragile slough, an empty garment. He remembered nothing more, like a man who has emerged from a long illness, like a dazed convalescent. Finally, he was in oblivion; he felt his soul enter gently into death . . . But, suddenly, from that kind of oblivious tranquillity a new pain burst forth, and the fallen idol surged up again, even taller, like an indestructible shoot. *She, she* was the idol who seduced all the willpower of his heart, broke all the strength of his intellect, kept closed all the most secret avenues of his soul to any other love, to any other pain, to any other dream, forever, forever . . ."

Andrea was lying; but his eloquence was so warm, his voice so penetrating, the touch of his hand so loving, that Elena was invaded by an infinite sweetness.

—Hush! she said. I must not listen to you; I am no longer yours; I can never be yours again. Hush! Hush!

—No, listen to me.

—I don't want to. Good-bye. I must go. Good-bye, Andrea. It's already late, let me go.

She slipped her hand out of the young man's grasp; and overcoming all her inner weakness, made as if to stand up.

—Why did you come, then? he asked her, his voice slightly hoarse, stopping her from getting up.

Although the violence of his gesture was but very slight, she frowned, and hesitated before answering.

—I came—she answered with a certain measured slowness, looking her lover in the eyes—I came because you asked me to. For the love we once had, for the way that love was interrupted, for the long, obscure silence of distance, I could not have refused that invitation without harshness. And then, I wanted to tell you what I have told you: that I am no longer yours, that I can never be yours again. I wanted to tell you this, in fairness, to spare you and me any painful deceit, any danger, any bitterness, in the future. Do you understand?

Andrea lowered his head almost onto her knees, in silence. She touched his hair, with a once-familiar gesture.

—And also—she continued, in a voice that gave him a shiver throughout every fiber—and also . . . I wanted to tell you that I love you, that I love you no less than I once did, that you are still the soul of my soul, and that I want to be your dearest sister, your sweetest friend. Do you understand?

Andrea did not move. Taking his temples between her hands, she lifted his forehead; she forced him to look her in the eyes.

—Have you understood? she repeated, her voice even more tender and soft.

Her eyes, in the shadow of her long lashes, seemed to be suffused with some pure and delicate oil. Her mouth, slightly open, had a light tremor in the upper lip.

—No; you did not love me, you do not love me! Andrea finally broke out, removing her hands from his temples and drawing back, because he already felt in his veins the insidious fire that those pupils exhaled even involuntarily, and he felt more piercingly the pain of having lost the material possession of the beautiful woman. —You did not love me! You, *then,* had the courage to kill your love, suddenly, almost treacherously, while it was giving you its greatest elation. You fled from me, you abandoned me, you left me alone, dismayed, aching all over, dispirited, while I was still blinded by your promises. You did not love me, you do not love me! After such a long absence, full of mystery, mute and inexorable; after such a long wait, in which I wasted the best part of my life nurturing a sadness that was dear to me because it came from you; after so much happiness and after so much hardship, lo and behold, you come back to a place where everything holds such an intense memory for us, and you say to me sweetly: "I am no longer yours. Goodbye." Ah, you do not love me!

—Ingrate! Ingrate! exclaimed Elena, wounded by the young man's almost irate voice. —What do you know about what happened, about what I suffered? What do you know?

—I don't know anything; I don't want to know anything, Andrea answered harshly, looking at her with a somewhat troubled gaze, at the base of which his exasperated desires glittered. —I know that you were mine, once, all of you, with unrestricted abandon, with unlimited voluptuousness, as no other woman has ever been; and I know that neither my spirit nor my flesh will ever forget that exhilaration . . .

—Hush!

—What do I care about your sisterly pity? You, against your will, offer it to me with the eyes of a lover, touching me with unsure hands. Too many times have I seen your eyes close in ecstasy; too many times have your hands felt me shiver. I desire you.

Incited by his own words, he grasped her wrists tightly and brought his face so close to hers that she could feel his warm breath in her mouth.

—I desire you as I never have, he continued, trying to draw her to his kiss, enclosing her upper body with one arm. —Remember! Remember!

Elena stood up, pushing him away. She was trembling all over.

—I don't want to. Do you understand?

He did not understand. He came still closer, his arms stretched out to take her: extremely pale, resolute.

—Could you bear—she cried with her voice slightly choked, unable to stand the violence—could you bear to share my body with others?

She had uttered that cruel question without thinking. Now, with her eyes wide open, she looked at her lover, anxious and almost dismayed, like one who in self-defense has struck a blow without gauging its strength, and fears that one has wounded too deeply.

Andrea's ardor suddenly vanished. And on his face there appeared such deep pain that the woman felt a stab in her heart.

Andrea said, after an interval of silence:

—Farewell.

In that one word was the bitterness of all the other words he had choked back.

Elena answered gently:

—Farewell. Forgive me.

Both felt the need to conclude, for that evening, the dangerous conversation. The one assumed a form of external courtesy that was almost overstated. The other became even gentler, almost humble; and an incessant tremor shook her.

She picked up her mantle from the chair. Andrea helped her with a concerned air. When she could not find the sleeve with her arm, Andrea guided it, barely touching her; then he handed her her hat and veil.

—Do you wish to go into the other room, to the mirror?

—No, thank you.

She went toward the wall, next to the fireplace, where a small antique mirror hung, with an ornate frame sculpted with figures in such an agile and candid style that it appeared to have been formed from some malleable gold rather than from wood. It was an exceedingly light thing, made surely by the hands of a delicate fifteenth-century artist for a Mona Amorrosisca or for a Laldomine.[9] Very often during the happy times, Elena had put on her veil before that clouded, tarnished glass, which had the appearance of dark, slightly greenish water. This came to her mind again now.

When she saw her image appear in those depths, it gave her a strange impression. A wave of sadness, heavier than before, passed through her spirit. But she did not speak.

Andrea was watching her with intent eyes.

When she was ready, she said:

—It must be very late.

—Not very. It must be around six, perhaps.

—I told my carriage to go, she added. —I would be very grateful if you could have a closed carriage called for me.

—Will you permit me to leave you alone here, for a moment? My manservant is out.

She nodded.

—Will you give the address to the coachman, please? Hotel Quirinale.

He went out, closing the door of the room behind him. She was left alone.

Rapidly, she cast her eyes about, encompassing the whole room with an indefinable gaze, and paused on the goblet of flowers. The walls seemed wider to her; the ceiling higher.

Looking around, she had the sensation of the beginnings of dizziness. She no longer smelled the scent; but certainly the air had to be as warm and heavy as that of a greenhouse. The image of Andrea appeared to her in a kind of intermittent flash; in her ears some indistinct wave of his voice resounded. Was she about to faint? And yet, what a delight to close one's eyes and abandon oneself to that languor!

Shaking herself, she went toward the window, opened it, and breathed in the wind. Revived, she turned once again to the room. The dim flames of the candles oscillated, stirring delicate shadows on the walls. The fireplace no longer had any flames, but the embers partially illuminated the sacred figures in the fire screen, which was made of a fragment of ecclesiastical stained glass. The cup of tea had remained on the edge of the table, cold, untouched. The cushion on the armchair still retained the imprint of the body that had been pressed into it. All the things around her exhaled an indistinct melancholy that flowed into and crowded the woman's heart. The weight was increasing on that weak heart, becoming a harsh oppression, an unbearable anguish.

—My God! My God!

She would have liked to flee. A stronger gust of wind swelled the curtains, agitated the small candle flames, stirred up a rustling sound. She started, with a shiver; and almost involuntarily called:

—Andrea!

Her voice and that name, in the silence, gave her a strange jolt, as if her voice and that name had not come from her own mouth. Why was Andrea taking so long? She began to listen. Nothing came to her except for the dull, bleak, jumbled sound of urban life, on the eve of the New Year. No carriage was passing on the square of Trinità de' Monti. As the wind was blowing hard in gusts, she closed the window again: she glimpsed the peak of the obelisk, black against the starry sky.

Perhaps Andrea had not immediately found a covered carriage in Piazza Barberini. She waited, sitting on the couch, trying to still the mad agitation within her, avoiding any examination of her soul, forcing her attention to external things. The glassy figures of the fire screen caught her eyes, barely lit by the half-dead coals. Higher up, on the mantelpiece, from one of the goblets, petals were falling from a huge white rose[10] that was falling apart slowly, languidly, softly, with something almost feminine, almost fleshlike about it. The concave petals were poised delicately on the marble, like falling flakes of snow.

How sweet, then, did that scented snow seem to the fingers! she thought. *All shredded, the roses were scattered over the carpets, the couches, the chairs; and she laughed, happy, amid the devastation; and her lover, happy, was at her feet.*

But she heard a coach stop before the front door, in the street; and she stood up, shaking her poor head, as if to chase away that kind of dullness that enveloped it. Immediately after, Andrea returned, panting.

—Forgive me, he said. —But I could not find the doorman, so I went right down to Piazza di Spagna. The coach is below, waiting.

—Thank you, Elena said, looking at him timidly through the black veil.

He was serious and pale, but calm.

—Mumps is arriving tomorrow, perhaps, she added, in a soft voice. —I will send you a note to tell you when I can see you.

—Thanks! Andrea said.

—Good-bye, then, she continued, holding out her hand to him.

—Would you like me to accompany you down to the street? There is no one about.

—Yes, come down with me.

She looked about, slightly hesitant.

—Have you forgotten anything? Andrea asked.

She looked at the flowers. But she answered.

—Oh yes, my cardholder.

Andrea ran to pick it up from the tea table. Handing it out to her, he said:

—*A stranger hither!*[11]

—*No, my dear. A friend.*

Elena uttered this reply with a very animated, vivacious voice. Then, suddenly, with a smile halfway between suppliant and flattering, of mingled fear and tenderness, above which trembled the edge of her veil, which reached her upper lip, leaving her whole mouth free:

—*Give me a rose.*

Andrea went to each vase; and removed all the roses, pressing them together into a great bunch that he could barely hold in his hands. Some fell, others fell apart.

—They were for you, all of them, he said, without looking at the woman he loved.

And Elena turned to go out, her head bent, in silence, followed by him.

They walked down the stairs still in silence. He saw the nape of her neck, so fresh and delicate, where below the knot of her veil the small black curls mingled with her ashen fur coat.

—Elena! he called, in a low voice, no longer able to conquer the consuming passion that was swelling his heart.

She turned, placing her index finger on her lips to indicate to him to be silent, with a suffering, imploring gesture, her eyes glittering. She quickened her pace, climbed up into the coach, and felt the roses being placed on her lap.

—Good-bye! Good-bye!

And as soon as the coach moved forward she lay back in the farthest corner, overcome, bursting into unrestrained tears, shredding the roses to pieces with her poor convulsed hands.

CHAPTER II

Beneath today's gray democratic flood, which wretchedly submerges so many beautiful and rare things, that special class of ancient Italic nobility in which from generation to generation a certain family tradition of elect culture, elegance, and art was kept alive is also slowly disappearing.

To this class, which I would call Arcadian because it rendered its greatest splendor in the sweet life of the eighteenth century, the Sperelli family belonged. Urbanity, elegant writing skills, a love of delicacy, a predilection for unusual studies, a mania for archaeology, refined gallantry, were all hereditary qualities of the house of Sperelli. A certain Alessandro Sperelli, in 1466, had carried to Federigo d'Aragona, the son of Ferdinando, King of Naples, and brother of Alfonso, Duke of Calabria, the codex in folio containing some "less coarse" poems of the old Tuscan writers, which Lorenzo de' Medici had promised in Pisa in '65; and that same Alessandro had written upon the death of the divine Simonetta,[1] in chorus with the sages of the time, a Latin elegy, melancholic and forsaken, in imitation of Tibullus. Another Sperelli, Stefano, in the same century, had been in Flanders amid a life of pomp, of exquisite elegance, of unparalleled Burgundian splendor; and he remained there at the court of Charles le Téméraire, marrying into a Flemish family. One of his sons, Giusto, studied painting under the instruction of Jan Gossaert; and together with his teacher he came to Italy in the retinue of Philippe de Bourgogne, ambassador of Emperor Maximilian to Pope Julius II, in 1508. He took up residence in Florence, where the main branch of his line continued to flourish; and had as a second teacher Piero di Cosimo, that jocund and easygoing painter, a strong and harmonious colorist who brought pagan fables freely back to life with his paintbrush. This Giusto was not a common artist, but he consumed all his strength in futile efforts to reconcile his primitive Gothic education with the recent spirit of the Renaissance. Toward the second half of the seventeenth century, the house of Sperelli relocated to Naples. There, in 1679, a Bartolomeo Sperelli published an astrological treatise, *De Nativitatibus;* in 1720 a Giovanni Sperelli gave the theater a comic opera entitled *La Faustina* and then a lyrical tragedy entitled *Progne;* in 1756 a Carlo Sperelli printed a book of amateur verse in which many lascivious mottos of classical derivation were rhymed with the Horatian elegance then in mode. A better poet was Luigi, a man of exquisite gallantry, at the court of the Beggar King[2] and Queen Caroline. He wrote verses with a certain melancholic and courteous Epicureanism, with great limpidity; and he loved like a very fine lover, and had abundant affairs, some of them celebrated, like the one with the Marchioness of Bugnano, who out of jealousy poisoned herself, and the one with the Countess of Chesterfield, whom, when she died of consumption, he mourned in songs, odes, sonnets, and elegies that were extremely sweet, though somewhat florid.

Count Andrea Sperelli-Fieschi of Ugenta, the sole heir, continued the family tradition. He was, in truth, the ideal type of young Italian gentleman of the nineteenth century, the legitimate defender of a lineage of gentlemen and elegant artists, the last descendant of an intellectual race.

He was, as it were, completely impregnated with art. His adolescence, nurtured with varied and profound studies, seemed prodigious. He had alternated, until the age of twenty, lengthy bouts of study with lengthy travels with his father and had been able to complete his extraordinary aesthetic education under his father's guidance, without the restrictions or constrictions of pedagogues. It was indeed from his father that he had inherited his taste for objects of art, his passionate cult of beauty, his paradoxical scorn for prejudice, his avidity for pleasure.

This father who had grown up amid the extreme splendors of the Bourbon court knew how to live to the full; he had a deep knowledge of the voluptuous life and also a certain Byronesque inclination toward fanciful romanticism. His own marriage had taken place in almost tragic circumstances, after a furious passion. After that he had disturbed and tormented conjugal harmony in every possible way. In the end he had separated from his wife and had always kept his young son with him, traveling with him throughout Europe.

Andrea's education had hence been, so to say, through life itself, namely not based so much on books as derived from the presence of human reality. His spirit was corrupted not only by high culture but also by experience: and his curiosity became ever sharper as his knowledge grew. Right from the start he had been lavish with himself; because his gift, the power of great sensibility, never tired of providing resources for his prodigality. But the expansion of that power of his led to the destruction in him of another strength, that of *moral strength,* which his own father had not been averse to discouraging. And he did not realize that his life was the progressive reduction of his own faculties, of his hopes, of his pleasure, almost a progressive renunciation; and that the circle was growing ever tighter around him, a process that was inexorable though slow.

His father had given him, among others, this fundamental maxim: "One must *fashion* one's life, as one fashions a work of art. A man's life must be of his own making. This is where true superiority lies."

Additionally, his father would warn him: "One must preserve, at every cost, one's liberty; keep it whole, to the point of exhilaration. The rule of a man of intellect is this:—*Habere, non haberi.*"[3]

He also used to say: "Regret is the fruitless pasture of an idle mind. One must avoid regret above all things, always keeping the mind occupied with new sensations and new imaginings."

But these *voluntary* maxims, which by their ambiguity could also be interpreted as high moral criteria, fell upon an *involuntary* nature, namely, in a man whose willpower was extremely weak.

Another paternal seed had perfidiously borne fruit in Andrea's soul: the seed of sophistry. "The sophism," that incautious educator would say, "is at the base of every human pleasure and pain. To intensify and multiply sophisms is therefore equal to intensifying and multiplying one's pleasure or pain. Perhaps the knowledge of life is to be found in the obscuring of truth. The word is a profound thing, in which for the man of intellect inexhaustible richness is hidden. The Greeks, craftsmen of the word, are in fact the most exquisite hedonists of all antiquity. The sophists flourished in great number in the century of Pericles, in the golden age."

Such a seed had found fertile ground in the morbid genius of the young man. Little by little, in Andrea falsehood had become not so much toward others as toward himself a habit so inherent to his conscience that he had reached a point where he could never be completely sincere, and could no longer regain his self-control.

After the premature death of his father, he found himself alone at the age of twenty-one, commanding a considerable fortune, distanced from his mother, under the sway of his passions and his tastes. He remained in England for fifteen months. His mother remarried to an old lover of hers. And he came to Rome, for which he had a predilection.

Rome was his great love: not the Rome of the Caesars but that of the popes; not the Rome of the arches, of the thermal baths, of the forums, but the Rome of the villas, of the fountains, of the churches. He would have given the entire Colosseum for Villa Medici, Campo Vaccino for Piazza di Spagna, the Arch of Titus for the Fontanella delle Tartarughe. The princely magnificence of the Colonnas, of the Dorias, of the Barberinis attracted him vastly more than the ruins of imperial grandeur. And his great dream was to possess a palace adorned by Michelangelo and embellished by the Caraccis, like Palazzo Farnese; a gallery full of paintings by Raphael, Titian, Domenichino, like the Galleria Borghese; a villa like that of Alessandro Albani where the deep box hedges, the red Oriental granite, the white Luni marble, the Grecian statues, the Renaissance paintings, the memories themselves of the place would cast a spell around one of his haughty lovers. At the home of his cousin the Marchioness of Ateleta, in an album of society confessions, alongside the question "What would you like to be?" he had written "Roman prince."

When he arrived in Rome toward the end of September 1884,

he established his abode in the Palazzo Zuccari at Trinità de' Monti, above that delightful Catholic tepidarium where the shadow of the obelisk of Pius VI marks the passage of Time. He spent the whole month of October absorbed in the decoration of his home; then, when the rooms were adorned and ready, he went through a few days of invincible sadness in his new house. It was an Indian summer, a springtime of the dead,[4] grave and sweet, in which Rome reclined, entirely golden like a city of the Far East, under an almost milky sky, as diaphanous as the heavens mirrored in the southern seas.

That languor of air and light where all things appear almost to lose their reality and become immaterial gave the young man an infinite exhaustion, an inexpressible sense of discontent, discomfort, solitude, emptiness, nostalgia. This vague malaise came perhaps from the change in climate, in habits, in occupation. The soul converts ill-defined impressions of the organism into psychic phenomena, in the way that dreams convert, according to their nature, events that occur during sleep.

Certainly, he was entering into a new phase. Would he finally find the woman and the work capable of taking charge of his heart, and of becoming his *purpose*? He had inside himself neither the confidence of strength nor the expectation of glory or happiness. Completely permeated and saturated with art as he was, he had not yet produced any work of note. Avid for love and pleasure, he had not yet loved anyone completely nor taken innocent pleasure in anything. Tormented by an Ideal, he did not yet have its image well defined at the forefront of his thoughts. Detesting pain by nature and by education, he was vulnerable and accessible to pain in every part of himself.

In the tumult of his contradictory inclinations he had lost all will and all morality. In abdicating his will, he had ceded power to his instincts; his aesthetic sense had substituted his moral sense. But precisely this aesthetic sense, extremely keen and powerful and constantly active, maintained a certain equilibrium in his spirit; hence one could say that his life was a constant struggle between opposing forces enclosed within the limits of a certain equilibrium. Men of intellect, educated in the cult of Beauty, always preserve even in the basest depravities a type of order. The concept of Beauty is, one could say, the *axis* of their interior being, around which all their passions gravitate.

Atop his sadness, the memory of Costantia Landbrooke still floated vaguely, like a faded scent. Conny's love had been a very fine love; and she had been a very pleasant woman. She appeared to be a creation of Thomas Lawrence; she possessed all the particular feminine graces that are dear to that painter of furbelows, laces, velvets, shining eyes, semi-open mouths; she was a second incarnation of the little Countess of Shaftesbury. Vivacious, loquacious, extremely fickle, lavish with childish diminutives and pealing laughter, easily prone to sudden tenderness, instant melancholy, rapid ire, she brought to a love affair much movement, much variety, and many whims. Her most lovable quality was freshness, a tenacious, constant freshness, at all hours of the day. When she awoke after a night of pleasure, she was all fragrant and clean as if she had just emerged from the bathtub. Her figure indeed appeared to Andrea's memory in a particular pose: with her hair partially loose on her neck and gathered partially atop her head with a comb patterned with a Greek design in gold; her irises swimming in white, like a pale violet in milk; her mouth open, dewy, all lit up by her teeth shining in the rosy blood of her gums, in the shadow of the screens, which diffused a glow over the bed that was something between pale blue and silver, similar to the light of a sea cave.

But the melodious chirping of Conny Landbrooke had passed over Andrea's soul like one of those light musical pieces that leaves its refrain in the mind for some time. More than once she had said to him, in one of her evening depressions, with her eyes misted in tears: *"I know you love me not . . ."*[5] In fact, he did not love her; he was not satisfied by her. His feminine ideal was less Nordic. Ideally, he felt attracted to one of those sixteenth-century courtesans who seem to wear some magic veil over their faces, a transparent enchanted mask, almost an obscure nocturnal charm, the divine horror of Night.

Meeting the Duchess of Scerni, Donna Elena Muti, he had thought: *Here is* my *woman.* His entire being felt an upliftment of joy in the anticipation of possessing her.

The first encounter had been at the house of the Marchioness of Ateleta. The salons of this cousin of Andrea's, who lived in

Palazzo Roccagiovine, were very well attended. Her attraction lay especially in her witty cheerfulness, the freedom of her movements, her indefatigable smile. The joyful features of her face recalled certain feminine profiles in the drawings of the young Moreau, or in Gravelot's vignettes. In her manner, in her tastes, in her dress style, there was something Pompadouresque, not without some affectation, because she did have a singular resemblance to Louis XV's favorite mistress.

Every Wednesday, Andrea Sperelli had a place at the marchioness's dining table. One Tuesday evening, in a box at the Valle Theater, the marchioness had laughingly said to him:

—Mind that you don't miss tomorrow, Andrea. We have among our guests an *interesting* person, or rather, *fatal*. Therefore, arm yourself against the spell . . . You are in a moment of weakness.

He had answered her, laughing:

—I shall come vulnerable, if you don't mind, cousin; rather, dressed as a victim. It's an outfit I wear as a seduction ploy, which I've been wearing for many evenings; in vain, alas!

—The sacrifice is at hand, cousin!

—The victim is ready!

The following evening he came to Palazzo Roccagiovine some minutes earlier than the customary hour, with a marvelous gardenia in his buttonhole and a vague disquiet at the base of his soul. His *coupé* had stopped in front of the main door, because the porte-cochère was already occupied by another carriage. The liveries, the horses, all the ceremony that accompanied the lady's descent had the stamp of a great noble family. The count glimpsed a tall and slim figure, a hairstyle shot through with many diamonds, a small foot placed on the step. Then, as he, too, was ascending the stairs, he saw the lady from behind.

She was going up before him, slowly, with a supple and measured pace. Her mantle lined with a snowy fur, like swansdown, no longer held up by its clasp, was lying loosely around her upper body, leaving her shoulders bare. Her shoulders emerged, pale as polished ivory, divided by a soft hollow with shoulder blades that, disappearing below the lace of her bodice, had a brief curve, like the sweet slope of wings; and from her shoulders rose her neck, agile and rounded; and from the nape of her neck her hair, gathered into a coil, folded over at the crown of her head to form a knot held in place by jeweled hairpins.

That harmonious ascension of the unknown woman gave such intense delight to Andrea's eyes that he stopped for an instant on the first landing to admire her. Her train rustled heavily on the stairs. Her manservant walked behind her, not in the wake of his lady on the red carpet, but to one side, along the wall, with an irreprehensible composure. The contrast between that magnificent creature and that rigid automaton was highly bizarre. Andrea smiled.

In the antechamber, while the manservant was taking her mantle, the woman cast a rapid glance toward the young man who was entering. He heard being announced:

—Her Excellency the Duchess of Scerni!

Immediately afterward:

—The Lord Count Sperelli-Fieschi of Ugenta!

And it pleased him that his name was uttered alongside the name of that woman.

In the reception room, the Marquis and Marchioness of Ateleta, the Baron and Baroness of Isola, and Don Filippo del Monte were already present. A fire burned in the fireplace; some couches were arranged in the glow of its heat; four *musae* palms stretched their wide red-veined leaves over the low backrests.

The marchioness, coming forward to the two who by now were standing next to each other, said with her lovely, inextinguishable laugh:

—As chance would have it, there's no need to introduce the two of you. Cousin Sperelli, bow to the divine Elena.

Andrea bowed deeply. The duchess gracefully offered him her hand, looking him in the eyes.

—I am very glad to meet you, Count. A friend of yours spoke to me so much about you at Lucerne last summer: Giulio Musèllaro. I was, I confess, a bit curious . . . Musèllaro also lent me your exceedingly rare *Fable of Hermaphrodite* to read, and gave me as a gift your etching of *Sleep*, a proof mark, a treasure. You have in me a cordial admirer. Remember that.

She spoke, pausing now and again. Her voice was so caressing that it gave the impression almost of a carnal embrace; and she had that involuntary loving and voluptuous gaze that agitates all men and immediately provokes desire in them.

A manservant announced:

—Cavalier Sakumi!

And the eighth and final dinner guest appeared.

He was a secretary of the Japanese Legation, small in stature, yellowish, with protruding cheekbones, long and slanting eyes, veined with blood, over which his eyelids constantly blinked. His body was too broad compared with his too-thin legs; and he walked with his feet turned inward, as if a belt were wound tightly around his hips. The tails of his dress coat were too wide; his trousers had many creases; the tie he wore bore very visible signs of an inexpert hand. He looked like a *daimyo*[6] hauled out of one of those suits of armor made of iron and lacquer that resemble the shells of monstrous crustaceans, then stuffed into the garments of a Western waiter. But even with his awkwardness he had a sharp expression, a kind of ironic refinedness at the corners of his mouth.

Halfway through the reception room, he bowed. His *gibus*[7] fell out of his hand.

The Baroness of Isola, a small blonde, her forehead covered in curls, graceful and coquettish like a young ape, said in her piercing voice:

—Come here, Sakumi, here, next to me!

The Japanese cavalier went forward, smiling and bowing over and over again.

—Will we see Princess Issé this evening? Donna Francesca of Ateleta asked him. She liked to gather in her salons the most bizarre exemplars of the exotic colonies in Rome, for the sake of picturesque variety.

The Asiatic spoke a barbaric language, barely intelligible, of English, French, and Italian mixed together.

Everyone, all at once, began to talk. It was almost a chorus, in the midst of which now and then there could be heard, like gushes of silver spurts, the fresh peals of laughter of the marchioness.

—I have certainly seen you before; I don't remember where, I don't remember when, but I have certainly seen you, Andrea Sperelli said to the duchess, standing very straight in front of her. —While I was watching you walk up the stairs, in the depths of my memory an indistinct recollection was reawakening, something that took form following the rhythm of your ascent, like an image springing from a musical aria . . . I have not yet managed to see the memory clearly; but, when you turned around, I felt that your profile had an undoubted correspondence to that image. It could not be an augury; it was therefore a strange phenomenon of memory. I have most certainly seen you, before. Who knows! Maybe in a dream, maybe in a work of art, maybe in another world, in a previous existence . . .

Uttering these last phrases, overly sentimental and chimeric, he laughed openly as if to thwart an incredulous or ironic smile from the woman. Elena, instead, remained serious. Was she listening or thinking about something else? Did she accept that kind of talk or was she mocking him with that seriousness? Did she mean to indulge the act of seduction initiated by him with such care, or was she withdrawing into indifference or uncaring silence? Was she, in short, able to be conquered by him or not? Andrea, perplexed, examined this mystery. In those who have the habit of seduction, especially the bold, this perplexity provoked by women who remain silent is well known.

A manservant opened the great door that led into the dining hall.

The marchioness placed her arm in that of Don Filippo del Monte and entered the hall first. The others followed.

—Let's go, said Elena.

It seemed to Andrea that she was leaning on him with some abandon. Was it not an illusion brought about by his desire? Perhaps. He tended toward doubt; but, with every moment that passed, he felt a sweet spell conquer him ever more deeply; and with every moment he grew more anxious to penetrate the woman's soul.

—Cousin, over here, said Donna Francesca, assigning him his place.

At the oval table he was seated between the Baron of Isola and the Duchess of Scerni with Cavalier Sakumi facing him. The latter was seated between the Baroness of Isola and Don Filippo del Monte. The marquis and marchioness were at each head. Porcelain, silver, crystal, and flowers glittered on the table.

Very few women could compete with the Marchioness of Ateleta in the art of giving dinner parties. She put more care into preparing a table than into her clothing. The exquisiteness of her taste was apparent in every object; and she was, truly, the arbiter of convivial elegance. Her fantasy and refined taste could be seen reflected in all the dinner tables of Roman nobility. She had, that winter, introduced the fashion of chains of flowers suspended from one side of the table to another, threaded through the great candelabra; and also the fashion of the slender vase of Murano glass, pale and shifting like an opal, containing one single orchid, placed between the various glasses in front of each diner.

—Diabolical flower, said Donna Elena Muti, taking the glass vase and observing from close up the bloodred and deformed orchid.

Her voice was so rich in tonalities that even the most vulgar words and the most common phrases appeared to take on, uttered by her mouth, an occult meaning, a mysterious accent and a new grace. In the same manner, King Midas turned everything he touched to gold.

—A symbolic flower, in your hand, Andrea murmured, gazing at the lady, who in that pose was wondrous to behold.

She was wearing a fabric of an exceedingly pale sky blue scattered with silver dots that sparkled beneath antique white Burano lace, an indefinable white, tending slightly toward fawn, but so slightly that it could barely be perceived. The flower, almost unnatural, as if made by some evil spell, waved about on its stalk, protruding from the fragile tube that its creator had surely forged with one breath into a liquid jewel.

—But I prefer roses, Elena said, replacing the orchid with a gesture of revulsion that contrasted with her previous act of curiosity.

Then she threw herself into the general conversation. Donna Francesca was talking about the latest reception given at the Austrian Embassy.

—Did you see Madame de Cahen? Elena asked her. —She wore a dress of yellow *tulle* scattered with innumerable hummingbirds with ruby eyes. A magnificent dancing birdcage. And Lady Ouless, did you see her? She had on a dress of white tarlatan fabric, with seaweed strewn all over it and I don't know how many goldfish, and over the seaweed and the goldfish there was another layer of sea-green tarlatan. Did you not see her? She was the most impressive beautiful aquarium . . .

And she laughed after making these little cutting remarks, a cordial laugh that lent a tremor to the underside of her chin and her nostrils.

In the presence of this incomprehensible volubility, Andrea was still perplexed. Those frivolous or cutting comments issued forth from the same lips that had just then, uttering a simple phrase, agitated him to the very depths of his soul; they came from the same mouth that just then had seemed to him like the mouth of Leonardo's *Medusa,* a human flower with a soul made divine by the flame of passion and the anguish of death. What, therefore, was the true essence of that creature? Did she have  any perception or consciousness of her constant metamorphosis or was she impenetrable even to herself, remaining on the outside of her own mystique? How much, in her expressions and manifestations, was artificial and how much was spontaneous? The need to know prickled him even amid the delight infused in him by the proximity of the woman he was beginning to love. The wretched habit of analysis continued to incite him still, still preventing him from forgetting; but every effort was punished, like Psyche's curiosity, by the distancing of love, by the eclipsing of every desired object, by the cessation of pleasure. Wasn't it better instead to surrender oneself innocently to the first ineffable sweetness of budding love? He saw Elena in the act of moistening her lips in wine as blond as liquid honey. He sought among the glasses before him the one in which the butler had poured the same wine, and drank with Elena. Both, at the same time, placed their glasses on the table. The commonality of the act made the one turn toward the other. And their look inflamed them both, much more than the sip of wine.

—You are not talking? Elena asked him, affecting lightness in her tone, which altered her voice slightly. —Rumor has it that you are an exquisite conversationalist. Bestir yourself, in that case!

—Oh, cousin, cousin! exclaimed Donna Francesca, with an air of commiseration, while Don Filippo del Monte murmured something in her ear.

Andrea started laughing.

—Cavalier Sakumi, we are the silent ones! Let us bestir ourselves!

The Asian's long eyes glittered with malice, even redder above the dark red flush that the wine was kindling on his cheekbones. Until that moment he had stared at the Duchess of Scerni with the ecstatic expression of a Buddhist priest in the presence of divinity. His wide face, which seemed to have come straight from the classic pages of the great comic illustrator Hokusai, glowed crimson like an August moon amid the chains of flowers.

—Sakumi—added Andrea in a low voice, leaning toward Elena—is in love.

—With whom?

—With you. Have you not noticed?

—No.

—Look at him.

Elena turned. And the loving contemplation of the *daimyo* in disguise prompted in Elena such an open laugh that he was hurt and visibly humiliated.

—Take this, she said to make up for it; and plucking a white camellia from the festoon, she threw it toward the envoy of the Rising Sun. —Find a simile in it, in my honor.

The Asian drew the camellia to his lips with a comic gesture of devotion.

—Ah, ah, Sakumi—said the small Baroness of Isola—you are being unfaithful to me!

He stammered a few words, becoming even more scarlet in the face. Everyone was laughing openly, as if that foreigner had been invited with the sole reason of providing them with a source of entertainment. And Andrea, laughing, turned toward Elena Muti.

Keeping her head lifted high and even tilted back slightly, she was glancing furtively at the young man from beneath her half-closed eyelids, with one of those indescribable female gazes that seem to absorb and almost drink in from the favored man everything in him that is most lovable, most desirable, most delectable, everything that has awoken in her that instinctive sexual exaltation from which passion is born. Her exceedingly long lashes veiled the iris slanted toward the corner of her eye; and the white floated as in a liquid, almost azure light; and an almost imperceptible tremor moved her lower eyelid. It seemed as if the range of her gaze were confined to Andrea's mouth, as if to the sweetest thing.

Elena was, indeed, captivated by that mouth. Pure in form, intense in color, swollen with sensuality, with a slightly cruel expression when firmly closed, that youthful mouth recalled, for its singular resemblance, the portrait of the unknown gentleman that is to be found in the Galleria Borghese, the profound and mysterious work of art in which fascinated minds believed they could perceive the figure of the divine Cesare Borgia painted by the divine Sanzio.[8] When his lips opened in a laugh, that expression vanished; and the white, square, even teeth, of an extraordinary brightness, lit up his mouth, which was as fresh and joyous as that of a young boy's.

As soon as Andrea turned, Elena dropped her gaze; but not so fast that the young man could not catch its blaze. It gave him such a fierce joy that he felt a flame rise to his cheeks. *She wants me! She wants me!* he thought, exulting in the certainty of having already conquered the rare creature. And he also thought: *It is a pleasure never felt before.*

There are certain glances from a woman that a lover would not exchange for the possession of her entire body. Whoever has never seen the radiance of tenderness glow for the first time in another person's clear eyes does not know the highest form of human happiness. After that, no other moment of joy will equal that moment.

While the conversation around them grew more vivacious, Elena asked:

—Will you remain in Rome for the whole winter?

—For the whole winter, and beyond, answered Andrea, for whom that simple question seemed to harbor a promise of love.

—You have a house, therefore!

—Palazzo Zuccari: *domus aurea.*[9]

—At Trinità de' Monti? Lucky you!

—Why lucky?

—Because you live in one of my favorite places.

—All the sovereign charm of Rome is gathered there, like an essence in a vase, isn't it?

—It is true! Between the obelisk of the Trinità and the column of the Conception, my Catholic and pagan heart is suspended *ex-voto*.

She laughed at that phrase. He had a madrigal on the topic of the suspended heart ready to recite, but did not utter it; because he did not like to prolong the dialogue in that false and light tone and thus disperse his intimate pleasure. He remained silent.

She was thoughtful for a while. Then she threw herself into the general conversation again, with even greater vivacity, lavishing witticisms and laughter, her teeth and her words scintillating. Donna Francesca was gossiping about the Princess of Ferentino, not without subtlety, alluding to her lesbian affair with Giovanella Daddi.

—By the way, the Princess of Ferentino is announcing another charity fair for the Epiphany, said the Baron of Isola. —Do you not know about it yet?

—I am the patroness, replied Elena Muti.

—You are a peerless patroness, said Don Filippo del Monte, a man of forty, almost completely bald, a fine crafter of epigrams, who wore on his face a kind of Socratic mask in which his mobile right eye scintillated with a thousand different expressions, while his left remained immobile and almost vitrified beneath the round lens, as if he used one for expressing himself and the other to see with. —At the May Fair, you received a cloud of gold.

—Ah, the May Fair! A folly, exclaimed the Marchioness of Ateleta.

While the butlers passed around the table pouring chilled champagne, she added:

—Do you remember, Elena? Our stalls were close by.

—Five *luigi*[10] for a sip! Five *luigi* for a bite! Don Filippo del Monte began to shout, jokingly imitating the voice of a town crier.

Elena Muti and the Marchioness of Ateleta were laughing.

—Right, right, it's true. You were proclaiming the wares, Filippo, said Donna Francesca. —It's a pity you weren't there, cousin of mine! For five *luigi* you could have eaten some fruit marked by my teeth, and for another five *luigi* you could have drunk champagne from Elena's cupped hands.

—What a scandal! interrupted the Baroness of Isola, with a grimace of horror.

—Ah, Mary! And did you not sell cigarettes lit by yourself, and much moistened, for a *luigi*? said Donna Francesca, still laughing.

And Don Filippo said:

—I saw something better. Leonetto Lanza obtained from the Countess of Lùcoli, for I don't know how much, a Havana cigar that she had held in her armpit . . .

—Goodness gracious! the small baroness interrupted again, comically.

—Every act of charity is blessed, the marchioness decreed. —I, with all my biting of fruit, managed to gather about two hundred *luigi*.

—And you? Andrea Sperelli asked of Elena Muti, smiling with difficulty. —And you, with your fleshly cup?

—I made two hundred and seventy.

Everyone continued to banter in this fashion, except for the marquis. Ateleta was already an old man, afflicted with an incurable deafness, well waxed, painted a blondish color, artificial from head to toe. He resembled one of those fake personages that one sees in wax museums. Every now and then, almost always inopportunely, he emitted a type of dry little laugh that sounded like the squeaking of a rusty machine that he had inside his body.

—But, at a certain point, the price of the sip went up to ten *luigi*. Do you understand? added Elena. —And finally that crazy Galeazzo Secìnaro came to offer me a five-hundred-lire note asking in return that I dry my hands in his blond beard . . .

The finale of the dinner was, as always in the d'Ateleta home, exceedingly splendid; as the true luxury of a dinner table consists of the dessert. All those delicious and rare things delight the eye in addition to the palate, artfully arranged on crystal plates adorned with silver. The festoons threaded with camellias and violets curled between the vine-leafed eighteenth-century candelabra, decorated with fauns and nymphs. And the fauns and the nymphs and the other graceful forms of that Arcadian mythology, and the Sylvanders and the Phyllises and the Rosalinds brought life to the tapestries on the walls with their tenderness, representing one of those luminous landscapes of Cythera that emerged from the imagination of Antoine Watteau.

The light erotic stimulation that invades the spirits at the end of a dinner embellished with women and flowers was revealed by the words being spoken, and revealed by the memories of that May Fair where the women, spurred on by a burning competitiveness to gather the largest possible sum through their vending efforts, had enticed buyers with unprecedented audacity.

—Did you accept? Andrea Sperelli asked the duchess.

—I sacrificed my hands for the sake of Charity, she replied. —Twenty-five *luigi* more!

—*All the perfumes of Arabia will not sweeten this little hand . . .*[11]

He laughed, repeating the words of Lady Macbeth, but deep down in him there was a confused suffering, an ill-defined torment that resembled jealousy. It now suddenly appeared to him that there was a certain excessive or almost courtesan-like air that in some moments dimmed the fine manners of the gentlewoman. From certain sounds of her voice and her laugh, from certain gestures, certain postures, certain glances, she exuded, perhaps involuntarily, a charm that was too aphrodisiacal. She dispensed too easily the visual enjoyment of her graces. From time to time, in front of everyone, perhaps involuntarily, she had a bearing or a position or an expression that in a bedroom would have made a lover thrill. Each person, looking at her, could steal from her a spark of pleasure, make her the object of their impure fantasies, visualize her secret caresses. She seemed to be created, truly, for the sole purpose of the act of love;—and the air she breathed was always inflamed by the desires she provoked around her.

How many have possessed her? Andrea thought. *How many memories does she foster, of the flesh and of the soul?*

His heart swelled as with a bitter wave, at the base of which simmered his tyrannical intolerance of every imperfect possession. And he could not take his eyes off Elena's hands.

In those incomparable hands, soft and white, of an ideal transparency, marked by a web of barely visible blue veins; in those slightly hollowed and rose-shadowed palms, where a clairvoyant would have found dark entanglements, ten, fifteen, twenty men had drunk, one after the other, at a price. He *saw* the heads of those unknown men bending over and sucking the wine. But Galeazzo Secìnaro was one of his friends: a handsome and cheerful gentleman, imperially bearded like a Lucius Verus, and a rival to be feared.

Then, incited by those images, his lust grew so fiercely and he was invaded by an impatience so tormenting that it seemed the dinner would never end. *I will have from her, this same evening, her promise,* he thought. Inside him, anxiety stung him as it would one who fears to see some precious object, coveted by many rivals, escape him. And his incurable and insatiable vanity made the exhilaration of victory tangible. Certainly, the more an object possessed by a man arouses the envy and the craving of others, the more the man takes pleasure and pride in this object. It is precisely this that makes women on the stage so enticing. When the whole theater resounds with applause and burns with desire, he who alone receives the glance and the smile of the star feels drunk with pride, as from a glass of too-strong wine, and loses his reason.

—You who are so innovative—Elena Muti was saying to Donna Francesca, while she cleansed her fingers in tepid water in a bowl of blue crystal edged with silver—you should bring back the custom of washing one's hands with the pitcher and bowl of old, away from the table. This modernity is ugly. Don't you think so, Sperelli?

Donna Francesca stood up. Everyone followed her example. Andrea offered his arm to Elena, bowing, and she looked at him without smiling, while placing her naked arm slowly on his. Her last words had been gay and light; her look, by contrast, was so grave and profound that the young man felt his soul overcome by it.

—Are you going—she was asking him—are you going to the ball at the French Embassy tomorrow evening?

—Are you? Andrea asked her in turn.

—I am, yes.

—So am I.

They smiled, like two lovers. And she added, while taking a seat:

—Sit down.

The couch was placed at some distance from the fireplace, along the rear of the piano, which was partly hidden by rich folds of fabric. A bronze crane at one side held in its uplifted beak a plate suspended from three chains, like a scale; and the plate contained a new book and a small Japanese saber, a *wakizashi,* decorated with silver chrysanthemums on the scabbard, on the guard, and on the hilt.

Elena picked up the book, of which half the pages were still uncut; she read the title; then she replaced it in the plate, which swung from side to side. The saber fell to the ground. As both she and Andrea leaned down to pick it up at the same time, their hands touched. Sitting up again, she examined the beautiful weapon with curiosity; and held it, while Andrea talked to her about that new novel, gradually and by stealth moving toward general topics of love.

—Why ever do you keep yourself so removed from the "grand public"? she asked him. —Have you sworn loyalty to the "Twenty-five Exemplars"?

—Yes, forever. Indeed, my dream is the "Unique Exemplar" to offer to the "Unique Woman." In a democratic society like ours, the creator of prose or verse must renounce every benefit except that of love. The true reader is not really the one who buys me, but the one who loves me. The true reader is therefore the benevolent lady. The laurel serves for nothing other than to attract the myrtle[12] . . .

—But glory?

—True glory is posthumous, and therefore not able to be enjoyed. What does it matter to me, for example, to have one hundred readers on the island of Sardinia, and another ten in Empoli, and five, say, in Orvieto? And what pleasure can I derive from being as well known as the pastry maker Tom and the perfumier Harry? I, the author, will go into posterity armed as best I can, but I, the man, do not desire any other crown of triumph but one . . . of beautiful naked arms.

He looked at Elena's arms, uncovered right to the shoulder. They were so perfect at the join and in their form that they recalled the Florentine simile about the ancient vase "made by the hand of masters"; those of "Pallas before the shepherd" would have been like these. Her fingers wandered over the engravings of the weapon; and her shining nails seemed to replicate the daintiness of the gems that adorned her fingers.

—You, if I am not mistaken—said Andrea, enveloping her in his flaming gaze—must have the body of Correggio's *Danäe*. I feel it, no, I see it in the shape of your hands.

—Oh, Sperelli!

—Can you not imagine the entire shape of the plant from the flower? You are, most certainly, like the daughter of Acrisius who receives the golden shower—not the one of the May Fair, for shame! Do you know the painting in Galleria Borghese?

—I know it.

—Am I wrong?

—Enough, Sperelli: please.

—Why?

She remained silent. By now, both felt the circle that was rapidly to enclose them and bind them together, coming closer. Neither one nor the other was conscious of its rapidity. Only two or three hours after seeing each other for the first time, the one was giving herself to the other, in spirit; and reciprocal surrender seemed natural.

She said, after a while, without looking at him:

—You are very young. Have you been in love many times?

He answered with another question.

—Do you believe that there is greater nobility of soul and of art to imagine in one sole woman the entire feminine Eternal, or that a man of discerning and intense spirit must traverse all the lips that pass by him, like the notes of an ideal harpsichord, until he finds the joyful Ut?[13]

—I don't know. And you?

—I can't either solve this great sentimental uncertainty. But, by instinct, I have traversed the harpsichord; and I fear I have found my Ut, judging at least by my internal warnings.

—You fear?

—*Je crains ce que j'espère.*[14]

He spoke that pretentious language with such naturalness, almost weakening the force of his feeling in the guile of his words. And Elena felt herself caught up by his voice, as in a net, and carried away from the life that moved around them.

—Her Excellency the Princess of Micigliano! announced the manservant.

—The Lord Count of Gissi!

—Madame Chrysoloras!

—The Lord Marquis and Lady Marchioness Massa d'Albe!

The reception rooms were filling up with people. Long sparkling trains traveled over the purple carpet; from bodices spangled with diamonds, embroidered with pearls, enlivened with flowers, emerged naked shoulders; almost every hairstyle sparkled with those wonderful heirloom jewels that make the nobility of Rome the envy of all.

—Her Excellency the Princess of Ferentino!

—His Excellency the Duke of Grimiti!

Already various groups were forming, the various hotbeds of gossip and gallantry. The largest group, consisting entirely of men, was near the piano around the Duchess of Scerni, who had stood up in order to better resist that siege. The Princess of Ferentino approached her friend, to greet her with a remonstration:

—Why didn't you come to Ninì Santamarta's today? We were waiting for you.

She was tall and thin, with two strange green eyes that seemed to be sunken deeply in her dark sockets. She was dressed in black with a neckline coming down to a point on her chest and on her back; she wore in her hair, which was of an ash-blond shade, a great crescent of diamonds, like Diana, and was waving a large fan made of red feathers, with twitching movements.

—Ninì is going to Madame Van Huffel's this evening.

—I'm also going there later for a short while, said Elena Muti. —I'll see her.

—Oh, Ugenta—the princess said, turning to Andrea—I was looking for you to remind you of our engagement. Tomorrow is Thursday. Cardinal Immenraet's auction begins tomorrow at midday. Come and fetch me at one.

—I will not fail, Princess.

—I must get that rock crystal, come what may.

—You will have some rivals, though.

—Who?

—My cousin.

—And who else?

—Me, Elena Muti said.

—You? We shall see.

The gentlemen standing about asked for clarification.

—A ladies' quarrel in the nineteenth century, over a vase of rock crystal that once belonged to Niccolò Niccoli; upon which vase is engraved the Trojan Anchises, who is loosening one of the sandals of Venus Aphrodite, Andrea Sperelli solemnly announced. —The show will be given by kind favor, tomorrow, after one o'clock in the afternoon, in the halls of the public auctions, in Via Sistina. Those contending are the Princess of Ferentino, the Duchess of Scerni, the Marchioness of Ateleta.

Everyone laughed at that proclamation.

The Duke of Grimiti asked:

—Are bets permitted?

—*La cote! La cote!*[15] Don Filippo del Monte began to warble, imitating the strident voice of the bookmaker Stubbs.

The Princess of Ferentino struck him on the shoulder with her red fan. But the jest seemed successful. The betting began. Drawn by the laughter and witticisms that emanated from the group, little by little other ladies and gentlemen approached to take part in the hilarity. The notice of the contest spread rapidly; it took on the proportions of a social event; it engaged all the wits present.

—Give me your arm and we'll go for a walk, said Donna Elena Muti to Andrea.

When they were far from the group, in the adjacent hall, Andrea murmured to her, pressing her arm:

—Thank you!

She leaned on him, stopping every now and then to reply to greetings. She seemed a bit tired; and she was as pale as the pearls of her necklaces. Every elegant young man paid her a hackneyed compliment.

—This stupidity is suffocating me, she said.

Turning around, she saw Sakumi, who was following her, wearing his white camellia in his buttonhole, in silence, his eyes bewildered, not daring to come closer to her. She smiled at him in pity.

—Poor Sakumi!

—Have you only seen him now? Andrea asked her.

—Yes.

—When we were sitting near the piano, he was standing in the embrasure of a window, constantly watching your hands, which were playing with a weapon from his own country, destined for cutting the pages of a Western book.

—Earlier?

—Yes, earlier. Maybe he was thinking: "How sweet it would be to commit *hara-kiri* with that small saber decorated with chrysanthemums that seem to burst forth from the lacquer and the iron, at the touch of her fingers!"

She did not smile. A veil of sadness and almost of suffering had descended over her face; her eyes seemed to be occupied by a darker shadow, vaguely illuminated below her upper lid, as in the glow of a lamp; an expression of pain weighed down the corners of her mouth slightly. She kept her right arm hanging down alongside her dress, holding her fan and her gloves in her hand. She no longer held her hand out to greeters and to flatterers; nor did she pay any more heed to anyone.

—What is the matter, now? Andrea asked her.

—Nothing. I must go to the Van Huffels'. Won't you take me to say good-bye to Francesca; and then accompany me down to my carriage?

They returned to the principal reception hall. Luigi Gullì, a young pianist who had come from his native Calabria in search of fortune, as dark and curly-haired as an Arab, was playing Ludwig van Beethoven's *Sonata in C sharp major* with great spirit. The Marchioness of Ateleta, who was a patroness of his, was standing alongside the piano watching the keyboard. Slowly, the solemn and sweet music caught up all those light spirits in its circles, like a slow but deep whirlpool.

—Beethoven, Elena said, with an almost religious tone, stopping and slipping her arm out from under Andrea's.

She paused to listen in this way, standing next to one of the banana palms. Holding her left arm straight out, she put on a glove with extreme slowness. In that pose, the arc of her back appeared slimmer; her whole figure, extended by her train, seemed taller and more erect; the shadow of the plant veiled and almost spiritualized the pallor of her skin. Andrea looked at her. And her clothes, for him, became mingled with her body.

She will be mine, he thought, with a sort of elation, as the pathos-filled music augmented his excitement. *She will hold me in her arms, on her heart!*

He imagined bending over and placing his mouth on her shoulder. Was it cold, that diaphanous skin which resembled a delicate milk shot through with a golden light? He felt an intense thrill; and half closed his eyelids, as if to prolong it. Her perfume reached him; an indefinable emanation, fresh and yet heady like a vapor of spices. His whole being was rising up and reaching with unrestrained vehemence toward the stunning creature. He would have liked to surround her, draw her inside himself, suck her, drink her, possess her in some superhuman way.

Almost compelled by the overwhelming desire of the young man, Elena turned slightly and smiled at him, with such a tender smile, almost so ethereal, that it did not seem to have been expressed by any movement of her lips but rather by the emission of the soul through the lips, while her eyes remained as sad as ever, as if lost in the distance of some internal dream. They were truly the eyes of Night, so enveloped in shadow, such as da Vinci would perhaps have imagined for an allegory after having seen Lucrezia Crivelli[16] in Milan.

And in the moment that the smile lasted, Andrea felt *alone* with her among the crowd. A huge pride swelled his heart.

Since Elena made as if to put on her other glove, he begged her softly:

—No, not that one!

Elena understood, and left her hand naked.

He had one hope, which was to kiss her hand before she left. Suddenly, in his mind, there arose a vision of the May Fair, when men were drinking wine from the palm of her hand. Again, an acute jealousy stung him.

—Let's go now, she said, taking his arm again.

The sonata had ended, and conversations were being taken up again, more intensely. The manservant announced another two or three names, among which that of the Princess Issé, who was entering with small uncertain steps, dressed in Western style, her oval face smiling, candid and tiny like a netsuke figurine.[17] A rustle of curiosity spread throughout the room.

—Good-bye, Francesca, Elena said, taking her leave of the Marchioness of Ateleta. —See you tomorrow.

—Leaving so early?

—They're waiting for me at the Van Huffels' place. I promised to go.

—What a pity! Mary Dyce is about to sing now.

—Good-bye. See you tomorrow.

—Take this. And good-bye. Sweet cousin, accompany her.

The marchioness gave her a bunch of double violets; and then turned to greet Princess Issé, graciously. Mary Dyce, dressed in red, tall and undulating like a flame, began to sing.

—I am so tired! Elena murmured, leaning on Andrea. —Please, would you ask for my fur coat?

He took the fur from the servant who was holding it out to him. Helping the lady to put it on, he brushed her shoulder with his fingers; and felt her shiver. The entire antechamber was full of valets in different liveries, who were bowing. The soprano voice of Mary Dyce reached them, carrying the words of a ballad by Robert Schumann: *"Ich kann's nicht fassen, nicht glauben . . ."*[18]

They descended the stairs in silence. The servant had gone ahead to call the carriage to the foot of the staircase. They heard the pawing of the horses resounding loudly under the porte-cochère. At every step Andrea felt the light pressure of Elena's arm. She was yielding slightly, holding her head lifted high, indeed tilted slightly back, with her eyes half closed.

—When you were ascending these stairs, you were followed by my unknown admiration. Descending them, you are accompanied by my love, Andrea said to her, in a low, almost humble tone, placing a hesitant pause between the last words.

She did not respond. But she brought the bunch of violets to her nostrils and inhaled their scent. In the act, the wide sleeve of her mantle slipped back along her arm, beyond the elbow. The sight of that living flesh, emerging from the fur like a mass of white roses from snow, once again inflamed longing in the young man's senses, even stronger than before, due to that strange provocative allure attained by the feminine nude when she is partly hidden by a thick, heavy garment. A small shiver moved his lips; and he could barely restrain his words of desire.

But the carriage was ready at the base of the stairs and the servant was at its door.

—The Van Huffel residence, the duchess ordered, mounting the carriage, assisted by the count.

The servant bowed, leaving the door; and took his place. The horses were scraping the ground vigorously, raising sparks.

—Watch out! Elena cried, holding her hand out to the young man; and her eyes and her diamonds glittered in the shadows.

To be with her there in the darkness, and to seek her neck with my mouth under that scented fur! He would have liked to say to her: Take me with you!

The horses pawed.

—Watch out! repeated Elena.

He kissed her hand, pressing it as if to leave a mark of passion on her skin. Then he closed the door. And at the thud, the carriage departed at speed, with a loud reverberation throughout the porte-cochère, exiting into the Forum.

CHAPTER III

Thus began Andrea Sperelli's affair with Donna Elena Muti.

The next day, the halls of the auction house in Via Sistina were crowded with elegant people who had come to watch the contest Andrea had announced.

It was raining hard. A gray light entered those damp and low-ceilinged rooms; along the walls were neatly arranged some pieces of furniture made of carved wood and some large triptychs and diptychs of the Tuscan school of the fourteenth century; four Flemish tapestries representing the *Story of Narcissus* hung to the floor; Metaurensian majolica ceramics took up two long shelves; fabrics, mostly ecclesiastical, were arranged either unfolded on chairs or piled onto tables; the rarest relics, ivories, enameled objects, glass pieces, carved jewels, medals, coins, prayer books, illuminated codices, ornate silverware, were gathered in another showcase behind the auctioneers' table; and a particular odor, emanating from the dampness of the place and from those ancient things, filled the air.

When Andrea Sperelli entered accompanying the Princess of Ferentino, he felt a secret quiver. He thought: *Has she already come?* and his eyes rapidly sought *her* out.

She had indeed already come. She was sitting in front of the table between Cavalier Dàvila and Don Filippo del Monte. She had placed her gloves and her otter muff, from which a bunch of violets peeped out, on the edge of the table. She held a small silver picture in her fingers, attributed to Caradosso Foppa; and was examining it with much attention. Objects were passing from hand to hand along the table; and the auctioneer was praising them loudly; the people standing behind the row of chairs leaned over to see; and then the auction sale began. The figures proceeded rapidly. At each step, the auctioneer would cry:

—Do I hear . . . ?

An amateur, incited by his cry, would call a higher sum, looking at his adversaries. The auctioneer would shout, his gavel raised:

—Going once, twice, third and final call: SOLD!

And would pound his gavel on the table. The object would go to the last bidder. A murmur would spread; then once again the contest would heat up. Cavalier Dàvila, a Neapolitan gentleman of gigantic proportions and almost feminine mannerisms, a celebrated collector and connoisseur of majolica ceramics, gave his judgment on each important piece. There were in truth three superior things in that cardinalitial sale: the *Story of Narcissus*, the rock crystal chalice, and a helmet made of embossed silver by Antonio del Pollajuolo, which the Signoria of Florence gave the Count of Urbino in 1472 as reward for services rendered by him at the time of the conquest of Volterra.

—Here is the princess, Don Filippo del Monte said to Elena Muti.

Elena arose to greet her friend.

—Already in the field! exclaimed the Princess of Ferentino.

—Already.

—And Francesca?

—She's not here yet.

Four or five elegant gentlemen, the Duke of Grimiti, Roberto Casteldieri, Ludovico Barbarisi, Giannetto Rùtolo, approached. Others arrived. The pouring rain drowned the sound of speech.

Donna Elena held out her hand to Andrea Sperelli, matter-of-factly, as to everyone else. He felt himself distanced by that handshake. Elena seemed cold and serious to him. All his dreams froze and collapsed in one moment; the memories of the preceding evening became confused; his hopes died. What was the matter with her? She was no longer the same woman. She wore a kind of long tunic made of otter and a kind of mortarboard cap on her head, also of otter. In her facial expression there was something sour and almost scornful.

—There's still time before the goblet, she said to the princess; and sat down again.

Every object passed through her hands. A centaur engraved in chalcedony, a very fine piece of work, perhaps originating from the dispersed museum of Lorenzo il Magnifico, tempted her. And she took part in the contest. She communicated her bids to the auctioneer in a low voice, without raising her eyes to him. At a certain point her competitors withdrew: she obtained the stone at a good price.

—An excellent purchase, said Andrea Sperelli, who was standing behind her chair.

Elena could not restrain a slight tremor. She picked up the chalcedony and gave it to him to look at, lifting her hand to shoulder height without turning around. It was truly a very beautiful thing.

—It could be the centaur that Donatello copied, Andrea added.

And in his soul, together with his admiration for the beautiful object, admiration arose for the noble taste of the woman who now possessed it. *She is therefore, in everything, an* elect spirit, he thought. *How much pleasure she could give a refined lover!* In his imagination she was growing in dimension; but in growing, she was escaping him. The great confidence of the evening before was changing into a kind of discouragement; and his original doubts rose up again. He had dreamed too much during the night; daydreaming, swimming in an endless happiness, while the memory of a gesture, a smile, a position of her head, a fold of her dress caught him and ensnared him like a net. Now, that entire imaginary world was collapsing miserably, coming into contact with reality. He had not seen in Elena's eyes the special greeting about which he had thought so much; he had not been singled out by her, from among the others, with any sign. *Why?* He felt humiliated. All those fatuous people around him made him angry; those things that attracted her attention made him angry; Don Filippo del Monte, who was leaning down toward her every now and then, perhaps to murmur some nasty gossip to her, made him angry. The Marchioness of Ateleta arrived. She was, as usual, cheerful. Her laughter, amid the men that already surrounded her, made Don Filippo turn around eagerly.

—The Trinity is perfect, he said, and got up.

Andrea immediately occupied his chair, next to Elena Muti. When the subtle scent of violets reached his nostrils, he murmured:

—They're not the ones from last night.

—No, said Elena, coldly.

In her mutability, undulating and caressing like a wave, there was always the threat of unexpected frost. She was prone to instant rigidity. Andrea remained silent, not comprehending.

—Do I hear . . . ? cried the auctioneer.

The numbers mounted. The competition was fierce for the helmet by Antonio del Pollajuolo. Even Cavalier Dàvila took up the gauntlet. It seemed that little by little the air was heating up and that the desire for those beautiful and rare objects was capturing every spirit. The mania spread like a contagion. That year in Rome, the love for *bibelots* and *bric-à-brac* had reached excesses; every salon of the nobility and of the upper bourgeoisie was cluttered with "curiosities"; every lady cut the cushions of her couch from a chasuble or from a cope, and placed her roses in an Umbrian pharmacist's vase or in a goblet made of chalcedony. The places of public auction were a favorite meeting place; and sales were very frequent. Ladies would arrive at afternoon tea, flaunting their elegance, saying, "I've just come from the sale of the painter Campos. Much hustle and bustle. His Arabo-Hispanic plates are magnificent! I bought a jewel that belonged to Maria Leczinska.[1] Here it is."

—Do I hear . . . ?

The figures rose. The table was thronged with amateurs. The elegant crowd devoted themselves to fine talk, among the Nativities and the Annunciations by Giotto. Ladies, amid that odor of mold and curios, bore the scent of their fur coats and, most noticeably, that of violets, because every muff contained a small bunch, as was charmingly decreed by fashion. With the presence of so many people a pleasant mist pervaded the air, as in a damp chapel where many faithful have congregated. The rain continued to pour down outside and the light to diminish. Gaslights were lit; and the two different intensities of light competed against each other.

—Going once, twice, third and final call: SOLD!

The thump of the gavel gave possession of the Florentine helmet to Lord Humphrey Heathfield. The sale began once more, of small objects, which passed along the table from hand to hand. Elena took them delicately, examined them, and then placed them in front of Andrea without saying anything. There were enamels, ivories, timepieces of the eighteenth century, jewelry made by Milanese goldsmiths from the time of Ludovico il Moro, prayer books written in gold letters on parchment illuminated with blue. In Elena's aristocratic hands, those precious materials seemed to acquire value. Her small hands appeared on occasion to tremble slightly, coming into contact with the most desirable things. Andrea watched intently; and in his imagination he transformed every motion of those hands into a caress. But why was Elena placing every object on the table, instead of holding them out to him?

He anticipated Elena's gesture, holding out his hand. And from then on, the ivories, the enamels, the jewelry passed from the fingers of the loved one to those of the lover, transmitting an indefinable delight. It seemed that a particle of the amorous charm of that woman passed into them, the way some of the qualities of a magnet pass into a piece of iron. It was truly a magnetic sensation of pleasure, one of those intense and profound sensations that one feels almost only at the beginning of a love affair, and that appear to have neither a physical basis nor a spiritual one, like all others, but have rather a basis in a neutral element of our beings, in an element one could almost call intermediate, unknown by nature, less simple than a spirit, more fragile than a shape, where passion is collected as in a bowl, from which passion radiates outward as from a hearth.

It is a pleasure never felt before, Andrea thought once more.

A slight torpor was invading his senses and he was slowly losing consciousness of place and time.

—I advise you to buy this timepiece, Elena said to him with a look whose significance he did not at first understand.

It was a small skull carved into ivory with extraordinarily good anatomical precision. Each jawbone bore a row of diamonds, and two rubies glinted at the base of the eye sockets. On the forehead a motto was inscribed: RUIT HORA;[2] on the occipital bone, there was another motto: TIBI, HIPPOLYTA.[3] The skull opened like a hinged box, although the joint was almost invisible. The inner heartbeat of the device gave that small skull an inexpressible semblance of life. That burial jewel, the gift of a mysterious craftsman to his woman, would have marked the hours of exhilaration and symbolized a warning for loving souls.

In truth, Pleasure could not wish for a more exquisite and more stimulating meter of time. Andrea thought: *Is she advising me to buy it* for us? And with that thought all his hopes revived and rose up again amid the uncertainty, confusedly. He threw himself into the contest with a kind of enthusiasm. Two or three ruthless competitors responded to him, among whom Giannetto Rùtolo, who, being the lover of Donna Ippolita Albónico, was attracted by the inscription: TIBI, HIPPOLYTA.

After a short while, only Rùtolo and Sperelli remained as contenders. The figures rose above the real price of the object, while the dealers smiled. At a certain point, Giannetto Rùtolo stopped bidding, beaten down by the obstinacy of his rival.

—Do I hear . . . ?

Donna Ippolita's lover, slightly pale, shouted out one last sum. Sperelli added to it. There was a moment of silence. The auctioneer looked at both bidders; then slowly lifted his gavel, watching them all the time.

—Going once, twice, third and final call: SOLD!

The death's head was Sperelli's. A murmur spread throughout the hall. A ray of light entered through the window, glittered on the gilded backgrounds of the triptychs and lit up the sorrowful forehead of a Sienese Madonna and the little gray hat of the Princess of Ferentino, which was covered in steel spangles.

—When's it going to be the goblet? the princess asked impatiently.

Her friends looked at the catalogues. There was no more hope that the goblet of the bizarre Florentine humanist would go up for sale that day. Due to the great deal of competition, the sale was proceeding slowly. A long list of tiny objects still remained, such as cameos, coins, medals. Some antique dealers and Prince Stroganow disputed every item. All those waiting felt disappointed. The Duchess of Scerni stood up to leave.

—Good-bye, Sperelli, she said. —I'll see you this evening, perhaps.

—Why "perhaps"?

—I feel very ill.

—Whatever is the matter?

Without answering, she turned to the others to say good-bye. But the others were following her example; they were going out together. The young men quipped about the spectacle that had not taken place. The Marchioness of Ateleta was laughing, but the Princess of Ferentino appeared to be in a filthy mood. The servants waiting in the corridor called the carriages forward, as at the door of a theater or a concert hall.

—Aren't you coming to Laura Miano's? the Marchioness of Ateleta asked Elena.

—No, I'm going home.

She waited on the edge of the pavement for her *coupé* to come forward. The rain was dispersing; between the great white clouds one could see some patches of blue; one area of light rays made the flagstones shine. And the lady, struck by that light, of a shade between blond and rose pink, in her magnificent cloak that fell with a few straight, almost symmetrical folds, was beautiful. The same dream of the evening before rose up in Andrea's mind when he glimpsed the interior of the *coupé* upholstered in satin as in a *boudoir,* with its shining silver cylinder full of hot water used for warming small noble feet. *To be there, with her, in that cozy intimacy, in that warmth made of* her *breath, in the scent of wilted violets, barely glimpsing the muddy streets, the gray houses, the humble masses through the clouded windowpanes!*

But she bowed her head slightly at the window, without smiling; and the carriage departed, toward Palazzo Barberini, leaving a vague sadness, an undefined discouragement in his soul. She had said "perhaps." Perhaps she would not come to Palazzo Farnese. And in that case?

This uncertainty afflicted him. The thought of not seeing her again was unbearable: every hour that he spent away from her already weighed heavily on him. He asked himself: *Do I already love her so much, then?* His spirit seemed to be enclosed in a circle within which whirled pell-mell all the phantasms of the feelings felt in the presence of that woman. Suddenly there would emerge from his memory with extraordinary precision a phrase of hers, an intonation of her voice, a pose, a movement of her eyes, the shape of a couch on which she was sitting, the finale of Beethoven's sonata, a note sung by Mary Dyce, the figure of the servant standing at the door of the coach, any detail, any fragment, and they obscured with the vividness of their image the things of his current existence; they superimposed themselves upon present things. He spoke to her mentally; he said mentally everything he would say to her later in reality, in their future talks. He foresaw the scenes, the incidents, the events, the entire unfolding of their love affair, according to the promptings of his desire. How would she give herself to him, for the first time?

While he ascended the stairs of Palazzo Zuccari to enter his apartment, this thought flashed across his mind. She, certainly, would come there. Via Sistina, Via Gregoriana, the square of Trinità de' Monti, especially at certain times, were almost deserted. The house was inhabited only by foreigners. She could therefore venture there without fear. But how to entice her? His impatience was so great that he would have liked to be able to say "She will come tomorrow!"

She is free, he thought. *No husband keeps guard on her. No one can ask her to account for long or even unusual absences. She is mistress of her every act, always.* To his mind, immediately, whole days and whole nights of passion presented themselves. He looked around in the hot, deep, secret room; and that intense and refined luxury all made of art, pleased him, for *her.* That air awaited *her* breath; those carpets asked to be pressed under *her* foot; those cushions wanted the imprint of *her* body.

She will love my house, he thought. *She will love the things that I love.* The thought gave him an unutterable sense of sweetness; and it seemed to him already that a new soul, conscious of imminent joy, palpitated under the high ceilings.

He asked his manservant for tea; and made himself comfortable in front of the fireplace to enjoy the fictions of his hope all the better. He took the small jeweled skull out of its case and began to examine it with care. In the light of the fire, the fragile diamond teeth glittered on the yellowed ivory, and the two rubies illuminated the shadows of the eye sockets. Beneath the polished cranium resounded the incessant beat of time—RUIT HORA. What kind of craftsman could ever have imagined for his

Ippolita such a proud and free fantasy of death, in the century when master enamelists were painting tender pastoral idylls on the little watches destined to mark the trysting hours of gallants with their ladies in Watteau's parks? The sculpture revealed an erudite, vigorous hand, master of its own style: it was in all ways worthy of a fifteenth-century artist as insightful as Verrocchio.[4]

"I advise you to buy this timepiece." Andrea smiled a little, remembering Elena's words uttered in such a strange way, after such a cold silence. Undoubtedly, in saying that phrase, she was thinking of love: she was thinking of imminent love trysts, without a doubt. But then why had she become so impenetrable again? Why had she taken no more notice of him? What was wrong with her? Andrea lost himself in the examination of this thought. However, the warm air, the softness of the armchair, the dim light, the flickering of the fire, the aroma of the tea, all those pleasant sensations brought his spirit back to errant pleasures. His mind was wandering aimlessly, as in a fantastical labyrinth. Sometimes his thoughts took on the effects of opium: they could intoxicate him.

—May I remind the Lord Count that he is awaited at the Doria residence at seven o'clock, the manservant said in a low voice, having also the duty of reminding Andrea of his appointments. —Everything is ready.

He went to dress in the octagonal room, which was, in truth, the most elegant and comfortable dressing room that a young modern gentleman could desire. When dressing, he had an infinite number of detailed attentions that he lavished upon his person. Upon a large Roman sarcophagus, transformed with much taste into a dressing table, there were neatly arranged his batiste handkerchiefs, dancing gloves, wallets, cigarette cases, essence vials, and five or six fresh gardenias in small blue porcelain vases. He chose a handkerchief with white initials and dabbed it with two or three drops of *pao rosa;*[5] he did not take a gardenia because he would find one on the table at the Doria residence; he filled with Russian cigarettes a case made of beaten gold, very slender, with a sapphire set into the thumb piece, slightly curved to fit around the thigh inside the pocket of one's trousers. Then he left.

At the Doria house, between one topic and another, after

mentioning the recent childbirth of Duchess Miano, Duchess Angelieri said:

—It appears as if Laura Miano and Elena Muti are quarreling.

—About Giorgio, perhaps? another lady asked, laughing.

—Rumor has it. The whole thing started this summer in Lucerne . . .

—But Laura wasn't in Lucerne.

—Exactly. Her husband was, though . . .

—I think that's just nasty gossip; nothing else, interrupted the Florentine countess, Donna Bianca Dolcebuono.

—Giorgio is in Paris now.

Andrea had heard this, even though on his right the talkative Countess Starnina kept him constantly occupied. The words of Countess Dolcebuono were not enough to soothe the piercing stab he felt. He would have liked, at least, to know everything. But Duchess Angelieri did not continue; and other conversations mingled amid the centerpieces fashioned from the magnificent roses of Villa Pamphily.

Who was this Giorgio? Elena's last lover perhaps? She had spent part of the summer in Lucerne. She had just returned from Paris. In leaving the auction sale, she had refused to go to the Miano residence. In Andrea's mind, it seemed as if everything was in her disfavor. An atrocious desire invaded him, to see her again, to speak to her. The invitation to Palazzo Farnese was for ten; at half past ten he was already there, waiting.

He waited for a long time. The halls were filling up rapidly; the dancing was beginning: in Annibale Caracci's gallery the demigoddesses of ancient Rome competed in comeliness with the Ariadnes, the Galateas, the Auroras, the Dianas of the frescoes; the whirling couples exuded perfumes; the gloved hands of the ladies pressed the shoulders of dance partners; the jeweled heads were bent over or held high; certain semi-open mouths shone like crimson; certain bare shoulders glistened, veiled with moisture; certain bosoms appeared to burst out of their corsets from the force of exertion.

—You aren't dancing, Sperelli? asked Gabriella Barbarisi, a girl as brown-skinned as the *oliva speciosa,* passing by on the arm of a dancer, waving her fan in her hand and causing a mole in a dimple near her mouth to shift with her smile.

—Yes, later, answered Andrea. —Later.

Indifferent to the introductions and greetings of others, he felt his torment grow in the futility of his wait; and wandered from room to room at random. The word "perhaps" made him fear that Elena was not coming. And if she really did not come? When would he see her again? Donna Bianca Dolcebuono passed by; and, without knowing why, he fell in beside her, saying many courteous things to her, feeling a sense almost of relief in her company. He would have liked to talk to her about Elena, to interrogate her, to reassure himself. The orchestra began a rather languid mazurka; and the Florentine countess entered the dance with her partner.

Then Andrea turned to a group of young men who were standing near a door. There was Ludovico Barbarisi, there was the Duke of Beffi, with Filippo del Gallo, with Gino Bommìnaco. They watched the couples circle the room, and gossiped, rather vulgarly. Barbarisi recounted having seen both curves of the bosom of the Countess of Lùcoli, while dancing the waltz. Bommìnaco demanded:

—But how?

—Try. Just look down her *corsage*.[6] I assure you it's worth the trouble . . .

—Have you noticed the armpits of Madame Chrysoloras? Look!

The Duke of Beffi indicated a lady dancing who had on her forehead, as white as the marble of Luni, a pile of red locks, like a high priestess painted by Alma-Tadema.[7] Her bodice was joined at the shoulders by a simple ribbon, and one could discern in each of her armpits an overabundant clump of reddish hair.

Bommìnaco started deliberating upon the singular odor of red-haired women.

—You know that odor well, Barbarisi said with malice.

—Why?

—Princess Micigliano . . .

The young man was manifestly smug at hearing one of his lovers mentioned. He didn't protest, but laughed; then, turning to Sperelli, he said:

—What's wrong with you this evening? Your cousin was

looking for you, a moment ago. She's dancing with my brother now. There she is.

—Look! exclaimed Filippo del Gallo. —Donna Albónico is back. She's dancing with Giannetto.

—Elena Muti also got back, a week ago, said Ludovico. —What a beautiful creature!

—Is she here?

—I haven't seen her yet.

Andrea felt his heart jump, fearing that some unpleasant gossip about her, too, would issue from one of those mouths. But the passage of Princess Issé on the arm of the minister of Denmark distracted his friends. Nonetheless he felt compelled by rash curiosity to bring the talk back to the name of his beloved, in order to know, to discover; but he did not dare. The mazurka was ending; the group was dispersing. *She is not coming! She is not coming!* His internal anxiety was becoming so powerful that he thought he would leave the halls, because the contact with that crowd was unbearable for him.

Turning, he saw the Duchess of Scerni appear at the entrance to the gallery on the arm of the ambassador of France. In a moment, he met her gaze; and their eyes, in that moment, seemed to mingle with each other, penetrate each other, drink each other in. Both felt that each sought the other; both felt, at the same time, silence descend upon their souls, amid all that noise, and something akin to an abyss open up into which all the surrounding world disappeared, under the force of one thought.

She came forward[8] through Caracci's frescoed gallery, to where the crowd was thinner, bearing a long white brocade train that followed her like a heavy wave on the floor. So white and simple, in passing she turned her head toward the many greetings, displaying an air of tiredness, smiling with a small visible effort that creased the corners of her mouth, while her eyes seemed wider under her bloodless forehead. Not only her forehead but all the lines of her face had taken on an almost psychic tenuity in its extreme paleness. She was no longer the woman seated at the d'Ateletas' table, nor the one at the table of the auction sale, nor the one standing for an instant on the sidewalk of Via Sistina. Her beauty now held an expression of sovereign ideality, which shone all the more in the midst of those other women, red in the face from dancing, excited, overactive, slightly agitated. Some men, observing her, became pensive. She elicited even in the most obtuse or fatuous of spirits a sense of commotion, uneasiness, an indefinable aspiration. Those whose heart was free imagined loving her, with a profound thrill; those who had a lover felt an obscure regret, their hearts unsatisfied, dreaming of some unknown delight; whoever harbored within themselves the open wound caused by the jealousy or deceit of some other woman, felt sure that they would be able to heal.

She came forward this way, receiving reverences on all sides, enveloped in the gaze of men. At the end of the gallery she joined a group of ladies who were talking excitedly, waving their fans, below the painting of Perseus and Phineus turned to stone. The Princess of Ferentino, the Marchioness Massa d'Albe, the Marchioness Daddi-Tosinghi, and Countess Dolcebuono were there.

—Why are you so late? the latter asked of her.

—I was very hesitant about coming, because I don't feel well.

—Indeed, you are pale.

—I think I'm getting neuralgia in my face again, like last year.

—I hope not!

—Look, Elena, Madame de la Boissière, said Giovanella Daddi, with that strange hoarse voice of hers. —Doesn't she look like a camel dressed as a cardinal, with a yellow wig?

—Mademoiselle Vanloo is going crazy over your cousin this evening, said the Marchioness Massa d'Albe to the princess, seeing Sofia Vanloo pass by on the arm of Ludovico Barbarisi. —I heard her begging, earlier, after a polka, next to me: *"Ludovic, ne faites plus ça en dansant; je frissonne toute . . ."*[9]

The ladies began to laugh in unison, waving their fans. The first notes of a Hungarian waltz reached them from the nearby ballrooms. Dancing partners presented themselves. Andrea could finally offer his arm to Elena and draw her away with him.

—Waiting for you, I thought I would die! If you had not come, Elena, I would have searched for you everywhere. When I saw you enter the room, I could barely restrain a shout. This is the second evening that I'm seeing you, but I seem to have loved you for I don't know how long. The one, incessant thought of you, is now the life of my life . . .[10]

He spoke these words of love in a humble tone, without looking at her, keeping his eyes fixed in front of him; and she listened to them in the same pose, seemingly impassive, almost marblelike. Few people remained in the gallery. Along the walls, among the busts of the Caesars, the opaque crystal lampshades shaped like lilies cast a uniform light, not overly bright. The profusion of green and flowered plants gave the impression of a sumptuous greenhouse. The waves of music undulated through the warm air below the concave and sonorous vaulted ceilings, passing along all those mythological figures like a breeze flowing over an opulent garden.

—Will you love me? asked the young man. —Tell me that you'll love me!

She answered slowly:

—I came here only for you.

—Tell me that you'll love me! the young man repeated, feeling all the blood in his veins flood to his heart in a torrent of joy.

She answered:

—Perhaps.

And she gazed at him with the same gaze that the evening before had seemed to him a divine promise, that indefinable gaze that almost gave one's flesh the sensation of a hand's loving touch. Then both fell silent; and they listened to the enveloping dance music, which now and then became as soft as a whisper or rose up like a sudden whirlwind.

—Would you like to dance? Andrea asked, trembling internally at the thought of holding her in his arms.

She hesitated briefly. Then she replied:

—No, I don't want to.

Seeing the Duchess of Bugnara, her maternal aunt, and Princess Alberoni entering the room with the French ambassador's wife, she added:

—Now, be prudent; leave me.

She held out her gloved hand to him; and went to meet the three women, alone, with a rhythmic and light step. The long white train gave a sovereign grace to her figure and her step, due to the contrast between the width and weight of the brocade and the narrowness of her waist. Andrea, watching her go, mentally repeated her phrase: "I came only for you." She was just so beautiful, for him, for him alone! Instantly, from the base of his heart, the residue of bitterness left there by the words of the Duchess Angelieri disappeared. The orchestra now threw itself enthusiastically into a reprise. And he never forgot those notes, nor that sudden anguish, nor the pose of the woman, nor the splendor of the fabric trailing behind her, nor the smallest fold, nor the slightest shadow, nor any detail of that supreme moment.

CHAPTER IV

Shortly afterward, Elena had left Palazzo Farnese almost in secret, without taking leave of Andrea or anyone else. She had therefore stayed at the ball for barely half an hour. Her lover searched for her through all the rooms, for a long time and in vain.

The next morning, he sent a servant to Palazzo Barberini to hear news of her; and heard that she was ill. That evening he went there in person, hoping to be received, but a maid told him that the lady was suffering greatly and could not see anyone. On Saturday, toward five in the afternoon, he returned, still hoping.

He left Palazzo Zuccari on foot. It was a violet and ashen sunset, somewhat doleful, which little by little was draping itself over Rome like a ponderous velarium.[1] Around the fountain of Piazza Barberini the streetlamps were already burning with small faint flames, like candles around a dead body; and the Triton was no longer spouting water, perhaps due to restoration or cleaning. Carts descended the slope drawn by two or three horses harnessed one behind the other, and throngs of workmen returned from the new construction sites. Some, linked arm in arm, were staggering and singing a rude song at the tops of their voices.

He stopped to let them pass. Two or three of those ruddy and sinister figures remained imprinted on his mind. He noted that one carter had a bandaged hand and the bandages were stained with blood. He also noted another carter kneeling on a cart, with a livid face, hollowed eye sockets, his mouth shrunken like that of a poisoned man. The words of the song mingled with the guttural shouts, the blows of the whips, the noise of the wheels, the jingling of the harness bells, the insults, the curses, and the harsh laughs.

His sadness worsened. He was in a strange state of mind. The sensitivity of his nerves was so acute that every minimal sensation that came to him from external things felt like a deep wound. While one fixed thought occupied and tormented his entire being, his entire being was exposed to the jolts of life surrounding him. Contrary to every mental derangement and sluggishness of will, his senses remained alert and active; and he had an imprecise consciousness of that activity. The clusters of sensations would suddenly pass through his spirit, similar to great illusions in the dark; and they disturbed and alarmed him. The clouds in the sunset, the shape of the dark Triton in a circle of unlit streetlamps, that barbaric descent of bestial men and enormous packhorses, those shouts, those songs, those curses, exasperated his sadness and aroused a vague fear in his heart, an ill-defined tragic foreboding.

A closed carriage was exiting the garden. He saw the face of a woman lean toward the glass pane, in the act of greeting; but he did not recognize her. The building rose up before him, as vast as a royal palace; the windows of the first floor glinted with purplish reflections; above it, a weak glow still lingered; from the vestibule emerged another closed carriage.

If only I could see her! he thought, stopping. He slowed his pace, to prolong his uncertainty and hope. She seemed very far away, almost lost, in that huge building.

The carriage stopped; and a man thrust his head out of the window, calling:

—Andrea!

It was the Duke of Grimiti, a relative.

—Are you going to the Duchess of Scerni's? he asked, with a subtle smile.

—Yes—Andrea replied—to get news. You know, she's ill.

—I know. I've just come from there. She's feeling better.

—Is she receiving visitors?

—Not me. But maybe she'll be able to receive you.

And the Duke of Grimiti began to laugh with malice, amid the smoke of his cigarette.

—I don't understand, said Andrea in a serious tone.

—Take heed; people are already saying that you are in favor. I heard it yesterday evening, at the Pallavicinis'; from a lady friend of yours: I swear it.

Andrea made a gesture of impatience and turned to go.

—*Bonne chance!*[2] the duke shouted to him.

Andrea entered beneath the portico. Deep down, his vanity relished the fact that rumors were already flying. He felt more confident now, lighter, almost happy, filled with an intimate complacency. The words of the Duke of Grimiti had suddenly lifted his spirits like a sip of liqueur. His hopes rose as he climbed the stairs. When he reached the door, he paused in order to control his anxiety. He rang the bell.

The servant recognized him; and immediately said:

—If the Lord Count would be so good as to wait a moment, I shall go and advise *Mademoiselle*.

He assented; and started pacing up and down the vast antechamber, throughout which, it seemed to him, the violent tumult of his blood reverberated. The wrought-iron lanterns cast an uneven light over the leather covering the walls, the sculpted chests, the ancient busts on *broccatello* marble pedestals. Below the canopy the ducal heraldic device was embroidered in gleaming silks: a golden unicorn on a red field. At the center of a table there was a bronze plate overflowing with visiting cards; and, glancing at it, Andrea saw the Duke of Grimiti's recent one. "*Bonne chance!*" The ironic greeting still resounded in his ears.

Mademoiselle appeared, saying:

—The duchess is slightly better. I think the Lord Count may go in for a moment. Please come with me.

She was a woman whose youth had already faded; rather thin, dressed in black, with two gray eyes that glinted strangely amid her fake blond curls. Her step and her gestures were extremely light, almost furtive, like one who has the habit of living around invalids or attending to delicate duties, or carrying out orders in secret.

—Come, Lord Count.

She preceded Andrea through the dimly lit rooms, over the thick carpets that muffled every sound; and the young man, even in the midst of the unrelenting tumult of his spirit, felt an instinctive sense of revulsion toward her, without knowing why.

Having reached a door that was covered by two panels of Medicean tapestry edged with red velvet, she stopped, saying:

—I shall enter first, to announce you. Please wait here.

A voice, Elena's voice, called from within:

—Cristina!

Andrea felt his veins tremble with such force at that unexpected sound that he thought: *That's it, now I'm going to faint.* He had a kind of indistinct foreshadowing of some supernatural happiness that went beyond his expectations, surpassed his dreams, overcame his strength. She was there, on the other side of that threshold. Every notion of reality was abandoning his spirit. It seemed to him that he had once imagined, picturesquely or poetically, a similar love affair, in that same way, with that same setting, with that same background, with that same mystery; and *another,* some imaginary character of his, was its hero. Now, by some strange phenomenon of his imagination, that ideal artistic fiction was becoming confused with the real event; and he felt an inexpressible sense of bewilderment.

Each heraldic panel bore a symbolic figure. Silence and Sleep, two youths, swift and rangy as only the Bolognese painter Primaticcio could have drawn them, guarded the door. And he, he himself, was standing there waiting; and beyond the threshold, perhaps in bed, his divine lover was breathing. He believed he could hear her breath in the beating of his arteries.

Mademoiselle exited, eventually. Holding up the heavy fabric with her hand, she said in a low voice, with a smile:

—You may enter.

And she withdrew. Andrea entered the room.

At first he had the impression of very warm air, almost suffocating; in the air he smelled the singular odor of chloroform; he discerned something red in the shadow, the red damask of the walls, the curtains of the bed; he heard Elena's tired voice, which murmured:

—I thank you, Andrea, for having come. I'm feeling better.

Slightly hesitant, because he could not see things distinctly in that faint light, he approached the bed.

She smiled, her head pressed back into the pillows, supine, in the half-light. A band of white wool was wrapped around her forehead and cheeks, passing under her chin like a nun's wimple; the skin of her face was as pale as that bandage. The outer corners of her eyelids clenched with the painful contraction of her inflamed nerves; at intervals, her lower lid had a small involuntary tremor; and her eyes were damp, infinitely sweet, as if veiled by a tear that could not brim over, almost imploring, between her trembling lashes.

An immense tenderness invaded the young man's heart, when he saw her from close up. Elena drew a hand from under the covers and held it out to him, very slowly. He bent over, almost kneeling against the side of the bed; and began to cover that burning hand, that fast-beating pulse, with light rapid kisses.

—Elena! Elena! My love!

Elena had closed her eyes as if to enjoy more intimately the stream of pleasure rising up her arm and spreading across her chest and insinuating itself into her most intimate fibers. She turned her hand under his mouth to feel his kisses on her palm, on the back of her hand, between her fingers, all around her wrist, along all her veins, in all her pores.

—Enough! she murmured, opening her eyes again; and with her hand, which seemed to her somewhat sluggish, she stroked Andrea's hair.

In that tender caress there was so much abandon that it was, for his soul, the rose petal placed on the brimming cup.[3] His passion overflowed. His lips trembled beneath the confused wave of words that he did not recognize, that he did not utter. He had a violent and divine sensation as of a vitality that was spreading beyond his limbs.

—How sweet! Isn't it? Elena said, in a low voice, repeating that gentle act. And a visible shiver ran through her body, through the heavy bedcovers.

As Andrea was about to take her hand again, she begged . . .

—No, like that, stay like that! I like it when you do that!

Pressing against his temple, she compelled him to place his head against the side of the bed, in such a position that he could feel the form of her knee against his cheek. Then she watched him for a while, still continuing to caress his hair; and in a voice faint with pleasure, while something like a white flash passed between her eyelashes, she added, stretching out the words:

—I like it so much!

There was an inexpressible voluptuous allurement in the opening of her lips when she pronounced that verb,[4] so liquid and sensual in the mouth of a woman.

—Again! the lover murmured, his senses becoming faint from passion from the stroking of her fingers, the enticement of her voice. —Again! Say it to me! Talk!

—I like it! Elena repeated, seeing that he was gazing fixedly at her lips, and perhaps knowing the allure that she evoked with that word.

Then both were silent. The one felt the presence of the other flow and mingle into his blood, until it became her life, and her blood became his. A profound silence made the room appear larger; the crucifixion by Guido Reni rendered spiritual the shadow cast by the bed hangings; the noise of the city of Rome reached them like the murmur of a distant wave.

Then, with a sudden movement, Elena sat up on the bed, pressed the young man's head between her two palms, breathed her wish onto his face, kissed him, fell back again, and offered herself to him.

Afterward an immense sadness invaded her; she was filled with that obscure sadness which is at the base of all human happiness, just as brackish water is to be found at the mouth of all rivers. Lying there, she kept her arms outside the covers, abandoned along her sides, her hands palm upward, almost dead, shaken every now and then by a light shudder; and she watched Andrea, her eyes wide open, with a constant gaze, immobile, intolerable. One by one, tears began to well up; and slid down her cheeks one by one, silently.

—Elena, what's wrong? Tell me: What's wrong? her lover asked her, taking both her wrists, bending over to suck her tears from her lashes.

She was clenching her teeth and her lips tightly together to contain her sobs.

—Nothing. Good-bye. Leave me; please! You will see me tomorrow. Go.

Her voice and her gesture were so pleading that Andrea obeyed.

—Good-bye, he said; and kissed her on her mouth, tenderly, tasting the salty drops, bathing in those warm tears. —Good-bye. Love me! Remember!

It seemed to him, crossing back over the threshold, that he heard her bursting into sobs. He went on, slightly uncertain, hesitant like a man whose vision is unclear. The smell of chloroform persisted, like an intoxicating vapor; but with each step something intimate escaped him, dispersed into the air; and with some instinctive impulse, he would have liked to contain himself, enclose himself, envelop himself, prevent that dispersion. The rooms were deserted and silent before him. *Mademoiselle* appeared at a door, her footsteps soundless, without any rustling of her clothes, like a ghost.

—This way, Lord Count. You will not find the way.

She smiled in an ambiguous and irritating way; and curiosity made her gray eyes even more piercing. Andrea did not speak. Once more the presence of that woman was irksome to him; it disturbed him, aroused in him an indistinct disgust, made him irate.

As soon as he was beneath the portico he breathed like a man freed from anguish. The fountain between the trees emitted a low warble, breaking into a noisy din every now and then; the whole sky sparkled with stars enwrapped in certain tattered clouds like long ashen strands of hair or vast black nets; between the stone colossi, through the gates, the headlamps of coaches rushing past appeared and disappeared; the breath of urban life spilled across the cold air; the bells rang, from far off and from close by. At last he had full consciousness of his own happiness.

From that point on, a full, oblivious, free, always new happiness held them both. Passion enveloped them and made them uncaring of anything that would not give them both immediate pleasure. Both, remarkably suited in spirit and body to the exercise of all the highest and rarest of delights, unceasingly sought the Peak, the Unsurpassable, the Unreachable, and they went so far that sometimes an obscure discomfort possessed them, even at the height of their oblivion, as if an admonishing voice rose up from the depths of their being to warn them of an unknown punishment, of an imminent end. From their tiredness itself, desire arose again, more subtle, more audacious, more imprudent; the more inebriated they became, the more the chimera of their heart became greater, became restless, generating new dreams; it seemed that they could find no repose except in exertion, just as the flame finds no life except in combustion. Sometimes, an unexpected source of pleasure opened up inside them, the way a wellspring of water suddenly gushes up under the heels of a man wandering through an entangled forest, and they drank from it without measure, until they consumed it all. Sometimes, their souls, under the effect of their desires, by some strange hallucinatory phenomenon, produced the illusory image of a wider, freer, stronger existence, "beyond pleasure," and they immersed themselves in it, reveling in it, breathing it in as if it were their own native atmosphere. The refinement and delicacy of their sentiment and their imagination followed the excesses of sensuality.

Neither had any reservations about the reciprocal prodigality of flesh and spirit. They felt an unspeakable joy in tearing every veil, uncovering all secrets, violating all mysteries, possessing each other right to the very depths, penetrating each other, fusing with each other, becoming one being.

—What a strange love! said Elena, remembering the very first days, her illness, her swift surrender. —I would have given myself to you the same evening that I met you.

She felt a kind of pride in this fact. And her lover would say:

—That evening when I heard my name announced alongside yours, on the threshold, I had the certainty, I don't know why, that my life would be bound to yours forever!

They believed what they said. They reread Goethe's[5] Roman elegy together: "*Laß dich, Geliebte, nicht reun, daß du mir so schnell dich ergeben!* . . . Don't regret, O beloved, having yielded yourself so promptly! Believe me, I harbor no base or impure thought of you. Love's arrows have varying effects: some barely scratch, and the heart suffers for many years from the poison that seeps into it; others, well feathered and armed with a sharp and piercing tip, penetrate into the spine and instantly inflame the blood. In heroic times, when gods and goddesses loved, desire followed the gaze; and pleasure followed desire. Do you believe that the goddess of love pondered for a long time when below the thickets of Mount Ida, she saw Anchises one day and became enamored of him? And the Moon? If she had hesitated, jealous Aurora would soon have awoken the beautiful shepherd! Hero sees Leander in the midst of a festival, and the inflamed lover throws himself into the nocturnal waves. Rhea Silvia, the royal virgin, goes to draw water from the Tiber and is seized by the god . . ."[6]

Just as it had been for Faustina's divine elegiac poet,[7] Rome was illuminated for them by a new voice. Wherever they went, they left a memory of love.[8] The remote churches of the Aventine: Saint Sabina on the beautiful columns made of Pario marble, the pleasant garden of Santa Maria del Priorato, the bell tower of Santa Maria in Cosmedin, like a sharp rosy stem in the blue sky, were witnesses to their love. The villas of cardinals and princes: Villa Pamphily, where one gazes at its fountains and its lake, graceful and soft, where every grove seems to harbor a noble idyll and where the stone balusters and woody trunks vie with one another in number; Villa Albani, as cold and mute as a cloister, a forest of marble effigies and a museum of centuries-old boxwoods, where from the vestibules and the porticoes, through the granite columns, caryatids,[9] and herms,[10] symbols of immobility, contemplate the unchanging symmetry of the greenery; and Villa Medici, which resembles a forest of branching emerald in a supernatural light; and Villa Ludovisi, somewhat wild, scented with violets, consecrated by the presence of Juno, whom Wolfgang adored,[11] where at that time the plane trees from the Orient and the cypresses of Aurora, which seemed immortal, shivered in the presentiment of the market and of death;[12] all the ancestral villas, sovereign glory of Rome, were witness to their love. The galleries of paintings and statues: the room in the Borghese Gallery with the *Danaë,* before which Elena smiled, almost in revelation, and the hall of mirrors where her image passed among the cherubs by Ciro Ferri and the garlands by Mario de' Fiori; the chamber of Heliodorus, masterfully animated by the most vigorous pulsation of life that the painter Sanzio could ever have infused into the inertia of a wall, and the Borgias' apartment, where Pinturicchio's great imagination transforms itself into a miraculous fabric of frescoes, fables, dreams, whims, artifices, and impudences; the Galatea room, from which emanates a sense of pure freshness and an inextinguishable serenity of light, and the room of Hermaphrodite, where the wondrous monster, born from the lust of a nymph and a demigod, reclines her ambiguous form amid the radiance of fine stones; all the solitary places of Beauty were witness to their love.

They understood the great call of the poet: "*Eine Welt zwar bist Du, o Rom!* You are a world, O Rome! But without love the world would not be the world, Rome itself would not be Rome." And the staircase of the Trinità, glorified by the slow ascension of Day, was the staircase of Happiness, due to the ascension of the beautiful Elena Muti.

It often pleased Elena to walk up those stairs to the *buen retiro* of Palazzo Zuccari. She walked up slowly, following the shade; but her soul raced rapidly to the top. Very many happy hours were measured by the small ivory skull dedicated to Ippolita, which Elena sometimes held to her ear with a childish gesture, while pressing her other cheek to her lover's chest, to listen to the fleeting seconds and the beating of that heart at the same time. Andrea seemed ever new to her. Sometimes, she was almost astonished by the untiring vitality of that spirit and that body. Sometimes, his caresses drew from her a cry that expressed all the terrible spasm of her being, overcome by the violence of the sensation. Sometimes, in his arms, a kind of torpor overcame her, almost, one could say, clairvoyant, in which she believed she was becoming, by the transfusion of another life, a diaphanous, light, fluid creature, penetrated by an immaterial, supremely pure element; while all the pulsations in their great multitude brought to her mind the image of the infinite trembling of a calm sea in summer. Also, sometimes, in his arms, on his chest, after the caresses, she felt the sensual pleasure quiet inside herself, level out, come to rest, like an effervescent water that slowly settles; but if her lover breathed more deeply or moved just a tiny bit, she felt once again an ineffable wave course through her entire body, from her head to her feet, vibrate ever more gently, and finally die. This "spiritualization" of fleshly enjoyment, caused by the perfect affinity of their two bodies, was perhaps the most notable among the phenomena of their passion. Elena, sometimes, had tears that were sweeter than kisses.

And in the kisses, what deep sweetness! There are women's mouths that seem to ignite with love the breath that opens them. Whether they are reddened by blood richer than purple, or frozen by the pallor of agony, whether they are illuminated by the goodness of consent or darkened by the shadow of disdain, whether they are opened in pleasure or twisted by suffering, they always carry within them an enigma that disturbs men of intellect, and attracts them and captivates them. A constant discord between the expression of the lips and that of the eyes generates the mystery; it seems as if a duplicitous soul reveals itself there with a different beauty, happy and sad, cold and passionate, cruel and merciful, humble and proud, laughing and mocking; and the ambiguity arouses discomfort in the spirit that takes pleasure in dark things. Two meditative fifteenth-century artists, untiring pursuers of a rare and celestial Ideal, perspicacious psychologists to whom one owes perhaps the most subtle analyses of human physiognomy, continuously immersed in their studies and in the search for the most arduous difficulties and the most occult secrets, Botticelli and da Vinci, understood and rendered in various ways all the indefinable seduction of such mouths in their art.

In Elena's kisses there was, in truth, the most sublime elixir, for her beloved. Of all the carnal couplings, that one seemed to them to be the most complete, the most satisfying. They believed, sometimes, that the living flower of their souls broke apart, pressed open by their lips, seeping a juice of delight through every vein all the way to their hearts; and sometimes, in their hearts they had the illusory sensation as of a soft and dewy fruit dissolving there. So perfect was their union that the one form seemed the natural complement of the other. Drinking each other in, to make it last longer they held their breaths until they felt themselves to be dying of distress, while the hands of the one trembled on the temples of the other, dazed. A kiss prostrated them more than the sexual act. Once separate, they looked at each other with eyes floating in a torpid mist. And she said, with her voice slightly hoarse, without smiling: —We shall die.

Sometimes, lying facedown, he closed his eyes, waiting. She, knowing that trick, bent over him with deliberate slowness to kiss him. In his voluntary blindness, the lover did not know where that vaguely anticipated kiss would land. In that moment of waiting and uncertainty, an indescribable anxiety shook all his limbs, similar in its intensity to the shivering of a blindfolded man who is being threatened with a fiery branding iron. When finally those lips touched him, he could barely stifle a yell. And he enjoyed the torture of that moment; because not infrequently, physical suffering in love is more enticing than caresses. Elena, too, because of that singular imitative spirit that compels lovers to reproduce a caress exactly, wanted to try.

—It seems to me—she said with closed eyes—that all the pores of my skin are like a million tiny mouths all craving yours, in spasms of desire to be chosen, the one envious of the other . . .

And he therefore, to be fair, would start covering her with rapid close kisses, covering her entire body, not leaving the tiniest space intact, never slowing down what he was doing. She laughed, happy, feeling herself surrounded as by an invisible garment; she laughed and moaned, maddened, feeling his passion growing; she laughed and cried, lost, no longer able to withstand the devouring ardor. Then, with a sudden effort, she would imprison his neck between her arms, ensnare him with her hair, holding him, palpitating like a quarry. Tired, he was happy to cede and to rest, thus trapped in those bonds. Looking at him, she would exclaim:

—How young you are! How young you are!

Against all corruptions, against all dispersions, his youth resisted, persisted, like an untarnishable metal, an indestructible aroma. The pure splendor of youth was, indeed, his most precious quality. In the great flames of his passion everything in him that was falsest, most wretched, most artificial, most frivolous, burned up as on a pyre. After the depletion of his strength, as a result of too much analysis and of the *separate* action of all his interior spheres, he now returned to the unity of strength, of action, of life; he regained his confidence and his spontaneity; he gave love and took pleasure in a youthful way. Some of the impulses to which he yielded seemed to be those of a young, unwitting boy; some of his fantasies were full of grace, of freshness, of impudence.

—Sometimes—Elena would say to him—my tenderness for you becomes more delicate than that of a lover. I don't know . . . It almost becomes maternal.

Andrea would laugh, because she was barely three years older than he.

—Sometimes—he would say to her—the communion of my soul with yours seems to me so chaste that I would call you "sister," kissing your hands.

These fallacious purifications and elevations of sentiment always occurred in the languid intervals of their pleasure, when the flesh being at rest, the soul felt some indistinct need for ideality. Then, too, there arose once more in the young man the ideality of the art he loved; and in his intellect tossed and turned all the forms he had once sought and contemplated, demanding to be released, and the words of the Goethean monologue incited him. "Of what use is blazing nature, before your eyes? What use is the form of art around you, if the passionate creative force does not fill your soul and flow to your fingertips, incessantly, to reproduce?"[13] The thought of bringing joy to his lover with a rhythmical verse or noble design encouraged him to create. He wrote *La Simona;* and made two etchings, of the *Zodiac* and of *Alexander's Goblet*.

He chose, when carrying out his art, difficult, exact, perfect, incorruptible instruments: meter and incision; and he intended to continue and renew the traditional Italian forms, with strict criteria, reconnecting with the poets of the *stil novo*[14] and the painters who were the forerunners of the Renaissance. His spirit was essentially *formal*. More than thought, he loved expression. His literary assays were exercises, diversions, studies, research, technical experiments, curiosities. He believed, along with Henri Taine,[15] that it was more difficult to compose six beautiful lines of poetry than to win a battle on the field. His *Fable of Hermaphrodite* imitated in structure the *Fable of Orpheus* by Poliziano; and had stanzas that were extraordinarily exquisite, powerful and musical, especially in the choruses sung by dual-natured monsters: Centaurs, Sirens, and Sphinxes. His new tragedy, *La Simona,* brief in extent, was of a decidedly original nature. Although it was rhymed in the ancient Tuscan manner, it seemed to have been created by an English poet of the Elizabethan age, inspired by a story from the *Decameron;* it possessed something of the sweet and strange enchantment that may be found in certain of William Shakespeare's minor plays.

The poet signed his works thus, in the frontispiece of the Sole Exemplar: A.S. CALCOGRAPHUS AQUA FORTI SIBI TIBI FECIT.[16]

Copper attracted him more than paper; nitric acid more than ink; the burin more than the pen. One of his forebears, Giusto Sperelli, had previously experimented with incision. Some of his prints, produced around 1520, manifestly revealed the influence of Antonio Pollajuolo, for the depth and almost acerbity of its mark. Andrea followed the style of Rembrandt, *a tratti liberi,*[17] and the *maniera nera*[18] technique favored by English engravers of the school of Green, Dixon, Earlom. He had shaped his education on all models, had separately studied the research of each engraver, had learned from Albrecht Dürer and from Parmigianino, Marcantonio Raimondi and Holbein, from Annibale Caracci and James MacArdell, from Guido and Callot, from Toschi and Gérard Audran; but the understanding that he had acquired of copper was this: how to illuminate with Rembrandt's effects of light the elegance of design of second-generation fifteenth-century Florentines such as Sandro Botticelli, Domenico Ghirlandajo, and Filippino Lippi.[19]

His two recent plates represented, in two love scenes, two aspects of Elena Muti's beauty; and the etchings took their title from the accessories they portrayed.

Among the most precious objects possessed by Andrea Sperelli was a quilt made of fine silk, of a faded pale blue on which the twelve embroidered signs of the zodiac revolved, with their names, Aries, Taurus, Gemini, Cancer, Leo, Virgo, Libra, Scorpius, Arcitenens, Caper, Amphora,[20] Pisces, in Gothic characters. The sun embroidered in gold occupied the center of the circle; the figures of the animals, designed with a slightly archaic style that recalled that of mosaics, had an extraordinary splendor; the entire fabric seemed worthy of draping an imperial nuptial bed. It originated, in fact, from the trousseau of Bianca Maria Sforza, niece of Ludovico il Moro; she had married Emperor Maximilian.

Elena's nudity could not, in truth, have a richer cloaking. Sometimes when Andrea was in the other room, she would undress rapidly, lie down on the bed under the marvelous cover, and would call Andrea loudly. And when he came running, she resembled a divinity wrapped in a band of the firmament. Also, sometimes, wanting to come nearer to the fireplace, she got out of bed pulling the cover with her. Feeling cold, she would draw the silk around her with both arms and walk barefoot, with little steps, in order not to trip in the abundant folds. The sun shone splendidly on her back through her loosened hair; the Scorpion took hold of one of her breasts; a great zodiacal strip of cloth dragged behind her on the carpet, drawing the roses along with it if she had already scattered them.

The etching represented Elena sleeping under the celestial signs. Her feminine form could be seen outlined by the folds of cloth, her head reclining slightly beyond the side of the bed, her hair trailing down to the floor, with one arm dangling and the other along her side. The parts that were not hidden, namely her face, the upper region of her bust, and her arms, were intensely luminous; and the burin had rendered with great potency the shine of the embroidery in the penumbra and the mystery of the symbols. A tall white greyhound, Famulus, brother to the one with his head resting on the lap of the Countess of Arundel in the painting by Peter Paul Rubens, stretched his neck toward the lady, gazing at her, standing solidly on all four legs, depicted with an apt boldness of foreshortening. The background of the room was opulent and dim.

The other etching concerned the great silver basin that Elena Muti had inherited from her aunt Flaminia.

This basin was historic: it was called Alexander's Cup. It had been donated to the Princess of Bisenti by Cesare Borgia before he left for France to deliver the bill of divorce and the dispensation for marriage to Louis XII; and it must have been included among the fabled baggage carried by sumpter-mules that Valentinois[21] brought with him when he entered Chinon, as described by the Seigneur de Brântome.[22] The design of the figures that encompassed it and of those that arose from the rim of the two ends was attributed to Sanzio.

The cup was called Alexander's because it had been created

in memory of that prodigious one from which, at his great feasts, the Macedonian would prodigiously drink. Throngs of Sagittariuses encircled the sides of the vase with bows drawn, rioting, in wonderful poses like those Raphael painted, naked and shooting arrows toward the herm in the fresco found in the Borghese Gallery, decorated by Giovan Francesco Bolognesi. They were pursuing a great Chimera, which rose up from the edge, like a handle, at one side of the vase, while on the opposite side bounded up the young Sagittarius Bellerophon with his bow drawn against the monster born of Typhon. The decorations of the base and the rim were of a pleasing elegance. The inside was gilded like that of a ciborium. The metal was as sonorous as a musical instrument. Its weight was five hundred pounds. Its entire form was harmonious.

Often, on a whim, Elena Muti would take her morning bath in that basin. She could immerse herself in it quite well if she did not stretch out; and nothing, in truth, was equal to the supreme grace of that body resting in the water which the gilt tinged with indescribably delicate reflections, because the metal was not yet silver, and the gold was fading.

In love with three such differently elegant forms, namely the woman, the basin, and the greyhound, the etcher conceived a composition of beautiful lines. The woman, naked, standing in the basin, leaning with one hand on the protruding Chimera, and with the other on the Bellerophon, stretched forward to mock the dog, which, arching with his front legs lowered and his back legs straight like a cat when it is about to spring, extended toward her his long, narrow muzzle like that of a pike, with intensity.

Never had Andrea Sperelli enjoyed and suffered with greater ardor the intent anxiety of the creator when watching over the action of the irrational and irreparable acid; never had he with greater ardor honed his patience in the subtle work of drypoint on the roughness of the transitions. He had been *born,* in truth, a copperplate engraver, like Luca d'Olanda. He possessed an admirable skill (which was perhaps a rare sense) for all the minutest details of timing and degree, which combine to vary the efficacy of the acid in infinite ways. It was not practice, not diligence, not intelligence alone, but that innate, almost infallible sense in particular that alerted him to the right moment, the precise instant at which the corrosion came to render the precise value of shadow that the craftsman intended the print to have. And mastering in such a spiritual way that brute energy, and infusing into it a certain spirit of art, and feeling some occult correspondence between the beating of his pulse and the progressive bite of the acid, was an intoxicating pride, a tormenting joy for him.

It seemed to Elena that she was deified by her lover, just like Isotta of Rimini in the indestructible medals that Sigismondo Malatesta had ordered to be minted in her honor.

But on the days when Andrea was attending to his work, she became sad and taciturn and sighing, almost as if an internal anguish possessed her. She had sudden effusions of tenderness so harrowing, mingled with tears and barely contained sobs, that the young man was astonished, suspicious, unable to comprehend.

One evening they were returning on horseback from the Aventino, down the Santa Sabina road, their eyes still filled with the great vision of imperial palaces aflame with sunset, glowing red among the black cypresses that penetrated a golden dust. They rode in silence, because Elena's sadness had transmitted itself to her lover. In front of Santa Sabina he halted his bay, saying:

—Do you remember?

Some chickens that were peaceably pecking among the tufts of grass dispersed at Famulus's barking. The clearing, infested with weeds, was tranquil and modest like the churchyard of a village; but the walls had that singular luminosity that is reflected by Rome's buildings "during Titian's hour."

Elena also came to a halt.

—How long ago that day seems! she said, with a slight tremor in her voice.

In fact, that memory was fading in time, vaguely, as if their love affair had been going on for many months, for many years. Elena's words had aroused in Andrea's soul a strange illusion, together with a sense of unease. She began to recall all the details of that visit, which they had made on a January afternoon under a spring sky. She persisted in describing every fine point, at length; and every now and then interrupted herself like one who is following, beyond her words, an unexpressed thought. Andrea thought he could hear regret in her voice. Whatever could she be regretting? Did their love not have even sweeter days to look forward to? Wasn't Rome already in the grip of spring? Perplexed, he almost stopped listening to her. The horses were descending, at a walking gait, one alongside the other, sometimes breathing strongly through their nostrils or bringing their muzzles together as if to confide a secret. Famulus ran up and down constantly.

—Do you remember—Elena continued—do you remember that monk who came to open for us, when we rang the bell?

—Yes, yes . . .

—He looked at us with such bewilderment! He was so small, beardless, all wrinkled. He left us alone in the entrance hall to go and fetch the keys of the church; and you kissed me. Do you remember?

—Yes.

—And all those barrels, in the entrance hall! And that odor of wine, while the monk explained to us the stories carved into the cypress door! And then, the Madonna of the Rosary! Do you remember? The explanation made you laugh; and I, hearing you laugh, couldn't stop myself; and we both laughed so much in front of that poor man that he became confused and did not open his mouth again even at the end to thank you . . .

After a pause, she continued:

—And at Sant'Alessio, when you didn't want to let me see the cupola through the keyhole! How we laughed, there, too!

She fell silent again. A crowd of men was coming up the road with a coffin, followed by a public coach full of weeping relatives. The deceased was being taken to the cemetery of the Israelites. It was a cold and mute funeral. All those men with their hooked noses and rapacious eyes resembled one another like blood kin.

The two horses separated, each taking one side, close to the wall, so that the crowd could pass; and the lovers looked at each other over the dead person in his coffin, feeling the sadness grow.

When they once again drew near to each other, Andrea asked:

—But what is wrong with you? What are you thinking about?

She hesitated before answering. She kept her eyes lowered on the neck of the animal, caressing him with the knob of the whip, irresolute and pale.

—What are you thinking about? the young man repeated.

—Well, I will tell you. I am leaving on Wednesday, I don't know for how long; maybe for a long time, forever; I don't know. This love affair is breaking up, because of me; but don't ask me how, don't ask me why, don't ask me anything: I beg you! I could not answer you.

Andrea looked at her, almost disbelieving. The thing seemed so impossible to him that it did not cause him pain.

—You're joking, aren't you, Elena?

She shook her head, indicating no, because her throat had seized up; and immediately she spurred her horse into a trot. Behind them, the bells of Santa Sabina and Santa Prisca started to toll in the dusk. They trotted in silence, causing echoes to resound under the archways, below the temples, in the solitary and empty ruins. They left San Giorgio in Velabro on their left, which still bore a vermilion glow on the bricks of its bell tower, as on the day of happiness. They skirted the Roman Forum, the Forum of Nerva, already possessed of a bluish shadow, similar to that of glaciers in the night. They stopped at the Arch of the Pantani, where their grooms and coaches awaited them.

As soon as she was out of the saddle, Elena held out her hand to Andrea, avoiding looking him in the eyes. It seemed as if she was in great haste to get away.

—Well, then? Andrea asked her, helping her to mount the carriage.

—I'll see you tomorrow. Not tonight.

CHAPTER V

The farewell on Via Nomentana, that *adieu au grand air*[1] that Elena had imposed, did not resolve any of the doubts in Andrea's soul. Whatever were the secret reasons of that sudden departure? In vain he tried to penetrate the mystery; doubts oppressed him.

In the first few days, the attacks of pain and desire were so cruel he thought he would die. Jealousy, which after its first appearances had vanished in the face of Elena's assiduous ardor, rose up again in him, awoken by impure fantasies; and the suspicion that a man could be concealed in that obscure entanglement gave him an unbearable torment. Sometimes, he was invaded by a deep anger toward the absent woman, a rancor full of bitterness, and almost a need for revenge, as if she had tricked and betrayed him in order to give herself to another lover. Also, sometimes he believed he did not desire her anymore, that he did not love her anymore, that he had never loved her; and it was not a new phenomenon in him, this momentary cessation of a sentiment, this type of spiritual elision that, for example, in the midst of a ball, rendered the favored woman completely irrelevant to him, and permitted him to participate in a lighthearted luncheon an hour after having drunk her tears. But these oblivions did not last. The Roman spring was flowering with unprecedented joy: the city made of travertine and brick drank in the light like an avid forest; the papal fountains soared into heavens more diaphanous than a jewel; Piazza di Spagna was scented like a rose garden; and the Trinità de' Monti, at the top of the stairs crowded with small children, resembled a golden dome.

With the incitements that came to him from Rome's new beauty, whatever remained in him of the spell of that woman, in his blood and in his soul, was revived and rekindled. And he was troubled, deep down, by invincible pains, implacable tumults, indefinable languors, which resembled somewhat those of puberty. One evening, at the Dolcebuono home, after a tea party, being the last to leave the salon full of flowers and still vibrating from a *Cachoucha* by Raff, he spoke of love to Donna Bianca and did not regret it, either that evening or afterward.

His affair with Elena Muti was by now very well known, just as sooner or later, or more or less, in the elegant society of Rome or in any other society, all affairs and flirtations are common knowledge. Precautions are futile. Everyone in these societies is such a good connoisseur of erotic body language that it is enough for them to witness by chance a gesture, a pose, or a glance in order to have sure evidence, while the lovers, or those who are about to become such, do not suspect anything. Indeed, there are in every society those inquisitive people who make a profession of discovering and following the traces of other people's love affairs, with no less perseverance than that of bloodhounds following the scent of game. They are always vigilant, without appearing so: they infallibly catch a murmured word, a slight smile, a small start of surprise, a faint blush, a flash of the eyes; at balls, at large parties, where imprudence is more probable, they circulate constantly, and know how to insinuate themselves into the densest areas with an extraordinary ability, as pickpockets do in large crowds; and their ear is pricked to steal a fragment of dialogue, their eye is ready behind the glinting of their spectacles, to note a squeeze of the hand, a faintness, a shiver, the nervous pressure of a feminine hand on the shoulder of a dancing companion.

One such terrible bloodhound was, for example, Don Filippo del Monte, who dined at the home of the Marchioness of Ateleta. But, in truth, Elena Muti did not concern herself much with society gossip; and in this latest passion of hers she had reached almost crazy heights of rashness. She screened every act of boldness with her beauty, her opulence, her high-ranking name; and was always accorded the same obeisance, the same admiration, the same adulation, due to that certain easygoing tolerance which is one of the most amiable qualities of Roman aristocracy, which perhaps it comes by precisely due to the abuse of gossip.

Hence, the affair had now suddenly raised Andrea Sperelli, in the eyes of the ladies, to a high level of power. An aura of favor surrounded him; and his success became in a short time a source of wonder. The contagion of desire is a very frequent phenomenon in modern societies. A man who has been loved by a woman of singular esteem excites the imagination in other women; and each one burns with desire to possess him, out of vanity and curiosity, competing with the others. The appeal of Don Giovanni is more in his fame than in his person. Moreover, Sperelli was benefited by that certain name he had made for himself as a mysterious artist; and two sonnets of his had become renowned, written in the visitors' book of the Princess of Ferentino, in which, as in an ambiguous diptych, he had praised a diabolical mouth and an angelical one, the one that draws souls to perdition and the one that says *Hail*. Common folk cannot imagine what profound and new pleasures the halo of glory, even if it is pale and false, brings to love. An obscure lover, even if he has the strength of Hercules and the beauty of Hippolytus and the grace of Hylas, will never be able to give his beloved the delights that the artist, perhaps unknowingly, disperses in abundance to ambitious feminine spirits. It must be a great sweetness for the vanity of a woman to be able to say: "In every letter that he writes me there is perhaps the purest flame of his intellect, at which I alone warm myself; in every caress he loses a part of his will and his strength; and his highest dreams of glory fall into the folds of my dress, into the circles formed by my breath!"

Andrea Sperelli did not hesitate for a moment in the face of enticement. That concentration produced in him by Elena's unparalleled dominion was now replaced by dissolution. No longer held by the fiery band that bound them tightly together, his forces returned to their original disorder. No longer able to conform itself, adapt itself, assimilate itself to a superior dominating form, his soul, chameleon-like, mutable, fluid, virtual, transformed itself, deformed itself, took on every form. He passed from one love to another with incredible lightness; he yearned for different loves at the same time; he wove without scruple a great web of deceits, fictions, lies, tricks, in order to gather the greatest number of quarries. The habit of falsity blunted his conscience. Due to the continuous absence of reflection, he gradually became impenetrable to himself, remained outside his mystery. Little by little he almost reached the stage of no longer seeing his inner life, in the way that the external hemisphere of the earth does not see the sun, despite being tied indissolubly to it. One instinct was always alive, ruthlessly alive in him: the instinct of detachment from everything that attracted him without binding him. And his will, as useless as a badly tempered sword, dangled as at the side of a Jew or a paralyzed man.

The memory of Elena filled him now and then, rising up suddenly; and he either tried to remove himself from the melancholy of regret or instead took pleasure in reliving in his marred imagination the excessiveness of that life, to draw stimulation from it for his new loves. He repeated to himself the words of the poem: "Remember the snuffed-out days! And place on the lips of the second woman kisses as sweet as those you gave to the first one, not too long ago!"[2] But already the second one had left his soul. He had spoken of love to Donna Bianca Dolcebuono, at first almost without thinking about it, instinctively attracted maybe by virtue of some undefined reflection that she possessed through being friends with Elena. Perhaps the small seed of affection, planted in him by the words of the Florentine countess at dinner at the Doria home, had begun to germinate. Who knows by what mysterious movement an arbitrary, even insignificant, spiritual or material contact between a man and a woman may generate and nurture in them both a latent, unperceived, unsuspected feeling, which after a long time suddenly emerges due to circumstance? It is the same phenomenon we find in the intellectual realm, when the seed of a thought or the shadow of an image surfaces again suddenly after a long interval, by some unconscious development, processed into a complete image, into complex thought. The same laws govern all the activities of our being; and the activities of which we are conscious are but a part of them.

Donna Bianca Dolcebuono was the ideal type of Florentine beauty, such as was depicted by Ghirlandajo in the portrait of

Giovanna Tornabuoni in Santa Maria Novella. She had a clear oval face, a wide, high, and pure forehead, a gentle mouth, a somewhat distinctive nose, and eyes of that mysterious tawny color praised by Firenzuola. She preferred her hair arranged with abundance on her temples, halfway across her cheeks, in the old-fashioned way. Her surname befitted her well, because she brought to society life an innate goodness, a great indulgence, an equal courtesy for all, and a melodious way of speaking. She was, in short, one of those affable women, without depth of spirit or intellect, somewhat indolent, who seem born to live in pleasantness and to indulge in discreet love affairs like birds in blossoming trees.

When she heard Andrea's phrases, she exclaimed with gracious amazement:

—Have you forgotten Elena so soon?

Then, after a few days of gracious hesitation, it pleased her to cede; and she spoke not infrequently of Elena to the unfaithful young man, without jealousy and with candor.

—But why on earth did she leave earlier than usual, this year? she asked him once, smiling.

—I don't know, answered Andrea, unable to hide a little impatience and bitterness.

—It's all really over?

—Bianca, I pray you, let's talk about us! he interrupted her with his voice distorted, because these discussions disturbed and irritated him.

She remained thoughtful for a moment, as if she wanted to solve some enigma; then she smiled shaking her head, as if relinquishing, with a fleeting shadow of melancholy in her eyes.

—Such is love.

And she caressed her lover.

Andrea, possessing her, possessed all those noble Florentine women of the fifteenth century, to whom the Magnificent sang:

> You can observe all around
> That what the proverb says is true
> That everyone changes his mind
> As soon as the eye is out of view
> You see love change for someone different

When the eye remains afar
So too does the heart stay distant
Because it's pierced by someone near
With whom it can soon unite
With great pleasure and delight . . .[3]

In the summer when she was about to leave, while saying good-bye, without hiding her well-bred emotion, she said:

—I know that when we see each other again, you will not love me anymore. Such is love. But remember me as a friend!

He did not love her. Still, on hot and tedious days, certain soft cadences of her voice returned to his mind like the magic of a rhyme, and aroused in him the vision of a freshwater garden in which she went about in the company of other women playing and singing as in a vignette from *Polyphilus's Dream*.

And Donna Bianca disappeared. And others came, sometimes in twos: Barbarella Viti, the *mascula*,[4] who had a superb boy's head all gilded and shining like certain Jewish heads by Rembrandt; the Countess of Lùcoli, the lady of the turquoises, a Circe by Dosso Dossi, with beautiful eyes full of perfidy, variable as autumn seas, gray, azure, green, indefinable; Liliana Theed, a lady of twenty-two, resplendent with that marvelous complexion composed of light, roses, and milk, which is possessed only by the babies of the great English families in the canvases of Reynolds, Gainsborough, and Lawrence; the Marchioness du Deffand, a Directoire-style beauty, a Récamier, with her long and pure oval face, her swan's neck, her surging breasts and Bacchic arms; Donna Isotta Cellesi, the lady of the emeralds, who moved her empress's head with a slow, bovine majesty amid the sparkling of her enormous heirloom gemstones; Princess Kalliwoda, the lady without jewels, who within the fragility of her form hid nerves of steel for pleasure and from whose waxy delicate features voracious leonine eyes gazed out, the eyes of a Scythe.

Each of these loves brought him a new degradation: each inebriated him with a malevolent elation, without satisfying him; each taught him some particularity and subtlety of the vice that was still unknown to him. He had within himself the germ of all infections. Corrupting himself, he corrupted. Fraud ensnared his soul, like some slimy and cold substance that became more tenacious every day. The perversion of his senses made him seek out and accentuate in his lovers whatever was least noble and least pure in them. A base curiosity compelled him to choose the women with the worst reputations; a cruel taste for contamination compelled him to seduce the women who had better reputations. In the arms of one he remembered the caresses of another, or a technique of pleasure learned from another. Sometimes (and it was especially when the news of Elena Muti's second marriage reopened for some time his wounds) he took pleasure in superimposing on the present nudity the evoked nudity of Elena, and to utilize the real figure as a sort of base on which he could enjoy the ideal figure. He nurtured the image with an intense effort, until his imagination reached the point of possessing the shadow that he had almost created.

However, all the same he did not venerate his memories of the past happiness. Sometimes, on the contrary, those memories gave him a pretext for some other arbitrary affair. In the Galleria Borghese, for example, in the memorable hall of mirrors, he obtained the first promise from Lilian Theed; in Villa Medici, upon the memorable green staircase that leads to the belvedere, he entwined his fingers with the long fingers of Angélique du Deffand; and the small ivory skull that had belonged to Cardinal Immenraet, the death jewel marked with the name of some obscure Hippolyte, aroused in him the whim to try his luck with Donna Ippolita Albónico.

This lady bore a great air of nobility, slightly resembling Maria Magdalena of Austria, the wife of Cosimo II de' Medici, in the portrait by Giusto Suttermans[5] that is in Florence, in the possession of the Corsinis. She adored sumptuous clothing, brocades, velvets, lace. Her wide Medicean collars seemed the best style to emphasize the beauty of her superb head.

One race day, up in the stands, Andrea Sperelli was endeavoring to obtain Donna Ippolita's promise to come to Palazzo Zuccari the next day to fetch the mysterious ivory dedicated to her. She was hedging, vacillating between prudence and curiosity. At every slightly impudent phrase of the young man, she frowned, while an involuntary smile tugged at her mouth; and her head beneath the hat decorated with white feathers, against the parasol decorated with white lace, was for a moment an image of singular harmony:

—*Tibi, Hippolyta!* Will you come, then? I will wait for you the entire day, from two until evening. All right?

—But are you crazy?

—What are you afraid of? I swear to Your Majesty that I will not remove from you even a glove. You will remain seated as on a throne, according to your regal custom; and even while taking a cup of tea, you will not be able to put down the invisible scepter that you always carry in your imperious right hand. Is this favor conceded to me, on these conditions?

—No.

But she smiled, because it pleased her to hear him emphasize this aspect of regality, which was her glory. And Andrea Sperelli continued to tempt her, always in a joking or beseeching tone, combining with the seduction of his voice a constant, subtle, penetrating gaze, that indefinable gaze that seems to undress women, to see them naked through their clothing, to touch them on their living skin.

—I don't want you to look at me like that, said Donna Ippolita, almost offended, with a faint blush.

Few people had remained on the stands. Ladies and gentlemen were walking on the grass, along the fence, some surrounding the victorious horse, some betting with the yelling public backers, below the inconstancy of the sun, which appeared and disappeared among the soft archipelagoes of the clouds.

—Let's go down, she added, unaware of the watchful eyes of Giannetto Rùtolo, who was leaning against the stair railing.

When they passed in front of him on their way down, Sperelli said:

—Good-bye, Marquis, till later. We will race.

Rùtolo bowed deeply to Donna Ippolita and a sudden flame colored his face. It had seemed to him that he heard a light mocking tone in the count's greeting. He stayed at the railing, still watching the couple in the enclosure. He was suffering visibly.

—Rùtolo, watch out! the Countess of Lùcoli said to him with a wicked laugh, passing by on Don Filippo del Monte's arm, going down the iron stairs.

He felt the stab in the center of his heart. Donna Ippolita

and the Count of Ugenta, having reached the observation point of the judges, were turning back toward the stands. The lady held the handle of her parasol on her shoulder, twirling it between her fingers: the white canopy rotated behind her head like a halo and the many lace trimmings fluttered and lifted up incessantly. Within that mobile circle she laughed every now and then at the words of the young man; and a light flush still tinged the noble pallor of her face. Every now and then the two stopped.

Giannetto Rùtolo, feigning to watch the horses entering onto the track, turned his binoculars on the two. His hands were trembling visibly. Every smile, every gesture of Ippolita's gave him an atrocious pain. When he lowered the binoculars he was extremely pale. He had caught in his beloved's eyes, which were gazing at Sperelli, that look he know so well, for he had once been lit up with hope by it. It seemed that everything was crashing down around him. A long love affair was ending, irreparably broken off by that look. The sun was no longer the sun; life was no longer life.

The stands were filling up again rapidly, now that the signal for the third race was imminent. Ladies were climbing up to stand on the seats. A murmur ran along the levels, like wind over a hanging garden. The bell rang. The horses set off like a cluster of arrows.

—I will race in your honor, Donna Ippolita, said Andrea Sperelli to the Albónico woman, taking his leave to go and prepare for the next race, which was for gentlemen. —*Tibi, Hippolyta, semper!*[6]

She squeezed his hand hard, for luck, not thinking that Giannetto Rùtolo, too, was among the contenders. When, a little later, she saw her pale lover descend the stairs, the candid cruelty of indifference reigned in her lovely dark eyes. The old love was falling from her soul like a lifeless slough, due to the invasion of the new one. She no longer belonged to that man; she was no longer tied to him by any bond. It is not conceivable how promptly and entirely the woman who loves no more takes back possession of her own heart.

He has taken her from me, he thought, walking toward the stands of the jockey club over grass that seemed to cede beneath his feet like sand. Before him, a short distance away, the other one walked with a jaunty and confident stride. His tall and slim figure in the ash-gray coat had that particular inimitable elegance that only lineage can bestow. He was smoking. Giannetto Rùtolo, coming behind him, smelled the odor of the cigarette with every puff of smoke; and it caused him an unbearable vexation, a disgust that rose up from his very entrails, as if it were poison.

The Duke of Beffi and Paolo Caligàro were on the threshold, already set for the race. The duke was crouching down, his legs apart, testing the elasticity of his leather trousers or the strength of his knees with an athletic movement. Little Caligàro was cursing the night rain, which had made the terrain heavy.

—Now—he said to Sperelli—you have a strong probability with Miching Mallecho.[7]

Giannetto Rùtolo heard that presage and felt a stab to the heart. He nurtured a vague hope of victory. In his imagination he saw the effects of a race won and a lucky duel against the enemy. While he undressed, every gesture betrayed his worry.

—Here's a man who, before mounting his horse, sees his grave open before him, said the Duke of Beffi, placing a hand on his shoulder with a comic gesture. —*Ecce homo novus.*[8]

Andrea Sperelli, who was in high spirits at that moment, broke out in one of his frank bursts of laughter, which was the most seductive effusion of his youthfulness.

—Why are you laughing? asked Rùtolo of him, extremely pale, distraught, staring at him from below corrugated brows.

—It seems to me—replied Sperelli, unperturbed—that you are speaking to me in a very sharp tone, dear Marquis.

—And so?

—Think what you like of my laughter.

—I think it is foolish.

Sperelli jumped to his feet, stepped forward, and lifted his whip against Giannetto Rùtolo. Paolo Caligàro managed to restrain his arm by some miracle. Other words burst out. Don Marcantonio Spada intervened; he heard the altercation, and said:

—Enough, lads. You both know what you must do tomorrow. Now you must race.

The two adversaries finished dressing in silence. Then they went outside. The news of the argument had already spread throughout the enclosure and was rising up the stands, increasing the anticipation of the race. The Countess of Lùcoli, with refined wickedness, passed it on to Donna Ippolita Albónico. She, without revealing any sign of perturbation, said:

—I'm sorry. They appeared to be friends.

The rumor spread, being transformed by beautiful female mouths. Eager crowds thronged around the public bookmakers. Miching Mallecho, the Count of Ugenta's horse, and Brummel, the horse of the Marquis Rùtolo, were the favorites; then came Satirist, of the Duke of Beffi, and Carbonilla of Count Caligàro. Expert connoisseurs were, however, diffident of the first two, thinking that the nervous agitation of the two riders would certainly harm the race.

But Andrea Sperelli was calm, almost cheerful.

His feeling of superiority over his adversary reassured him; besides, that chivalric tendency for dangerous adventure, inherited from his Byronic father, induced him to see his fortune in a glorious light; and all the inherent generosity of his young blood was reawakening in the face of risk. Donna Ippolita Albónico suddenly arose at the summit of his soul, more desirable and more beautiful.

He went toward his horse, his heart beating fast as if he were going toward a friend who was bringing him the anticipated announcement of some good fortune. He stroked its muzzle gently; and the animal's eye, that eye in which all the nobility of its pedigree glittered with an inextinguishable flame, elated him like the magnetic gaze of a woman.

—Mallecho—he murmured, stroking him—it's a great day! We must win.

His trainer, a short, ruddy man, fixing his sharp pupils on the other horses, which were passing by led by their grooms, said in a hoarse voice:

—*No doubt.*[9]

Miching Mallecho Esq. was a magnificent bay, originating from the stables of the Baron of Soubeyran. The slender elegance of his form was combined with extraordinary lumbar strength. From his shining fine chest, beneath which a network of veins was visible, spreading down to his thighs, a steaming heat seemed to radiate, so ardent was his vitality. Being possessed of very strong jumping ability, he had very often carried his owner on hunts, beyond all the obstacles of the Roman countryside, on any terrain, never refusing in the face of a triple-bar fence or a drystone wall, always right behind the dogs, dauntless. One "hup" from the rider spurred him on more than a stroke from the whip; and a caress made him quiver.

Before mounting, Andrea carefully examined the entire harness and checked every buckle and every strap; then he leaped into the saddle, smiling. The trainer demonstrated his faith with an expressive gesture, watching his master as he moved away.

Around the betting table the throng of betters continued to surge. Andrea felt everyone's gaze upon him. He looked toward the right-hand stands to see Donna Albónico, but he could distinguish no one among the crowd of women. He greeted Lilian Theed nearby, who well knew Mallecho's gallops after foxes and chimeras. The Marchioness of Ateleta made him a gesture of reproach from afar, for she had heard of the quarrel.

—How is Mallecho ranked? he asked Ludovico Barbarisi.

Heading toward the starting point, he thought coolly about the method he would employ in order to win; and he looked at his three rivals who preceded him, calculating the strength and the technique of each. Paolo Caligàro was a cunning devil, wise to all the tricks of the game, like a jockey; but Carbonilla, though fast, did not have much stamina. The Duke of Beffi, a rider skilled in *haute école* dressage,[10] who had won more than one race in England, was riding an animal of difficult temperament, which was liable to refuse obstacles. Giannetto Rùtolo instead was riding an excellent and very well-disciplined one; but although he was strong, he was too impetuous and was taking part in a public race for the first time. Besides, he must have been in a terrible state of nerves, judging by the many signs he displayed.

Andrea thought, watching him: *My victory today will influence tomorrow's duel, without a doubt. He will lose his head, certainly, here and there. I must be calm on both fields.* Then, also, he thought: *What frame of mind will Donna Ippolita be in?* It seemed to him that there was an unusual silence all around. He measured with his eyes the distance to the first hedge; he noted a glittering stone on the track; he realized he was being observed by Rùtolo; he shivered throughout his entire body.

The bell gave the signal; but Brummel had already sped off; and the start, therefore, not being simultaneous, was deemed to be a false one. The second was a false start, too, because of Brummel. Sperelli and the Duke of Beffi smiled at each other fleetingly.

The third start was judged to be fair. Brummel immediately separated himself from the group, grazing the fence. The other three horses followed him, running head to head for a stretch; and jumped the first hedge successfully; then the second one. Each of the three riders was playing a different game. The Duke of Beffi tried to stay within the group so that before any obstacles, Satirist could be set an example. Caligàro was moderating Carbonilla's enthusiasm in order to conserve her strength for the last five hundred meters. Andrea Sperelli was gradually increasing his speed, wanting to place pressure on his enemy near the most difficult obstacle. Shortly thereafter, in fact, Mallecho overtook his two companions and began to close in on Brummel.

Rùtolo heard the pursuing gallop behind him and was overcome by such anxiety that he could no longer see a thing. Everything was blurring in his vision, as if he were about to lose his senses. He made an enormous effort to keep his spurs planted in the horse's belly; and he was dismayed by the thought that his strength was abandoning him. He had a constant roar in his ears and in the midst of the roar he heard the brief and sharp cry of Andrea Sperelli:

—*Hup! Hup!*

Highly sensitive to voice commands, more than to any other incitement, Mallecho was devouring the space between them; he was not more than three or four meters from Brummel; he was about to reach him, to overtake him.

—*Hup!*

Another barrier crossed the track. Rùtolo did not see it, because he had lost all consciousness, preserving only a furious instinct to adhere to the animal and to push it onward to chance.

Brummel jumped; but, not assisted by his rider, he hit his back legs and landed on the other side so badly that the rider lost his stirrups, although remaining in the saddle. He continued, however, to race. Andrea Sperelli was now holding first place; Giannetto Rùtolo, without having regained his stirrups, was coming second, pursued by Paolo Caligàro; the Duke of Beffi, having suffered a refusal by Satirist, was coming last. They passed below the stands in this order; they heard an indistinct clamor, which then faded away.

On the stands everyone was rapt with attention. Some were commenting aloud on the succession of events in the race. At every change in the order of the horses, many exclamations would be heard amid a constant murmur; it provoked a shudder in the ladies. Donna Ippolita Albónico, standing upright on her seat and supporting herself on the shoulders of her husband, who was below her, watched without altering expression, with marvelous control; unless her tightly pressed lips and a very light wrinkling of her forehead could perhaps reveal the strain to anyone examining her. At a certain point, she withdrew her hands from her husband's shoulders for fear of betraying herself with some involuntary movement.

—Sperelli has fallen, the Countess of Lùcoli announced loudly.

Mallecho, in fact, while jumping had placed a foot wrong on the damp grass and had buckled forward onto his knees, getting up again immediately. Andrea had slipped forward over his neck, without any damage done; and with lightning speed had returned to the saddle, while Rùtolo and Caligàro were catching up to him. Brummel, although his back legs were injured, was doing wonderfully, by virtue of his pure blood. Carbonilla finally was unleashing all her speed, guided with admirable skill by her rider. There were about eight hundred meters left to the finish line.

Sperelli saw victory elude him; but he gathered all his energy to grasp it once more. Standing taut in the stirrups, bent over the mane, he launched from time to time that brief, slight, penetrating cry which had so much power over the noble animal. While Brummel and Carbonilla, tired from the difficult terrain, were losing vigor, Mallecho was increasing the intensity of his momentum, was about to regain his place, and already was caressing victory with his flaming nostrils. After the last obstacle, having overtaken Brummel, his head was abreast of Carbonilla's shoulder. Approximately one hundred meters from the end he grazed the hedge, moving forward, forward, leaving between himself and Caligàro's black mare the space of ten lengths. The bell sounded; applause rang out throughout the stands like the dull crackle of hail; clamor spread throughout the crowd on the lawn flooded by sunlight.

Andrea Sperelli, returning to the enclosure, was thinking: *Luck is with me today. Will it be with me tomorrow, too?* Sensing the aura of triumph draw near to him, he felt almost a surge of anger at the unknown danger. He would have liked to confront it immediately, this same day, at this same moment, without any delay, in order to enjoy a double victory and hence to bite at the fruit that Donna Ippolita's hand was offering him. His entire being was becoming enflamed with a savage pride at the thought of possessing that pale and haughty woman by right of violent conquest. His imagination visualized a sense of never-experienced joy, almost a voluptuousness of bygone days, when gentlemen loosened the hair of their lovers with murderous and caressing hands, burying in it their brows still dripping from the exertions of the felling and their mouths still bitter from the insults they had uttered. He was invaded by that inexplicable elation brought to certain men of intellect by acts of physical strength, by trials of courage, by the revelation of brutality. Whatever has remained deep inside us of primeval ferocity returns to the surface, at times, with a strange vehemence, and even beneath the narrow-minded gentility of modern dress, our heart sometimes swells with a certain bloodthirsty craving and yearns for carnage. Andrea Sperelli inhaled deeply of the warm and pungent exhalations of his horse, and none of the many delicate scents he had favored until that moment had ever given his senses more acute pleasure.

As soon as he dismounted, he was surrounded by female and male friends who congratulated him. Miching Mallecho, exhausted, all steaming and foaming, panted, stretching out his neck and shaking his bridle. His flanks were heaving continuously, so strongly that they appeared to burst; his muscles beneath the skin trembled like the strings of bows after releasing the arrow; his eyes, injected with blood and dilated, now held the atrocity of those of a wild animal; his hide, now blotched with wide darker patches, parted here and there in a herringbone pattern beneath the rivulets of sweat; the incessant vibration of his entire body evoked compassion and tenderness, as would the suffering of a human creature.

—Poor fellow! murmured Lilian Theed.

Andrea examined the horse's knees to see whether the fall had injured them. They were intact. Then, patting him softly on the neck, he said with an indefinable tone of sweetness:

—Go, Mallecho, go.

And he watched the horse walk away.

Then, having removed his racing silks, he sought out Ludovico Barbarisi and the Baron of Santa Margherita.

Both accepted the appointment to assist him in the matter with Marquis Rùtolo. He urged them to speed up the arrangement.

—Settle everything by this evening. Tomorrow, by one p.m., I must already be free. But tomorrow morning let me sleep at least until nine. I am lunching with the Princess of Ferentino; and then I am going to drop in at the Giustinianis'; and then, later on, at the club. You know where to find me. Thank you, and I'll see you later, fellows.

He went up into the stands; but avoided approaching Donna Ippolita straightaway. He smiled, feeling feminine glances alight on him from all around. Many lovely hands stretched out to him; many lovely voices called him "Andrea" with familiarity; some indeed called him so with a certain ostentation. The ladies who had bet on him told him the amount of their winnings: ten *luigi*, twenty *luigi*. Others asked him, with curiosity:

—Are you going to fight a duel?

It seemed to him that he had reached the summit of adventurous glory in one sole day, more so than the Duke of Buckingham and De Lauzun.[11] He had emerged as the victor of a heroic race; he had acquired a new lover, as magnificent and serene as a doge's wife; he had provoked a mortal duel; and now he was strolling calmly and courteously, no more or less than usual, among the smiles of ladies of whom he had known more than the grace of their mouths. Could he not perhaps indicate among many of them a secret habit or a particular voluptuous inclination? Could he not see the blond mole, similar to a small golden coin, through that luminous freshness of spring fabrics, on the left hip of Isotta Cellesi; or the incomparable abdomen of Giulia Moceto, as polished as an ivory goblet, as pure as that of a statue, due to that perfect absence, lamented by the poet of the *Musée secret*,[12] in ancient sculptures and paintings? Could he not hear in the resonant voice of Barbarella Viti another indefinable voice, which constantly repeated an immodest word; or another indefinable sound in the naive laugh of Aurora Seymour, raucous and guttural, which recalled somewhat the purring of cats on the hearth or the cooing of doves in the woods? Did he not know the exquisite depravations of the Countess of Lùcoli, who was inspired by erotic books, by engraved stones and miniatures; or the invincible prudishness of Francesca Daddi, who at the highest point of rapture gasped out, like someone dying, the name of God? Almost all the women whom he had deceived, or who had deceived him, were there and were smiling at him.

—Here comes the hero! said the husband of Donna Ippolita Albónico, holding his hand out to him with unusual amicability and squeezing his hand hard.

—Truly a hero, added Donna Ippolita, with the insignificant tone of an obligatory compliment, appearing to be unaware of the drama.

Sperelli bowed and passed on, because he felt a certain embarrassment in the face of that strange benevolence of the husband. A suspicion flashed into his mind, that the husband was grateful to him for having picked a quarrel with his wife's lover; and he smiled at the cowardice of the man. As he turned, Donna Ippolita's eyes met and held his.

Returning home, from the mail coach of the Prince of Ferentino he saw Giannetto Rùtolo fleeing toward Rome in a small two-wheeled coach, driving a large roan at a rapid trot, hunched forward, holding his head low and his cigar between his teeth, without paying any heed to the guards who were ordering him to get in line. Rome, in the background, was a dark outline above a zone of sulfur-yellow light; and the statues at the summit of the basilica of San Giovanni towered in a violet sky, beyond the zone. At that moment Andrea became fully conscious of the hurt he was causing that soul to suffer.

In the evening at the Giustiniani home he said to Donna Albónico:

—It's confirmed, then, that tomorrow, between two and five o'clock, I will wait for you.

She wished to ask him:

—How so? Aren't you fighting tomorrow?

But she did not dare. She replied:

—I have promised.

Shortly afterward, the husband approached Andrea, taking his arm with affectionate solicitude to ask for news of the duel. He was a still-youthful man, blond, elegant, with very sparse hair, milky eyes, and with his canine teeth protruding from his lips. He had a slight stammer.

—And so? And so? Tomorrow, eh?

Andrea could not overcome his repugnance; and he held his arm stiffly alongside his hip, to show that he did not appreciate that familiarity. As soon as he saw the Baron of Santa Margherita enter, he freed himself, saying:

—I urgently need to speak with Santa Margherita. Excuse me, Count.

The baron met him with these words:

—Everything is arranged.

—Good. For what time?

—Ten thirty, at Villa Sciarra. Sword and gauntlet. To the death.

—Who are the other two?

—Roberto Casteldieri and Carlo de Souza. We sorted it out immediately, avoiding formalities. Giannetto's were already organized. We drew up the protocol of the encounter at the club, with no discussion. I advise you to try not to go to bed too late. You must be tired.

Out of braggadocio, when he left the Giustinianis', Andrea went to the Hunting Club; and he began to play cards with the Neapolitan sportsmen. Toward two, Santa Margherita came upon him, forced him to leave the table, and insisted on accompanying him on foot right to Palazzo Zuccari.

—My dear fellow—he admonished him while walking—you

are too reckless. In these cases, imprudence could be fatal. To keep his strength intact, a good swordsman must take the same care with himself as a tenor does with his voice. The wrist is as delicate as the larynx; the articulations of the legs are as delicate as the vocal cords. Do you understand? The mechanism suffers from any minimal disorder; in this case the instrument is ruined; it does not obey anymore. After a night of love or gambling or debauchery, even the rapier thrusts of Camillo Agrippa[13] would not go straight and his parries would be neither exact nor rapid. Now, it is enough to miss by one millimeter to receive three inches of steel in one's body.

They were at the beginning of Via de' Condotti; and could see at its end Piazza di Spagna illuminated by the full moon, the stairs gleaming white, the tall Trinità de' Monti in the sweet azure sky.

—You, certainly—continued the baron—have many advantages over your adversary: among other things, you have sang-froid and knowledge of the terrain. I saw you in Paris against Gavaudan. Do you remember? Splendid duel! You fought like a god.

Andrea began to laugh with gratification. The elegy of that illustrious dueler swelled his heart with pride; it infused his nerves with a great abundance of strength. His hand clutching the cane instinctively repeated the movement of the famous thrust that pierced the arm of the Marquis de Gavaudan on December 12, 1885.

—It was—he said—a *contre-tierce* parry[14] and a *coulé.*[15]

And the baron continued:

—Giannetto Rùtolo, on the piste, is a fairly good fencer; on the ground, he is impetuous. He has fought only once, with my cousin Cassìbile; and he came out of it badly. He makes excessive use of "one, two" and "one, two, three" when attacking. You should make use of "arrests in time" and especially of "inquartata."[16] My cousin, indeed, hit him with a clean "inquartata" on the second assault. And you have a good sense of timing. Always keep your eye vigilant, however, and try to keep your measure. It is best that you do not forget that you are facing a man whose lover you have taken, they say, and against whom you have raised your whip.

They were in Piazza di Spagna. The Barcaccia Fountain[17] emitted a hoarse and modest gurgle, glinting in the light of the moon, which was reflected in it from the summit of the Catholic column. Four or five public coaches were stationary in a row, their headlamps lit. From Via del Babuino, a tinkling of bells and a dull sound of footsteps could be heard, like a herd on the move.

At the foot of the stairs the baron took his leave.

—Good-bye, until tomorrow. I will come a few minutes before nine with Ludovico. You will do some practice moves to warm up. We will take care of informing the doctor. Go; sleep soundly.

Andrea started up the stairs. At the first landing he stopped, attracted by the tinkling of the bells, which was drawing closer. In truth, he felt somewhat tired; and also somewhat sad, deep in his heart. After the pride roused in his blood by that talk of the science of weaponry and by the memory of his skill, a sort of uneasiness invaded him, not very distinct, mixed with doubt and discontent. His nerves, too strained in that violent and troubled day, were relaxing now in the clemency of the spring night. Why, without passion, out of pure whim, out of mere vanity, out of mere arrogance, had it pleased him to rouse hatred and bring pain to a man's soul? The thought of the horrible distress that certainly would be afflicting his enemy in such a gentle night almost moved him to a sense of pity. The image of Elena passed through his heart, in a flash; the anguish from the year before, when he had lost her, and the jealousy and the rages and the inexpressible sorrows, returned to his mind. Then, too, the nights had been clear, tranquil, crisscrossed with scents; and how they had weighed upon him! He inhaled the air, through which the exhalations of flowering roses drifted up from the small side gardens; and he looked down at the flock passing through the square.

The thick, grubby white wool of the massed-together sheep moved forward with a constant surging fluctuation, similar to muddy water flooding a pavement. A few tremulous bleats mingled with the tinkling; other bleats, shriller, shyer, answered them; the herdsmen gave a shout every now and then and stretched out their staffs, riding behind and alongside the flock;

the moon lent that passing of the flock, in the midst of the great sleeping city, a certain mystery almost as of something seen in a dream.

Andrea remembered that in a calm February night, emerging from a ball held by the English ambassador in Via Venti Settembre, he and Elena had encountered a flock; and the carriage had had to stop. Elena, leaning toward the windowpane, had watched the sheep passing by very close to the wheels, and had pointed out the smallest lambs, with a childlike gaiety; and he had held his face next to hers, half closing his eyes, listening to the shuffling, the bleats, the tinkling.

Why ever were all those memories of Elena returning to mind now? He continued climbing, slowly. He felt his tiredness become heavier as he climbed; his knees were buckling. Suddenly the thought of death flashed into his mind. *What if I am killed tomorrow? What if I am badly wounded and am left with some impediment for the rest of my life?* His eagerness for living and taking pleasure rose up against that dismal thought. He said to himself: *I must win.* And he saw all the advantages he would derive from this other victory: the prestige of his luck, the fame of his gallantry, the kisses of Donna Ippolita, new loves, new enjoyments, new caprices.

Then, controlling all his agitation, he began to attend to the hygienics of his strength. He slept until he was awakened by the arrival of his two friends; he took his customary shower; he had the oilcloth strip laid down on the floor; and he invited Santa Margherita to perform some "disengagements" with him; and then Barbarisi to a short free-fencing bout, during which he carried out with precision many timed actions.

—Excellent hand position, said the baron, congratulating him.

After the fencing, Sperelli had two cups of tea and some light biscuits. He selected a pair of wide trousers, a pair of comfortable shoes with a very low heel, a lightly starched shirt; he prepared the gauntlet, wetting it slightly on the palm and spreading some powdered Greek pitch on it; he placed with it a leather cord to tie the hilt to his wrist; he examined the blade and the point of the two swords; he did not forget any precaution, any small detail.

When he was ready, he said:

—Let's go. It's best if we get to the ground before the others. The doctor?

—He's waiting there.

Going down the stairs he met the Duke of Grimiti, who was coming also on behalf of the Marchioness of Ateleta.

—I'll follow you to the villa, and then I will take the news immediately to Francesca, said the duke.

They all went down together. The duke got into his carriage, waving. The others climbed into the covered coach. Andrea did not flaunt a good mood, because he deemed witticisms before a serious duel to be in extremely bad taste; but he was very calm. He smoked, listening to Santa Margherita and Barbarisi discuss, with regard to a recent case that had occurred in France, whether it was or was not permissible to use one's left hand against an adversary. Every now and then he leaned toward the window to look out onto the road.

Rome shone in the May morning, embraced by the sun. Along the way, a fountain illuminated with its silvery chuckle a small square that was still in shadow; the door of a building displayed a view through to a courtyard decorated with porticoes and statues; from the baroque lintel of a travertine church dangled the hangings that denoted the month of Mary. From the bridge the Tiber could be seen, shining, receding among the greenish houses toward the island of San Bartolomeo. After an uphill stretch, the city appeared, immense, august, radiant, bristling with bell towers, columns, and obelisks, crowned with cupolas and rotundas, clearly carved like an acropolis in the blue heights.

—*Ave, Roma, Moriturus te salutat,*[18] said Andrea Sperelli, throwing the remains of his cigarette toward the city.

Then he added:

—In truth, dear friends, to be hit by a sword today would annoy me.

They were at Villa Sciarra, half of it already blemished by the builders of new houses; and they passed along an avenue of tall slender bay trees, espaliered on each side by roses. Santa Margherita, leaning out of the window, saw another carriage stationary on the square in front of the villa; and said:

—They are waiting for us already.

He looked at his watch. There were still ten minutes to go until the scheduled time. He ordered the carriage to stop; and together with the witness and the surgeon headed toward the adversaries. Andrea remained in the avenue, waiting. Mentally, he began to carry out certain offense and defense actions, which he intended to carry out with probable success; but he was distracted by the vague marvels of light and shadow cast by the intricate web of the bay trees. His eyes roamed behind the appearance of the branches moved by the morning wind, while his mind meditated upon injury; and the trees, as kind as in the loving allegories of Francesco Petrarch, sighed above his head, in which the thought of the good hit reigned.

Barbarisi came up to him to call him, saying:

—We are ready. The custodian has opened the villa. We have the ground floor at our disposal; it's very convenient. Come and get undressed.

Andrea followed him. While he undressed, the two doctors opened their pouches in which the small steel instruments glinted. One was still young, pale, bald, with feminine hands, his mouth somewhat severe, with a constant visible friction of his bottom jaw, which was extraordinarily developed. The other was already mature, robust, covered with freckles, with a thick ruddy beard and a bull neck. One appeared to be the physical contradiction of the other; and their diversity attracted Sperelli's inquisitive attention. They were preparing on a table the bandages and the carbolic acid for disinfecting the blades. The odor of the acid spread throughout the room.

When Sperelli was ready, he went out with his witness and the doctors onto the square. Once more, the spectacle of Rome through the palm trees drew his gaze and made his heart pound strongly. Impatience invaded him. He would have liked already to be on guard and to hear the command to attack. It seemed to him that he already had the decisive hit, victory, in his grasp.

—Ready? Santa Margherita asked him, coming to meet him.

—Ready.

The chosen ground was alongside the villa, in the shade, scattered with fine gravel and rollered. Giannetto Rùtolo was already at the other end with Roberto Casteldieri and Carlo de Souza. Each had assumed a grave air, almost solemn. The two adversaries were placed facing each other; and they observed each other. Santa Margherita, who was in charge of the duel, noted Giannetto Rùtolo's heavily starched shirt, too stiff, with his collar too high; and he pointed this out to Casteldieri, who was his second. The latter spoke to his principal; and Sperelli saw his enemy suddenly become inflamed in the face and with a resolute gesture take off his shirt. With cold tranquillity he followed this example; he rolled up his trousers; took the gauntlet, the cord, and the sword from Santa Margherita's hands; he armed himself with much care and then shook the sword to ensure that he had it firmly gripped. In that movement, his biceps emerged very visibly, revealing the extensive exercise of his arm and the strength he had acquired.

When the two held out their swords to take measure, Giannetto Rùtolo's wavered in his convulsed fist. After the warning regarding fair play, the Baron of Santa Margherita commanded in a ringing and virile voice:

—Gentlemen, on guard!

Both assumed the on-guard position at the same time, Rùtolo tapping his foot, Sperelli arching lightly. Rùtolo was of mediocre stature, very slender, full of nervous energy, with an olive-skinned face made haughty by his upturned mustaches and the small pointed beard on his chin, in the style of Charles I in the portraits by Van Dyck. Sperelli was taller, more willowy, more composed, of beautiful posture, steady and calm with a balance of grace and strength, containing in his entire figure the disdain of a great gentleman. Each stared the other in the eye; and each felt inside himself an indefinable shiver at the sight of the other's naked flesh against which his sharp blade was pointed. In the silence, the cool babbling of the fountain could be heard, mingled with the rustle of the wind through the climbing roses where innumerable white and yellow roses quivered.

—Gentlemen, fence! the baron commanded.

Andrea Sperelli expected an impetuous attack by Rùtolo; but the latter did not move. For a minute both continued to study each other, without having any contact of the blades, almost immobile. Sperelli, crouching even farther down on his ankles in low guard, was exposing himself completely, by bringing his sword very much into third position; and he provoked his adversary with insolence in his eyes and by tapping his foot. Rùtolo advanced, feinting a direct thrust, accompanying it with a yell in the manner of certain Sicilian swordsmen; and the fencing began.

Sperelli was not building up any decisive action, limiting himself almost always to parries, forcing his adversary to disclose all his intentions, to exhaust all his means, to carry out all the varieties of his game. He was parrying cleanly and fast, without ceding ground, with an admirable precision, as if he were on the piste in a fencing academy facing an innocuous foil; while Rùtolo was attacking with ardor, accompanying every thrust with a dull cry, similar to that of tree fellers wielding their axe.

—Halt! commanded Santa Margherita, whose vigilant eyes did not miss any movement of the two blades.

And he approached Rùtolo, saying:

—You have been touched, if I am not mistaken.

In fact, he had a scratch on his forearm, but so light that there was no need even for taffeta.[19] He was panting, however; and his extreme pallor, as somber as a bruise, was a sign of his contained ire. Sperelli, smiling, said in a low voice to Barbarisi:

—I know my man now. I'll give him a carnation below the left breast. Watch out in the second assault.

Since without thinking he had rested the tip of his sword on the ground, the bald doctor, the one with the great jaw, came to him with the sponge soaked in carbolic acid and once again disinfected the sword.

—By God! murmured Andrea to Barbarisi. —He looks like a jinx to me. This blade is going to break.

A blackbird began to whistle in the trees. Among the rosebushes, a few roses were shedding petals and dispersing in the wind. Some clouds in midair were rising up to meet the sun, sparse, similar to the fleece of sheep; and broke up into tufts; and gradually vanished.

—On guard!

Giannetto Rùtolo, conscious of his inferiority vis-à-vis his enemy, resolved to work in close measure, recklessly, and thus to block every action taken by the other. He had for this purpose the short stature and the agile, slender, flexible body that offered very little target for hits.

—Fence!

Andrea Sperelli already knew that Rùtolo would advance in that way, with the usual feints. He stood on guard arched like a crossbow ready to let fly, intent on choosing his time.

—Halt, shouted Santa Margherita.

Rùtolo's chest was bleeding slightly. His adversary's sword had hit him below the right breast, injuring the tissues almost to the rib. The doctors ran to him. But the wounded man said immediately to Casteldieri, with a harsh voice in which a tremor of rage could be heard:

—It's nothing. I want to continue.

He refused to go back into the villa to be medicated. The bald doctor, after having squeezed the small hole, which was bleeding slightly, and after having cleansed it with antiseptic, applied a simple piece of plaster; and said:

—He can continue.

The baron, by invitation of Casteldieri, commanded the third assault without hesitating.

—On guard!

Andrea Sperelli perceived the danger. Before him his enemy, all hunched on his ankles, almost hidden behind the point of his sword, seemed determined to make a supreme effort. His eyes were glinting strangely and his left thigh, under the excessive tension of the muscles, was trembling badly. Andrea, this time, against this attack, was preparing to throw himself across in order to replicate Cassìbile's decisive hit, and the white disc of the plaster on the hostile chest served him as a target. He aimed to place the thrust there once again but to find the intercostal space, not the rib. All around, the silence appeared deeper; all the onlookers were conscious of the murderous will that drove those two men; and anxiety gripped them, and the thought that they would perhaps be taking home a dead or dying man bound them together. The sun, veiled by the little sheep, cast an almost milky light; the trees rustled now and again; the blackbird still whistled, invisible.

—Fence!

Rùtolo launched himself at close measure, with two circles of the sword and a thrust in second. Sperelli parried and riposted, taking a step backward. Rùtolo pursued him, furious, with rapid thrusts, almost all of them low, no longer accompanying them with yells. Sperelli, without becoming disconcerted at that fury, wishing to avoid contact, parried hard and riposted with such fierceness that each of his thrusts could have passed right through his enemy. Rùtolo's thigh, near the groin, was bleeding.

—Halt! thundered Santa Margherita when he noticed it. But at that exact moment Sperelli, executing a parry in low fourth and not meeting the adversary's blade, received a hit full in the chest; and fell in a faint into Barbarisi's arms.

—Thoracic wound, at the fourth right intercostal space, penetrating into the cavity, with superficial lesion of the lung, the bull-necked surgeon announced in the room, once he had completed his examination.

SECOND BOOK

CHAPTER I

Convalescence is a purification and a rebirth. Never is the sense of life as sweet as it is after the anguish of pain; and never is the human soul more inclined to goodness and faith than after having gazed into the abyss of death. Man understands, when healing, that thought, desire, will, consciousness of life, are not life. Something in him is more vigilant than thought, more constant than desire, more potent than will, more profound even than consciousness; and it is the substance, the nature of his being. He understands that his real life is, as it were, the one not lived by him; it is the combination of involuntary, spontaneous, unconscious, instinctive sensations; it is the harmonious and mysterious activity of living vegetation; it is the imperceptible development of all metamorphoses and all renewals. It is precisely that life within him that carries out the miracles of convalescence: it closes wounds, remedies losses, reconnects broken tissues, mends lacerated flesh, restores the mechanism of organs, reinfuses the veins with the richness of blood, ties once more around the eyes the blindfold of love, weaves once more the crown of dreams around the head, rekindles the flame of hope in the heart, opens once more the wings of the chimeras of fantasy.

After the mortal wound, after a kind of long and slow hovering at the point of death, Andrea Sperelli little by little was now being reborn, almost with another body and another spirit, like a new man, like a creature emerged from a cool Lethean bath,[1] forgetful and vacuous. It seemed to him that he had taken on a more elementary form. The past, in his memory, was all equally distant, just as the starred sky is, to the eye, an equal and diffuse field, even though the stars are at different distances. Turmoil was pacified, mud receded to the lowest level, the soul cleansed itself; and he returned to the womb of Mother Nature, feeling goodness and strength infuse maternally into him.

Hosted by his cousin at the villa of Schifanoja, Andrea Sperelli was once again facing existence in the presence of the sea. Since the *sympathetic* nature still persists within us, and since our old soul, embraced by the great natural soul still palpitates at this contact, the convalescent measured his breathing against the wide and tranquil respiration of the sea, stretched out his body the way powerful trees do, calmed his thoughts with the calmness of the horizon. Little by little, in that attentive and absorbed leisure, his spirit relaxed, unfolded, unfurled, lifted itself gently like grass crushed on a path; finally it became real, ingenuous, original, free, open to pure knowledge, ready for pure contemplation; he attracted things to himself, conceived of them as forms of his own being, as forms of his own existence; he felt himself finally being penetrated by the truth proclaimed by the Upanishad[2] of the Vedas:[3] "*Hae omnes creaturae in totum ego sum, et praeter me aliud ens non est.*"[4] The great gust of ideality exhaled by the sacred Indian books, once studied and loved, appeared to uplift him. And repeatedly, the Sanskrit formula glowed for him in a remarkable way: "TAT TWAM ASI"; which means: "This living thing, that you are."

It was the last days of August. An ecstatic quietness held the sea; the waters were of such transparency that they reflected any image with perfect exactness; the farthest line of the waters mingled with the sky in such a way that the two elements appeared to be one single, impalpable, unnatural element. The vast amphitheater of the hills, studded with olive trees, orange trees, pines, all the noblest forms of Italic vegetation, embracing that silence, was no longer a multitude of things but one single thing, under the common sun.

The young man, stretched out in the shade or leaning against a tree trunk or seated on a rock, believed he could feel the river of time flowing within him; with a kind of catalectic tranquillity, he believed he could feel the entire world living in his heart; with a kind of religious exaltation, he believed he possessed the infinite. What he felt was ineffable, not expressible even in the words of the mystic: "I am admitted by nature into the most secret of her divine seats, to the source of all life. Here I discover the cause of movement and hear the first song of living beings, in all its freshness."[5] His sight slowly mutated into a profound and continuous vision; the branches of the trees above his head seemed to him to hold up the sky, to amplify the blueness, to shine like the crowns of immortal poets; and he contemplated and listened, breathing with the sea and the earth, placid as a god.

Wherever were all his vanities and his cruelties and his expedients and his lies? Where were the loves and the betrayals and the disillusionments and the disgust and the incurable repugnance after pleasure? Where were those impure and rapid love affairs that left in his mouth the strange sourness of fruit cut with a steel knife? He could no longer remember anything. His spirit had made a great renunciation. Another beginning of life was entering into him; *someone* was entering into him, secretly, who profoundly felt the peace. He rested, because he did not desire anymore.

Desire had abandoned its realm; during activity, intellect freely followed its own laws and reflected the objective world like a pure subject of knowledge; things appeared in their true form, in their true color, in their true and full meaning and beauty, precise and very clear; every sentiment of the person disappeared. In this temporary death of desire, in this temporary absence of memory, in this perfect objectivity of contemplation, was to be found the cause of never-experienced pleasure.

Die Sterne, die begehrt man nicht,
Man freut sich ihrer Pracht.

"The stars, man does not desire them—but takes pleasure in their splendor."[6] For the first time, in fact, the young man discovered all the harmonious nocturnal poetry of the summer skies.

They were the last moonless nights of August. The ardent life of innumerable constellations pulsated in the deep basin. The Ursus constellations, the Swan, Hercules, Boötes, Cassiopeia, scintillated with such a rapid and strong throb that they almost seemed to draw closer to the earth, to have entered the earth's atmosphere. The Milky Way unfolded like a regal aerial river, like an assembly of heavenly coasts, like an immense silent stream that drew into its *"miro gurge"*[7] a dust of starry minerals, passing above a crystal hive, between phalanxes of flowers. At intervals, shining meteors streaked the immobile air, with the infinitely soft and silent slide of a drop of water on a sheet of diamond. The breathing of the sea, slow and solemn, was enough to measure the tranquillity of the night without disturbing it; and the pauses were sweeter than the sound.

But this period of visions, of abstractions, of intuitions, of pure contemplations, this sort of Buddhistic and almost, one could say, cosmogonic mysticism, was extremely brief. The causes of the rare phenomenon, over and above the plastic nature of the young man and his aptitude toward objectivity, were perhaps to be sought in the singular tension and extreme impressionability of his cerebral nervous system. Little by little, he began to recover consciousness of himself, to regain the sentiment of himself, and to return to his original corporeity. One day at the noon hour, while the life of things appeared to be suspended, the great and terrible silence suddenly allowed him to perceive within himself vertiginous abysses, inextinguishable needs, indestructible memories, accumulations of suffering and regret, all the misery he had once felt, all the vestiges of his vice, all the residues of his passions.

From that day on, a subdued and constant melancholy occupied his soul; and he saw in every aspect of things a state of his spirit. Instead of transmuting into other forms of existence, or placing himself in different states of consciousness or losing his particular being in general life, he now presented contrary phenomena, wrapping himself up in a nature that was a completely subjective conception of his intellect. The countryside became for him a symbol, an emblem, a sign, an escort that guided him through his internal labyrinth. He discovered secret affinities between the apparent life of things and the intimate life of his desires and his memories. *"To me—high mountains are a feeling."* Just like mountains in George Byron's verse, so, too, was the seashore, for him, *a feeling.*

Clear September seashores! The sea, calm and innocent like a sleeping boy, spread out under angelic pearly heavens. Sometimes it appeared to be completely green, the fine and precious green of malachite; and on it, the small red sails resembled errant flamelets. Sometimes it appeared to be completely blue, of an intense azure, almost, one could say, heraldic, shot through with veins of gold like a lapis lazuli; and on it, the decorated sails resembled a procession of ensigns and banners and Catholic shields. Also, sometimes it took on a diffused metallic gleam, a pale silvery color, mingled with the greenish hue of a ripe lemon, something indefinably strange and delicate; and on it, the sails were pious and as innumerable as the wings of cherubs in the background of Giotto's panels.

The convalescent discovered forgotten childhood sensations, that impression of coolness lent to childish blood by the gusts of salty wind, those inexpressible effects lent by the lights, shadows, colors, smells of water on the virgin soul. The sea was not only a delight for his eyes but also a perennial wave of peace at which his thoughts drank, a magical fountain of youth in which his body regained its health and his spirit its nobility. The sea held for him the mysterious attraction of a fatherland; and he surrendered himself to it with filial familiarity, like a weak son in the arms of an omnipotent father. And he took comfort from it; because no one has ever confided his pain, his desire, his dream to the sea in vain.

The sea always had a profound word for him, full of sudden revelations, unexpected illuminations, unforeseen meanings. It uncovered in his secret soul a still-living, though hidden, ulcer and made it bleed; but the balm thereafter was sweeter. It shook awake in his heart a sleeping chimera and incited it so that he could once again feel its nails and its beak; but then it killed it and buried it in his heart forever. It awoke in his memory a recollection and it revived it such that he suffered all the bitterness of regret for things that were irremediably lost; but then it lavished upon him the sweetness of an endless oblivion. Nothing remained hidden in that soul, in the presence of the great consoler. In the same way that a strong electrical current makes metals luminous and reveals their essence by the color of their flame, the virtue of the sea illuminated and revealed all the powers and the potentialities of that human soul.

At certain times the convalescent, under the assiduous dominion of such a virtue, under the assiduous yoke of such fascination, felt a sort of bewilderment and almost of dismay, as if that dominion and that yoke were unbearable, due to his weakness. At certain times he derived from the incessant exchange between his soul and the sea a vague sense of prostration, as if that great discourse caused too much violence to his distressed intellect, eager to comprehend the incomprehensible. Any sadness of the waters upset him like a misfortune.

One day, he saw himself lost. Bloody and evil vapors burned on the horizon, casting splashes of blood and gold onto the dark waters; a tangle of purple clouds arose from the vapors, resembling a skirmish of enormous centaurs above a flaming volcano; and in that tragic light a funeral procession of triangular sails was etched in black on the farthest rim. They were sails of an indescribable hue, as sinister as the insignia of death; marked with crosses and shadowy figures; they resembled the sails of fleets carrying plague-infested cadavers to some cursed island populated by ravenous vultures. A human sense of terror and pain loomed over that sea; an agonizing dejection burdened that air. The gush spurting from the wounds of the brawling monsters did not ever abate; rather it grew into rivers that reddened the waters throughout the entire area, right up to the shore, becoming tinted here and there with violet and greenish shades as if it were decaying. Every now and then the knot collapsed, the bodies became deformed or tore apart, bleeding strips dangled down from the crater or disappeared, swallowed by the abyss. Then, after the great collapse, the giants, regenerated, once again sprang into battle, more atrocious than before; the mound recomposed itself, more enormous than before; and the massacre began again, redder than before, until the combatants were left drained of blood amid the ashes of dusk, lifeless, defeated, on the semi-extinct volcano.

It seemed like an episode from some primitive Titanomachia,[8] a heroic spectacle, seen over a long succession of epochs in the fabled sky. Andrea, his heart suspended, followed the entire succession of events. Accustomed to the tranquil descent of shadow in that serene decline of summer, he now felt himself shaken, uplifted, and confused by the unusual contrast, with a strange violence. At first, it was like a confused anguish, tumultuous, full of unwitting tremors. Fascinated by the bellicose sunset, he was not yet able to see clearly inside himself. But when the ash of dusk rained down extinguishing every war, and the sea resembled an immense leaden swamp, he believed he could hear in the shadow the shout of his soul, the shout of other souls.

It was inside him, like a gloomy shipwreck in the shadow. Many, many voices called for help, imploring for help, cursing death; familiar voices, voices to which he had once listened (voices of human beings or of phantoms?); and now he could not distinguish the one from the other! They called, they implored, they cursed uselessly, feeling themselves perish; they grew feebler, suffocated by the voracious wave; they became weaker, distant, interrupted, unrecognizable; they became a moan; they died away; they rose up no more.

He was left alone. Of his entire youth, of his entire interior life, of all his ideals, nothing remained. Inside him there was nothing but a cold empty abyss; around him was impassive nature, the perennial source of pain for the solitary soul. Every hope was dimmed; every voice was mute; every anchor was broken. What was there to live for?

At once, the image of Elena rose up again in his memory. Other images of women superimposed themselves upon it, mingled with it, dispersed it, became dispersed. He could not stop any one of them. All appeared to smile, an enemy smile, when vanishing; and all, in vanishing, seemed to take away with them something of his. What? He did not know. An unspeakable disheartenment oppressed him; a sense almost of oldness chilled him; his eyes filled with tears. A tragic warning sounded in his heart: "Too late!"

The recent sweetness of peace and melancholy seemed already distant; it seemed to be an illusion that had already escaped him; it almost seemed to him that it had been enjoyed by some other spirit, new, foreign, which had entered him and then disappeared. It seemed to him that his old spirit by now could neither renew nor uplift itself again. All the wounds that he had inflicted without restraint on the dignity of his internal being bled. All the degradations that he had inflicted on his conscience without repugnance emerged like stains and spread like leprosy.

All the violations that he had without shame committed on his ideals roused an acute remorse in him, desperate, terrible, as if inside him wept the souls of his daughters whom he, their father, had stripped of their virginity while they slept, dreaming.

And he wept with them; and it seemed to him that his tears did not go down to his heart like a balm, but rebounded as if from some slimy or cold substance with which his heart was bound. The ambiguity, the simulation, the falsity, the hypocrisy, all the forms of falsehood and fraud in the life of sentiment, all adhered to his heart like tenacious mistletoe.

He had lied too much, had deceived too much, had debased himself too much. Revulsion of himself and his vice invaded him. For shame! For shame! The dishonorable ugly deed seemed indelible to him; the wounds seemed untreatable; it seemed to him that he would have to bear the nausea forever, forever, like an interminable torment. For shame! He wept, bent over the windowsill, collapsed beneath the weight of his misery, overcome like a man who cannot see salvation; and he did not see the stars twinkle one by one on his piteous head, in the depth of evening.

With the new day he had a pleasant awakening, one of those fresh and limpid awakenings that are experienced only by the Adolescent during his triumphant springs. The morning was a wonder; to breathe in the morning was an immense beatitude. All things were living in the bliss of the light; the hills seemed to be draped in a diaphanous silver awning, stirred by an agile quiver; the sea appeared to be crossed by milky coasts, by crystal rivers, by emerald streams, by a thousand veins that formed the fickle web of a liquid labyrinth. A sense of nuptial joy and religious grace emanated from the concordance of sea, sky, and earth.

He breathed, watched, listened, slightly astonished. In his sleep, his fever had healed. He had closed his eyes in the night, lulled by the chorus of the waters as by a friendly and faithful voice. Those who fall asleep to the sound of that voice find repose full of therapeutic tranquillity. Not even a mother's words induce sleep as pure and beneficial to the son who suffers.

He watched, listened, mute, engrossed, touched, allowing that wave of immortal life to enter him. Never had the sacred music of a supreme master, an Offertory by Joseph Haydn or a Te

Deum by Wolfgang Mozart, moved him as much as he was now moved by the simple bells of the distant churches, greeting the ascension of Day into the heavens of the One God in Three Divine Persons. He felt his heart fill and overflow with emotion. Something like a vague but great dream rose in his soul, something like an undulating veil through which the mysterious treasure of happiness shone. Until now he had always known what he desired, and had almost never desired in vain. Now he could not tell what he desired; he did not know. But certainly, the desired thing would be infinitely sweet, because it was sweet even to desire it.

The verses of the Chimera in the "King of Cyprus," ancient verses, almost forgotten, returned to his memory, and sounded like an enticement.

> Do you want to fight?
> Kill? See rivers of blood?
> great mounds of gold? herds of captive
> females? slaves? other, other preys? Do you want
> to bring marble to life? Erect a temple?
> Compose an immortal hymn? Do you want (do you hear me,
> young man, do you hear me?) do you want to love
> divinely?

The Chimera repeated to him in his secret heart, in a subdued voice, with obscure pauses:

> Do you hear me,
> young man, do you hear me: do you want to love
> divinely?

He smiled a little. And he thought: *Love whom? Art? A woman? Which woman?* Elena seemed far away, lost, dead, no longer his; the others seemed even farther, lost forever. He was free, therefore. Why ever would he once more carry out a futile and perilous search? Deep in his heart there was the desire to give himself, freely and for acknowledgment, to a higher and purer being. But where was this being? The Ideal poisons every imperfect possession; and in love every possession is imperfect and deceiving, every pleasure is mixed with sadness, every enjoyment is halved, every joy carries within it a seed of suffering, every surrender carries within it a seed of doubt; and doubts destroy, contaminate, corrupt all delights just as Harpies rendered all foods inedible for Phineas. Why ever, therefore, would he once again stretch out his hand to the tree of knowledge?

> The tree of knowledge has been pluck'd—all's known—

as George Byron intones in *Don Juan*. In truth, for the future, his health would be found in "ευλαβεια,"[9] namely, in prudence, in refinement, in caution, in wisdom. This understanding of his seemed to be well expressed in the sonnet of a contemporary poet,[10] whom he favored for a certain affinity of literary tastes and commonality of aesthetic education.

> I will be like he who lies down
> beneath the shade of a great laden tree
> sated, by now, of drawing crossbow or arch;
> and over his head ripe fruit is suspended.
>
> He does not shake that branch, nor does he stretch out
> his hand, nor lie in wait for his prey.
> He lies there; and gathers with a frugal gesture
> the fruits bestowed by that branch to the earth.
>
> Of such sweet pulp he does not bite
> into the depth, to seek its inner essence,
> because he fears the bitterness; rather he sniffs it,
>
> then sucks, with clear pleasure, without
> greed, neither sad nor joyful.
> His brief fable is already done.

But "ευλαβεια," if it serves to exclude pain, in part, from life, also excludes every lofty ideal. Health therefore was to be found in a type of Goethian equilibrium between a cautious and refined practical Epicureanism and the profound and passionate worship of Art.

Art! Art! Here was the faithful Lover, always young, immortal; here was the Source of pure joy, forbidden to the multitude, conceded to the elect; here was the precious Food, which makes man similar to a god. How could he have drunk from other cups after bringing his lips to that one? How could he have sought other pleasures after having tasted the supreme one? How could his spirit have held other turbulences after having felt within it the unforgettable tumult of creative force? How could his hands have idled and frolicked wantonly over the bodies of women after having felt a tangible form erupt from his fingers? How, ultimately, could his senses have weakened and become perverted into base lust after having been illumined by a sensibility that discerned invisible lines in the appearance of things, perceived the imperceptible, gauged the hidden thoughts of Nature?

A sudden enthusiasm invaded him. In that religious morning, he wanted to kneel again at the altar and, as in Goethe's poem, read his acts of devotion in Homer's liturgy.[11]

But what if my intelligence has fallen into decline? What if my hand has lost its skill? If I were no longer worthy? At this doubt, such strong dismay assailed him that with a puerile frenzy, he began to seek out some immediate proof to be sure that his fear was unreasonable. He would have liked immediately to carry out a real experiment: compose a difficult verse, draw a figure, engrave a copperplate, solve some problem of form. And so? And then? Would that not be a failed experiment? The slow decline of intellect can also be unconscious: here lies the terrible fact. The artist who slowly loses his faculties is not aware of his progressive weakness; because together with the power of producing and reproducing, his critical judgment and criteria also abandon him. He can no longer distinguish the defects of his work; he does not know that his work is bad or mediocre; he deludes himself; he believes that his painting, his statue, his poem are within the laws of Art, whereas they are outside of them. Here lies the terrible fact. The artist who has been struck in his intellect may have no conscience of his own imbecility, just as the madman has no conscience of his own aberration. And so?

It was a kind of panic for the convalescent. He pressed his temples between the palms of his hands; and remained for a few moments subject to the jolt of that fearsome thought, beneath the horror of that threat, as if annihilated. Better, better to die! Never, as in that moment, had he felt the divine merit of the *gift;* never, as in that moment, had the *spark* seemed sacred to him. His entire being trembled with a strange violence, at the sole doubt that that gift could be destroyed, that that spark could be extinguished. Better to die!

He lifted his head; shook all inertia from himself; went down to the park; walked slowly beneath the trees, not having any definite thought. A light breeze drifted through the treetops; at intervals, the leaves were disturbed by a strong rustling, as if a scurry of squirrels were passing through them; small fragments of sky appeared between the branches, like blue eyes below green eyelids. In a favorite place, a kind of small sacred grove dominated by a four-headed herm intent upon a fourfold meditation, he stopped; and he sat down on the grass, his shoulders leaning against the base of the statue, his face turned toward the sea. Before him, certain tree trunks, straight and gradually decreasing in length like the reeds of Pan's pipes, intersected the ultramarine; around him, the acanthus plants opened the basket of their leaves with sovereign elegance, symmetrically incised like Callimachus's capital.[12]

The verses of Salmacis in the *Fable of Hermaphrodite* came to his mind.

> Noble acanthi, O ye in the earthly
> forests, signs of peace, lofty coronas,
> of pure form; O ye, slender baskets
> that Silence composes with a light hand
> to gather the flower of sylvan
> Dreams, which virtue did you spill onto the beautiful boy
> from the dark, sweet leaves?
> He sleeps, naked; his head supported by his arm.

He recalled other verses, and others still, others still, tumultuously. His soul filled up completely with music made up of rhymes and rhythmic syllables. He rejoiced; that spontaneous sudden poetic agitation gave him an inexpressible delight. He listened to those sounds inside himself, pleased with the rich images, the precise epithets, the lucid metaphors, the studied harmonies, the exquisite combinations of hiatus and diaeresis, of all the most subtle refinements that varied his style and his meter, of all the mysterious artifices of the hendecasyllable learned from the admirable poets of the fourteenth century, and especially from Petrarch. The magic of the verses subjugated his spirit once again; and the sentential hemistich of a contemporary poet cheered him in particular. "The Verse is everything."[13]

The verse is everything. In the imitation of Nature, no instrument of art is more alive, agile, acute, varied, multiform, plastic, obedient, sensitive, faithful. More compact than marble, more malleable than clay, more subtle than fluid, more vibrating than a cord, more luminous than a gem, more fragrant than a flower, sharper than a sword, more flexible than a germinating shoot, more caressing than a murmur, more terrible than thunder, the verse is everything and is capable of everything. It can render the smallest motions of sentiment and the smallest motions of sensation; it can define the indefinable and say the unutterable; it can embrace the unlimited and penetrate the abyss; it can have dimensions of eternity; it can represent the superhuman, the supernatural, the awesome; it can inebriate like wine, ravish like ecstasy; it can possess at the same time our intellect, our spirit, our body; it can, ultimately, reach the Absolute. A perfect verse is absolute, immutable, immortal; it holds within it words with the coherence of a diamond; it encloses thought as in a precise circle that no force will ever manage to break; it becomes independent of any bond and any dominion; it belongs no longer to its creator, but to everyone and to no one, like space, like light, like immanent and perpetual things. A thought expressed exactly in a perfect verse is a thought that already existed *preformed* in the obscure depths of language. Extracted by the poet, it *continues* to exist in the consciousness of men. The greatest poet is therefore the one who knows how to uncover, extricate, extract a greater number of these ideal preformations. When the poet is near to the discovery of one such eternal verse, he is alerted by a divine torrent of joy that suddenly invades his entire being.

What joy is stronger? Andrea half closed his eyes, almost as if to prolong that particular thrill which was the herald of inspiration within him, when his spirit was preparing itself for the work of art, especially that of writing poetry. Then, full of delight never experienced before, he began to explore rhymes with a slender pencil on the small white pages of his notebook. The first verses of a song by Lorenzo the Magnificent came to his mind:

> Lightly and quickly depart
> my thoughts from within my soul . . .[14]

Almost always, in order to start composing, he needed to be given a musical intonation by another poet; and it was his custom almost always to derive it from the ancient Tuscan versifiers. A hemistich by Lapo Gianni, by Cavalcanti, by Cino, by Petrarch, by Lorenzo de' Medici, the memory of a cluster of rhymes, the conjunction of two epithets, any concordance of beautiful and well-sounding words, any rhythmical phrase, was enough to open the vein for him, to give him, as it were, the note *La*[15] that would serve him as foundation of the harmony of the first stanza. It was a kind of rhetorical topic applied to the search not for an argument, but for preludes. The first Medicean septenarius in fact offered him the rhyme; and he distinctly *saw* everything that he wished to show his imaginary listener in the figure of the herm; and together with the vision, at the same time, in his mind the metrical form spontaneously presented itself, into which he had to pour, like wine into a goblet, the poetry. Since his poetic sentiment was twofold, or rather, arose from a contrast, namely from the contrast between his past wretchedness and his present resurrection, and since in his lyrical activity he worked toward spiritual elevation, he chose the sonnet; the architecture of which consists of two orders: the higher one represented by two quatrains and the lower one represented by two tercets. Thought and passion, therefore, expanding in the first order, would be concentrated, reinforced, elevated in the second. The form of the sonnet, although being wonderfully beautiful and magnificent, is in some ways imperfect; because it resembles a figure with the torso too long and the legs too short. Indeed the two tercets are in reality not only shorter than the quatrains, by number of lines; but they also *seem* shorter than the quatrains, for the rapidity and fluidity of their pace in comparison with the slowness and majesty of the quatrain. Whoever knows how to conceal these deficiencies is the greatest craftsman; whoever, namely, reserving for the tercets the most precise and most visible image and the strongest and most sonorous words, succeeds in making the tercets stand out and harmonize with the upper stanzas without, however, losing any of their essential lightness and rapidity. The Renaissance painters knew how to balance an entire figure with a simple flourish of a ribbon or the edge of a garment or a fold.

Andrea, while composing, studied himself with curiosity. He had not written verse for a long time. Had that interval of idleness harmed his technical skill? It seemed to him that the rhymes, emerging gradually from his brain, had a new flavor. Consonance was coming to him spontaneously, without his having to search for it; and thoughts were emerging from him already in rhyme. Then, suddenly, an obstacle stopped the flow; a line rebelled against him; all the rest broke up like a disconnected mosaic; the syllables struggled against the constraints of the meter; a musical and luminous word, which pleased him, was excluded by the severity of the rhythm despite every effort; from one rhyme a new idea arose, unexpectedly, to seduce him, to distract him from the original idea; an epithet, despite being appropriate and exact, had a weak sound; coherence, the quality so long searched for, was completely missing; and the stanza was like a medal that has turned out imperfectly through the fault of an inexperienced founder who could not properly calculate the quantity of molten metal necessary for filling the mold. With intense patience, he would replace the metal in the crucible; and start the work over from scratch. In the end, the stanza would turn out complete and precise; some lines, here and there, had a certain pleasing asperity; through the undulations of the rhythm, the symmetry became very evident; the repetition of the rhymes made clear music, recalling to mind with the harmony of its sounds the harmony of thoughts and reinforcing with a physical bond the moral bond; the whole sonnet lived and breathed like an independent organism, in its unity. To pass from one sonnet to the other, he *held* a note, just as in music the modulation from one tone to the other is prepared by the seventh chord, in which one holds the key note in order to make it the dominant one of the new tone.

He composed in such a way, sometimes rapidly, sometimes slowly, with a pleasure he had never experienced; and the quiet place, in truth, seemed to have emerged from the fantasy of a solitary egipane[16] devoted to lyrical poetry. The sea, as the day advanced, flashed between the tree trunks as between the intercolumniations of a jasper portico; the Corinthian acanthi resembled coronations felled from those arboreal columns; now and then in the air, pale bluish green as the shade of a lacustrine cavern, the sun shot forth golden darts and rings and discs. Certainly, Alma-Tadema would have imagined there a Sappho with violet locks, seated below the marble herm, versifying on a seven-stringed lyre, amid a chorus of pale girls with flame-colored hair intent on drinking from the Adonic verse the accomplished harmony of each stanza.

When he had completed the four sonnets, he drew a breath and recited them silently, with an internal emphasis. The apparent break of the rhythm in the fifth line of the last sonnet, caused by the lack of a tonic accent and hence of a grave pause in the eighth syllable, seemed effective to him and he kept it. Then he wrote the four sonnets on the quadrangular base of the herm: one sonnet on each face, in this order.

I

Four-sided herm, do your four faces
know my wondrous tidings?
Light and quick, spirits leave singing
from my heart's hidden places.

My valiant heart barred all corrupted sources
and cast out every single impure thing
it smothered every flame which could be shaming
and broke all bridges against besieging forces.

Singing, spirits rise upward. Well do I hear
the hymn; and unquenchable, powerful
laughter seizes me, concerning my great peril.

Pale, yes,[17] but like a king, I take great pleasure
in hearing in my heart the laughing soul,
while I stare at the already vanquished Evil.

II

The soul smiles on its dear ones who are distant
while I stare at the already vanquished Evil
which thrust me into those fiery tangles
as into volcano-nourished forests.

Now the great circle of human suffering
she enters, a novice in robes of hyacinth,[18]
abandoning behind her the false labyrinth
where beautiful pagan monsters[19] were roaring.

No more does the Sphinx seize her with golden nails
nor does the Gorgon leave her turned to stone
or the Siren enchant her with its long ode.

Up high, atop the circle, a very pale
woman, making the act of communion
holds between her pure fingers the sacred Host.

III

Away from the snares and away from the anger
and away from the harm, she stands calmly and strong
like the one who can, right till Death comes along
know Evil, without suffering its danger.

—O you who make all the winds so fragrant
and under whose rule all harbors are embraced
At your feet my destiny is placed:
My Lady, please will you grant me your consent!

In your pure hand it dazzles so,
that longed-for sacred Host, like the sun.
Will I thus not see the sign that consents?

And she, so benign to those who bow down low
says the words, giving them communion:
—Your Love has been offered; indeed it is present.

IV

I—she says—am the supernatural Rose
begotten in the breast of Beauty
It is I who impart the most supreme ecstasy
It is I who bring exaltation and repose.

Plow with sad cries, soul that is suffering,
in order to harvest with songs of gladness.[20]
After long affliction, my sweetness
will exceed in sweetness every other thing.—

—Let it be so, My Lady; and from my heart may there be
much blood gushing, and rivers flowing on the earth,
and may immortal pain make it new once more,

and let those whirlpools overwhelm me,
cover me; but may I see from the depths
the light that on my undefeated soul you pour.

DIE XII SEPTEMBRIS MDCCCLXXXVI.[21]

CHAPTER II

Schifanoja[1] rose up on the hill, at the point where the range, after following the coastline and embracing the sea as in an amphitheater, turned inward and curved down toward the plain. Although it had been built by Cardinal Alfonso Carafa of Ateleta in the second half of the eighteenth century, the villa had a certain purity of style in its architecture. It formed a quadrilateral, two stories high, in which porticoes alternated with apartments; and the arched openings of the porticoes lent the building agility and elegance, as the Ionic columns and pillars appeared to have been designed and harmonized by Vignola.[2] It was truly a summer house, open to the sea winds. On the side facing the gardens, on the slope, a vestibule led to a beautiful two-flight staircase descending to a landing enclosed by stone balustrades, like a vast balcony, decorated with two fountains. Other stairs extended from each end of the balcony down the slope, stopping on other levels until they ended almost at the sea, and from this lower area, they appeared to one's view like a kind of sevenfold path meandering among the magnificent greenery and the dense rosebushes. The marvels of Schifanoja were its roses and its cypresses. The roses, of every kind, in every season, were sufficient *pour en tirer neuf ou dix muytz d'eaue rose,*[3] as the poet of the *Vergier d'honneur*[4] would have said. The cypresses, pointed and dark, more solemn than the pyramids, more enigmatic than obelisks, were inferior neither to those of Villa d'Este nor to those of Villa Mondragone, nor to any other similarly gigantic ones that tower over the glorious villas of Rome.

It was the custom of the Marchioness of Ateleta to pass the summer and part of the autumn at Schifanoja, since she, despite being one of the most worldly among the ladies, loved the countryside and rustic freedom and hosting friends. She had shown infinite care and concern to Andrea during his illness, like an elder sister, almost like a mother, tirelessly. A deep affection bound her to her cousin. She was full of indulgence and forgiveness for him; she was a good and sincere friend, able to understand many things, quick, always gay, always shrewd, witty and spiritual at the same time. Although she had crossed the threshold of thirty about a year before, she maintained a wonderful youthful vivacity and a greatly pleasing quality, for she possessed the secret of Madame Pompadour, that *beauté sans traits*[5] that can enliven itself with unexpected graces. She also possessed a rare virtue, the one commonly called "tact." A delicate feminine gift was her infallible guide. In her relations with innumerable acquaintances of both sexes, she always knew, in every circumstance, how to comport herself; and she never made mistakes, she never weighed upon the lives of others, was never inopportune or importunate; she did everything and said every word at the right time. Her behavior toward Andrea, in this slightly strange and moody period of convalescence, could not be, in truth, more delicate. She sought in every way not to disturb him and to ensure that no one disturbed him; she gave him full freedom; she appeared not to notice any eccentricities or gloominess; she never bothered him with indiscreet questions; she made sure that her company was easy when being in each other's presence was unavoidable; she even stopped making witticisms in his presence, to save him the trouble of making a forced smile.

Andrea, who understood that delicacy, was grateful.

On September 12, after the herm sonnets, he returned to Schifanoja with unusual joy; he met Donna Francesca on the stairs and kissed her hands, saying to her in a playful tone:

—Cousin, I have found Truth and the Way.

—Hallelujah! said Donna Francesca, lifting her lovely rounded arms. —Hallelujah!

And she went down into the gardens and Andrea went up to his rooms, his heart uplifted.

After a short while, he heard knocking on the door and Donna Francesca's voice asking:

—May I come in?

She entered carrying in her overall and in her arms a great bunch of pink, white, yellow, vermilion, and russet roses. Some, large and pale, like those of Villa Pamphily, very fresh and all pearled with dewdrops, had something almost vitreous between each leaf; others had dense petals and an abundance of color that brought to mind the celebrated magnificence of the purples of Elissa and Tyre;[6] others resembled clumps of scented snow and provoked in one a strange desire to bite and swallow them; others were made of flesh, truly of flesh, voluptuous as the most voluptuous forms of a woman's body, with a few subtle venations. The infinite gradations of red, from violent crimson to the discolored hue of the ripe strawberry, mingled with the finer and almost imperceptible variations of white, from the candor of immaculate snow to the indefinable color of freshly drawn milk, of the communion host, of the marrow of a reed, of opaque silver, of alabaster, of opal.

—Today is a holiday, she said, laughing; and the flowers covered her chest almost to the throat.

—Thank you! Thank you! Thank you! Andrea said, helping her to place the bundle on the table, on top of the books, on the albums, on the covers of his drawings. —*Rosa rosarum!*[7]

After she had freed herself, she brought together all the vases in the room and began to fill them with roses, composing many small bouquets with a choice that revealed a rare taste in her, the taste of the great hostess. Choosing and composing, she spoke of a thousand things with that gay volubility of hers, almost as if she wanted to compensate for the parsimony of words and laughter she had employed until then with Andrea, out of respect for his taciturn gloominess.

Among other things, she said:

—On the fifteenth we will have a lovely guest: Donna Maria Ferres y Capdevila, wife of the plenipotentiary minister of Guatemala. Do you know her?

—I don't think so.

—Indeed, you couldn't possibly know her. She has been back in Italy for only a few months; but she will spend next winter in Rome, because her husband has been appointed to that post. She is a very dear childhood friend of mine. We were together in

Florence for three years, at the Annunziata Institute; but she is younger than I am.

—Is she American?

—No; she is Italian, and from Siena, what's more. She was born a Bandinelli, and baptized with the water of the Gaia Fountain. But she is quite melancholic by nature; and so sweet. The story of her marriage, also, is not very happy. That Ferres is not a nice man at all. However, they have a little girl who is a darling. You'll see: very pale, with so much hair, and two immense eyes. She looks a lot like her mother . . . Look, Andrea, at this rose! Doesn't it look like velvet? And this one? I could eat it. But look, really, doesn't it look like an ideal custard? What a delight!

She carried on selecting roses and talking amiably. A full scent, as inebriating as a hundred-year-old wine, arose from the bunch; some corollas were disintegrating and their petals were being caught among the folds of Donna Francesca's skirt; through the window, in the blond sun, the dark point of a cypress could just be seen. And in Andrea's mind, a line of Petrarch's was singing insistently, like a musical phrase:

> Thus he distributed the roses and the words.[8]

Two mornings later, he offered as a reward to the Marchioness of Ateleta a sonnet, quaintly formed in the old-fashioned way, and handwritten on a parchment adorned with decorations in the style of those that illuminate the missals of Attavante and Liberale da Verona.

> Schifanoja in Ferrara (O glory of the Estes!),
> where Cossa emulated Cosimo Tura
> depicting triumphs of gods in his murals,
> never bore witness to such joyous feasts.
>
> So many roses she bore in her dress,
> Mona Francesca, to nurture her guest's soul
> as Heaven ever by chance did hold,
> little white angels, to garland your tresses.

She spoke and selected those blooms
with such beauty that I thought:—Has perchance
a Grace come, along the paths the Sun burns?

My eyes were mistaken, drunk on perfumes.
A verse of Petrarch rose up to the heavens
"Thus he distributed the roses and the words."

Thus Andrea began once again to approach Art, experimenting, inquisitively, with little exercises and dalliances, but meditating deeply on less frivolous works. Many ambitions that had once stimulated him began once again to stimulate him; many old projects surfaced again in his mind, modified or complete; many old ideas presented themselves to him again in a new light or a better light; many images, once merely glimpsed, shone out at him brightly and clearly, without him able to realize how they had developed. Sudden thoughts rose up from the mysterious depths of consciousness and surprised him. It seemed to him that all these jumbled elements accumulated deep inside him, now combined with his particular disposition of will, transformed into thoughts with the same method by which stomach digestion processes foods and changes them into bodily matter.

He intended to conceive a form of modern Poem, this unattainable dream of many poets; and he intended to compose a lyric that was truly modern in content but adorned with all the ancient elegance, profound and limpid, passionate and pure, strong and seemly. Moreover, he longed to compile a book of art on the Primitives, the artists who foreran the Renaissance, and a book of psychological and literary analysis on the poets of the thirteenth century who were mostly unknown.

He would have liked to write a third book on Bernini, a great study of decadence, assembling around this extraordinary man, the favorite of six popes, not only all the art but also all the life of his century. For each of such works, naturally, many months, much research, much labor, a great intensity of ingenuity, a vast ability for coordination would be required.

As far as design was concerned, he intended to illustrate with etchings the third and fourth Days of the *Decameron,* taking as example the "Story of Nastagio degli Onesti,"[9] in which Sandro Botticelli displays so much refinement of taste in the skill of grouping and expression. Furthermore, he aspired to create a series of Dreams, Whims, Grotesques, Customs, Fables, Allegories, Fantasies, in the loose style of Callot, but with a very different sentiment and a very different style, in order to abandon himself freely to all his predilections, all his imaginings, all his most intense curiosities and wildest temerities as a designer.

On September 15, a Wednesday, the new guest arrived.

The marchioness went together with her firstborn son, Ferdinando, and Andrea to meet her friend at the nearby station of Rovigliano. As the phaeton descended the road shaded by tall poplars, the marchioness spoke of her friend to Andrea with much benevolence.

—I think you will like her, she concluded.

Then she began to laugh, as if at some thought that had suddenly crossed her mind.

—Why are you laughing? Andrea asked her.

—About an analogy.

—Which?

—Guess.

—I don't know.

—This is it: I was thinking about another announcement about an introduction and another introduction that I made for you, almost two years ago, linking it with a cheerful prophecy. Do you remember?

—Ah!

—I'm laughing because this time, too, we're dealing with an unknown lady and again this time, I am . . . the involuntary patroness.

—Oh dear!

—But it's a different case, or at least, the character of the possible drama is different.

—Namely?

—Maria is a *turris eburnea.*[10]

—I am now a *vas spirituale.*[11]

—Fancy! I had forgotten that you had finally found Truth and the Way. "*The soul smiles on its dear ones who are distant . . .*"

—Are you reciting my verses?

—I know them by heart.

—How sweet!

—Besides, dear cousin, that "very pale woman" with the Host in her hand seems suspect to me. She seems to be completely fictitious, a bodiless stole, at the mercy of any angel or demon's soul who'd like to enter it, to administer communion to you and make *"the sign that consents."*

—Sacrilege! Sacrilege!

—Watch out for yourself, and guard the stole well, and do a lot of exorcisms . . . I'm falling back into prophecies! Really, prophecies are one of my weaknesses.

—We're there, cousin.

They were both laughing. They entered the station with only a few minutes to spare until the arrival of the train. The twelve-year-old Ferdinando, a sickly young boy, carried a bouquet of roses to present to Donna Maria. Andrea, after that dialogue, felt cheerful, light, very vivacious, almost as if he had suddenly returned to his former life of frivolity and fatuity: it was an inexplicable sensation. It seemed to him that something like a feminine whiff, an undefined temptation, was passing through his spirit. He selected a tea rose from Ferdinando's bouquet and put it in his buttonhole; he glanced rapidly at his summer clothing; he looked complacently at his well-cared-for hands, which had become thinner and whiter with his illness. He did all this without reflection, almost as if an instinct of vanity had suddenly reawoken in him.

—Here's the train, Ferdinando said.

The marchioness went forward to welcome her guest, who was already at the window and was waving and nodding, her head all wrapped in a great veil the color of pearls, which half covered her black straw hat.

—Francesca! Francesca! she was calling, with a tender effusion of joy.

That voice made a singular impression on Andrea; it vaguely reminded him of a voice he knew. Which?

Donna Maria descended with a rapid and agile movement; and with a gesture full of grace she lifted the dense veil, uncovering her mouth to kiss her friend. Immediately, that tall and supple lady beneath her traveling cloak, veiled so that he could see nothing of her but her mouth and her chin, was profoundly seductive for Andrea. His entire being, which had been deceived in the past few days by an appearance of freedom, was ready to take in the allure of the "eternal feminine." No sooner were they agitated by a woman's breath, the ashes gave off sparks.

—Maria, I present my cousin, Count Andrea Sperelli-Fieschi of Ugenta.

Andrea bowed. The lady's mouth opened in a smile that seemed mysterious, since the shine of her veil hid the rest of her face.

Next, the marchioness introduced Andrea to Don Manuel Ferres y Capdevila. Then she said, stroking the hair of the little girl who was gazing at the young man with two sweet astonished eyes:

—This is Delfina.

In the phaeton, Andrea sat facing Donna Maria and alongside her husband. She had not yet removed her veil; she held Ferdinando's bouquet on her lap and every now and then brought it to her nose, while answering the marchioness's questions. Andrea had not been mistaken: in her voice could be heard some accents of Elena Muti's voice, perfectly alike. A strange impatience invaded him to see her hidden face, the expression, the color.

—Manuel—she said, continuing to talk—will leave on Friday. Then he'll come back to fetch me later on.

—Much later, we hope, Donna Francesca said cordially. —Indeed, the best thing to do would be to leave all on the same day. We will stay at Schifanoja until the first of November, no later.

—If Mother weren't waiting for me, I would happily stay with you. But I promised to be in Siena at all costs by the seventeenth of October, which is Delfina's birthday.

—What a pity! The twentieth of October is the feast day of gifts at Rovigliano, so beautiful and unusual.

—What can I do? If I don't go, Mother will surely be terribly upset. Delfina is her darling . . .

Her husband remained silent: he was likely taciturn by nature. Of medium height, slightly obese, slightly bald, he had skin of a peculiar color, of a pallor somewhere between greenish and purplish, against which the white of his eyes, in the movements he made as he looked around, shone like that of an enamel eye in certain ancient bronze heads. His mustaches, black, stiff, and trimmed as evenly as a brush, shadowed a severe sardonic mouth. He seemed to be a man completely irrigated with bile. He was possibly forty years old or slightly more. In his person there was something hybrid and shifty, which did not escape an observer; it was that indefinable aspect of debauchery which is borne in generations stemming from a mixture of bastardized races, proliferating amid turbulence.

—Look, Delfina, the orange trees are all in blossom! exclaimed Donna Maria, extending her hand from the window, as they passed, to grab a twig.

The road indeed ascended amid two citrus woods near Schifanoja. The trees were so high that they created shade. A sea breeze blew softly and sighed in the shade, laden with a scent that one could almost drink in, like cooling water.

Delfina had gotten onto her knees on the seat and was leaning out of the carriage to grab the branches. Her mother wrapped an arm around her to support her.

—Careful! Careful! You could fall. Wait until I take my veil off, she said. —Sorry, Francesca; help me.

And she leaned her head toward her friend so that her veil could be disentangled from her hat. In doing so, the bouquet of roses fell to her feet. Andrea was ready to pick it up; and, sitting back up again, he finally saw the entire face of the lady, uncovered.

—Thank you, she said.

She had an oval face, perhaps slightly too elongated, but with only a hint of that aristocratic elongation overemphasized by fifteenth-century artists in search of elegance. In her delicate features there was that subtle expression of suffering and fatigue which constitutes the human enchantment of the Virgins in the Florentine tondos of Cosimo's era. A soft, tender shadow, similar to the fusion of two diaphanous tints, of an ideal violet and blue, encircled her eyes, which had the tawny irises of dark angels. Her hair encumbered her forehead and temples like a heavy crown; it was gathered and twisted on her nape. The locks in front had the density and form of those that cover, like a helmet, the head of the Antinous Farnese. Nothing surpassed the grace of her refined head, which appeared to be afflicted by the great mass, like a divine punishment.

—My God! she exclaimed, trying to lift the weight of the braids bound together below the straw hat. —My entire head is as painful as if I had been hung by the hair for an hour. I can't go for very long without undoing it; it tires me out too much. It's an enslavement.

—Do you remember—asked Donna Francesca—in the conservatory, when so many of us wanted to brush your hair? There were such great arguments every day. Just imagine, Andrea, that even blood was drawn! Ah, I will never forget the scene between Carlotta Fiordelise and Gabriella Vanni. It was a craze. To brush the hair of Maria Bandinelli was the aspiration of all the boarders, big and little. The contagion spread throughout the conservatory; prohibitions, penalties, even threats of tonsure were imposed. Do you remember, Maria? All our hearts were bound by that beautiful black snake that hung down to your heels. How much desperate crying went on, at night! And when Gabriella Vanni, out of jealousy, gave you a treacherous snip of the scissors! Gabriella really lost her head! Do you remember?

Donna Maria was smiling, a particular smile, melancholic and almost bewitched, like that of a person dreaming. In her half-closed mouth, her upper lip emerged slightly over the lower one, but so slightly that it was barely perceptible, and the corners twisted down in pain and in their gentle hollow they held a shadow. These things formed an expression of sorrow and goodness, but tempered by that pride which reveals the moral elevation of those who have suffered greatly and have known how to suffer.

Andrea thought that in none of his lady friends had he possessed such tresses, such a vast and somber forest, in which one could lose oneself. The story of all those girls in love with a braid, fired up with passion and jealousy, in a frenzy to place the comb and their fingers within the living treasure, seemed to him a gentle and poetic episode of cloistral life; and the girl with flowing hair lit up gracefully in his imagination like the heroine of a fable, like the heroine of a Christian legend describing the girlhood of a saint, destined to martyrdom and future glorification. At the same time, an illusion of art arose in his soul. How much richness and variety of lines that voluble and divisible mass of hair could bring to the design of a female figure!

It was not truly black. He was looking at it the next day at table, at the point where the glint of the sun struck it. It had reflections of dark purple, those reflections that have the hue of logwood or even sometimes of steel tested by fire or even a certain type of polished rosewood; and it seemed dry, so that even in its compactness the strands remained separated from one another, penetrated by air, almost breathing. The three luminous and melodious epithets by Alcaeus were naturally destined for Donna Maria: "'Ἰόπλοκ' ἄγνα μελλιχόμειδε . . ."[12] She spoke with refinement, displaying a delicate spirit inclined toward things of intelligence, toward rarity of taste, toward aesthetic pleasure. She was a woman of abundant and varied learning, with an extensive imagination, the colorful speech of those who have seen many countries, lived in diverse climates, met different people. And Andrea felt an exotic aura envelop her form, felt a strange seduction emanating from her, an enchantment composed of the vague phantasms of the distant things she had looked at, of the sights she still preserved in her mind's eye, in the memories that filled her soul. And it was an indefinable, inexpressible enchantment; it was as if she carried in her person a trace of the light in which she had been immersed, of the scents she had breathed, of the idioms she had heard; it was as if she carried within her, mingled, faded, indistinct, all the magic of those lands of the sun.

In the evening, in the large hall that led into the vestibule, she approached the piano and opened it to test it, saying:

—Do you still play, Francesca?

—Oh no, replied the marchioness. —I stopped studying many years ago. I think that simply listening is a preferable pleasure. However, I do fancy myself as protecting the art; and in winter at my house, I always preside over a little good music. Don't I, Andrea?

—My cousin is terribly modest, Donna Maria. She's something more than a patroness; she is a restorer of good taste. This very year, in February, at her house, she organized the performance of two quintets, a quartet, and a trio by Boccherini, and a quartet by Cherubini: music almost completely forgotten, but admirable and ever young. Boccherini's adagio and minuets are of an exquisite freshness; only the finales seem to me to be slightly stale. You, certainly, know something about him . . .

—I remember having heard a quintet four or five years ago, at the Brussels Conservatory; and it seemed magnificent to me, and also very innovative, full of unexpected episodes. I remember well that in some parts, the quintet, through the utilization of unison, was reduced to a duet; but the effects obtained with the difference of timbres were of the most extraordinary refinement. I have never found anything similar in the other instrumental compositions.

She spoke of music with the subtlety of a connoisseur; and in expressing the sentiment that a particular composition or the entire art of a particular maestro aroused in her, she used inspired terms and bold images.

—I have performed and listened to a great deal of music, she said. —And of every symphony, every sonata, every nocturne, of every single piece, in sum, I retain a visible image, an impression of form and color, a figure, a group of figures, a landscape; so much so that all my favorite pieces bear a name, according to the image. I have, for example, the *Sonata of Priam's Forty Daughters-in-law,* the *Nocturne of Sleeping Beauty,* the *Gavotte of the Yellow Ladies,* the *Gigue of the Mill,* the *Prelude of the Water Droplet,* and so on.

She began to laugh, a soft laugh that on that afflicted mouth had an inexpressible grace and was as surprising as an unexpected flash of lightning.

—Do you remember, Francesca, at boarding school, how many comments in the margins we afflicted upon the music of that poor Chopin, of *our* divine Frederick? You were my accomplice. One day we changed all Schumann's titles, with grave discussions; and all the titles had a long explanatory note. I still keep all those papers as a reminder. Now, when I play the *Myrthen* and the *Albumblätter* again, all those mysterious significations are incomprehensible to me; the emotion and the vision are very different; and it is a subtle pleasure, now, to be able to compare the present sentiment with the past one, the new image with the old. It is a pleasure similar to what one feels when one reads one's own journal; but it is perhaps more melancholy and more intense. The journal, generally, is the description of real events, the chronicle of happy days and sad days, the gray or rosy trace left by fleeting life; while the notes made in the margin of a book of music in one's youth are the fragments of the secret poem of a soul that is opening, they are the lyrical effusions of our intact ideality, they are the story of our dreams. What language! What words! Do you remember, Francesca?

She spoke with complete assurance, perhaps with a slight spiritual exaltation, like a woman who, having long been oppressed by the forced frequenting of inferior people or by a vulgar scene, has an irresistible need to open her intellect and her heart to a breath of higher life. Andrea listened to her, feeling a sweet sentiment for her that resembled gratitude. It seemed to him that she, talking of such things to him and with him, was granting him a kindly proof of benevolence and almost that she was permitting him to draw closer. He believed that he could glimpse the edges of that internal life not so much from the meaning of the words she was saying as from the sounds and modulations of her voice. Again, he recognized the accents of the *other.*

It was an ambiguous voice, one could almost say bisexual, twofold, androgynous; with two timbres. The male timbre, low and slightly veiled, softened, became clearer, became effeminate at times with such harmonious passages that the listener's ear was surprised and delighted by it at the same time, and perplexed. Just as when music passes from a minor tone to a major tone, or when music that has been formed of painful dissonances returns, after many beats, to a key tone, so, too, did that voice make its changes at intervals. The feminine timbre was the one that recalled the *other.*

And the phenomenon was so notable that it was enough to occupy the listener's mind independently of the sense of the words. These, however much they acquire in musical value from a rhythm or a modulation, so much do they lose in symbolic value. The mind, indeed, after a few minutes of attention, yielded to the mysterious charm; and remained suspended, waiting and desiring the sweet cadence as it would a melody wrought from an instrument.

—Do you sing? Andrea asked the lady, almost shyly.

—A little, she replied.

—Sing, a little, Donna Francesca begged her.

—All right—she acquiesced—but just a few notes, because really, for more than a year now, I have lost all my strength.

In the adjacent room, Don Manuel was playing cards with the Marquis of Ateleta, without a sound, without a word. In the room, the light was diffused through a great Japanese lampshade, tempered and red. The sea air drifted in between the columns of the vestibule, moving from time to time the tall Karamanieh curtains, carrying the scent of the gardens below. In the spaces between the columns appeared the peaks of the cypresses, black, solid, like ebony, above a diaphanous sky all palpitating with stars.

Donna Maria placed herself at the piano, saying:

—Seeing as we're evoking old times, I will sing a few notes of a melody by Paisiello from *Nina pazza,* something divine.

She sang, accompanying herself. In the ardor of the song the two timbres of her voice fused like two precious metals, forming one sole sonorous, warm, flexible, vibrating metal. Paisiello's melody, simple, pure, spontaneous, full of sorrowful sweetness and winged sadness, over a very clear accompaniment, pouring from the beautiful afflicted mouth lifted itself with such a flame of passion that the convalescent, agitated to his very depths, felt the notes pass through his veins one by one, as if within his body his blood had stopped to listen. An insidious chill gripped the roots of his hair; rapid and thick shadows fell over his eyes; anxiety pressed upon his breathing. And the intensity of the sensations in his heightened nerves was such that he had to make an effort to contain an outburst of tears.

—Oh, my Maria, exclaimed Donna Francesca, tenderly kissing the singer on her hair, once she fell silent.

Andrea did not speak; he remained seated in his armchair with his shoulders against the light, his face in the shadows.

—More! added Donna Francesca.

She sang in addition an arietta by Antonio Salieri. Then she played a toccata by Leonardo Leo, a gavotte by Rameau, and a gigue by Sebastian Bach. Beneath her fingers the music of the eighteenth century came wondrously to life, so melancholy in the dance melodies, which seem composed to be danced on a languid afternoon in an Indian summer, in an abandoned park, between silent fountains, among pedestals without statues, above a carpet of dead roses, by pairs of lovers who are soon to love no more.

CHAPTER III

—Throw down your braid, so that I may come up! shouted Andrea, laughing, from the first landing of the stairs to Donna Maria, who was on the balcony adjoining her rooms, between two columns.

It was morning. She was standing in the sun to dry her damp hair, which cloaked her entirely like beautiful deep violet velvet, amid which appeared the opaque pallor of her face. The linen curtain, half lifted, of a bright orange color, held suspended above her head the lovely black frieze of its edge, in the style of the friezes that circle the ancient Greek vases of Campania; and if she had had a crown of narcissi around her temples and near her, one of those large nine-stringed lyres, which bear an effigy of Apollo and a greyhound in encaustic painting, she would certainly have resembled a student of the school of Mytilene, a Lesbos lyre player at rest, but as a Pre-Raphaelite could have imagined her.

—Throw me a madrigal, she replied, in jest, drawing back slightly.

—I'm going to write it on the marble of a baluster on the last terrace, in your honor. Come and read it when you're ready, later.

Andrea continued, slowly descending the stairs that led to the last terrace. On that September morning, his soul swelled together with his breathing. The day had a kind of sanctity; the sea seemed to shine with its own light, as if in its depths there lived magical sources of light rays; all things were penetrated by the sun.

Andrea descended, stopping every now and then. The thought

that Donna Maria had remained on the balcony to watch him caused him a vague uneasiness, brought to his breast a strong throbbing, almost intimidated him, as if he were a youth experiencing his first love. He felt an ineffable beatitude breathing in that warm and limpid atmosphere where she, too, breathed, where her body, too, was immersed. An immense wave of tenderness gushed from his heart, spreading over the trees, the rocks, the sea, as over friendly and knowing beings. He was driven as if by a need for submissive, humble, pure adoration; as if by a need to bend his knees and join his hands and offer up that vague and mute affection, which he did not recognize. He believed that he could feel the goodness of things coming to him and mixing with his own goodness, and overflowing. *Do I love her, then?* he wondered; and did not dare to look inside himself and reflect, because he feared that that delicate enchantment would disperse and disappear like a dream at dawn.

Do I love her? And what does she think? And, if she comes alone, will I tell her that I love her? He took pleasure in interrogating himself and not answering and interrupting the answer of his heart with a new question and prolonging that fluctuation, which was tormenting and delicious at the same time. *No, no, I will not tell her that I love her. She is above the others.*

He turned; and saw still, up high on the balcony, her indistinct figure in the sun. Perhaps she had followed him, with her eyes and her thoughts, assiduously, right down to the bottom. Out of childish curiosity he pronounced her name in a clear voice on the solitary terrace; he repeated it two or three times, listening to himself. —Maria! Maria! No word ever, no name had seemed sweeter, more melodious, more caressing to him. And he thought that he would be happy if she permitted him to call her simply Maria, like a sister.

That creature, so spiritual and elect, inspired a supreme sense of devotion and submission in him. If anyone had asked him what the sweetest thing would be for him, he would have answered sincerely: To obey her. Nothing would cause him as much pain as having her believe him to be a common man. By no other woman, as much as by her, would he like to be admired, praised, understood for his works of intelligence, taste, research, his artistic aspirations, his ideals, his dreams, the noblest part of his spirit and his life. And his most ardent ambition was to fill her heart.

She had already been staying at Schifanoja for ten days; and in those ten days, how entirely she had conquered him! Their conversations, on the terraces or on the chairs scattered in the shade or along the avenues flanked by roses, lasted sometimes for hours and hours, while Delfina ran like a little gazelle among the winding paths of the citrus grove. In conversing, she had an admirable fluidity; she was profuse with delicate and penetrating observations; she opened up, sometimes, with a candor that was full of grace; regarding her travels, sometimes with a single picturesque phrase she roused in Andrea broad visions of distant lands and seas. And he expended assiduous care in showing her his worth, the extent of his learning, the refinement of his breeding, the exquisiteness of his sensibility; an enormous pride lifted his entire being when she said to him with a sincere tone after reading his *Fable of Hermaphrodite:* "No music has intoxicated me as this poem did, and no statue has given me a more harmonious impression of beauty. Certain verses pursue me without respite and they will continue to pursue me for a very long time, perhaps; they are so intense."

Now, sitting on the balusters, he thought about those words again. Donna Maria was no longer on the balcony; indeed, the curtain covered the entire space between the columns. She would perhaps come down shortly. Should he write the madrigal for her, as promised? The small torment of having to compose verse under pressure seemed unbearable to him, in that majestic and joyful garden where the September sun caused a kind of supernatural spring to be revealed. Why disperse that rare emotion in a hurried game of rhymes? Why reduce that vast sentiment into a short metrical sigh? He resolved to break his word; and he remained seated, watching the sails on the farthest line of the water, which glinted like fires overpowering the sun.

But anxiety gripped him the more the minutes passed; and he turned every minute to see whether at the top of the stairs, between the columns of the vestibule, a feminine form appeared. —Was that perhaps a lovers' rendezvous? Was that woman coming, perhaps, to a secret meeting in that place? Could she imagine his anxiety?

Here she is! his heart said. And she was.

She was alone. She descended slowly. On the first terrace, she paused near one of the fountains. Andrea watched her, suspended, feeling trepidation at every movement, every step, every pose of hers, as if her movement, her step, her pose had a meaning, or were a language.

She began to walk along that succession of stairs and terraces, interposed with trees and shrubs. Her figure appeared and disappeared; now completely whole, now from the belt up, now emerging with her head above a rosebush. At times the web of branches hid her for a goodly stretch: one could see only in the sparsest patches her dark dress passing by, or the light straw of her hat glimmering. The closer she came, the more slowly she walked, hesitating near the hedges, stopping to look at the cypresses, bending down to gather a fistful of fallen leaves. From the second-to-last terrace she waved to Andrea, who was standing and waiting on the last step; and she threw the gathered leaves to him, scattering them like a cloud of butterflies, trembling, some drifting in the air, landing lightly on the stone with the softness of snow.

—Well? she asked, halfway down the staircase.

Andrea knelt on the step, lifting his palms.

—Nothing! he confessed. —I ask forgiveness; but you and the sun, this morning, fill the skies with too much sweetness. *Adoremus.*[1]

The confession was sincere, as was the adoration, even though both were made with the semblance of jest; and certainly Donna Maria understood that sincerity, because she blushed a little, saying with particular concern:

—Get up, get up.

He stood up. She held her hand out to him, adding:

—I forgive you, because you are convalescing.

She was wearing a dress in a strange rust color, the color of saffron, murky, indefinable; one of those so-called aesthetic colors that one finds in the pictures of divine Autumn, in those of the Primitives, and in those of Dante Gabriele Rossetti. The skirt was composed of many pleats, straight and regular, which commenced below her arms. A wide sea-green ribbon, as pallid as a wan turquoise, formed her belt and fell with a single large loop down her side. The wide, soft sleeves, with close pleats at the shoulder, became tighter around her wrists. Another sea-green ribbon, a narrow one, circled her neck, knotted on the left with a small loop. An identical ribbon bound the end of the prodigious braid that fell from beneath a straw hat crowned with a corona of hyacinths similar to those of Alma-Tadema's Pandora. A large Persian turquoise, her only jewelry, in the shape of a scarab, incised with letters like a talisman, fastened her collar beneath her chin.

—Let's wait for Delfina, she said. —Then we shall go up to the Cybele gate. Do you wish to?

She was very kind and considerate toward the convalescent. Andrea was still very pale and very thin, and his eyes had become extraordinarily large in that thinness; and the sensual expression of his mouth, a little swollen, made a strange and alluring contrast with the upper part of his face.

—Yes, he answered. —Rather, I am grateful to you.

Then, after a slight hesitation:

—Would you permit me a few moments of silence, this morning?

—Why do you ask me this?

—It seems to me that I do not have a voice, and do not know how to say anything. But silences, at certain times, can be heavy, and irritate and even disturb one if they go on for too long. Therefore I'm asking if you will permit me to be silent during the walk, and to listen to you.

—Then, we shall be silent together, she said, with a slight smile.

And she looked upward toward the villa, with visible impatience.

—Delfina is so late!

—Was Francesca already up, when you came down? Andrea asked.

—Oh, no! She is incredibly lazy . . . Here is Delfina. Can you see her?

The little girl descended rapidly, followed by her governess. Invisible on the stairs, she reappeared on all the terraces that she ran across. Her loose hair undulated over her shoulders, in the breeze created as she ran, beneath a wide straw hat crowned with poppies. When she reached the last step, she opened her arms to her mother and kissed her many times on the cheeks. Then she said:

—Good morning, Andrea.

And she offered her forehead to him, with an infantile gesture of adorable grace.

She was a fragile creature, and as vibrant as an instrument formed from sensitive material. Her limbs were so delicate that they seemed almost as if they could not hide nor veil the splendor of the living spirit within, like a flame in a precious lamp, of an intense and sweet life.

—My love! whispered her mother, looking at her with an indescribable gaze, from which emanated all the tenderness of her soul occupied by that sole affection.

And Andrea felt from that word, from that gaze, from that expression, from that caress, a sort of jealousy, a sort of discouragement, as if he felt her soul distance itself, escape him forever, become inaccessible.

The governess asked permission to go back up; and they headed along the avenue of the orange trees. Delfina ran ahead, pushing her hoop; and her straight legs, encased in their black stockings, fairly long, of that slender length of ephebic design, moved with rhythmic agility.

—You seem quite sad to me now—said the Sienese woman to the young man—whereas before, while coming down, you were happy. Is some thought bothering you? Or are you not feeling well?

She asked these things with an almost sisterly manner, grave and sweet, persuading him to confide in her. A shy desire, almost a vague temptation, overcame the convalescent, to place his arm under that of the woman and allow himself to be guided by her in silence, through that shade, through that scent, over that ground scattered with orange blossom, on that path marked out by the ancient Termini[2] covered with moss. It seemed to him almost to have returned to the first days after his illness, to those unforgettable days of languor, of happiness, of unconsciousness; and to need friendly support, an affectionate guide, a familiar arm. That desire grew so strongly in him that the words rose spontaneously to his mouth to express them. But instead, he replied:

—No, Donna Maria; I feel all right. Thank you. It is September that is putting me in somewhat of a daze . . .

She looked at him as if she doubted the truth of that answer. Then, to avoid silence after the evasive phrase, she asked:

—Do you prefer, of the neutral months, April or September?

—September. It's more feminine, more discreet, more mysterious. It's like spring seen in a dream. All the trees, slowly losing their strength, also lose some part of their reality. Look at the sea, down there. Doesn't it resemble an atmosphere rather than a mass of water? Never, as in September, are the alliances of sky and sea as mystical and profound. And the earth? I don't know why, but looking at a landscape during this time of year, I always think of a beautiful woman who has given birth and is resting in a white bed, smiling a startled, pale, inextinguishable smile. Is it a correct impression? There is something of the amazement and beatitude of the woman who has just given birth, in a September countryside.

They had almost reached the end of the path. Certain herms adhered to certain tree trunks, forming with them almost one single trunk, arboreal and lapidary; and the abundant fruit, some already all golden, others stained with gold and green, others all green, hung over the heads of the Termini, which appeared to guard intact and intangible trees, to be their genius loci.[3]—Why was Andrea assailed by sudden uneasiness and anxiety approaching the place where, two weeks before, he had written the sonnets of liberation? Why did he struggle between fear and hope that she would discover and read them? Why did some of those verses return to his memory detached from the others, as if representing his present feeling, his present aspiration, the new dream that he held in his heart?

—O you who make all the winds so fragrant
and under whose rule all harbors are embraced
At your feet my destiny is placed:
My Lady, please will you grant me your consent!

It was true! It was true! He loved her; he was placing at her feet his entire soul; he had one single desire, humble and immense:—to be earth beneath her footprints.

—How beautiful it is here! exclaimed Donna Maria, entering the dominion of the four-sided herm, in the acanthus paradise. —What a strange odor!

Indeed, an odor of musk pervaded the air, as if due to the invisible presence of a musk-secreting insect or reptile. The shade was mysterious, and the lines of light that filtered through the foliage already touched by autumn's damage were like lunar rays passing through the stained glass panes of a cathedral. A mixed sentiment, pagan and Christian, emanated from the place, as from a mythological painting by a pious quattrocento[4] artist.

—Look, look, Delfina! she added, with the excitement of one who sees an object of beauty, in her voice.

Delfina had ingeniously braided a garland from flowering orange twigs; and, with sudden childish imagination, now wanted to place it on the head of the stone divinity. But as she could not reach the top, she was exerting herself to accomplish this task by rising up on tiptoes, lifting her arm, stretching as far as she could; and her slender, elegant, and lively form contrasted with the rigid, square, and solemn form of the statue, like a lily stalk at the base of an oak tree. Every effort was in vain.

Then, smiling, her mother came to her aid. She took the garland from her hands and placed it on the four pensive foreheads. Involuntarily, her gaze fell on the inscriptions.

—Who wrote here? You? she asked Andrea, surprised and pleased. —Yes, it is your handwriting.

And immediately, she knelt on the grass to read; curiously, almost avidly. Imitating her, Delfina leaned over behind her mother, circling her neck with her arms and pushing her face against her cheek, almost covering it. Her mother murmured the rhymes. And those two feminine figures, crouching at the base of the tall, garlanded stone, in the uncertain light, among the symbolic acanthi, formed such a harmonious composition of lines and colors that the poet remained for a few moments under the sole dominion of aesthetic pleasure and pure admiration.

But the obscure jealousy still stung him. That tenuous creature, so wound around her mother, so intimately mingled with her soul, seemed an enemy to him; she seemed to him to be an insurmountable obstacle that rose up against his love, against his desire, against his hope. He was not jealous of the husband and he was jealous of the daughter. He wanted to possess not the body but the soul of that woman; and to possess her entire soul, with all her tenderness, all her joys, all her fears, all her anguish, all her dreams, in other words, the entire life of her soul; and to be able to say: *I am the life of her life.*

The daughter, instead, had that possession, uncontested, absolute, continuous. It seemed as if the mother lacked some essential element of her existence when her adored child was far from her even for a short time. A sudden, very visible transfiguration took place on her face when she heard the childish voice after a brief absence. Sometimes, involuntarily, due to some secret correspondence, almost, one could say, by the laws of some common vital rhythm, she imitated the gesture of her daughter, a smile, a pose, a position of the head. Sometimes she had, at quiet times or when her daughter slept, moments of such intense contemplation that she seemed to have lost consciousness of every other thing, in order to become similar to the being that she was contemplating. When she spoke to her adored child, the word was a caress and her mouth lost every trace of pain. When she received kisses, a tremor shook her lips and her eyes filled with an indescribable joy, between the palpitating lashes, like the eyes of a beatified person at being taken up to heaven. When she conversed with others, or listened, she seemed every now and then to have a kind of sudden suspension of thought, like a momentary absence of spirit; and it was for her daughter, for her, always for her.

Who could ever break that chain? Who could conquer even a minimal part of that heart? Andrea suffered as from an irremediable loss, as from a necessary renouncement, as from hope that has died. Even now, even now, was the daughter not removing something from him?

In fact, in play, she wanted to force her mother to remain kneeling. She was leaning on her and pressing her arms around her neck, shouting and laughing:

—No, no, no; you can't get up.

And as her mother opened her mouth to talk, she placed her small hands on her mouth to stop her from talking; and made her laugh; and then she blindfolded her with her braid; and would not stop, excited and elated by this game.

Watching her, Andrea had the impression that with those actions she was shaking from her mother and destroying and dispersing everything that the reading of the verses had perhaps caused to blossom in her spirit.

When finally Donna Maria managed to free herself from the sweet tyrant, she said to him, reading his vexation in his face:

—Forgive me, Andrea. Sometimes Delfina has these silly whims.

Then, with a light hand, she tidied the folds of her skirt. A slight flame suffused the area beneath her eyes, and she was also breathing slightly irregularly. She added, smiling a smile which in that unusual animation of her blood was of remarkable luminosity:

—And forgive her, as a reward for her unconscious augur; because earlier she had the inspiration of placing a nuptial crown on your poem, which sings of a nuptial communion. The symbol is a seal of the alliance.

—To Delfina and to you, my thanks, replied Andrea, who had heard her calling him for the first time not by his ancestral title but simply by name.

That unexpected familiarity and the kind words brought confidence back to his soul. Delfina had run on ahead up one of the avenues.

—These verses therefore are a spiritual document, continued Donna Maria. —You must give them to me, so that I may keep them always.

He wanted to tell her: *They come to you today, naturally. They are yours, they speak of you, they entreat you.* But instead he simply said:

—I will give them to you.

They took up their walk again toward the Cybele. Before leaving the herm's dominion, Donna Maria turned toward it, as if she had heard some call; and her forehead seemed very pensive. Andrea asked her with humbleness:

—What are you thinking about?

She replied:

—I'm thinking about you.

—What are you thinking of me?

—I'm thinking about your earlier life, which I do not know about. Have you suffered very much?

—I have sinned very much.

—And loved very much, also?

—I don't know. Perhaps love is not as I experienced it. Perhaps I must still love. I don't know, truly.

She fell silent. They walked alongside each other for a stretch. To the right of the path grew tall laurel trees, interposed by a cypress at regular intervals; and the sea sparkled here and there in the background, between dainty foliage, as blue as flax blossoms. On the left against the embankment there was a kind of wall, similar to the backrest of a very long stone seat, bearing the Ateletas' escutcheon[5] repeated along its entire length, alternating with an alerion.[6] Below each escutcheon and each alerion was to be found a sculpted mask, from the mouth of which a small water pipe emerged, emptying itself into underlying basins that had the shape of sarcophagi placed alongside each other, decorated with mythological stories in bas-relief. There must have been one hundred mouths, because the avenue was named One Hundred Fountains; but some no longer dispensed water, having become clogged over time, while others barely dripped. Many shields were broken and moss had covered the heraldic device; many alerions had been decapitated; the figures in bas-relief appeared amid the moss like pieces of silver imperfectly concealed beneath an old torn velvet cloth. In the basins, upon the water that was clearer and greener than an emerald, maidenhair fern trembled or a few rose leaves floated, fallen from the shrubs above; and the surviving water pipes emitted a hoarse, gentle sound that flowed over the sound of the sea, like a melody over its accompaniment.

—Can you hear that? Donna Maria asked, stopping, straining her ears, captivated by the enchantment of those sounds. —The music of bitter water and of sweet water!

She stood in the middle of the path, bending slightly toward the fountains, attracted more by the melody, with her index finger lifted to her mouth in the involuntary gesture of those who fear that their listening will be disturbed. Andrea, who was nearer the basins, saw her stand out against a background of foliage as delicate and graceful as an Umbrian painter could have placed behind an Annunciation or a Nativity.

—Maria, murmured the convalescent, whose heart was swollen with tenderness. —Maria, Maria . . .

He felt an inexpressible voluptuousness in mingling her name with that music of the waters. She pressed her finger against her mouth, indicating that he must be quiet, without looking at him.

—Forgive me—he said, overcome by emotion—but I cannot stand it anymore. It is my soul that is calling you!

A strange sentimental excitement had overcome him; all the lyrical peaks of his spirit had ignited and were flaming; the hour, the light, the place, all surrounding things suggested love to him; from the farthest end of the sea right to the humble maidenhair fern of the fountains, a single magical circle was being drawn; and he felt that its center was that woman.

—You will never know—he added, his voice low, almost fearing to offend her—you will never know the extent to which my soul is yours.

She became even paler, as if all the blood in her veins had gathered in her heart. She said nothing; she avoided looking at him. She called, her voice agitated:

—Delfina!

Her daughter did not answer, perhaps because she had gone deeper into the thicket at the end of the path.

—Delfina! she repeated, more loudly, with a kind of alarm.

In the wait, after her shout, one could hear the two waters singing in a silence that seemed to expand.

—Delfina!

A rustling came from amid the foliage, as if from the passing of a roebuck; and the little girl burst forth nimbly from the depths of the laurel trees, carrying her straw hat full of small red fruit that she had gathered from an arbutus. She was red from the effort and from running; many thorns had become stuck in the wool of her tunic; and some leaves were entangled in the rebellion of her hair.

—Oh, Mommy, come, come with me!

She wanted to drag her mother to gather the rest of the fruit.

—Down there there's a wood; so so many! Come with me, Mommy, come!

—No, love, please. It's late.

—Come!

—But it's late.

—Come! Come!

This insistence forced Donna Maria to yield and allow herself to be led by the hand.

—There is a way to get to the arbutus wood without passing through the thicket, Andrea said.

—Did you hear, Delfina? There is a better way.

—No, Mommy! Come with me!

Delfina pulled her between the wild laurels on the side facing the sea. Andrea followed; and he was happy to be able to gaze freely upon the figure of his beloved before him, to drink her in with his eyes, to be able to watch all her different movements and rhythms, constantly interrupted by the passage along the uneven slope, among the obstacles formed by trunks, between the hindrances of the saplings, between the resistance of the branches. But while his eyes fed on those things, his mind retained one pose, one expression, above all the others. Oh, the pallor, the pallor he had just seen, when he had uttered those subdued words! And the indefinable sound of that voice which had called Delfina!

—Is it still far off? Donna Maria asked.

—No, no, Mommy. Here we are, we're there already.

A kind of shyness invaded the young man at the end of the walk. After those words, his eyes had not met hers even once. What was she thinking? What was she feeling? With what expression in her eyes would she look at him?

—Here we are! shouted the little girl.

The laurel thicket was indeed thinning out and the sea appeared more clearly; suddenly the thicket of *Arbutus andrachne* revealed itself, glowing red like a grove of earthly coral, bearing at the tips of their branches abundant bunches of flowers.

—How wonderful! murmured Donna Maria.

The beautiful grove flowered and bore fruit within an inlet curved like a hippodrome, deep and sun-drenched, in which all the mildness of that shore was delightfully assembled. The slender trunks of the shrubs, mostly vermilion, some yellow, rose up tall, bearing large shiny leaves, green above and pale blue below, immobile in the quiet air. The florid clusters, similar to bunches of lily of the valley, white and rose-colored and innumerable, hung from the tops of the young branches; the red and orange berries hung from the tops of the old branches. Every plant was laden with them; and the magnificent pomp of the flowers, the fruit, the leaves, and the stems displayed itself against the vivid azure of the sea with the intensity and incredibility of a dream, like the remains of some legendary kitchen garden.

—How wonderful!

Donna Maria entered slowly, no longer held by the hand by Delfina, who was running around crazy with joy, with one sole desire: to strip the entire bush.

—Can you forgive me? Andrea dared to say. —I did not wish to offend you. Rather, seeing you so elevated, so far from me, so pure, I thought that I would never ever speak to you of my secret, that I would never ask your consent, nor would I ever cross your path. Since I met you, I have dreamed very much of you, by day and by night, but without any hope or any goal. I know that you do not love me and that you cannot love me. And yet, believe me, I would renounce all the promises of life, just to live in a small part of your heart . . .

She continued to walk slowly, beneath the brilliant trees that spread their dangling bunches, their delicate white and rose-colored clusters above her head.

—Believe me, Maria, believe me. If they told me now to abandon all vanity and all pride, every desire and every ambition, any dearest memory of the past, the sweetest future enticement, and to live uniquely in you and for you, without any tomorrow, without any yesterday, without any other bond, without any other preference, out of the world, entirely lost in your being, forever, until death, I would not hesitate, I would not hesitate. Believe me. You have looked at me, spoken with me, and smiled and answered; you have sat beside me, and you have been silent and thought; and you have lived, alongside me, your internal existence, that invisible and inaccessible existence that I do not know, that I will never know; and your soul has possessed mine right down to the depths, without changing, without even knowing it, like the sea drinks a river . . . What does my love do for you? What does love do for you? It is a word that has been profaned too many times, a sentiment that has been falsified too many times. I do not offer you love. But will you not accept the humble tribute of religion that the spirit addresses to a nobler and higher being?

She continued to walk slowly, her head bent, extremely pale, bloodless, toward a seat that was placed at the edge of the wood facing the shore. As soon as she reached it, she sat down with a kind of abandon, in silence; and Andrea sat down near her, still talking to her.

The seat was a large semicircle of white marble, edged along its length with a smooth, shining backrest, with no other ornament but for a lion's paw carved at each end serving as an armrest; and it recalled those ancient ones upon which, in the Archipelago islands and in Magna Graecia and in Pompeii, women lazed and listened to poets reading in the shade of oleanders, overlooking the sea. Here the arbutus bushes cast shade more with flowers and fruit than with leaves; and the coral stems, contrasting with the marble, appeared more vivid.

—I love all those things that you love; you possess all those things that I seek. The mercy that came from you would be dearer to me than the passion of any other woman. Your hand on my heart would, I feel, cause a second youth to germinate, much purer than the first, much stronger. That eternal oscillation which is my interior life, would find repose in you; it would find calmness and security in you. My restless and discontented spirit, tormented by attractions and revulsions and by pleasure and disgust in constant conflict, eternally, irremediably alone, would find in yours a refuge from the doubt that contaminates all ideality and defeats all will and diminishes all strength. Others are unhappier; but I don't know if there has been a man less happy than I, in the world.

He was making Obermann's words[7] his own. In that kind of sentimental elation, all gloomy thoughts rose to his lips; and the very sound of his voice, humble and slightly trembling, increased his emotion.

—I dare not express my thoughts. Being near you over these few days since I met you, I have had moments of such complete oblivion that it almost seemed to me to have returned to the earliest days of my convalescence, when I was experiencing the deep sentiment of another life. The past, the future, were no more; rather it was as if the one had never been and the other would never be. The world was like a shapeless and obscure illusion. Something like a vague but great dream was rising up in my soul: a fluttering veil, sometimes opaque, sometimes diaphanous, through which now and again the intangible treasure of happiness shone. What did you know about me, in those moments? Perhaps you were far away, in your soul; very, very far! But still, your visible presence alone was enough to intoxicate me; and I felt it flow in my veins like blood and invade my spirit like a superhuman sentiment.

She was silent, with her head erect, immobile, her torso upright, her hands placed on her knees in the position of one who is keeping herself awake with a fierce effort of courage against a sense of languor that invades her. But her mouth, the expression of her mouth, with lips fruitlessly and fiercely pressed together, betrayed a sort of painful voluptuousness.

—I dare not express my thoughts. Maria, Maria, do you forgive me? Do you forgive me?

Two small hands, from behind the seat, stretched out to blindfold her and a voice palpitating with joy shouted:

—Guess who! Guess who!

She smiled, leaning against the backrest because Delfina was pulling her, holding her fingers on her eyelids, and Andrea saw lucidly, with a strange clarity, that light smile dispersing on that mouth all the obscure contrast of her earlier expression, deleting every trace that could signal to him the indication of consent or confession, routing every dubious shadow that could convert itself into a glimmer of hope in his heart. And he was left like a man who has been deceived by a cup that he thought was almost brimming, which offers nothing but air to his thirst.

—Guess who!

The daughter was covering the mother's head with hard and rapid kisses, in a kind of frenzy, perhaps hurting her slightly.

—I know who you are, I know who you are, the blindfolded woman said. —Let me go!

—What will you give me, if I let you go?

—Whatever you want.

—I want a mule to carry my berries home! Come and see how many I've got!

She went around the seat and took her mother by the hand. She stood up with some difficulty; and once on her feet, she blinked several times as if to clear a dazzle from her vision. Andrea also stood up. They both followed Delfina.

The terrible creature had stripped almost half the thicket of its fruit. The lower plants no longer displayed even one berry on their branches. She had used a cane found heaven knows where, and had collected a prodigious quantity, lastly gathering all the berries into a single heap that resembled a pile of burning coals for the intensity of their hue on the brown earth. But the bunches of flowers had not attracted her: they hung, white, pink, faintly yellow, almost diaphanous, more delicate than the clusters of an acacia, gentler than lily of the valley, immersed in the indistinct light as in the transparence of an amber milk.

—Oh, Delfina, Delfina, exclaimed Donna Maria, looking at that devastation. —What have you done?

The little girl was laughing, happy, in front of her vermilion pyramid.

—You are really going to have to leave everything here.

—No, no . . .

She did not want to, at first. Then she changed her mind; and said almost to herself, with shining eyes:

—The deer will come and eat it.

She had perhaps seen the lovely animal roaming free in the park, in that vicinity; and the thought of having gathered the food for it gratified her and fired her imagination, already nourished with fairy tales in which deer are kind and powerful fairies that recline on satin cushions and drink from sapphire goblets. She fell silent, immersed in thought, perhaps already seeing the lovely blond animal gorge on berries beneath the flowering trees.

—Let's go, said Donna Maria. —It's late.

She held Delfina by the hand and walked beneath the flowering plants. At the edge of the woods she stopped and looked at the sea.

The waters, receiving the reflections of the clouds, gave the appearance of an immense silken fabric, soft, fluid, changing, undulating in broad folds; and the clouds, white and golden, one detached from the other but emerging from a common strip, resembled chryselephantine[8] statues wrapped in thin veils, lifted atop a bridge without arches.

In silence, Andrea plucked from an arbutus a bunch so dense that its branch was bending under its weight; and he offered it to Donna Maria. Taking it, she looked at it, but she did not open her mouth.

They set off down the paths once more. Delfina was now talking and talking, copiously, repeating the same things endlessly, infatuated with the deer, mingling the strangest fantasies, inventing long, monotonous stories, confusing one fairy tale with another, composing tangled stories in which she herself became lost. She talked and talked, with a kind of unconsciousness, almost as if the morning air had inebriated her; and around that deer of hers she invoked sons and daughters of kings, Cinderellas, little queens, wizards, monsters, all the characters of imaginary kingdoms, in crowds, in tumults, as in the continuous metamorphosis of a dream. She spoke in the same way that a bird warbles, with melodious modulations, sometimes with successions of sounds that were not words, from which the already-begun musical wave was emitted, like the quivering of a string during a pause, when in that infantile spirit the link between the verbal sign and the idea was interrupted.

The other two were not speaking or listening. But it seemed to them that that singsong refrain covered their thoughts, the murmur of their thoughts, because in thinking they had the impression that something sonorous was escaping from their innermost minds, something that in silence one would have been able to perceive physically; and if Delfina was quiet for a short time, they felt a strange sense of disquiet and suspension, as if silence would reveal and almost strip bare their souls.

The avenue of the One Hundred Fountains appeared in a vanishing perspective, in which the needles and mirrors of water gave off a fine vitreous sparkle, a mobile translucent transparency. A peacock that was perched on one of the escutcheons took flight, causing some disintegrating roses to tumble into the basin below. Andrea recognized, a few steps farther on, the basin in front of which Donna Maria had said to him, "Can you hear that?"

Within the herm's dominion the odor of musk could no longer be perceived. The herm, musing beneath its garland, was entirely spangled by the rays that penetrated between the gaps in the foliage. The blackbirds sang, replying to one another.

Delfina, seized by a new whim, said:

—Mommy, give me back the garland.

—No, let's leave it there. Why do you want it back?

—Give it back to me; I want to take it to Muriella.

—Muriella will spoil it.

—Give it back to me, please!

The mother looked at Andrea. He approached the stone, took the garland off it, and gave it to Delfina. In their exalted spirits, superstition, which is one of the obscure perturbations brought by love even to intellectual creatures, gave the insignificant episode the mysteriousness of an allegory. It seemed to them that in that simple deed a symbol was concealed. They did not know precisely what; but they thought about it. A verse tormented Andrea:

Will I thus not see the sign that consents?

An enormous sense of anxiety compressed his heart, the closer they came to the end of the path; and he would have given half his blood for a word from the woman. But she was on the point of speaking one hundred times, and she did not speak.

—Look, Mommy, down there, there's Ferdinando, Muriella, Riccardo . . . said Delfina, catching sight of Donna Francesca's children at the bottom of the path; and she flew off, shaking the crown. —Muriella! Muriella! Muriella!

CHAPTER IV

Maria Ferres had always remained faithful to her youthful habit of noting daily in an intimate journal her thoughts, joys, sadness, dreams, troubles, aspirations, regrets, hopes, all the events of her inner life, all the episodes of her outer life, composing almost an Itinerary of the Soul, which from time to time she loved to reread, in order to draw from it a rule for her future journey and to rediscover the trace of things that had long been dead.

Forced by circumstances constantly to withdraw into herself, always locked in her purity as in an incorruptible and inaccessible ivory tower, she felt relief and comfort in that kind of daily confession entrusted to the white page of a secret book. She complained about her troubles, she gave herself up to tears, she sought to penetrate the enigmas of her heart, she interrogated her conscience, she drew courage from prayer, she fortified herself through meditation, she banished all weakness and every vain image from herself, she placed her soul in the hands of the Lord. And every page shone with a common light, that of Truth.

> *September 15, 1886 (Schifanoja).* —How tired I feel! The journey fatigued me somewhat and this new sea and country air has dazed me somewhat. I need rest; and it already seems to me that I can foretaste the goodness of sleep and the sweetness of reawakening tomorrow. I will awaken in a kindly home, to Francesca's cordial hospitality, in this Schifanoja that has such beautiful roses and tall cypresses; and I will awaken with a few weeks of peace before me, twenty days of spiritual existence, maybe more. I am very grateful to Francesca for the invitation. Seeing her again, I saw a sister once more. How many changes have taken place in me, and what deep ones, since the lovely Florentine years!

Francesca was remembering today, with regard to my hair, all the passions and melancholy of that time, and Carlotta Fiordelise, and Gabriella Vanni, and that whole long-ago story that now doesn't seem to me to have been lived through, but rather read about in an old forgotten book, or seen in a dream. My hair has not fallen out, but very many other more living things have fallen from me. As many hairs I have on my head, so many wheat spikes of pain do I have in my destiny.

But why is sadness overcoming me once more? And why do the memories cause me pain? And why is my resignation being shaken from time to time? It's pointless lamenting over a grave; and the past is like a grave that does not give up its dead. My God, let me remember this, once and for all!

Francesca is still young, and still preserves that lovely frank geniality of hers that exerted such a strange charm at boarding school on my somewhat dark spirit. She has a great and rare virtue: she is cheerful, but she can understand the sufferings of others and also knows how to soothe them with her mindful compassion. She is, above all, an intellectual woman, a woman of refined tastes, a perfect woman, a friend who is not a burden. She takes perhaps a little too much pleasure in witticisms and clever phrases, but her arrows always have a golden point and are shot with an inimitable grace. Certainly, among all the worldly ladies I have known, she is the finest; among my friends, she is my favorite.

Her children do not resemble her; they are not beautiful. But the little girl, Muriella, is very kind; she has a clear laugh and her mother's eyes. She played hostess to Delfina with the courtesy of a little noblewoman. She, certainly, will inherit her mother's "great style."

Delfina seems happy. She has already explored most of the garden, she has gone down to the sea, she has descended all the staircases; she has come to tell me about the wonders, panting, gobbling her words, with a kind of dazzle in her eyes. She often repeated the name of her new friend: Muriella. It is a pretty name, and on her mouth it becomes prettier still.

She is sleeping deeply. When her eyes are closed, her lashes cast a long, long shadow over the top of her cheeks. Francesca's cousin was marveling at their length, this evening, and repeated a verse by William Shakespeare from *The Tempest,* very beautiful, about Miranda's eyelashes.

There is too much scent here. Delfina wanted me to leave the bunch of roses next to the bed, before falling asleep. But now that she is sleeping, I will remove it and place it on the veranda, where it is calm.

I am tired, yet I have written three or four pages. I am sleepy, and yet I would like to prolong being awake in order to prolong this undefined languor of my soul, fluttering in some strange tenderness diffused outside of me, around me. It has been so long, so long, since I felt a little benevolence surrounding me!

Francesca is very good, and I am very grateful to her.

*

I carried the vase of roses onto the veranda; and I stayed out there for a few minutes to listen to the night, kept there by the regret of missing, in the blindness of sleep, the hours that pass beneath such a beautiful sky. The harmony between the voice of the fountain and the voice of the sea is strange. The cypresses before me seemed to be the columns of the firmament: the stars shone right above their peaks, lighting them up.

Why, by night, do scents have in their waves something that speaks, has meaning, has a language?

No, flowers do not sleep at night.

*

September 16. —Delightful afternoon, spent almost entirely in conversing with Francesca on the verandas, on the terraces, along the avenues, in all the open spaces of this villa, which appears to have been built by a poet prince in order to forget anguish. The name of the Ferrarese mansion suits it perfectly.

Francesca let me read a sonnet by Count Sperelli, written on parchment: a very fine trifle. This Sperelli is an elect and intense spirit. This morning at table, he said two or three very beautiful things. He is convalescing from a mortal wound received in a duel, in Rome, last May. He has in his gestures, his words, his gaze, that kind of affectionate and delicate abandon which is typical of convalescents, of those who have emerged from the hands of death. He must be very young; but he must have lived a great deal, and a restless life at that. He carries the marks of battle.

*

Delightful evening, of intimate conversation, intimate music, after dinner. I, perhaps, talked too much; or, at least, too fervently. But Francesca listened to me and indulged me; as did Count Sperelli. One of the greatest pleasures, in nonvulgar conversation, is indeed to feel that the same degree of fervor animates all intelligent spirits present. Only then do words take on the sound of sincerity and give those who utter them, and those who hear them, supreme pleasure.

Francesca's cousin is a refined connoisseur of music. He greatly loves the masters of the eighteenth century, and especially, among the composers for harpsichord, Domenico Scarlatti. But his most ardent love is Sebastian Bach. He likes Chopin little; Beethoven penetrates too deeply inside him and agitates him too much. In sacred music he can find no one to compare with Bach aside from Mozart. "Perhaps," he said, "in no Mass does the voice of the supernatural reach religiosity and terribleness to the extent that Mozart does in the *Tuba mirum* of the Requiem. It is not true that he who had so deep a sense of the supernatural as to create musically the Commendatore's ghost, and who, creating Don Giovanni and Donna Anna, was able to push the analysis of the inner being so far, had to be a Greek, a Platonist, a pure seeker of grace, beauty, serenity . . ."

He said these words and others, with that particular emphasis employed by men who are constantly absorbed in the search for elevated and complex things, when talking of art.

Then, while listening to me, he had a strange expression, as if of astonishment, and at times, of anxiety. I was almost always addressing myself to Francesca, looking at her; and yet, I felt his gaze fixed on me with an insistence that bothered me but did not offend me. He must still be ill, weak, prey to his sensibilities. He asked me, finally: "Do you sing?"—in the same way that he would have asked me: "Do you love me?"

I sang an aria by Paisiello and one by Salieri. I played a little eighteenth-century music. My voice was warm and my hand skillful.

He did not give me any praise. He remained in silence. Why?

Delfina was sleeping already, up here. When I came up to see her, I found her sleeping but with her eyelashes wet as if she had cried. Poor love! Dorothy told me that my voice had reached here clearly and that Delfina had shaken off her drowsiness and had begun to sob and wanted to come downstairs.

When I play, she always cries.

Now she is sleeping; but every now and then her breath quickens; it resembles a muffled sob, and it gives my own breathing a vague anxiety, almost a need to respond to that unconscious sob, to that suffering that has not been appeased in her sleep. Poor love!

Who is playing the piano downstairs? Someone is softly playing a few notes of Luigi Rameau's gavotte,[1] a gavotte full of fascinating melancholy, which I was playing earlier. Who can it be? Francesca came upstairs with me; it is late.

I looked out on the veranda. The vestibule hall is dark; only the adjacent room, where the marquis and Manuel are still playing, is lit.

The gavotte is ceasing. Someone is going down the stairs into the garden.

My God, why am I so alert, so vigilant, so curious? Why are noises churning me up so much, inside, tonight?

Delfina has woken up and is calling me.

September 17. —Manuel left this morning. We accompanied him to the station at Rovigliano. Toward October 10 he will return to fetch me; and we will go to Siena, to my mother's. Delfina and I will remain in Siena probably until the new year: for two or three months. I will once again see the Pope's Loggia and the Gaia Fountain and my beautiful black-and-white Dome, the beloved house of the Blessed Virgin Assunta, where a part of my soul is still praying, alongside the Chigi chapel, in the place that knows my knees.

In my mind, the image of the place is always clear; and when I return I will kneel down in the exact place where I used to, with precision, better than if I had left two deep hollows there. And there I will once again find that part of my soul that still prays, beneath the spangled blue vault, which is reflected in the marble like a nocturnal sky in calm water.

Nothing, certainly, has changed. In the precious chapel, full of a pulsing shade, of a darkness animated by the jeweled reflections of the stones, the lamps burned; and the light seemed to gather itself entirely within the small circle of oil in which the flame was nourished, as in a clear topaz. Little by little, beneath my intent gaze, the sculpted marble took on a less cold pallor, almost the warmth of ivory; little by little the pale life of the celestial creatures entered the marble, and through the marble forms diffused the vague transparency of angelic flesh.

How ardent and spontaneous my prayer was! If I read Saint Francis's *Philotea,* it seemed that the words descended to my heart like tears of honey, like drops of milk. If I began to meditate, it seemed that I was walking along the secret paths of the soul, as in a garden of delight where nightingales sang on flowering trees and doves cooed on the banks of the streams of divine Grace. Devotion infused in me a sense of calm full of freshness and perfumes, opened up the holy springtimes of the *Fioretti* in my heart, garlanded me with mystical roses and supernatural lilies. And in my old Siena, in the ancient city of the Virgin, I heard above all the voices the calls of the bells.

September 18. —Indefinable hour of torture. I seem to have been condemned to repiece together, to rejoin, to reunite, to recompose the fragments of a dream, of which one part seems to be materializing confusedly outside of me and the other floundering confusedly deep in my heart. And I am toiling, I am toiling, without ever managing to put it back together in its entirety.

September 19. —Another torture. Someone sang to me, a long while ago; and did not finish the song. Someone is singing to me now, taking up the song at the point where it left off; but for a long time now I have forgotten the beginning. And my restless soul, while it tries to remember it in order to connect it to the continuation, loses itself; and neither finds the old tones nor enjoys the new ones.

September 20. —Today, after breakfast, Andrea Sperelli invited me and Francesca to go and see in his rooms the drawings that he received yesterday from Rome.

One can say that an entire art passed today before our eyes, an entire art studied and analyzed by the pencil of a sketcher. I had one of the most intense pleasures of my life.

These drawings are by Sperelli; they are his studies, his sketches, his notes, his memories gathered here and there in all the galleries of Europe; they are, I'll express it this way, his breviary, a wonderful breviary in which every ancient master has his supreme page, the page in which his style is synthesized, where the noblest and most original beauties of the work are noted, where the *punctum saliens*[2] of the entire production is gathered. Glancing through this wide collection, not only did I manage to gain a precise sense of the different schools, the different movements, the different trends, the different influences through which painting is developed in a given region; but I penetrated into the intimate spirit, into the essential substance of the art of every single painter. How deeply I now understand, for example, the fourteenth and the fifteenth centuries, the Trecentisti and the Quattrocentisti, the simple, noble, great Primitives!

The drawings are stored in lovely cases made of engraved leather with studs and silver clasps imitating those of missals. The variety of the technique is ingenious. Certain drawings, of Rembrandt's work, are executed on a type of slightly reddish paper, warmed with hematite pencil, watercolor-painted with bistre; and the areas of light are emphasized with white tempera. Certain other drawings, of the Flemish masters' work, are executed on rough paper very similar to paper prepared for oil painting, where the bistre watercolor takes on the character of sketches done in bitumen. Others are in hematite pencil, in black pencil, in three pencils with a few touches of pastel, in watercolors with bistre over pen strokes, watercolor painted with China ink, on white paper, on yellow paper, on gray paper. Sometimes the hematite pencil seems to contain purple; the black pencil renders a velvety mark; the bistre is warm, tawny, blond, of a fine tortoiseshell color.

All these details I have derived from the sketcher; I feel a strange pleasure in remembering them, in writing them; I seem to be intoxicated by art; my brain is full of a thousand lines, a thousand figures; and in the midst of the jumbled tumult I always *see* the women of the Primitives, the unforgettable heads of the Saints and the Virgins, the ones that smiled on my religious childhood, in old Siena, from the frescoes of Taddeo and Simone.

No masterpiece of the most advanced and most refined art leaves such a strong, enduring, tenacious impression in the soul. Those long, slim bodies, like lily stalks; those slender reclining necks; those rounded protruding foreheads; those mouths full of suffering and affability; those hands (O Memling!)[3] as thin, waxen, diaphanous as a host, more meaningful than any other feature; and that hair red as copper, tawny as gold, blond as honey, one strand made almost distinct from the other by the religious patience of the paintbrush; and all those noble and grave poses, either receiving a flower from an angel or placing their fingers upon an open book or bending over toward the infant or holding on their laps the body of Jesus or in the act of blessing or dying or ascending to Paradise, all those pure, sincere, and profound things make one feel tenderness or pity deep down in one's intimate soul; and are imprinted forever in memory, like a spectacle of human sadness seen in the reality of life, in the reality of death.

One by one, today, the women of the Primitives passed beneath our eyes. Francesca and I were seated on a low divan, with a large reading desk in front of us, on which was placed the leather holder with the drawings that the sketcher, sitting opposite us, paged through slowly while commenting. With each gesture, I saw his hand take the sheet and place it on the other side of the holder with a singular delicacy. Why, at each gesture, did I feel inside me the beginning of a shiver, as if that hand were about to touch me?

At a certain point, perhaps finding the chair uncomfortable, he knelt on the carpet and continued to turn over the sheets. In talking, he addressed himself almost always to me; and he did not have the air of teaching me but of reasoning with a connoisseur on equal terms; and deep inside me fluttered a slight satisfaction, mingled with gratitude. When I made an exclamation of wonder, he looked at me with a smile that is still with me and that I do not know how to define. Two or three times Francesca leaned her arm on his shoulder, with familiarity, carelessly. Seeing the head of Moses' firstborn son, taken from Sandro Botticelli's fresco in the Sistine Chapel, she said: "He looks a bit like you, when you are melancholic." Seeing the head of the archangel Michael, which is a fragment of the *Madonna of Pavia* by Perugino, she said: "He looks like Giulia Moceto; doesn't he?" He did not answer; and he turned the sheet with less slowness. Then she added, laughing: "Far be from us any image of sin!"

Is this Giulia Moceto perhaps a woman whom he once loved? When the page was turned, I felt an incomprehensible desire to see the archangel Michael again, to examine it with greater attention. Was it only curiosity?

I don't know. I don't dare to look inside myself, into the secret; I much prefer to delay things, to deceive myself; I don't think that sooner or later all ambiguous lands fall into the dominion of the Enemy; I don't have the courage to confront the battle; I am pusillanimous.

Meanwhile, it is a sweet hour. My mind is stimulated with intellectual visual images, as if I had drunk many cups of strong tea. I have no desire to go to bed. The night is warm, as in August; the sky is clear but veiled, like a fabric made of pearls; the sea has a slow and subdued respiration, but the fountains fill in the pauses. The veranda attracts me. Let's dream a bit! Which dreams?

The eyes of the Virgins and the Saints persecute me. I still *see* those hollow eyes, low and narrow, with the eyelids lowered, from below which they watch with a fascinating gaze, as mild as that of a dove, slightly oblique like that of a snake. "Be simple as a dove and prudent as a serpent,"[4] Jesus Christ said.

Be prudent. Pray, go to bed and sleep.

September 21. —Alas, it is necessary to begin the hard task again, to climb up the steep slope already climbed, reconquer the territory already conquered, once again fight the battle already won!

September 22. —He has given me one of his books of poetry, *The Fable of Hermaphrodite,* the twenty-first of the twenty-five sole exemplars, printed on parchment, with two frontispiece proof marks.

It is an extraordinary work, in which a mysterious and deep sense is enclosed, although the musical element prevails, drawing one's spirit into an unprecedented magic of sounds and enveloping one's thoughts, which shine like a golden and diamond dust in a clear river.

The choruses of the Centaurs, of the Sirens, and of the Sphinxes lend an indefinable uneasiness; awaken an unsatisfied restlessness and curiosity in the ear and the soul, produced by the continuous contrast of a twofold sentiment, a twofold aspiration, of human nature and of the bestial nature. But with what purity, and how *visibly,* the ideal form of the Androgyne delineates itself amid the troubled choruses of the monsters! No music has intoxicated me as this poem has, and no statue has given me a more harmonious impression of beauty. Certain verses haunt me without respite and will pursue me for a very long time, perhaps; they are so intense.

*

He conquers my intellect and my soul, more and more each day, more and more each hour, without respite, against my will, against my resistance. His words, his glances, his gestures, his slightest movements enter my heart.

September 23. —When we talk together, sometimes I feel that his voice is like the echo of my soul.

It happens at times that I feel myself being pushed by a sudden fascination, by a blind attraction, by an unreasonable violence, toward a phrase, toward a word that could reveal my weakness. I save myself by some miracle; and then an interval of silence falls, in which I am agitated by a terrible internal tremor. If I begin to talk again, I say something frivolous and insignificant, with a light tone; but it seems to me that a flame surges beneath the skin of my face, almost as if I am about to blush. If he chose that moment to look me resolutely in the eyes, I would be lost.

*

I have played much music, by Sebastian Bach and Robert Schumann. He was sitting, like that evening, on my right, slightly behind me, on the leather armchair. Every now and then, at the end of every piece, he stood up and, bending over my shoulder, paged through the book to indicate another fugue, another intermezzo, another improvviso to me. Then he would sit down again; and listen, without moving, deeply absorbed, his eyes fixed above me, letting me *feel* his presence.

Could he understand how much of myself, of my thoughts, of my sadness, of my intimate being, was passing through the music of others?

*

"Music,—Silver key of the fountain of tears / Where the spirit drinks till the brain is wild, Softest grave of a thousand fears / Where their mother Care, like a drowsy child / Is laid asleep on flowers . . ." SHELLEY.[5]

The night is menacing. A warm and humid wind blows in the garden; and the dark shudder protracts itself in the darkness, then falls, then begins again more strongly. The peaks of the cypresses oscillate in an almost-black sky, where the stars appear half doused. A strip of clouds stretches across the space, from one horizon to the other, ragged, contorted, blacker than the sky, similar to the tragic head of hair of a Medusa. The sea is invisible in the darkness; but it sobs, as if for an immense and inconsolable pain, alone.

Whatever is this consternation? It seems that the night is warning me of an imminent disaster and that the warning corresponds, deep down inside me, to an undefined remorse. Sebastian Bach's prelude still pursues me; it mingles in my soul with the shuddering of the wind and the sobbing of the sea.

Wasn't there some part of me crying, in those notes, earlier?

Someone was crying, moaning, oppressed by anguish; someone was crying, moaning, calling God, asking forgiveness, beseeching help, praying with a prayer that ascended to heaven like a flame. He was calling and being heard; was praying and his prayers were being answered; he was receiving light from above, emitting cries of joy, was finally grasping Truth and Peace, and was resting in the clemency of the Lord.

*

My daughter always comforts me; and she heals me from every fever, like a sublime balm.

She is sleeping in the shadow lit by the lamp, which is as mild as the moon. Her face, of the fresh whiteness of a white rose, is almost buried in the abundance of her dark hair. It seems that the fine texture of her eyelids barely manages to hide her luminous eyes within. I bend over her, I gaze at her again; and all the voices of the night die away, for me; and the silence is measured, for me, by nothing other than the rhythmic breathing of her life.

She feels the closeness of her mother. She lifts an arm and lets it fall again; she smiles with her mouth, which opens like a pearly flower; and for an instant, between her lashes there appears a splendor similar to the damp silvery splendor of the flesh of the asphodel. The longer I contemplate her, she becomes to my eyes an immaterial creature, a being formed from the element *such as dreams are made on.*[6]

Why, in giving an idea of her beauty and her spirituality, do images and words of William Shakespeare rise spontaneously to my memory? Of this powerful savage atrocious poet who has such mellifluous lips?

She will grow, nourished and enveloped by the flame of my love, of my great *only* love . . .

Oh, Desdemona, Ophelia, Cordelia, Juliet! Oh, Titania! Oh, Miranda!

September 24. —I cannot make any resolutions; I cannot define any purpose. I am abandoning myself little by little to this very new sentiment, closing my eyes to the distant danger, closing my ears to the wise warnings of my conscience, with the anxious rashness of one who, wanting to gather violets, ventures onto the edge of an abyss, at the bottom of which roars a voracious river.

He will know nothing from my mouth; I will know nothing from his. The Souls will ascend together, for a brief way, up the hills of the Ideal; they will drink a few sips from the perennial fountains; then each will take his own path, with greater confidence, and less thirst.

*

What tranquillity there is in the air, after midday! The sea has the milky bluish-white color of an opal, of Murano glass; and here and there it is like a crystal glass clouded by a puff of breath.

*

I am reading Percy Shelley, a poet he loves, the divine Ariel who feeds on light and speaks the language of the Spirits. It is nighttime. This allegory lifts itself before me, visibly.

"A door of somber diamond is flung open on the great path of life that we all traverse, an immense and corroded cavern. All around a perpetual war of shadows rages, similar to the restless clouds that crowd around the fissure of some steep mountain, losing themselves up high among the whirlwinds of the highest heavens. And many pass with a careless step before that door, not knowing that a shadow follows in the tracks of every traveler as far as the place where the dead await, in peace, their new companion. Others, however, stimulated by a more curious thought, stop to watch. There are very few of these; and very little do they understand, if not that shadows follow them wherever they go."[7]

Behind me, so close that it almost touches me, is the Shadow. I feel it watching me; in the same way that yesterday, while playing, I felt his gaze on me without seeing him.

September 25. —My God, my God!

When he called me, with that voice, with that tremor, I believed that my heart had dissolved in my chest and that I was about to faint. "You will never know," he said, "you will never know the extent to which my soul is yours."

We were in the avenue of the fountains. I was listening to the waters. I saw nothing more; I heard nothing more; it seemed that everything was receding from me and that the ground was sinking in and that with it all, my life was dispersing. I made a superhuman effort; and Delfina's name came to my lips, and I felt a mad impulse to run to her, to escape, to save myself. I shouted that name three times. In the pauses, my heart did not pulsate, my pulse did not beat, from my mouth no breath was exhaled . . .

September 26. —Is it true? Is it not a deception of my misguided spirit? But why does that time yesterday seem so far away, so *unreal*?

He spoke, again, for a long time, standing close to me while I walked beneath the trees, lost in reverie. Beneath what trees? It was as if I were walking along the secret paths of my soul, among flowers born of my soul, listening to the words of an invisible Spirit that once nourished itself on my soul.

I still hear the sweet and dreadful words.

He said: "I would renounce all the promises of life, just to live in a small part of your heart . . ."

He said: "Out of the world, entirely lost in your being, forever, until death . . ."

He said: "The mercy that came from you would be dearer to me than the passion of any other woman . . ."

"Your visible presence alone was enough to intoxicate me; and I felt it flow in my veins like blood, and invade my spirit, like a superhuman sentiment . . ."

September 27. —When, at the edge of the woods, he picked this flower and offered it to me, did I not call him *Life of my life*?

When we passed back along the avenue of the fountains, before that fountain where he had first spoken to me, did I not call him *Life of my life*?

When he took the garland from the herm and gave it back to my daughter, did he not lead me to understand that the Woman exalted in the verses had already fallen, and I alone, I alone was his hope? And did I not call him *Life of my life*?

September 28. —How long this meditation has been in coming!

So many times, since that hour, I have struggled, I have suffered, to return to my true conscience, to see things in their true light, to judge what has happened with firm and calm judgment, to resolve this, to decide, to recognize my duty. I fled from myself; my mind was bewildered; my will was retreating; every effort was futile. Almost by instinct, I avoided remaining alone with him; I always stayed close to Francesca and my daughter, or remained here in my room, as in a refuge. When my eyes met his, I seemed to read in his a deep and imploring sadness. Doesn't he know how much, how much, how much I love him?

He doesn't know; he will never know. This is how I wish it to be. This is how it must be. May I find strength!

My Lord, help me.

September 29. —Why did he speak? Why did he want to break the spell of silence where my soul was being lulled, almost without remorse and almost without fear? Why did he want to tear away the hazy veils of uncertainty and place me in the presence of his unveiled love? By now I can no longer delay, or delude myself, or concede myself any weakness, nor abandon myself to any languor. The danger is there, certain, open, manifest; and it attracts me with its dizzying height, like an abyss. One moment of languor, of weakness, and I am lost.

*

I ask myself: *Is this a sincere pain? Is it sincere regret, for that unexpected revelation?* Why do I always think about those words? And why, when I repeat them to myself, does an ineffable wave of voluptuousness pervade me? And why does a shiver run through my marrow, if I imagine that I could hear other words, more words still?

*

A verse by William Shakespeare, in *As You Like It:*

> Who ever lov'd, that lov'd not at first sight?[8]

Nighttime. —The motions of my spirit assume the form of examinations, of enigmas. I question myself constantly and never answer. I have not had the courage to look right into the depths, to understand my state with precision, to make a resolution that is truly strong and loyal. I am pusillanimous; I am cowardly; I am afraid of pain; I want to suffer as little as possible; I still want to waver, to procrastinate, to dissimulate, to save myself with subterfuges, to hide, instead of confronting openly the decisive battle.

The fact is this: that I *fear* to remain alone with him, to have a serious discussion with him, and that my life here is reduced to a succession of small deceptions, small expedients, small pretexts to avoid his company. This artifice is unworthy of me. Either I want to renounce this love absolutely; and he will hear my sad but firm word. Or I want to accept him, in his purity; and he will have my spiritual consensus.

Now I ask myself: *What do I want? Which of the two paths do I choose? Do I renounce? Do I accept?*

My God, my God, *you* answer for me, *you* illuminate me!

To renounce it, by now, is to tear a living part of my heart out with my nails. The anguish will be supreme; the agony will surpass the limits of all endurance; but heroism, by the grace of God, will be crowned with resignation, will be rewarded by the divine sweetness that follows every strong moral elevation, every triumph of the soul over the fear of suffering.

I will renounce it. My daughter will retain the possession of my entire being, of my entire life. This is my duty.

> Plow with sad cries, soul that is suffering,
> in order to harvest with songs of gladness.

September 30. —Writing these pages, I feel slightly calmer: I am regaining, at least for now, a little equilibrium and I am considering my disaster with greater lucidity and it seems that my heart is becoming lighter, as after making confession.

Oh, if I could confess! If I could ask for advice and help from my old friend, my old consoler!

In this turbulence, the thought that I will see Don Luigi in a few days' time sustains me more than any other thing, that I will speak to him and show him all my wounds, and I will reveal to him all my fears and I will ask him for a balm for all my ills, as I once did; as when his mild and deep words drew tears of tenderness from my eyes, which did not yet know the bitter salt of other tears, or the parching thirst, much more terrible, of aridity.

Will he still understand me? Will he understand the obscure anguish of the woman, in the same way that he understood the undefined and fleeting melancholy of the girl? Will I see him bend toward me, in a posture of mercy and sympathy, his lovely forehead crowned with white hair, illuminated with saintliness, pure as the host in the ciborium, blessed by the hand of the Lord?

*

I played music by Sebastian Bach and Cherubini on the chapel organ after Mass. I played the prelude from the other evening.

Someone was crying, moaning, oppressed by anguish; someone was crying, moaning, calling God, asking forgiveness, beseeching help, praying with a prayer that ascended to heaven like a flame. He was calling and being heard; was praying and his prayers were being answered; he was receiving light from above, emitting cries of joy, was finally grasping Truth and Peace, and was resting in the clemency of the Lord.

This organ is not large; the chapel is not large; and yet my soul swelled as if I were in a basilica; it rose up as if in an immense cupola; it touched the summit of the ideal church steeple where the sign of signs glitters, in the heavenly blue, in the sublime ether.

I think about the greatest organs in the greatest cathedrals, those in Hamburg, Strasbourg, Seville, in Weingarten Abbey, Subiaco Abbey, that of the Benedictines in Catania, at Monte Cassino,[9] at Saint-Denis. What voice, what choir of voices, what multitude of cries and prayers, what songs, and what weeping of the people are equal to the terribleness and the sweetness of this marvelous Christian instrument that can combine within itself all the intonations perceptible to the human ear, and all those that are imperceptible, too?

I dream:—a solitary Dome, immersed in shadow, mysterious, unadorned, similar to the depth of a dull crater that receives a starry light from above; and a Soul intoxicated with love, as ardent as that of Saint Paul, as sweet as that of Saint John, as multiple as a thousand souls in one, needing to exhale his elation in a superhuman voice; and a vast organ like a forest of wood and metal that, like the one at Saint-Sulpice, has five keyboards, twenty pedals, one hundred and eight organ stops, more than seven thousand pipes, all the sounds.

Nighttime. —Futile! Futile! Nothing calms me; nothing gives me an hour, a minute, a second of oblivion; nothing will ever heal me; no dream of my mind will cancel out the dream of my heart. Futile!

My anguish is mortal. I feel that my ailment is incurable; my heart aches exactly as if someone had squeezed it, had pressed upon it, had damaged it forever; the moral pain is so intense that it changes into a physical pain, into atrocious agony, unbearable. I am infatuated, I know; I am prey to a kind of madness; and I cannot restrain myself, I cannot contain myself, I cannot regain my reason; I cannot, I cannot.

Is this, then, love?

He left this morning, on horseback, with a servant, without my seeing him. My morning was spent almost entirely in the chapel. He did not return for breakfast. His absence made me suffer so much that I was stunned by the acuteness of that suffering. I came here to my room; in order to lessen my pain, I wrote a page of my journal, a religious page, becoming excited at the memory of my morning faith; then I read a few passages of Percy Shelley's *Epipsychidion;* then I went down to the park to look for my daughter. In all these actions, the intense thought of him gripped me, occupied me, tormented me without respite.

When I heard his voice again, I was on the first terrace. He was talking to Francesca in the vestibule. Francesca had leaned out, calling me from above: "Come up!"

Climbing the stairs again, I felt my knees give way. In greeting me, he held out his hand; and he must have noticed the tremor in mine, because I saw something pass across his expression, rapidly. We sat down on the long wicker chairs in the vestibule, facing the sea. He said he was very tired; and he began to smoke, talking about his horse ride. He had reached Vicomìle, where he had stopped for a rest.

"Vicomìle," he said, "possesses three wonders: a pine forest, a tower, and an ostensorium[10] dating back to the fifteenth century. Imagine a pine forest between the sea and the hill, full of ponds that multiply the woods to infinity; a bell tower in the pagan Lombard style, which certainly dates back to the eleventh century, a stone stalk laden with sirens, peacocks, serpents, Chimeras, hippogriffs, with a thousand monsters and a thousand flowers; and an ostensorium of gilded silver, enameled, engraved, and carved, in a Gothic-Byzantine style with a foretaste of the Renaissance, made by Gallucci, an almost-unknown craftsman, who is a great precursor of Benvenuto . . ."

He was addressing himself to me, while talking. It is strange how I remember all his words so exactly. I could write down his conversation in full, with the most insignificant and minute details; if there were the means, I could reproduce every modulation of his voice.

He showed us two or three small pencil drawings in his notebook. Then he continued to talk about the wonders of Vicomìle, with that ardor he has when talking about beautiful things, with that enthusiasm for art which is one of his greatest seductions.

"I promised the Canon that I would return on Sunday. We'll go, won't we, Francesca? Donna Maria simply must see Vicomìle."

Oh, my name on his mouth! If there were a way, I could reproduce exactly the position, the opening of his lips in pronouncing each syllable of the two words: Donna Maria. But I could never express my sensation; I could never recount all the unknown, unexpected, unsuspected feelings that awaken in my being in the presence of that man.

We remained seated there until lunchtime. Francesca seemed slightly melancholic, unusually for her. At a certain point, a grave silence descended upon us. But between him and me one of those *discussions of silence* began, where the soul exhales the Unutterable and comprehends the murmur of thoughts. He said things to me that made me faint with sweetness upon my cushion: things that his mouth could never repeat to me and my ear could never hear.

In front of us the unmoving cypresses, as insubstantial to the eye as if they were immersed in a sublimating ether, lit by the sun, appeared to bear a flame at their tips, like twisted votive candles. The sea had the green shade of an aloe leaf, and here and there the palest blue of a liquefied turquoise: an indescribable delicacy of paleness, a diffusion of angel-like light, where every sail gave the impression of an angel swimming. And the harmony of scents rendered weaker by autumn was like the spirit and the sentiment of that afternoon spectacle.

O serene September death!

This month, too, is finished, lost, fallen into the abyss. Adieu.

An immense sadness oppresses me. How much of me this period of time is taking away with it! I have lived more in fifteen days than in fifteen years; and it seems that none of my long weeks of suffering equals in acuteness of agony this brief week of passion. My heart hurts; my mind has gone astray; a dark and burning thing is deep inside me, something that suddenly appeared like an infection and that is beginning to contaminate my blood and my soul, against my will, against every remedy: Desire.

I am ashamed and horrified by it, as by something dishonorable, a sacrilege, a violation; I am desperately and madly afraid of it, as of a deceitful enemy who knows ways to penetrate into the city that are unknown even to me.

And now and then I stay awake at night; and writing this page with the agitation with which lovers write their love letters, I do not hear the breath of my daughter who is sleeping. She sleeps in peace; she does not know how far away her mother's soul is . . .

October 1. —My eyes see something in him that they did not see before. When he talks, I watch his mouth; and the position and color of his lips engage me more than the sound and meaning of his words.

October 2. —Today is Saturday; today is the eighth day since the unforgettable day—SEPTEMBER 25, 1886.

*

By some remarkable fate, although I now no longer avoid being alone with him, although on the contrary I want that terrible and heroic moment to come; by some remarkable fate, the moment has not come.

Francesca has always been with me today. This morning we went for a ride along the Rovigliano road. And we spent the afternoon almost entirely at the piano. She wanted me to play her some dance music of the sixteenth century, then the Sonata in F sharp minor and the famous toccata by Muzio Clementi, then two or three caprices by Domenico Scarlatti; and she wanted me to sing her some parts of Robert Schumann's *Frauenliebe*. What contrasts!

Francesca is no longer cheerful, like she was once, like she was also in the first days of my stay here. She is often pensive; when she laughs, when she jokes, her gaiety seems artificial to me. I asked her: "Is there some thought that is bothering you?" She answered, appearing astonished: "Why?" I added: "You seem a bit sad." And she: "Sad? Oh no; you're mistaken." And she laughed, but a laugh that was involuntarily bitter.

This thing afflicts me and gives me a vague sense of disquiet.

*

Tomorrow, then, we are going to Vicomìle, after midday. He asked me:—"Do you have the strength to go on horseback? If we are on horses we can cross the entire pine forest . . ."

Then he also said to me: "Reread, among Shelley's lyrics to Jane, the *Recollection*."

Therefore we will be going on horseback; Francesca will also ride with us. The others, including Delfina, will go by mail coach.

What a strange frame of mind I find myself in this evening! I have a kind of dull and acrid wrath at the base of my heart, and I don't know why; I have a kind of intolerance of myself and of my life and of everything. The nervous agitation is so strong that now and then I am gripped by a mad impulse to shout, to sink my nails into my flesh, to break my fingers against the wall, to provoke whatever sort of material agony in order to extract myself from this unbearable internal malaise, this unbearable torment. I seem to have a knot of fire at the top of my chest, my throat blocked by a sob that does not want to come out, my head empty, now cold, now burning; and from time to time I feel myself invaded by a kind of sudden anxiety, by an absurd dismay that I can never repel nor repress. And at times, involuntary images and thoughts flicker through my mind, arising from heaven knows what depths of my being: base images and thoughts. And I feel languid and faint, like one who is immersed in a binding love; and yet it is not a pleasure, it is not a pleasure!

October 3. —How weak and wretched our soul is, without defense against the reawakening and the assaults of everything that is least noble and pure, dormant in our unconscious life, in the unexplored abyss where blind dreams are born of blind sensations!

A dream can poison a soul; one sole involuntary thought can corrupt the will.

*

We are going to Vicomìle. Delfina is in a state of joy. It is a religious day. Today is the name day of Mary, Virgin of the Rosary. Have courage, my soul!

October 4. —No courage.

The day yesterday was, for me, so full of little episodes and great emotions, so happy and so sad, so strangely troubled that I become bewildered remembering it. And already all the other memories fade away and vanish in the face of one single one.

After visiting the tower and admiring the ostensorium, we prepared to leave Vicomìle toward five thirty. Francesca was tired; and she preferred to return with the mail coach rather than remount the horse. We followed for a while, trotting at times behind, at times alongside it. From the coach, Delfina and Muriella shook long flowered canes toward us, and laughed, threatening us with the lovely violet plumes.

It was a very peaceful evening, windless. The sun was about to set behind the Rovigliano hill, in a sky all rosy like one in the Far East. Everywhere, roses roses roses drifted down, slowly, densely, delicately, like snowfall at dawn. When the sun disappeared, the roses multiplied, spreading out almost as far as the opposite horizon, vanishing, dissolving in an infinitely pale azure, in a silvery azure, indefinable, similar to the hue that curves over the peaks of ice-covered mountains.

It was he who said to me from time to time: "Look at the tower of Vicomìle. Look at the cupola of San Consalvo . . ."

When the pine forest was in view, he asked me: "Shall we cross it?"

The main road skirted the woods, describing a wide curve and approaching the sea, almost right on the shore, at the summit of the arch. The woods appeared to be already dark, a somber green, as if the shadows had gathered on the tops of the trees, leaving the air above it still clear; but within them, the ponds shone with an intense deep light, like fragments of a sky much purer than the one that stretched above our heads.

Without waiting for my answer, he said to Francesca:

"We're going to ride through the pine forest. We'll meet you on the road, at the Convito bridge, on the other side."

And he held back his horse.

Why did I consent? Why did I enter the woods with him? In my eyes, I had a kind of dazzle; it seemed to me that I was under the influence of a confused fascination; it seemed that that countryside, that light, that event, all that combination of circumstance was not new to me, but had already existed once, almost, I could say, in a previous existence, which was now existing again . . . The impression is inexpressible. It seemed to me then that that hour, those moments, had already been lived through by me, were not happening outside of me, independently of me, but rather belonged to me, had a natural and indissoluble bond with my person, so that I could not withdraw myself to relive them in that given way, but that I *necessarily* had to relive them, rather. I had a very clear feeling of this necessity. The inertia of my will was absolute. It was like when an episode of life returns in a dream with something more than truth, and different from truth. I can't even describe a minimum part of that extraordinary phenomenon.

And there was a secret correspondence, a mysterious affinity between my soul and the countryside. The image of the woods in the water of the ponds appeared in fact, to be the *dreamed* image of the real scene. As in Percy Shelley's poem, each pond seemed to be a brief sky engulfed in a subterranean world; a firmament of rose-colored light, spread out above the dark earth, more infinite than the infinite night and purer than day; where the trees developed in the same way as in the air above but more perfect in form and shade than any of the others undulating there.[11] And delicate views, such as have never been seen in our world above, were painted there by the love of the waters for the beautiful forest; and all their depth was penetrated by a faint heavenly light, by an unchanging atmosphere, by an evening that was gentler than the one above.[12]

From what remote time did that hour come to us? We rode along at walking pace, in silence. The occasional cries of magpies, the gait and the breathing of the horses did not disturb the tranquillity, which seemed to become greater and more magical as each minute passed.

Why did he have to shatter the magic we ourselves had created? He spoke; he poured into my heart a wave of ardent, crazy, almost senseless words, which in that silence of the trees alarmed me, because there was something not human about them, something indefinably strange and fascinating. He was not humble and meek as in the park; he did not tell me about his timid and discouraged hopes, his almost mystical aspirations, his incurable sadness; he did not beseech; he did not implore. He had the voice of passion, audacious and strong; a voice that I did not recognize in him.

"You love me, you love me, you *cannot not love me*! Tell me that you love me!"

His horse was walking alongside mine, very close by. And I felt him brush against me; and I also thought I could feel his breath on my cheek, the ardor of his words; and I thought I would faint from the great agitation I felt, and that I would fall into his arms.

"Tell me that you love me!" he repeated, obstinately, without pity. "Tell me that you love me!"

Out of my mind, in the terrible exasperation his demanding voice caused me, I believe that I said, I don't know whether with a cry or with a sob:

"I love you, I love you, I love you!"

And I urged my horse into a gallop along the road that was barely visible in the density of the tree trunks, not knowing what I was doing.

He followed me shouting:

"Maria, Maria, stop! You're going to get hurt . . ."

I did not stop; I don't know how my horse avoided the trees; I don't know how I did not fall. I cannot describe the impression given to me during this ride by the dark forest interrupted here and there by the wide shining patches of the ponds. When finally I emerged from it onto the road, at the opposite side near the Convito bridge, it seemed that I was emerging from a hallucination.

He said to me with some severity:

"Did you want to kill yourself?"

We heard the sound of the coach approaching; and we moved toward it. He still wanted to talk to me.

"Be quiet, I pray you; please!" I implored, because I felt that I could take no more.

He fell silent. Then, with a confidence that amazed me, he said to Francesca:

"What a pity that you did not come! It was enchanting . . ."

And he continued to talk, frankly, simply, as if nothing had occurred; rather, with a certain gaiety. And I was grateful to him for his dissimulation, which seemed to save me, because certainly, if I had had to talk, I would have betrayed myself; and if we had both been silent it would have perhaps seemed suspicious to Francesca.

After a while, the ascent toward Schifanoja began. What immense melancholy in the evening! The first quarter of the moon shone in a delicate sky, slightly green, in which my eyes, or maybe my eyes only, still saw a faint appearance of rose, of the rosy hue that illuminated the ponds, down there in the forest.

October 5. —He now knows that I love him; he knows it from my own mouth. I have no escape other than flight. This is the point I have reached.

When he looks at me, there is deep in his eyes a singular glitter that was not there before. Today, in a moment when Francesca was not present, he took my hand and made as if to kiss it. I managed to withdraw it; and I saw his lips disturbed by a small tremor; I caught on his lips, for a second, almost the shape of a kiss not planted, an expression that has remained in my memory and that does not leave me, does not leave me!

October 6. —On September 25, on the marble seat, in the arbutus woods, he said to me: "I know that you do not love me and that *you cannot love me.*" And on October 3: "You love me, you love me, you *cannot not love me.*"

*

In Francesca's presence, he asked me if I would permit him to do a study of my hands. I consented. He will begin today.

And I am apprehensive and anxious, as if I had to offer up my hands to an unknown torture.

Nighttime. —The slow, sweet, indefinable torture has begun.

He was drawing with black pencil and hematite pencil. My right hand was resting on a piece of velvet. On the table there was a Korean vase, yellowish and spotted like the skin of a python; and in the vase was a bunch of orchids, those grotesque multiform flowers that are Francesca's sophisticated idiosyncrasy. Some green ones, of the almost *animal* green of certain locusts, hung down in the form of small Etruscan urns, with the lid slightly lifted. Others bore at the top of a silver stem a five-petaled flower with a small calyx at the center, yellow on the inside and white on the outside. Others bore a small purplish ampulla and, on the sides of the ampulla, two long filaments;

and they brought to mind some minuscule king in fairy tales, greatly affected with goiter, and with a beard divided into two braids in the Oriental style. Still others bore a quantity of yellow flowers, similar to little angels in a long dress, hovering in flight with their arms raised high and their halo behind their head.

I looked at them, when it seemed I could no longer bear the torment; and their unusual shapes engaged me for an instant, evoked a fleeting memory of their countries of origin, induced in my spirit some momentary sense of bewilderment. He drew without talking; his eyes went constantly from the paper to my hands; then, two or three times, they turned toward the vase. At a certain point, standing up, he said:

"Forgive me."

And he took up the vase and took it farther away, to another table; I don't know why.

Then he began to draw with greater openness, as if liberated from an irritation.

I cannot say what his eyes made me feel. It seemed to me that I was not offering to his scrutiny my naked hand, but rather a naked part of my soul; and that he had penetrated it with his gaze right down to the very base of it, uncovering all its innermost secrets. I had never felt such a sentiment from my hand; it had never appeared to me so alive, so expressive, so intimately tied to my heart, so dependent on my internal existence, so revealing. An imperceptible but constant vibration caused it to quiver under the influence of his gaze; and the vibration spread right to the depths of my being. At times the tremor became stronger and more visible; and if he was looking at me with too much intensity, I was gripped by an instinctive impulse to withdraw it; and sometimes this impulse was one of modesty.

At times he gazed at me intently for a long time, without drawing; and I had the impression that he was drinking in some part of me with his pupils, or that he was caressing me with a caress softer than the velvet on which my hand was resting. Every now and then, while he was bent over the paper, perhaps instilling into the line whatever he had drunk from me, a faint smile drifted over his lips, but so light that I could barely glimpse it. And that smile, I don't know why, gave me a tremor of pleasure in the upper part of my chest. Again, two or three times, I saw the shape of the kiss reappear on his mouth.

Now and then, curiosity overcame me; and I asked: "Well?"

Francesca was sitting at the piano, her back toward us; and was touching the keys, trying to remember Luigi Rameau's gavotte, the *Gavotte of the Yellow Ladies,* which I played so often and which will remain the musical memory of my holiday at Schifanoja. She was muffling the notes with the pedal, and interrupting herself often. And those interruptions in the aria and in the cadences that were so familiar to me, which the ear would complete in advance, were another source of disquiet for me. Suddenly, she struck a key hard, repeatedly, as if incited by cranky impatience; and she got up and went to bend over the drawing.

I looked at her. And I understood.

This bitterness was the last thing I needed. God held aside this cruelest test for last. May His will be done.

October 7. —I have but one single thought, one single desire, one single purpose: to leave, to leave, to leave.

I am at the limit of my strength. I am swooning, I am dying from my love; and the unexpected revelation multiplies my mortal sadness. What does she think of me? What does she believe? Does she love him, then? And since when? And does he know? Or does he not even have the slightest suspicion? . . .

My God, my God! I am losing my reason, my strength is abandoning me; my sense of reality is slipping away from me. At times my suffering pauses, similar to the lull that occurs during hurricanes when the furies of the elements are balanced in a terrible immobility, just to break out again with even greater violence. I find myself in a kind of stupefaction, my head heavy, my limbs tired and worn out as if someone had been beating me; and while the pain gathers itself to launch a new assault on me, I cannot manage to gather my will.

What does she think of me? What does she think? What does she believe?

To be snubbed by her, my best friend, the one who is dearest to me, the one to whom my heart was always open! It is the greatest bitterness; it is the cruelest test reserved by God for one who has made sacrifice the law of her life.

I must talk to her before I leave. She must know everything from me, and I must know everything from her. This is my duty.

Nighttime. —Toward five o'clock she proposed that we go for a ride in the carriage along the Rovigliano road. We went alone, in an open carriage. I thought, trembling: *I will talk to her now.* But the internal tremor deprived me of all courage. Was she waiting for me to speak? I don't know.

We remained silent for a long time, listening to the regular trot of the two horses, observing the trees and the hedges alongside the road. Now and then, with a brief phrase or a nod, she brought to my attention some detail of the autumnal countryside.

All of autumn's human enchantment was being disseminated at that hour. The oblique rays of evening lit up against the hill the diffuse, harmonious richness of dying foliage. Due to the constant blowing of the northeast wind with the new moon, premature death throes grip the trees of the coastal lands. Gold, amber, crocus, sulfur yellow, ocher, orange, bistre, copper, sea green, maroon, purple, crimson, the dullest hues, the most violent and most delicate shades mingled in a profound harmony that will never be surpassed in sweetness by any spring melody.

Pointing out a cluster of black locust trees, she said: "Don't they look as if they are full of flowers!"

Already withered, they appeared to be of a slightly rose-colored white, like great almond trees in March, against the turquoise sky, which was already inclining toward ash-gray.

After an interval of silence, I said, to begin with: "Manuel will come on Saturday, most likely. I'm awaiting his telegram, tomorrow. And we will depart on Sunday, with the morning train. You have been so good to me, these last days; I am so grateful to you . . ."

My voice was trembling slightly; an immense tenderness swelled my heart. She took my hand and kept it in hers, without speaking, without looking at me. And we remained for a long time in silence, holding hands.

She asked me: "How long will you stay at your mother's?"

I answered: "Until the end of the year, I hope; and maybe longer."

"So long?"

Again, we fell silent. I already felt that I would not have the courage to confront the explanation; and I also felt that it was less necessary now. It seemed that she was drawing closer to me now, that she understood me, acknowledged me, was becoming my good sister. My sadness attracted her sadness, the way the moon attracts the waters of the sea.

"Listen," she said; because the sound of a chant, sung at the top of their voices by women of the village, was reaching us, a slow, extensive, religious song like a Gregorian chant.

Farther on we saw the singers. They were emerging from a field of desiccated sunflowers, walking in line, like a sacred procession. And the sunflowers at the top of the long, leafless sulfur-yellow stalks bore their wide disks neither crowned with petals nor laden with seeds, but resembling in their bareness liturgical emblems, pale golden ostensories.

My emotion grew. The chant behind us dispersed in the evening. We crossed Rovigliano, where the lights were already being lit; then we emerged again onto the main road. Behind us, the sound of the bells faded. A damp wind blew across the tops of the trees, which cast a bluish shadow on the white street, and an almost liquid shadow, as in water, in the air.

"Aren't you cold?" she asked me; and ordered the lackey to unfold a plaid blanket and the coachman to turn the horses around for the return journey.

In the Rovigliano bell tower a bell still tolled, with slow tolls, as if for a religious rite; and it seemed to propagate, in the wind, a wave of frost along with the wave of sound. Of common accord we drew close to each other, pulling the blanket over our knees, infecting each other with the shiver of cold. And the carriage entered the village at a walking pace.

"Whatever is that bell tolling for?" she murmured, in a voice that no longer seemed hers.

I replied: "Unless I'm mistaken, the viaticum is coming out."

Farther on, in fact, we saw the priest enter a doorway while a cleric held a raised umbrella and two others held lit lanterns aimed directly on the doorposts, on the threshold. In that house one single window was illuminated, the window of the Christian on his deathbed awaiting the holy oil. Slight shadows appeared in the glow; on that rectangle of yellow light, there could be seen, faintly traced, the entire silent drama enacted around whoever is about to enter into death.

One of the two servants asked in a low voice, bending down slightly from above: "Who is dying?" The person questioned gave the name of a woman, in his dialect.

And I would have liked to attenuate the noise of the wheels on the cobblestones, I would have liked to silence our passage through that place where the breath of a spirit was about to depart. Certainly, Francesca had the same sentiment.

The carriage reached the Schifanoja road, speeding up to a trot. The moon, encircled by auras, shone like an opal in diaphanous milk. A bank of clouds arose from the sea and slowly transformed into globe shapes, like fickle smoke. The choppy sea drowned all other sounds with its din. Never, I think, has a heavier sadness bound two souls.

I felt a sense of warmth on my cold cheeks, and I turned to Francesca to see whether she had realized that I was crying. I met her eyes full of tears. And we remained mute, alongside each other, our mouths pressed shut, squeezing our hands together, knowing that we were crying for him; and the tears descended drop by drop, silently.

Near Schifanoja I dried mine and she hers. Each of us hid our own weakness.

He was waiting for us with Delfina, Muriella, and Ferdinando in the atrium. Why did I feel toward him, deep in my heart, an indistinct sense of diffidence, as if instinct were warning me of an obscure damage? What suffering did the future hold for me? Will I be able to escape the passion that attracts me, blinding me?

Yet those few tears have done me so much good! I feel less oppressed, less parched, more trustful. And I feel an inexpressible tenderness repeating the last excursion to myself, while Delfina sleeps, content with all the crazy kisses I placed on her face, and while the melancholy of the moon, which earlier saw me cry, smiles on the windowpanes.

October 8. —Did I sleep last night? Did I remain awake? I cannot say.

Obscurely, terrible thoughts and images of unbearable suffering flashed through my brain like thick shadows; and my heart was subject to sudden jolts and palpitations, and I would find myself with my eyes open in the darkness, not knowing whether I had come out of a dream, or whether until then I had been awake, thinking and imagining. And this sort of ambiguous drowsiness, much more tormenting than insomnia, continued, continued, continued.

Nonetheless, when I heard the voice of my daughter calling me in the morning, I did not answer; I pretended to be sleeping deeply, to avoid getting up, to remain there still, to procrastinate, to postpone for a while the inexorable certainty of necessary realities. The tortures of my thoughts and my imagination seemed less cruel than the unforeseen tortures my life is preparing for me in these last two days.

After a short while, Delfina came in on tiptoe, holding her breath, to look at me; and she said to Dorothy, her voice agitated by a slight tremor: "She's sleeping so deeply! Let's not wake her."

Nighttime. —I seem not to have a drop of blood left in my veins. While ascending the stairs it felt that with every effort I made to climb one step, my blood and my life escaped through all my open-ended veins. I am weak like a dying woman . . .

Courage, courage! There are still a few hours left; Manuel will arrive tomorrow; we will leave on Sunday; by Monday we will be at my mother's.

Earlier, I gave him back two or three books that he had lent me. In the book by Percy Shelley, at the end of a stanza, I underlined two lines with my nail and made a visible sign on the page. The lines said:

> And forget me, for I can *never*
> Be thine![13]

October 9, nighttime. —The entire day, the entire day he sought a moment to talk to me. His suffering was manifest. And the entire day I tried to escape from him, so that he could not cast into my soul other seeds of suffering, of desire, of regret, of remorse. I won; I was strong and heroic. I thank you, my Lord.

This is the last night. We are leaving tomorrow morning. Everything will be over.

Will everything be over? Deep down, a voice speaks to me; and I don't understand it, but I know that it speaks to me of distant disasters, unknown yet inevitable, mysterious yet detestable as death. The future is dismal, like a field full of graves already dug and ready to receive cadavers; and on the field, here and there, pale lamps glow, which I can barely distinguish; and I don't know whether they are burning to attract me toward danger or to signal a path of salvation for me.

I read my journal again, attentively, slowly, from September 15, the day I arrived. What a difference between that first night and this last one!

I wrote: "I will awaken in a kindly home, to Francesca's cordial hospitality, in this Schifanoja, which has such beautiful roses and tall cypresses; and I will wake up with a few weeks of peace before me, twenty days of spiritual existence, maybe more." Alas, where has the peace gone? And the roses, so beautiful, why were they also so treacherous? Perhaps I have opened my heart too much to fragrances, starting with that night, on the veranda, while Delfina was sleeping. Now the October moon is flooding the sky; and I see the tips of the cypresses through the windowpanes, black and unchanging, which were touching the stars that night.

I can repeat one single phrase from that prelude in this wretched ending. "So much hair on my head, so many wheat spikes of pain in my destiny." The spikes multiply, rise up, undulate like a sea; and the iron to form the scythe has not yet been extracted from the mines.

I am leaving. What will become of him, when I am far away? What will become of Francesca?

Francesca's change is still incomprehensible, inexplicable; it is an enigma that tortures and confuses me. She loves him! And *since when*? And does he know?

My soul, confess the new misery. A new infection is poisoning you. You are jealous.

But I am ready for ever more atrocious suffering; I know the agony that awaits me; I know that the torments of these days are nothing compared to the torments to come, to the terrible cross to which my thoughts will bind my soul in order to devour it. I am ready. I ask only for a respite, O Lord, a brief respite for the remaining hours. I will need all my strength tomorrow.

How strangely, sometimes, in the different events of life, external circumstances resemble each other, correspond to each other! This evening, in the vestibule hall, it seemed as if I had returned to the evening of September 16, when I sang and played; when he began to invade me. Tonight, too, I was sitting at the piano, and the same dim light illuminated the hall and in the adjacent room Manuel and the marquis were playing cards; and I played the *Gavotte of the Yellow Ladies,* the one that Francesca likes so much, the one that on September 16 I heard being repeated while I was awake during the first indeterminate nocturnal restlessness.

Certain fair-haired ladies, no longer young but just out of their youth, dressed in a dull silk the color of a yellow chrysanthemum, dance it with adolescent dancing partners, dressed in rose, somewhat listless; they carry in their hearts the image of other, more beautiful women, the flame of a new desire. And they dance it in a hall that is too large, which has all the walls covered in mirrors; they dance it upon a floor inlaid with amaranthus and cedar, beneath a great crystal chandelier in which the candles are about to burn out, but never do. And on their slightly faded mouths the women have a faint but never-dimming smile; and the gentlemen have an infinite boredom in their eyes. And a pendulum clock is always sounding the same hour; and the mirrors always repeat repeat repeat the same poses; and the gavotte continues continues continues, always sweet, always slow, always the same, eternally, like a prison sentence.

That sadness entices me.

I don't know why, but my soul inclines toward that form of torment; it is seduced by the perpetuity of a single suffering, by uniformity, by monotony. It would willingly accept for its entire life a tremendous weight, but a defined and unchanging one, rather than changeability, than unforeseeable events, than unforeseeable alternatives. Even though it is accustomed to suffering, it is afraid of the uncertain, it fears surprises; it fears sudden jolts. Without hesitating for an instant, tonight it would accept any heavier sentence of suffering, as long as it were protected against unknown ambushes in the future.

My God, my God, where does such a blind fear come from? Please will *You* protect me! I am placing my soul in Your hands!

And now, enough of this wretched raving, which unfortunately increases the anguish rather than relieving it. But I already know that I will not be able to close my eyes, even though they hurt.

He, surely, is not sleeping. When I came upstairs, he, having been invited to do so, was about to take the marquis's place at the card table, opposite my husband. Are they still playing? Perhaps he is thinking and suffering, while playing. What might his thoughts be? What might be his suffering?

I am not sleepy, I am not sleepy. I am going onto the veranda. I want to know if they are playing still; or whether he has returned to his rooms. His windows are at the corner, on the second floor.

*

The night is bright and damp. The gaming hall is illuminated; and I remained there on the veranda for a long time, looking down toward the light, which was reflected against a cypress, mingling with the light of the moon. I am trembling all over. I cannot describe the almost tragic impression exerted on me by those illuminated windows, behind which the two men are playing, one opposite the other, in the great silence of the night barely interrupted by the muffled sobs of the sea. And they will, perhaps, play until dawn, if he wishes to gratify my husband's terrible passion. Three of us will remain awake until dawn, without rest, out of passion.

But what does he think? What is his torment? I don't know what I would give, at this moment, to be able to see him, to be able to remain gazing at him until dawn, even through the window, in the dampness of the night, trembling as I now tremble.

The craziest thoughts flash inside me and dazzle me, rapid, confused; I feel something akin to the beginning of an unpleasant drunkenness; I feel something akin to a dull incitement to do something audacious and irreparable; I feel something like the fascination of perdition.

I would remove, I feel, this enormous weight from my heart, I would remove this suffocating knot from my throat, if now, in the night, in the silence, with all the strength of my spirit I began to shout that I love him, I love him, I love him.

THIRD BOOK

CHAPTER I

The departure of the Ferres family was followed after a few days by the departure of the Ateletas and of Sperelli for Rome. Donna Francesca insisted on cutting short her holiday at Schifanoja, a change from her usual custom.

After a brief stop in Naples, Andrea arrived in Rome on October 24, a Sunday, with the first heavy morning rain of autumn. Reentering his apartment in Palazzo Zuccari, his precious and exquisite *buen retiro,* he felt an extraordinary pleasure. It seemed to him that he was regaining some part of himself in those rooms, something that was missing. Almost nothing in the place had changed. Everything still preserved, for him, that inexpressible appearance of life taken on by material objects amid which man has loved, dreamed, taken pleasure, and suffered for a long time. Old Jenny and Terenzio had taken care of the smallest details; Stephen had prepared with great delicacy every comfort for the return of his master.

It was raining. For a while, he remained with his forehead against the windowpanes, looking out at his Rome, the great beloved city, which appeared ash-gray in the background, with silver here and there among the rapid alternations of the rain thrust this way and that by the caprice of the wind in an environment that was consistently gray, in which at intervals a patch of brightness would spread, only to extinguish itself immediately afterward like a fleeting smile. The square of Trinità de' Monti was deserted, contemplated by the solitary obelisk. The trees on the avenue along the wall that joins the church to Villa Medici were tossing about in the wind and the rain, already semibare, blackish and russet. The Pincian Hill still shimmered green, like an island in a misty lake.

Looking out, he did not have any definite thought but rather a confused tangle of thoughts; and one sentiment occupied his mind overwhelming any other: the full and lively reawakening of his old love of Rome, for sweetest Rome, for immense august unique Rome, for the city of cities, the one that is always young and always new and always mysterious, like the sea.

It rained and rained. Above Monte Mario the sky grew dark, the clouds grew denser and took on a dark cerulean color of a mass of water; they expanded toward the Janiculum Hill; they sank low over the Vatican. The cupola of Saint Peter touched that enormous accumulation with its peak and appeared to be holding it up like a gigantic leaden pile. Amid the innumerable oblique stripes of water, vapor slowly advanced, resembling a delicate veil passing through rigid and constantly vibrating cords of steel. The monotony of the downpour was not interrupted by any other greater clamor.

—What's the time? he asked Stephen, turning around.

It was about nine. He felt somewhat tired. He thought about going to sleep. Then, too, he thought that he would not see anyone during the day and that he would spend the evening at home in contemplation. The life of the city, society life, was once again starting up for him. He wanted, before taking up that old practice, to engage in some brief meditation and preparation, to establish a rule, to discuss with himself what his future conduct should be.

He ordered Stephen:

—If anyone comes to ask after me, tell them that I have not yet returned. Let the porter know. Tell James that I won't need him today but that he must come and take orders this evening. Have some lunch prepared for me at three o'clock, very light, and dinner at nine. Nothing else.

He fell asleep almost immediately. At two, the manservant awoke him; and announced that the Duke of Grimiti had come before midday, having heard from the Marchioness of Ateleta of their return.

—Well?

—The duke left a message that he would return before evening.

—Is it still raining? Open the shutters completely.

It was no longer raining. The sky had cleared. A band of muted sunlight entered the room, shedding its light over the tapestry of *The Virgin with Baby Jesus and Stefano Sperelli,* over the ancient tapestry that Giusto had brought from Flanders in 1508. And Andrea's eyes roved across the walls, slowly, regarding the fine wall-hangings, the harmonious shades, the pious figures that had been witness to so many pleasures and had smiled upon joyful reawakenings and had rendered the vigils of the wounded man less miserable, too. All those well-known and beloved things seemed to be greeting him. He regarded them with singular delight. The image of Donna Maria arose in his mind.

He raised himself slightly on the pillows, lit a cigarette, and began to follow the course of his thoughts with a sort of sensual pleasure. An unusual sense of well-being spread through his limbs and his spirit was in a happy disposition. He mingled his fantasies with the undulations of the smoke, in that temperate light in which colors and shapes assumed a milder haziness.

Spontaneously, his thoughts did not return to the last few days but went to the future. He would see Donna Maria again in two or three months' time, who knows? Perhaps even much sooner; and he would then resume that love affair which harbored so many mysterious promises and so many secret attractions for him. It would be his true *second love,* with the depth and the sweetness and the sadness of a second love. Donna Maria Ferres appeared to be, for a man of intellect, the Ideal Lover, the *Amie avec les hanches,*[1] as Charles Baudelaire expresses it, the unique *Consolatrix,* the one that comforts and forgives knowing how to forgive. Assuredly, marking in Shelley's book the two painful lines, she must have repeated other words deep within her heart; and reading the poem in its entirety, she must have cried like the magnetic Lady and thought at length about the merciful cure, the miraculous healing. *"I can* never *be thine!"* Why *never*? That day, in the woods at Vicomìle, she had answered with too much anguish born of passion: "—I love you, I love you, I love you!"

He could still hear her voice, the unforgettable voice. And Elena Muti entered his thoughts, drew near the other woman, mingled with the other, evoked by that voice; and little by little this turned his thoughts to images of voluptuous pleasure. The bed in which he rested, and all the things around it, witnesses and accomplices to his bygone raptures, little by little were beginning to prompt images of lust in him. Inquisitively, in his imagination he began to undress the Sienese woman, to envelop her in his desire, to shape her in uninhibited positions, to picture her in his arms, to take pleasure in her. The material possession of that woman, so chaste and so pure, seemed to him to be the highest, newest, rarest pleasure that he could reach; and that room seemed to him to be the worthiest place to accommodate that pleasure, because it would render more intense the singular note of profanation and sacrilege that the secret act, according to him, would have.

The room was religious, like a chapel. In it were gathered almost all the ecclesiastical fabrics he possessed, and almost all the wall-hangings of a sacred nature. The bed was raised on a platform reached by three steps, shadowed by a canopy of carved Venetian velvet dating from the sixteenth century, with a background of gilded silver and decorations of a faded red color with raised embroidery in spun gold, which in times gone by must have been a sacred covering, because the design portrayed Latin inscriptions and the fruits of the Sacrifice: grapes and wheat. A small, extremely fine Flemish hanging interwoven with Cyprian gold, representing an Annunciation, covered the headboard of the bed. Other hangings, with the coat of arms of the Sperelli house in the pattern, covered the walls, edged at the top and at the bottom with strips like a frieze on which were embroidered scenes from the life of the Virgin Mary, and the deeds of martyrs, of apostles, of prophets. An altar frontal, representing the parable of the wise virgins and the foolish virgins, and two parts of a cope, formed the upholstery of the chimney place. Other precious sacristy furniture made of sculpted wood from the fifteenth century completed the pious décor, together with some pieces of majolica by Luca della Robbia and some large armchairs covered on the headrest and on the seat with pieces of ecclesiastical tunics representing the events of Creation. Everywhere, with ingenious taste, other liturgical fabrics were used as ornaments and for comfort: chalice bags, baptism bags, chalice covers, chasubles, maniples, stoles, embroidered copes, tabernacle veils. On the mantelpiece, as on the table of an altar, a great triptych by Hans Memling shone forth, an *Adoration of the Magi,* infusing the room with the radiance of a masterpiece.

In certain woven inscriptions, the name of Mary recurred among the words of the Angelic Salutation; and in many places the great initial *M* was repeated; in one, it was even embroidered with pearls and garnets. *Entering this place*—the sensitive decorator thought—*will she not believe she is entering her glory?* And he took pleasure imagining for a long time the profane event amid the sacred events; and once again aesthetic sense and the refinement of sensuality overwhelmed and falsified in him the frank and human sentiment of love.

Stephen knocked on the door, saying:

—May I advise the Lord Count that it is already three o'clock.

Andrea got up, and went into the octagonal room to dress. The sun entered through the lace curtains, sparkling on the Arabic-Hispanic tiles, the innumerable silver and crystal objects, the bas-reliefs of the ancient sarcophagus. Those diverse glimmers gave the air a dynamic gaiety. He felt cheerful, perfectly healed, full of vitality. Being back in his home gave him an inexpressible joy. Everything in him that was most fatuous, vainest, most worldly, was suddenly reawakening. It seemed as if the surrounding things had the power to call forth in him the man he had once been. His curiosity, his elasticity, his spiritual ubiquity were reappearing. He was already beginning to feel the need to spread himself out, to see friends again, to see lady friends, to experience pleasure. He realized he was very hungry; and he ordered the servant to serve his lunch.

He rarely dined at home; but on extraordinary occasions, for dainty romantic luncheons or small intimate suppers, he had a room decorated with Neapolitan high-warp tapestries, dating back to the eighteenth century, which Carlo Sperelli had ordered from the royal tapestry weaver, the Roman Pietro Duranti, in 1766, to the designs of Girolamo Storace. The seven wall-pieces depicted, with a certain plentiful Rubenesque abundance, Bacchic episodes of love; and the doors, the overdoor panels, the transoms, portrayed fruit and flowers. The pale, tawny golds, which predominated, and the pearly flesh and the cinnabars and the dark azures, formed a soft and rich harmony.

—When the Duke of Grimiti returns—he said to the servant—let him in.

There, too, the sun setting over Monte Mario cast its rays. The clatter of coaches on the square of Trinità de' Monti could be heard. It seemed that after the rain all the luminous fairness of the Roman October was being diffused over Rome.

—Open the shutters, he said to the servant.

And the din became louder; the tepid air entered; the curtains fluttered slightly.

Divine Rome! he thought, observing the sky between the tall curtains. And an irresistible curiosity drew him to the window.

Rome appeared, of a very light slate color with slightly hazy outlines as in a washed-out painting, beneath a sky by Claudio Lorenese,[2] damp and cool, scattered with diaphanous clouds in lofty groups, which lent the open spaces an indescribable subtlety, just as flowers bring greenery a novel grace. In the distance, in the uppermost heights, the slate was gradually changing to amethyst. Long and narrow bands of vapor were winding themselves through the cypresses on Monte Mario, like hair flowing through a bronze comb. Nearby, the pines on the Pincian Hill lifted their gilded umbrellas. On the square, Pius VI's obelisk resembled an agate flower stalk. Everything took on a richer aspect in that rich autumnal light.

Divine Rome!

He could not take his fill of the vision. He watched a throng of red-robed clerics pass by below the church; then the black carriage of a prelate with two black long-tailed horses; then other open-top coaches, which carried ladies and children. He recognized the Princess of Ferentino with Barbarella Viti; then the Countess of Lùcoli who was driving two ponies, followed by her Great Dane. A gust of the old life passed over his spirit and disturbed him and gave him a feeling of perturbation, made up of indeterminate desires.

He withdrew and sat down at the table again. Before him, the sun was igniting the crystal and illuminating, on the wall, a dance of satyrs around Silenus.

The manservant announced:

—The Lord Duke with two other gentlemen.

And the Duke of Grimiti, Ludovico Barbarisi, and Giulio Musèllaro entered, while Andrea was rising to meet them. They all embraced him, one after the other.

—Giulio! exclaimed Sperelli, seeing his friend again after more than two years. —How long have you been in Rome?

—For a week. I wanted to write to you at Schifanoja, but then I decided to wait until you got back. How are you? You seem a bit thinner, but in good health. I heard about what happened to you only when I got back to Rome; otherwise, I'd have left India to come and help take care of you. At the beginning of May I was in Padmavati, in Bahar. I've got so many things to tell you about!

—And I have so many to tell you!

They squeezed each other's hands again, heartily. Andrea seemed very happy. Musèllaro was dearer to him than any other friend, due to his high intelligence, his acute mind, the sophistication of his learnedness.

—Ruggero, Ludovico, sit down. Giulio, sit here.

He offered cigarettes, tea, liqueurs. The conversation became very animated. Ruggero Grimiti and Barbarisi were recounting the news regarding Rome, reporting on local goings-on. Smoke rose in the air, becoming tinged in the sun's rays, now almost horizontal; the wall-hangings blended together in a warm, mellow hue; the aroma of tea mingled with the odor of tobacco.

—I brought you a bag of tea—said Musèllaro to Sperelli—much better than the one your famous Kien-Lung drank.

—Ah, do you remember, in London, when we composed tea according to the poetic theory of the great emperor?

—You know, said Grimiti. —Clara Green, the blonde, is in Rome. I saw her on Sunday at Villa Borghese. She recognized me, greeted me, and stopped the carriage. She's staying, for now, at the Albergo d'Europa, in Piazza di Spagna. She's still lovely. Do you remember what a passion she had for you, and how she pursued you when you were in love with the Landbrooke girl? She immediately asked about your news, before asking for mine . . .

—I'd willingly see her again. But does she still wear green and put sunflowers on her hat?

—No, no. She has abandoned aestheticism for good, it appears. She's now thrown herself into feathers. On Sunday she was wearing a huge hat in the Montpensier style with an incredible plume.

—This year—remarked Barbarisi—we have an extraordinary abundance of *demi-mondaines*.[3] There are three or four who are quite pleasing. Giulia Arici has a beautiful body and fairly aristocratic limbs. The Silva woman is also back; the day before yesterday our friend Musèllaro conquered her with a panther skin. Maria Fortuna has returned, but she's on bad terms with Carlo de Souza, who for the moment is being substituted by Ruggero . . .

—So the season is already in full swing?

—This year it's earlier than ever, as far as sinners and impeccables are concerned.

—Which of the impeccable ladies are already in Rome?

—Almost all of them: Moceto, Viti, the two Daddis, Micigliano, Miano, Massa d'Albe, Lùcoli . . .

—I saw the Lùcoli woman earlier from my window. She was driving. I also saw your cousin with the Viti woman.

—My cousin is here until tomorrow. Tomorrow she is going back to Frascati. On Wednesday she is throwing a party at the villa, a type of garden party, in the manner of the Princess of Sagan. It's not obligatory to wear any particular fancy dress, but all the ladies will wear Louis XV or Directoire hats. We're going.

—You're not leaving Rome for now, are you? Grimiti asked Sperelli.

—I'll stay until the beginning of November. Then I'm going to France for two weeks to restock with horses. And I'll come back here toward the end of the month.

—By the way, Leonetto Lanza is selling Campomorto, said Ludovico. —You know him: he is a magnificent animal and a great jumper. You'd be well advised to buy him.

—How much?

—Fifteen thousand, I think.

—We'll see.

—Leonetto is about to get married. He got engaged this summer at Aix-les-Bains to the Ginosa girl.

—I forgot to tell you—said Musèllaro—that Galeazzo Secìnaro says hello. We came back together. I wish I could tell you everything he got up to on the trip! He's in Palermo now, but he's coming to Rome in January.

—Gino Bommìnaco also sends his greetings, added Barbarisi.

—Ha, ha! exclaimed the duke, laughing. —Andrea, you must get Gino to tell you about his adventure with Donna Giulia Moceto . . . You're in a situation, I believe, to be able to give us a few explanations in this regard.

Ludovico also began to laugh.

—I've heard—said Giulio Musèllaro—that here in Rome you wrought awe-inspiring havoc. *Gratulor tibi!*[4]

—Tell me, tell me about the adventure, Andrea urged with curiosity.

—You have to hear it from Gino, to have a good laugh. You know his powers of mimicry. You have to see his face when he reaches the climax. It's a tour de force!

—I'll hear it from him, too—insisted Andrea, piqued by curiosity—but tell me about it in brief, please.

—Here it is, in a few words, Ruggero Grimiti assented, placing his cup on the table, setting about recounting the anecdote without scruples and without reticence, with that astonishing ability with which young gentlemen make public the sins of their ladies and those of others. —Last spring (I don't know if you noticed) Gino was paying court to Donna Giulia, extremely ardent and very visible court. At Le Capannelle racecourse, this courtship changed to a very spirited flirtation. Donna Giulia was on the point of capitulating; and Gino, as usual, was all aflame. The opportunity presented itself. Giovanni Moceto departed for Florence, to take his worn-out horses onto the turf at Le Cascine. One evening, one of the usual Wednesday evenings, indeed the last Wednesday evening, Gino thought that his great moment had come; and he waited for everyone to leave, one by one, and for the salon to remain empty, and finally to be alone with her . . .

—Here—interrupted Barbarisi—we would need Bommìnaco now. He is inimitable. You need to hear him recount, in Neapolitan dialect, the description of the *ambient,* and the analysis of his state of being, and then the reproduction of the *psychological* and the *physiological* moment, as he says, in his way. It's irresistibly funny.

—So—continued Ruggero—after the prelude, which you will hear from him, in the languor and the erotic excitement of a *fin de soirée,* he knelt in front of Donna Giulia, who was sitting in a very low armchair, an armchair "stuffed with complicity." Donna Giulia was already drowning in sweetness, defending herself weakly; and Gino's hands were getting ever more daring, while she was already sighing the sigh of surrender . . . But oh dear, from an attitude of extreme daring, those hands snapped back with an instinctual movement as if they had touched the skin of a snake, something revolting . . .

Andrea broke out in peals of laughter so frank that his hilarity spread to all his friends. He had understood, because he knew. But Giulio Musèllaro said, with great concern, to Grimiti:

—Explain it to me! Explain it to me!

—You explain, said Grimiti to Sperelli.

—All right—explained Andrea, still laughing—do you know Théophile Gautier's most beautiful poem, the *Musée secret*?

—*O douce barbe feminine!*[5] recited Musèllaro, remembering. —And so?

—And so, Giulia Moceto is a very delicate blonde; but if you had the luck, which I hope you do, to draw aside *le drap de la blonde qui dort,*[6] certainly you would not find, as did Philippe de Bourgogne, the golden fleece.[7] She is, they say, *sans plume et sans duvet*[8] like the marble sculptures of Paros, of which Gautier sings.

—Ah, a very rare rarity, which I appreciate greatly, said Musèllaro.

—A rarity that we know how to appreciate, repeated Andrea. —But Gino Bommìnaco is an ingenue, a simpleton.

—Listen, listen to the rest—said Barbarisi.

—Oh, if only the hero were here! exclaimed the Duke of Grimiti. —The story told by another mouth loses all its taste. Just imagine that the surprise was so great, and the confusion so great, as to extinguish any fire. Gino had to withdraw prudently, with the absolute impossibility of going any further. Can you imagine? Can you imagine the terrible mortification of a man who, having managed to obtain everything, can take nothing? Donna Giulia was green; Gino pretended to be listening out for noises, to procrastinate, hoping . . . Oh, the story of the retreat is a marvel! Anabasis[9] was nothing compared with this! You'll hear about it.

—And did Donna Giulia become Gino's lover after that? asked Andrea.

—Never! Poor Gino will never eat of that fruit; and I think that he will die of regret, of desire, of curiosity. He vents by laughing about it with his friends, but watch him well, when he talks about it. Underneath the joking, there's anguish.

—Nice topic for a short story, said Andrea to Musèllaro. —Don't you think? A short story entitled "The Obsessed" . . . One could make something very refined and intense. The man, continually possessed, pursued, tormented by the fantastic vision of that rare form he has touched and therefore imagined but never enjoyed, nor seen with his eyes, consumes himself with passion little by little and goes mad. He cannot remove from his fingers the impression of that contact; but the first instinctual revulsion has mutated into an inextinguishable ardor . . . One could, in short, make a work of art based on the real event; accomplish something like an erotic Hoffmann story, written with the plastic precision of a Flaubert.

—Try.

—Who knows! Anyway, I'm sorry for poor Gino. The Moceto woman has, I've heard, the most beautiful belly of all Christendom . . .

—I like that "I've heard"—interrupted Ruggero Grimiti.

—. . . the belly of an infertile Pandora, an ivory bowl, a radiant shield, *speculum voluptatis;*[10] and the most perfect belly button that one has ever seen, a small rounded belly button, as in the Clodion's terra-cotta statuettes, a pure seal of grace, an eye that is blind but more splendid than a star, *voluptatis ocellus,*[11] to celebrate in an epigram worthy of Greek anthology.

Andrea was becoming excited by these discussions. Supported by his friends, he entered into a dialogue on female beauty, much less restrained than Firenzuola's. His sensuality of old was reawakening in him, after his long abstinence; and he spoke with intimate and profound fervor, as a great connoisseur of the *nude,* priding himself on his more colorful words, drawing fine distinctions like an artist and a libertine. And, in truth, the dialogue of those four young men amid those enchanting Bacchic tapestries, had it been recorded, could well have been the *Breviarium Arcanum*[12] of elegant corruption at this turn of the nineteenth century.

The day was ebbing away; but the air was still permeated with light, retaining light within it the way a sponge retains water. Through the window one could see, on the horizon, an orange strip against which the cypresses on Monte Mario were clearly traced, like the teeth on a great ebony rake. Now and then one could hear the cries of crows flying in flocks to reunite on the roofs of Villa Medici, then descending to Villa Borghese, in the small valley of sleep.

—What are you doing this evening? Barbarisi asked Andrea.

—I really don't know.

—Come with us, then. We're having dinner at the Doney, at eight, at the Teatro Nazionale. We're inaugurating the new restaurant, rather, the *cabinets particuliers*[13] of the new restaurant, where at least we will not have to resign ourselves,[14] after the oysters, to the aphrodisiac uncovering of *Judith* and of the *Bather,* as at the Caffè di Roma.[15] Academic pepper upon fake oysters . . .

—Come with us, come with us, urged Giulio Musèllaro.

—It's the three of us—added the duke—with Giulia Arici, the Silva girl, and Maria Fortuna. Ah, a wonderful idea! Come with Clara Green.

—Wonderful idea! repeated Ludovico.

—And where do I find Clara Green?

—At the Albergo d'Europa, near here, in Piazza di Spagna. A card from you would make her happy. You can be sure that she would abandon any previous engagements.

Andrea liked the proposal.

—It would be better—he said—for me to pay her a visit. She's probably back by now. Don't you think so, Ruggero?

—Get dressed and we'll go immediately.

They went out. Clara Green had just returned to the hotel. She greeted Andrea with a childlike joy. Most certainly, she would have preferred to dine alone with him; but she accepted the invitation without hesitation; she wrote a note to free herself from a previous commitment; she sent the key of a theater box to a friend. She seemed happy. She began to tell him about a number of her sentimental affairs; she asked him numerous sentimental questions; she swore to him that she had never been able to forget him. She held his hands while talking.

—*I love you more than any words can say, Andrew . . .*[16]

She was young still. With her pure, straight profile, crowned with blond hair, parted above her forehead in a low style, she resembled a Greek beauty in a keepsake.[17] She had a light dusting of aesthetic cultivation, left to her by her love for the poet-painter Adolphus Jeckyll,[18] who followed John Keats in poetry and Holman Hunt in painting, composing obscure sonnets and painting subjects taken from the *Vita Nuova*. She had "posed" for a *Sibylla palmifera*[19] and for a *Madonna of the Lily*.[20] She had also once "posed" for Andrea, for a head study he required for his etching of *Isabetta* in Boccaccio's story.[21] She was therefore ennobled by art. But, deep down, she did not possess any spiritual quality; on the contrary, ultimately, that certain exalted sentimentalism she affected, to be encountered not uncommonly in Englishwomen of pleasure, and which makes a strange contrast with the depravations of their lasciviousness, rendered her somewhat tedious.

—*Who would have thought we would be together again, Andrew!*[22]

After an hour, Andrea left her and returned to Palazzo Zuccari, ascending the staircase that leads from Piazza Mignanelli to the Trinità. The noise of the city in the mild October evening reached the solitary staircase. Stars scintillated in a humid, clear sky. Down below at the Casteldelfino house, on the other side of a small gate, shrubs immersed in a mysterious dim light cast indistinct fluttering shadows, without a rustle, like marine plants undulating at the bottom of an aquarium. From the house, through an illuminated window with red curtains, came the sound of a piano. The church bells tolled. All of a sudden he felt his heart grow heavy. A memory of Donna Maria filled him, suddenly; and provoked in him, confusedly, a sense of regret and almost of repentance. What was she doing right now? Thinking? Suffering? With the image of the Sienese woman, the old Tuscan city appeared in his memory: the white-and-black Dome, the loggia, the fountain. A heavy sadness possessed him. It seemed to him that something had vanished from the base of his heart; and he did not know precisely what it was, but he was afflicted by it as if by an irremediable loss.

He thought once again about the resolution he had made that morning. One evening in solitude, in the house where she would perhaps come one day; a melancholic but pleasant evening, in the company of his memories and dreams, in the company of her spirit; an evening of meditation and concentration! In truth, his resolution could hardly have been better kept. He was about to go to a dinner with friends and women; and, without a doubt, he would spend the night with Clara Green.

His repentance was so unbearable, and gave him such torment, that he dressed with unusual speed, jumped into the *coupé,* and was driven to the hotel, arriving early. He found Clara ready. He suggested to her that they go for a ride in the *coupé* along the streets of Rome, to fill the time that remained till eight o'clock.

They passed along Via del Babuino, around the obelisk in Piazza del Popolo, and from there up the Corso and then right, along Via della Fontanella di Borghese; they returned via Montecitorio on the Corso to Piazza di Venezia, and then up to the Teatro Nazionale. Clara prattled constantly, and now and then leaned toward the young man to place a half kiss on the corner of his mouth, hiding the furtive act with a fan made of white feathers, from which drifted a very subtle scent of white rose.[23] But Andrea appeared not to be listening and at her gesture barely smiled.

—What are you thinking about? she asked, pronouncing the Italian words with a slight graceful uncertainty.

—Nothing, Andrea answered, taking one of her hands, which was not yet gloved, and looking at her rings.

—Who knows! she sighed, giving singular expression to those two monosyllables that foreign women learn immediately; in which they believe all the melancholy of Italian love to be enclosed. —Who knows!

Then she added, with an almost pleading tone:

—*Love me this evening, Andrew!*[24]

Andrea kissed her ear, passed an arm around her waist, told her a quantity of silly trifles, and changed his mood. The Corso was full of people, shopwindows gleamed, newspaper vendors shouted, public and elegant carriages intersected with the *coupé,* and from Piazza Colonna to Piazza di Venezia extended all the evening bustle of Roman life.

When they entered the Doney, it was ten past eight. The other six dining companions were already present. Andrea Sperelli greeted the company and, holding Clara Green by the hand, said:

—*Ecce*[25] Miss Clara Green, *ancilla Domini, Sibylla palmifera, candida puella.*[26]

—*Ora pro nobis,*[27] Musèllaro, Barbarisi, and Grimiti answered in chorus. The women laughed, but without understanding. Clara smiled; and having slipped off her cloak, appeared in a white, simple, short dress, with a décolletage coming down to a point on her chest and on her back, with a sea-green ribbon on her left shoulder, two emeralds at her ears, self-assured under the triple scrutiny of Giulia Arici, Bébé Silva, and Maria Fortuna.

Musèllaro and Grimiti knew her. Barbarisi was introduced to her. Andrea was saying:

—Mercedes Silva, known as Bébé, *chica pero guapa.*[28]

—Maria Fortuna, the lovely Talisman, who is a real public Fortune . . . for this Rome of ours, which has the fortune of possessing her.

Then, turning to Barbarisi:

—Do us the honor of introducing us to that lady who, if I am not mistaken, is the divine Giulia Farnese.

—No: Arici, interrupted Giulia.

—I beg your pardon, but to believe it I need to gather all my good faith and consult the Pinturicchio[29] in the Sala Quinta.[30]

He uttered these nonsensical things without laughing, taking pleasure in astonishing or irritating the sweet ignorance of these lovely foolish women. When he happened to be in the *demimonde,* he had his own particular manner and style. In order not to be bored, he started to compose grotesque phrases, to spout huge paradoxes, atrocious impertinences that he dissimulated with the ambiguity of his words, incomprehensible subtleties, enigmatic madrigals, in an unorthodox language, mingled like slang, with a thousand flavors as in a Rabelaisian *olla podrida,*[31] laden with strong spices and succulent flesh. No one knew better than he how to recount a coarse tale, a scandalous anecdote, a Casanovian deed. No one, in the description of something pertaining to sensual pleasure, knew better than he how to choose a lewd word, but one that was precise and powerful, a real word made of flesh and bones, a sentence full of substantial marrow, a phrase that lives and breathes and palpitates like the object of which it depicts the form, communicating to the worthy listener a double pleasure, an enjoyment not only of the intellect but of the senses, a joy partly similar to that produced by certain paintings of the great master colorists, blended with purple and milk, bathed as if in the transparency of liquid amber, impregnated with a warm and unquenchably luminous gold like immortal blood.

—Who is Pinturicchio? asked Giulia Arici of Barbarisi.

—Pinturicchio? exclaimed Andrea. —A superficial interior decorator, who some time ago had the whim to paint a portrait of you above a door in the apartment of the Pope. Don't worry about it. He's dead.

—But how? . . .

—Oh, in a frightful manner! His wife was the lover of a soldier from Perugia, who was garrisoned at Siena. Ask Ludovico about it. He knows everything; but he has never spoken to you about it, for fear of troubling you. Bébé, I would like to caution you that the Prince of Wales, at table, begins to smoke between the second and the third course; not before. You are somewhat premature.

The Silva woman had lit a cigarette; and was swallowing oysters while smoke issued from her nostrils. She resembled a sexless schoolboy, a small, depraved hermaphrodite: pale, thin, with eyes made bright by fever and charcoal, an excessively red mouth, and short, woolly, slightly curly hair, which covered her head like an astrakhan pageboy. In her left eye socket was wedged a round lens; she wore a high starched collar, a white cravat, an open waistcoat, a black jacket with a masculine cut, a gardenia in her buttonhole, affecting the manners of a dandy, talking in a hoarse voice. She was attractive, tempting, because of that stamp of vice, of depravity, of monstrosity that was in her appearance, in her poses, in her words. *Sal y pimiento.*[32]

Maria Fortuna, instead, was of a more bovine type, a Madame de Parabère,[33] tending toward corpulence. Like the lovely mistress of the Regent, she possessed a white skin, of an opaque and profound whiteness, one of those untiring and insatiable bodies on which Hercules could have carried out his labor of love, his thirteenth task, without being asked for a respite. And her eyes swam, soft violets, in a shadow such as Tranquillo Cremona would have painted, and her mouth, always half open, displayed an indistinct mother-of-pearl gleam in a rosy shadow, like a half-opened seashell.

Sperelli found Giulia Arici very pleasing, with her golden coloring, from which gazed elongated velvet eyes, of a soft chestnut velvet that at times took on almost tawny glints. Her slightly fleshy nose and her swollen, fresh, bloodred, firm lips lent the lower part of her face an expression of overt wantonness, rendered even racier by the restlessness of her tongue. Her canine teeth, being too prominent, lifted the corners of her mouth; and as the corners lifted in this way became dry or perhaps caused her some slight irritation, every now and then she moistened them with the tip of her tongue. And each time one saw that tip run along the enclosure formed by her teeth, like the moistened petal of a plump rose along a row of small bare almonds.

—Julia[34]—said Andrea Sperelli, watching her mouth—San Bernardino[35] has a wonderful epithet for you in one of his sermons. And you don't know this, either!

The Arici woman began to laugh, a stupid but beautiful laugh, which revealed her gums slightly; and with the commotion of her hilarity, a stronger scent emanated from her, as when a bush is shaken.

—What would you give me—added Andrea—what would you give me as a reward if, extracting that sensual word from the saint's sermon, like an aphrodisiac stone from a theological treasury, I offered it to you?

—I don't know, answered the Arici woman, still laughing, holding between her rather long, fine fingers a glass of Chablis wine. —Whatever you want.

—The noun of the adjective.

—What are you saying?

—We'll talk about it. The word is: *linguatica*.[36] Mister Ludovico, add this epithet to your litany: *"Rosa linguatica, glube nos."*[37]

—Pity—said Musèllaro—that you aren't at the dining table of a sixteenth-century duke, between a Violante and an Imperia,[38] with Giulio Romano, Pietro Aretino, and Marc Antony!

The conversation grew more and more inflamed with the wine, the aged French wines, fluid and ardent, which lend wings and flames to words. The majolica tableware was not made by Durantino, nor decorated by the cavalier Cipriano dei Piccolpasso; nor was the silverware from Milan, of Ludovico the Moor; but neither were they too common. In the center of the table a vase of pale blue crystal stood, containing a great bouquet of chrysanthemums—yellow, white, violet—gazed at by the melancholic eyes of Clara Green.

—Clara—inquired Ruggero Grimiti—are you sad? What are you thinking about?

—*À ma chimère!*[39] answered the ex-lover of Adolphus Jeckyll, smiling; and she hid her sigh within a brimming glass of champagne.

That clear and sparkling wine, which has such an immediate and strange effect on women, was already beginning to excite the minds and wombs of those four dissimilar *hetaerae*[40] in different ways, to reawaken and stimulate in them the small hysterical demon, and to cause it to run amok through their veins, spreading madness as it went. Bébé Silva was uttering horrendous witticisms, laughing a choked, convulsive, almost sobbing laugh, like a woman who is being tickled to death. Maria Fortuna was crushing *fondants* with her naked elbow and offering them for free, pressing her sweetened elbow onto Ruggero's mouth. Giulia Arici, tyrannized by Sperelli's madrigals, was blocking her ears with her lovely hands, leaning back against the chair; and her mouth, in that act, attracted bites like a juicy fruit.

—Have you ever eaten—Barbarisi was saying to Sperelli—certain sweetmeats from Constantinople, as soft as dough, made from bergamot, orange blossom, and roses, which perfume your breath for the rest of your life? Giulia's mouth is an Oriental sweetmeat.

—Please, Ludovico—said Sperelli—let me try her. Seduce Clara Green for me and give me Giulia for a week. Clara also has a novel flavor: a julep of Parma violets between two Peek Frean[41] vanilla biscuits . . .

—Watch, gentlemen! shouted Bébé Silva, taking a *fondant*.

She had seen the attention Maria Fortuna was attracting, and had made a gymnastic bet that she could eat a *fondant* from her own elbow by pulling it toward her lips. To accomplish the feat, she uncovered her arm: a thin and pale arm, covered with a dark down; she stuck the *fondant* on her sharp bone; and taking her right forearm with her left hand and pressing on it hard, managed to win the bet, with the ability of a clown, amid applause.

—And that's nothing, she said, covering her spectral nudity. —*Chica pero guapa;* not so, Musèllaro?

And she lit her tenth cigarette.

The odor of the tobacco was so delicious that everyone wanted to smoke some. The Silva woman's cigarette case was passed from hand to hand. Maria Fortuna read aloud from the engraved enameled silver of the case:

—"*Quia nominor Bébé.*"[42]

Then everyone wanted a saying, a motto to place on their handkerchiefs, their notepaper, their shirts. It seemed to them to be a very aristocratic, supremely elegant thing.

—Who will find me a motto? exclaimed Carlo de Souza's ex-lover. —I want it in Latin.

—I will, said Andrea Sperelli. —Here it is: "*Semper parata.*"[43]

—No.

—"*Diu saepe fortiter.*"[44]

—What does it mean?

—What do you care what it means? It just has to be Latin. Here's another one, a magnificent one: "*Non timeo dona ferentes.*"[45]

—I don't like it much. It's not new to me . . .

—All right then, this one: "*Rarae nates cum gurgite vasto.*"[46]

—It's too common. I read it so often in the newspaper columns.

Ludovico, Giulio, Ruggero laughed in chorus, loudly. The smoke of their cigarettes wafted over their heads forming light pale-bluish clouds. Every now and then, a wave of sound drifted over in the hot air from the theater orchestra; and it made Bébé hum. Clara Green was shredding petals from chrysanthemums into her plate, in silence, because the light white wine had been converted in her veins to a dismal listlessness. For those who already knew her, such Bacchic sentimentalism was not new; and the Duke of Grimiti was amusing himself by provoking it even more. She did not reply, continuing to tear off chrysanthemum petals and pressing her lips together, almost to stop herself from crying. Since Andrea Sperelli was paying little attention to her and had thrown himself into a crazy jollity of actions and words, amazing even his own companions in pleasure, she said with a pleading voice, amid the chorus of the other voices:

—*Love me tonight, Andrew!*[47]

And from then on, almost at regular intervals, lifting her blue gaze from her plate, she began languidly to beseech:

—*Love me tonight, Andrew!*

—Oh, what a drag, said Maria Fortuna. —But whatever does it mean? Does she feel ill?

Bébé Silva smoked, drank small glasses of *vieux cognac,* and said outrageous things with artificial vivacity. But she had, every now and then, very peculiar moments of tiredness, of prostration, in which it seemed as if something dropped from her face, and that her audacious and obscene form was occupied by some small, sad, miserable, sick, pensive, older figure, the oldness of a consumptive monkey that withdraws to the back of its cage to cough after having made people laugh. They were fleeting moments. She would shake herself out of it to take another sip or to make another outrageous comment.

And Clara Green continued to repeat:

—*Love me tonight, Andrew!*

CHAPTER II

Thus, with a bound, Andrea Sperelli dived back into Pleasure.

For two weeks he was kept occupied by Giulia Arici and Clara Green. Then he left for Paris and London, together with Musèllaro. He returned to Rome toward mid-December; found winter life already very active; and was immediately absorbed back into the great social circle.

But he had never found himself to be in such a restless, uncertain, confused state of mind. He had never experienced a more irritating sense of discontent, a more inconvenient malaise. Neither had he ever felt toward himself crueler impulses of anger and feelings of disgust. Sometimes, in some tired solitary moment, he felt bitterness rise up from his deepest innards, like sudden nausea; and he sat there mulling over it, troubled, without the strength to expel it, with a kind of dull resignation, like a sick person who has lost all faith in being healed and is inclined to live with his illness, to withdraw into his suffering, to sink down into his mortal misery. It seemed to him that once again the old leprosy was spreading through his soul and once again his heart was emptying out, never to fill up again, like a leather water sac that has been irreparably pierced. The sense of this emptiness, the certainty of this irreparability, sometimes moved him to a sort of desperate anger, and then to a crazy scorn of himself, of his willpower, of his last hopes, his last dreams. He had reached a terrible time, pursued by the inexorability of life, by the implacable passion of life; he had reached the supreme moment of salvation or of perdition, the decisive moment in which great hearts reveal all their strength and small hearts all their cowardice. He allowed himself to be overcome; he did not have the courage to save himself with any voluntary act; despite being in the grip of pain, he was afraid of a more virile pain; despite being tormented by disgust, he was afraid of giving up whatever disgusted him; even though he had the intense and ruthless instinct to detach himself from the things that most appeared to attract him, he was afraid to distance himself from such things. He allowed himself to be beaten down; he abdicated his will, his energy, his inner dignity, entirely and forever; he sacrificed forever whatever remained to him of faith and idealism. He threw himself into life, as into a great pointless adventure, seeking out pleasure, the opportunity, the moment of happiness, entrusting himself to destiny, to chance, to the fortuitous confusion of cause. However, while he believed with this kind of cynical fatalism that he was putting a check on suffering and achieving, if not calm, at least dullness, his sensitivity to pain became more acute, his ability to suffer multiplied; his needs and his disgusts increased without end. He was now experiencing the profound truth of the words he had said one day to Maria Ferres, in a moment of sentimental intimacy and melancholy: "Others are unhappier; but I don't know if there has been a man less happy than I, in the world." He was now experiencing the truth of those words said in a very sweet moment, when the illusion of a second youth and the prescience of a new life were illuminating his soul.

And yet, that day, talking to that person, he had been sincere as never before; he had expressed his thought with naiveté and candor, as never before. Why, in a flash, had everything dispersed, had everything vanished? Why had he not known how to nurture that flame in his heart? Why had he not been able to safeguard that memory and keep that faith? His law was hence mutability; his spirit had the inconsistency of fluid; everything in him was transforming and deforming, without respite; moral strength was completely lacking in him; his moral being was composed of contradictions; unity, simplicity, and spontaneity evaded him; through the tumult, the voice of duty no longer reached him; the voice of will was overpowered by that of the instincts; his conscience, like a star without any light of its own, at every stage was eclipsing itself.

It had always been so; it would always be so. Why, therefore, should he fight against himself? *Cui bono?*[1]

But this precise struggle was a necessity of his life; this precise restlessness was an essential condition of his existence; this precise suffering was a punishment from which he would never, ever be able to extract himself.

Any attempt at analyzing himself resulted in greater uncertainty, in greater obscurity. As he was completely unequipped with the ability to synthesize, his analysis became a cruel destructive game. And after an hour of reflection upon himself, he emerged confused, undone, desperate, lost.

When, on the morning of December 30, in Via de' Condotti, he unexpectedly encountered Elena Muti, he was filled with an inexpressible emotion, as if he were seeing some wondrous destiny come to pass, as if the reappearance of that woman in that exceedingly sad moment of his life occurred by virtue of predestination and she had been sent to him as a last aid, or to cause the final damage in his mysterious shipwreck. The first impulse of his soul was to join himself to her, to retake her, reconquer her, to repossess her entirely, as he had once done; to revive the old passion with all its elations and all its splendors. His first impulse was one of jubilation and hope. Then, without hesitation, diffidence, doubt, and jealousy arose; without hesitation, he was invaded by the certainty that no miracle would ever be able to resuscitate even a minimum part of the happiness that had died, or reproduce even one spark of the joy that had been extinguished, or even one shadow of the illusion that had vanished.

She had come! She had come! She had returned to the place where everything conserved a memory for her, and had said: "I am no longer yours; I can never be yours again." She had cried out at him: "Would you tolerate sharing my body with others?" She had really dared to shout those words at him, in that place, in front of all those things!

An atrocious, enormous pain, consisting of a thousand stings, each distinct from the other, and each more acute than the other, possessed him for some time and exasperated him. Passion enveloped him with a thousand fires, provoking an inextinguishable carnal ardor in him for that woman who was no longer his, reawakening in his memory all the tiniest details of those remote pleasures, the images of all the caresses and all her postures during pleasure, all the mad couplings that never sated or slaked their craving, which was constantly being reborn. And yet always, in all his imaginings, that strange difficulty persisted in matching up the Elena from then with the Elena of now. While the memories of possession inflamed and tortured him, the certainty of possession eluded him: the Elena of now seemed to him to be a new woman, never enjoyed, never held. His desire gave him such spasms of pain that he thought he would die of them. Impurity infected him like a toxin.

Impurity, which *then* the winged flame of the soul had veiled with a sacred veil, and surrounded with an almost divine mystery, now appeared without the veil, without the mystery of the flame, like an entirely carnal lust, like a base libido. And he felt that that ardor of his was not Love, and that it no longer had anything in common with Love. It was not Love. She had shouted at him: "Would you tolerate sharing my body with others?" Well, yes, he would have tolerated it!

He would have taken her, without repugnance, just as she came to him, contaminated by the embrace of another; he would have placed his caress on top of another man's caress; he would have pressed his kiss over another man's kiss.

Nothing more, nothing, therefore, remained intact in him. Even the memory of that great passion was becoming miserably corrupted, soiled, degraded, within him. The last flicker of hope had been dampened. Finally, he was touching the bottom, never to raise himself up again.

But now a terrible frenzy invaded him, to cast down the idol that yet remained before him, lofty and enigmatic. With a cynical cruelty he began to undermine it, to obscure it, to corrode it. This destructive analysis, which he had already experimented on himself, he now used on Elena. To all the doubting questions he had once wished to evade, he now sought an answer; of all the suspicions that had once appeared and dissipated without leaving a trace, he now studied the source, found justifications, and obtained confirmation. He believed he found relief in this wretched exercise of demolition; and increased his suffering, irritated his malaise, enlarged his blemishes.

What had been the real reason for Elena's departure, in March 1885? There had been many rumors in that period and at the time of her marriage to Humphrey Heathfield. There was only one truth. He had heard it from Giulio Musèllaro one evening, by chance, amid irrelevant chitchat, while coming out of the theater; and he did not doubt it. Donna Elena Muti had left for financial reasons, in order to conclude a "transaction" that would extract her from very serious pecuniary difficulties caused by her excessive extravagance. Marriage with Lord Heathfield had saved her from ruin. This Heathfield, Marquis of Mount Edgcumbe and Count of Bradford, possessed considerable wealth and was allied with the highest British nobility. Donna Elena had managed to settle her affairs with great acumen; she had been able to remove herself from peril with extraordinary skill. Certainly, her three years of widowhood did not appear to have been a chaste interval preparatory to her second marriage. Neither chaste nor cautious. But, without doubt, Donna Elena was a great woman . . .

—Ah, my dear chap, a great woman! repeated Giulio Musèllaro. —And you know it well.

Andrea remained silent.

—But I don't advise you to approach her again, added his friend, throwing away his cigarette, which had gone out between one piece of gossip and another. —Relighting a love affair is like relighting a cigarette. The tobacco becomes bitter; love, too. Shall we go and have a cup of tea with the Moceto woman? She told me that one can drop by after the theater: it is never too late.

They were outside Palazzetto Borghese.

—You go, said Andrea. —I'm going home, to sleep. Today's hunt tired me out somewhat. Say hello to Donna Giulia for me. *Comprends et prends.*[2]

Musèllaro went upstairs. Andrea continued down along the Fontanella de Borghese and Via Condotti, toward the Trinità. It was a cold and tranquil January night, one of those prodigious wintry nights that transform Rome into a silver city enclosed within a diamond sphere. The full moon, in mid-sky, poured out its triple purity of light, frost, and silence.

He walked under the moon like a somnambulist, conscious of

nothing but his pain. The last blow had been struck; the idol was crumbling; nothing else remained on the great ruins; everything thus was ending, forever. She had never loved him, therefore. Without hesitating, she had ended their love in order to rectify a financial problem. Without hesitating, she had contracted a marriage of convenience. Now, before him, she was putting on the air of a martyr, was wrapping herself in the veil of an inviolable bride! A bitter laugh rose up from deep down inside him; and then a dull rage stirred in him against the woman and blinded him. The memories of passion counted for nothing. Everything from that period seemed to him to be one great deceit, enormous and cruel, like one great lie; and this man who had made deceit and lies a habit in his life, this man who had deceived and lied so many times, felt, at the thought of other people's fraud, offended, scornful, disgusted, as by an unforgivable sin, as by an inexcusable, and also inexplicable, monstrosity. He could not manage to understand how Elena could have committed such an offense; and despite not understanding, could not concede her any justification, could not entertain the doubt that some other secret cause had pushed her to the sudden flight. He could see nothing but the brutal act, the baseness, the vulgarity: the vulgarity, above all—crude, overt, odious, not extenuated by any emergency. All in all, it amounted to this: a passion, which had seemed sincere and was sworn to be great and inextinguishable, had been interrupted by a commercial affair, a material benefit, a deal.

"Ingrate! Ingrate! What do you know about what happened, about what I suffered? What do you know?" Elena's words returned to his memory with precision; all her words, from the beginning to the end of the conversation held in front of the fireplace, returned to his memory: the words of tenderness, the offers of sisterhood, all those sentimental phrases. And he thought again of the tears that had veiled her eyes, the changing expression of her face, her trembling, her voice choked by her words of farewell when he had placed the bunch of roses on her lap. Why ever had she agreed to come to his house? Why had she decided to play that role, to provoke that scene, to plot that new drama or comedy? Why?

He had reached the top of the stairs in the deserted square.

The beauty of the night gave him, suddenly, a vague but anxious aspiration toward some unknown Good; the image of Donna Maria passed through his mind; his heart pounded strongly, as under the impetus of desire; he had the sudden thought of holding Donna Maria's hands in his, to rest his forehead against her heart and feel her console him wordlessly, mercifully. That need for pity, refuge, sympathy, was like the last piece of the soul that did not resign itself to perishing. He bowed his head and reentered the house, without turning to regard the night any longer.

Terenzio was waiting for him in the entrance, and followed him right into his bedroom, where the fire was lit. He asked:

—Will the Lord Count go to bed immediately?

—No, Terenzio. Bring me some tea, his master answered, sitting down in front of the fireplace and holding his hands out toward the flames.

He was trembling, a slight nervous tremor. He had uttered those words with a strange sweetness; he had called his servant by name; he had been familiar with him.[3]

—Is the Lord Count cold? asked Terenzio, with affectionate concern, encouraged by the benevolence of the master.

And he bent down over the andiron to stoke the fire, adding other pieces of wood. He was an old servant of the Sperelli household; he had served Andrea's father for many years; and his devotion toward the young man reached idolatry. No human being seemed more handsome, nobler, more sacred to him. He belonged, in truth, to that ideal race that provides faithful servants for adventure or sentimental novels. But unlike fictional servants, he spoke rarely, gave no advice, and devoted himself only to obeying.

—I'm fine, said Andrea, trying to overcome the convulsive trembling, drawing nearer to the fire.

The presence of the old man in that painful moment moved him in a singular way. It was an emotion partly similar to the weakness that overcomes men in the presence of a good person, before suicide. Never before, as he did now, had the old man stirred up thoughts of his father, memories of the dear dead man, sorrow for the great friend now lost. Never before, as he did now, had Andrea felt the need of familiar comfort, of the paternal voice and hand. What would his father have said if he had seen his son cast down in this horrible misery? How would he have consoled him? With what strength?

He thought about the dead man with immense regret. But within him there was not even the shadow of a suspicion that the distant cause of his misery was to be found in the early teachings of his father.

Terenzio brought the tea. Then he began to prepare the bed, slowly, with almost feminine care, emulating Jenny, forgetting nothing, seeming to want to ensure his master perfect repose, imperturbable sleep, until morning. Andrea watched him, noting every action with growing emotion, at the base of which there was also some indefinable sense of modesty. It pained him to see the goodness of that old man moving around the bed through which so many tainted love affairs had passed; it almost seemed to him that those senile hands were unconsciously stirring up all the impurities.

—Go to sleep, Terenzio, he said. —I don't need anything else.

He remained alone in front of the fireplace, alone with his soul, alone with his sadness. He got up, troubled by his inner torment, and began to pace around the room. He was pursued by the vision of Elena's head on the uncovered pillow on the bed. Each time, when he reached the window, he turned around, believing that he would see her; and he jumped. His nerves were so exhausted that they indulged every disorder of his imagination. The hallucination became more intense. He stopped and hid his face in his hands, to contain the agitation. Then he drew the cover up over the pillow and went to sit down again.

Another image rose up in his mind: Elena in the arms of her husband: yet again, with an inexorable precision.

He now knew this husband better. That same evening, at the theater, in a box, he had been introduced to him by Elena and had observed him attentively, in fine detail, with sharp inquiry, as if to achieve some revelation about him, as if to root out a secret from him. He still heard his voice, a voice with a notable timbre, somewhat shrill, with a questioning tone at the beginning of every sentence; and he still saw those pale eyes beneath the great convex forehead, those eyes that at times had the dead glints of glass or became animated with an indefinable gleam, somewhat similar to the eyes of a maniac. And he also saw those moist whitish hands, strewn with pale blond fuzz, which had something immodest in every movement, whether picking up his binoculars, unfolding his handkerchief, resting on the sill of the box, leafing through the libretto of the opera, in every movement: hands marked by vice, *sadistic* hands, because certain characters of the Marquis de Sade's must have hands like those.

He saw those hands touch Elena's nakedness, contaminating the beautiful body, attempting a curious lasciviousness . . . Oh, horror!

The torture was unbearable. He rose to his feet again; went to the window, opened it, shivered in the cold air, shook himself. The Trinità de' Monti shone in the azure light with clean lines, as if carved into marble ever so slightly tinged with rose. Rome, down below, had a crystalline glitter, like a city carved out of a glacier.

That frozen, precise quietness brought his mind back to reality and gave him true consciousness of his state. He closed the window again and went to sit down once more. The enigma of Elena still attracted him; questions arose in a tumult and harried him. But he had the strength to place them in order, to coordinate them, examine them one by one, with strange lucidity. The further he progressed in his analysis, the more lucidity he acquired; and he enjoyed that cruel psychology as he would a vendetta. At last, he seemed to have bared a soul, to have penetrated a mystery. It seemed to him, at last, to possess Elena deeper within than he ever had during the time of ecstasy.

Whoever was she?

She was an unbalanced spirit in a voluptuary body. Like all beings who are greedy for pleasure, she had at the base of her moral constitution a boundless egoism. Her chief skill, her intellectual *axis,* so to speak, was her imagination: a romantic imagination, nourished by diverse readings, deriving directly from her womb, constantly stimulated by hysteria. Possessing a certain intelligence and having been educated amid the luxury of a princely Roman household, in that papal luxury consisting of art and history, she had veiled herself with a vague aesthetic dusting, had acquired an elegant taste; and having also understood the nature of her beauty, she sought, with extremely subtle simulations and a masterly talent for mimicry, to increase its spirituality, radiating an insidious light of the ideal.

She hence brought very dangerous elements to the human comedy; and was cause for more devastation and pandemonium than if she had made a public profession of immodesty.

Beneath the ardor of her imagination, every whim of hers took on a sentimental appearance. She was a woman of sudden passions, unexpected conflagrations. She concealed the erotic needs of her flesh with ethereal flames and could transform a base appetite into high sentiment . . .

Thus, in this way, with this ferocity, Andrea judged the woman he had once adored. He proceeded in his ruthless examination without pausing at any of the most intense memories. At the base of every act, in every manifestation of Elena's love, he found cunning, design, skill, an admirable self-confidence in implementing a theme of fantasy, in acting a dramatic role, in arranging an extraordinary scene. He did not leave untouched any of the most memorable episodes: the first encounter at dinner at the Ateleta house, Cardinal Immenraet's auction, the ball at the French Embassy, her sudden surrender in the red room at Palazzo Barberini, nor the farewell on Via Nomentana in the March sunset. That magical wine which once had intoxicated him now seemed to him a perfidious potion.

All the same, in some respects, he was perplexed as if, penetrating into the woman's soul, he was penetrating into his own soul and recognizing his own falsity in her falsity; such was the affinity of their two natures. And little by little his scorn evolved into an ironic indulgence, because he *understood*. He understood everything that he found within himself.

Then, with cold clarity, he defined his comprehension.

All the details of the conversation that had taken place on New Year's Eve, more than a week before, all returned to his memory; and he took pleasure in reconstructing the scene, with a kind of cynical inner smile, without any more scorn, without any agitation, smiling at Elena, smiling at himself. Why had she come? She had come because that unexpected meeting with an old lover, in a familiar place, after two years, had seemed *unusual* to her, had tempted her spirit, which was avid for rare emotions, had tempted her fantasy and her curiosity. Now she wanted to see what new situations and new combinations of facts this singular game would bring her to. Perhaps she was drawn by the novelty of a platonic affair with the same person who had already been the object of a sensual passion. As always, she had given herself over to imagining such a sentiment with a certain ardor; and perhaps, too, she had believed she was being sincere, and from that imagined sincerity she had drawn those tones of profound tenderness and the sorrowful poses and the tears. A phenomenon was occurring in her that was very familiar to him. She went so far as to believe that a fictitious and fleeting movement of the soul was genuine and momentous; she had, so to say, a sentimental hallucination the way others have a physical hallucination. She lost consciousness of her lie; and she no longer knew whether the situation she was in was true or false, fictional or sincere.

Now, at this point, it was the same moral phenomenon that constantly repeated itself in him. In fairness, therefore, he could not point any fingers at her. But naturally, this discovery deprived him of all hope of any pleasure that was not carnal. By now, suspicion was impeding any pleasant abandon, any spiritual elation. Deceiving a good and faithful woman, warming oneself at a great flame stirred up with a fallacious dazzle, dominating a soul with trickery, possessing her completely and making her vibrate like a musical instrument, *habere non haberi*, may be a great delight. But to deceive knowing that one is being deceived is a foolish and sterile effort; it is a boring and futile game.

He wanted, therefore, to persuade Elena to give up the idea of fraternizing with him and to return to his arms, where she once had been. He had to regain the material possession of the beautiful woman, to extract from her beauty the greatest possible enjoyment, and hence, by sating himself on it, to free himself from it forever. But in this task it was necessary to exercise prudence and patience. Already in their first conversation, his violent ardor had proved to be a bad move. It seemed clear that she founded her project of impeccability on the famous phrase "Would you tolerate sharing my body with others?" The great Platonic mechanism was driven by this saintly horror of promiscuity. It was also possible that deep down, this horror was sincere. Almost all women who have led an amorous life, if they succeed in marrying, affect in the early days of marriage a ferocious purity and cast themselves in the role of chaste wives with good intentions. It was also therefore possible that Elena was subject to this common scruple. There could hence be nothing worse than confronting her head-on and openly jarring her newfound virtue. Rather, it would be better to support her in her spiritual aspirations, accept her as "the dearest sister, the sweetest friend," exalt her with ideals, Platonizing with shrewdness; and little by little to lure her from a chaste sisterly relationship to a sensuous friendship, and from a sensuous friendship to the total surrender of the body. Probably, these transitions would be extremely rapid. Everything depended on circumstance . . .

Thus cogitated Andrea Sperelli, seated in front of the fireplace that had cast its light upon his naked lover Elena, wrapped in the zodiacal quilt, laughing amid the scattered roses. And he was pervaded by an immense tiredness, a tiredness that did not demand sleep, a tiredness so empty and disconsolate that it almost seemed a need to die; while the fire dwindled on the andiron and his drink grew cold in the cup.

Over the following days, he waited in vain for the promised note. "I will send you a note to tell you when I can see you." Elena therefore intended to arrange a new rendezvous. But where? At Palazzo Zuccari again? Would she commit a second reckless act? The uncertainty gave him unspeakable torment. He spent all his time thinking up some way to meet her, to see her. More than once he went to the Albergo del Quirinale, hoping to be received, but never found her home. He saw her one evening with her husband, Mumps, as she called him, again at the theater. Speaking of trivial things, music, singers, ladies, he injected a pleading sadness into his expression. She displayed much concern about her apartment: she was returning to Palazzo Barberini, to her old quarters, which had now been amplified; she spent all her time with decorators, giving orders and organizing.

—Will you be staying in Rome for a while? Andrea asked her.

—Yes, she answered. —Rome will be our winter residence.

Shortly after that, she added:

—You, truly, could give us some advice about the décor. Come to the palazzo one of these mornings. I'm always there between ten and noon.

He took advantage of a moment in which Lord Heathfield was talking to Giulio Musèllaro, who had just then arrived at the theater box; and he asked her, looking her in the eyes:

—Tomorrow?

She answered, simply, as if she had not heeded the tone of the question:

—So much the better.

The following morning, toward eleven, he walked along Via Sistina, through Piazza Barberini, and up the hill. It was a well-known walk. He seemed to be feeling the same sensations he had once felt; he had a momentary illusion: his heart lifted. The Bernini Fountain was sparkling in the sun in a most particular way, as if the dolphins, the scallop shells, and the Triton had become more translucent, neither stone nor crystal, as if by some interrupted metamorphosis. The industrious activity of new Rome filled the entire square and nearby roads with noise. Small boys from Ciociaria[4] darted among the carts and the horses, offering violets for sale.

When he passed through the gate and entered the garden, feeling a tremor seize him, he thought:—But do I still *love her*? Do I still *dream* about *her*?—It seemed to him that the tremor was the one he used to feel in the past. He looked at the great luminous building and his spirit flew to the time when that residence, in certain cold misty dawns, took on an air of enchantment for him. It was at the very beginning of the happy time: he would leave warm with kisses, filled with recent joy; the bells of Trinità de' Monti, of Sant'Isidoro, of the Capuchins[5] were tolling the *Angelus* in the dusk, indistinctly, as if they were much farther away; at the corner of the road, fires burned red around the asphalt boilers; a flock of goats stood along the grubby white wall, next to a silent house; the weak shouts of the liqueur hawkers[6] disappeared into the mist . . .

He felt those forgotten sensations rise up again from deep down; for a moment, he felt a wave of the old love pass through his soul; for a moment, he tried to imagine that Elena was the Elena of old and that the sad things were not real and that the happiness was continuing. All this deceptive turmoil fell away as soon as he crossed the threshold and saw the Marquis of Mount Edgcumbe coming toward him, smiling that shrewd, slightly ambiguous smile of his.

Then the torment began.

Elena appeared, and held her hand out to him very cordially, in front of her husband, saying:

—Good man, Andrea! Help us, help us!

She was very vivacious in her words and in her gestures. She had a very youthful air. She wore a jacket made of a deep blue fabric, trimmed with black astrakhan on the edges, on the straight collar, and on the cuffs; and a woolen cord formed an elegant embroidered pattern, interwoven over the astrakhan. She held one hand in her pocket in a graceful posture; and with the other, pointed out the installation of the hangings in progress, the furniture, the paintings. She was asking for advice.

—Where would you place these two chests? Look: Mumps found them in Lucca. The paintings are by *your* Botticelli. Where would you place these tapestries?

Andrea recognized the four wall-hangings depicting the story of Narcissus that had been at Cardinal Immenraet's auction. He looked at Elena, but did not meet her eyes. A veiled irritation gripped him, at her, at her husband, at those objects. He would have liked to leave; but it was necessary for him to place his good taste at the service of the Heathfield couple; it was also necessary for him to suffer the archaeological erudition of Mumps, who was an ardent collector and insisted on showing him some of his collections. He recognized a helmet by Pollajuolo in one display cabinet, and in another, the rock crystal chalice that had belonged to Niccolò Niccoli. The presence of that goblet in that place agitated him strangely and caused mad suspicions to flash to his mind. Had it, then, fallen into the hands of Lord Heathfield? After the famous quarrel, which had not been resolved, no one had paid heed to the heirloom, no one had returned to the sale the day after; the ephemeral excitement had languished, died out, and dissipated as everything dissipates in worldly life; and the crystal had remained, in contrast with other things. It was a very natural thing, but at that moment it seemed extraordinary to Andrea.

Deliberately, he stopped in front of the cabinet and examined at length the precious goblet on which the story of Anchises and Venus scintillated as if it had been carved into pure diamond.

—Niccolò Niccoli, said Elena, pronounced with an indefinable tone, in which the young man believed he could hear a little sadness.

Her husband had passed into the adjacent room to open an armory cabinet.

—Remember! Remember! murmured Andrea, turning.

—I remember.

—When will I see you, then?

—Who knows!

—You promised . . .

Mount Edgcumbe reappeared. They passed into the next room, going on with the tour. Everywhere, decorators were busy hanging wallpaper, lifting curtains, transporting furniture. Every time the woman asked him for advice, Andrea had to make an effort to answer, to overcome his unwillingness, to control his impatience. During a moment when the husband was talking to one of the men, he said to her in a low voice, showing his vexation clearly:

—Why cause me this torment? I was hoping to find you alone.

While she was passing through a doorway, Elena's little hat bumped against a badly hung curtain and was dented along one side. Laughing, she called to Mumps to undo the knot of her veil. And Andrea saw those odious hands untying the knot on the nape of the woman he desired, brushing against the small black curls, those living curls that once had emitted a mysterious scent under his kisses, not comparable to any known perfumes, but sweeter than any others, more intoxicating than any others.

Without delay he said good-bye, claiming that he was being awaited for lunch.

—We will move in permanently on the first of February, on Tuesday, Elena said to him. —Thereafter you will be, I hope, a regular visitor of ours.

Andrea bowed.

He would have given anything not to touch Lord Heathfield's hand. He went away full of rancor, jealousy, disgust.

Later the same evening, finding himself by chance at the club, where he had not been for a long time, he saw Don Manuel Ferres y Capdevila, the minister of Guatemala, seated at a gaming table. He greeted him solicitously; asked him news of Donna Maria, of Delfina.

—Are they still in Siena? When are they coming?

The minister, mindful of having won a few thousand lire playing cards with the young count on the last night at Schifanoja, responded to the solicitousness with great courtesy. He had found Andrea Sperelli to be an admirable player, perfect, with superb style.

—They've both been here for a few days. They arrived on Monday. Maria is very sorry not to have found the Marchioness of Ateleta in town. I think that a visit from you would be very much appreciated by her. We are staying in Via Nazionale. Here is the exact address.

He gave him one of his cards. Then he turned back to his card game. Andrea heard his name being called by the Duke of Beffi, who was in a group with other gentlemen.

—Why didn't you come to Centocelle[7] this morning? the duke asked him.

—I had another engagement, Andrea replied, without thinking, just as an excuse.

The duke began to snigger in chorus with the other friends.

—At Palazzo Barberini?

—Perhaps.

—Perhaps? Ludovico saw you going in.

—And where were you? Andrea asked Barbarisi.

—At my aunt Saviano's.

—Ah!

—I don't know if you had a better hunt—continued the Duke of Beffi—but we had a fast gallop of forty-two minutes and two foxes. Thursday, at the Three Fountains.

—Do you understand? Not at the Four Fountains . . . Gino Bommìnaco warned, with his usual comic gravity.[8]

The friends laughed at the witticism; and the laughter also spread to Sperelli. He did not mind that malice. Rather, precisely now that there was no foundation to it, he enjoyed the fact that his friends believed his relationship with Elena Muti to be renewed. He turned to talk with Giulio Musèllaro, who had arrived. From some words he overheard, he realized that they were talking about Lord Heathfield in the group.

—I met him in London six or seven years ago, the Duke of Beffi was saying. —He was Lord of the Bedchamber of the Prince of Wales, I think . . .

Then his voice was lowered. The duke must be recounting outrageous things. Andrea heard, two or three times, amid fragments of erotic phrases, the title of a newspaper famous in the history of London scandals: *Pall Mall Gazette*. He would have liked to listen: a terrible curiosity invaded him. He once again saw in his mind's eye Lord Heathfield's hands, those pale hands, so expressive, so significant, so revealing, unforgettable. But Musèllaro was continuing to talk. Musèllaro said to him:

—Let's go. I'll tell you about it . . .

Going down the stairs they met Count Albónico, who was coming up. He was dressed in mourning due to the death of Donna Ippolita. Andrea stopped: he asked him some details regarding the sorrowful event. He had heard about the misfortune in November, in Paris, from Guido Montelatici, Donna Ippolita's cousin.

—But was it typhus?

The fair, pale widower took advantage of the opportunity to pour out his grief. He wore his heartache as a sign of distinction, the way he had once worn his wife's beauty. His stutter made his afflicted words even more wretched: and it seemed that his pale eyes were about to deflate, like two blisters full of serum, at any moment.

Giulio Musèllaro, seeing that the widower's plaintive lament was going on a little too long, urged Andrea to hurry, saying:

—Listen, they're waiting for us.

Andrea took his leave, adjourning the continuation of the commemoration of the dead to their next meeting. And he left the building with his friend.

Albónico's words had revived that strange feeling, a combination of a tormenting desire and a kind of complacence, which had preoccupied him for a few days in Paris after the news of the death. In that period, the image of Donna Ippolita, almost shrouded in oblivion, had appeared to him, through the time of his sickness and convalescence, through so many other events, through the love for Donna Maria Ferres, very distant but shrouded in a vague ideality. He had obtained her consent; and, although he had not succeeded in possessing her, he had derived from this one of the greatest human elations: the euphoria of victory over a rival, a sensational victory, in the presence of the desired woman. In those days, the desire he had not managed to satisfy had been roused again; and beneath the dominion of his imagination, the impossibility of satisfying it had given him an unspeakable restlessness, several hours of real torment. Then, between desire and regret another sentiment was born, almost of complacency, perhaps almost of lyrical elevation. It pleased him that his affair had ended in such a way, forever. He had almost been killed in acquiring her, that almost unknown woman he had not possessed, and now she rose up, unique and intact, at the uppermost pinnacle of his spirit, in the divine ideality of death. *Tibi, Hippolyta, semper!*

—So—Giulio Musèllaro was recounting—she came today, toward two p.m.

He was relating the surrender of Giulia Moceto with a certain enthusiasm, with many details regarding the rare and secret beauty of the infertile Pandora.

—You're right. It is an ivory cup, a radiant shield, *speculum voluptatis*.

Andrea felt once again a particular light sting he had felt a few days before, in the moonlit night after the theater, when his friend had gone up alone to Palazzetto Borghese. It now evolved into an ill-defined resentment, at the base of which broiled, mingled with memories, jealousy, envy, and that supreme egoistical and tyrannical intolerance that were in his nature and that often pushed him to desire, almost, the destruction of a woman he had already favored and enjoyed, so that she could never be enjoyed by any others. No one should drink from the glass where he had once drunk. The memory of his passage should be sufficient to fill an entire life. His lovers must remain eternally faithful to his infidelity. This was his secret proud dream. And in addition, he disliked the broadcasting, the divulgence of a secret beauty. Certainly, if he had possessed Myron's *Discobulos* or Polyclitus's *Doryphoros* or the Cnidian *Venus*, his first concern would have been to lock the masterpiece in an inaccessible place and enjoy it alone, so that the enjoyment of others could not diminish his own. And so why had he himself rushed to disclose the secret? Why had he himself piqued the curiosity of his friend? Why had he himself wished him luck? The ease with which that woman had given herself to Giulio provoked anger and disgust in Andrea, and also humiliated him somewhat.

—But where are we going? asked Giulio Musèllaro, stopping in Piazza di Venezia.

At the base of the various emotions in his soul and his various thoughts, Andrea still felt the agitation aroused in him by the encounter with Don Manuel Ferres, and the thought of Donna Maria, a flashing thought. And indeed, amid those fleeting contrasts, a sort of anxiety was drawing him toward her house.

—I'm going home, he replied. —Let's go along Via Nazionale. Walk with me.

From that point, he did not listen to the words his friend spoke. The thought of Donna Maria dominated him completely. When he arrived in front of the theater he had a moment of hesitation, not knowing whether to choose the sidewalk on the right or the one on the left. He wanted to find the house by reading the numbers on the doors.

—But what is going on with you? Musèllaro asked him.

—Nothing. I'm listening to you.

He looked at the number and calculated that the house must be on the left, not very far off, perhaps in the vicinity of Villa Aldobrandini. The great pine trees of the villa could be seen, delicate in the starry sky, because the night was freezing but serene; the Tower of the Milices rose up, square and massive, dark among the stars; the palm trees that grew along the Servian Wall appeared to be sleeping, immobile, in the brightness of the headlamps.

Only a few numbers remained until he reached the one marked on Don Manuel's card. Andrea was as anxious as if Donna Maria were about to walk toward him. The house was nearby, in fact. He passed the closed front door, almost brushing against it; he could not stop himself from glancing up.

—But what are you looking at? Musèllaro asked him.

—Nothing. Give me a cigarette. Let's walk faster, it's cold.

They walked along Via Nazionale as far as the Four Fountains in silence. Andrea's preoccupation was evident. His friend said:

—You certainly have something that's bothering you.

And Andrea's heart felt so swollen that he was on the point of giving in and confiding. But he restrained himself. He was still feeling troubled by the malicious things he'd heard at the club, by Giulio's story, by all those indiscreet frivolities he himself had provoked, frivolities he had professed himself. The complete lack of mystery in the affair, the vain complacency of lovers in receiving the witticisms and smiles of others, the cynical indifference with which erstwhile lovers praise the qualities of a woman to those who are just about to enjoy them, and the affectation with which the former give advice to the latter so that they may reach their objective more easily, and the concern with which the latter give the former the most finely detailed reports regarding a first rendezvous, in order to know whether the *manner* in which the lady gave herself could be compared with the one in which she gave herself on other occasions, and the cessions, and the concessions, and the successions, and in short all the small and great depravities that accompany sweet society adulteries, seemed to him to reduce love to a banal and dirty promiscuity, an ignoble vulgarity, a prostitution without name. The memories of Schifanoja traversed his mind, like cordial scents. The image of Donna Maria shone inside him with such intensity that he was almost astonished by it; and he saw one attitude distinct from all the others, more luminous than all the others: her attitude when she had uttered the burning word in the woods at Vicomìle. Would he hear that word from that mouth again? What had she done, what had she thought, how had she lived during the time they were apart? His internal agitation grew with every step. Fragments of visions passed through his mind like mobile and fleeting phantasmagorias: a strip of countryside, a strip of sea, a flight of stairs amid rosebushes, the interior of a room, all the places in which a feeling had been born, where sweetness had been diffused, where she had transmitted the allure of her presence. And he felt an intimate and profound tremor thinking that perhaps passion still lived in her heart, that perhaps she had suffered and cried, and perhaps even dreamed and hoped. Who knows!

—Well? said Giulio Musèllaro. —How are things going with Lady Heathfield?

They were walking down the Four Fountains road and were in front of Palazzo Barberini. Through the gates, between the great marble statues, the dark garden was visible, enlivened by a faint murmur of water, dominated by the gleaming building where only the portico was still illuminated.

—What did you say? said Andrea.

—How are things going with Donna Elena?

Andrea looked at the mansion. At that moment it seemed to him that he felt a great indifference in his heart, the true death of desire, the final renunciation; and he came up with an arbitrary answer.

—I'm following your advice. I'm not relighting the cigarette . . .

—And yet, see, maybe this time it would be worth the trouble. Have you looked at her properly? She seems more beautiful to me; I don't know, she seems to have something new, inexpressible about her . . . Maybe I'm wrong in saying *new.* It's as if she's become more intense, preserving all her characteristic beauty; and, well, I'll put it like this, *more Elena* than the Elena of two or three years ago: "the quintessence." Perhaps it is the effect of her second spring; since, I believe, she's very nearly thirty. Don't you think so?

These words stung Andrea, and inflamed him once more. Nothing can revive and exasperate a man's desire as much as hearing other men praise a woman he has possessed for too long, or for whom he has yearned, in vain, for too long. There are dying love affairs that still drag on due to the envy or the admiration of others; since the repulsed or tired lover is afraid of giving up his possession or his siege in favor of the happiness of whoever might succeed him.

—Don't you think so? And, making a Menelaus[9] out of that Heathfield must be an extraordinary delight.

—I think so, too, said Andrea, making an effort to imitate his friend's frivolous tone. —We'll see.

CHAPTER III

—Maria, let this moment keep its sweetness, let me express my thought fully!

She stood up. She said softly, without indignation, without severity, with evident emotion in her voice:

—Forgive me. I cannot listen to you. You are causing me a lot of pain.

—I'll keep quiet. Stay, Maria, I beg you.

She sat down again. She was the same as she had been at Schifanoja. Nothing surpassed the grace of her delicate head, which seemed to be afflicted by the great mass of hair, like a divine punishment. A soft, tender shadow, similar to the fusion of two diaphanous hues, of a perfect violet and blue, surrounded her eyes, with their tawny irises like those of dark angels.

—I only wanted—added Andrea humbly—I only wanted to remind you of the words I once spoke, the ones you heard one morning in the park, on the marble bench under the arbutus trees, a time that is unforgettable for me, and almost sacred in my memory . . .

—I remember them.

—Well, Maria, since that moment my misery has become more abject, gloomier, crueler. I will never be able to tell you about all my suffering, all my desolation; I can never tell you how many times my soul has cried out for you, believing I was going to die; I can never describe to you the shiver of joy, the upliftment of my entire being toward hope, if for a moment I dared to think that the memory of me still lived, perhaps, in your heart.

He was speaking in the same tone as on that distant morning;

he seemed to be in the grip, once more, of that same sentimental elation. All his sadness once again rose to his lips. And she listened, her head bowed, immobile, almost in the same position as that other time; and her mouth, the expression of her mouth, violently pressed shut, in vain, like that other time, betrayed a sort of sorrowful lust.

—Do you remember Vicomìle? Do you remember the forest, in that October evening, when we were riding through it on our own?

Donna Maria nodded slightly.

—And the word that you said to me? the young man added, more softly, but with an intense expression of contained passion in his voice, leaning toward her closely as if trying to look into her eyes, which she still kept lowered.

She raised them, those good, merciful, sorrowing eyes, to him.

—I remember everything—she answered—everything, everything. Why should I hide my soul from you? You are a noble and great spirit; and I have faith in your generosity. Why should I behave toward you like a vulgar woman? That evening, didn't I tell you that I loved you? I perceive another question in your question. You are asking me if I still love you.

She hesitated for a moment. Her lips were trembling.

—I love you.

—Maria!

—But you must renounce my love forever; you must go away from me; you must be noble and great, and generous, by sparing me a struggle that scares me. I have suffered greatly, Andrea, and I have borne this suffering; but the thought of having to fight against you, to have to defend myself against you, causes me mad fear. You don't know what sacrifices it cost me to manage to achieve peace in my heart; you don't know what high and dear ideals I renounced . . . Poor ideals! I have become another woman, because it was necessary for me to become another; I became a common woman, because this is what my duty required.

She had a grave and gentle sadness in her voice.

—When I met you, I suddenly felt all my old dreams rise up in me again; I felt my old soul revive; and during the first few days I abandoned myself to the pleasure, closing my eyes to the distant danger. I thought: "He will never know anything from my mouth; I will never know anything from his." I was almost without regret, almost without fear. But you spoke; you said words to me that I had never heard; you wrested a confession from me . . . The danger appeared to me, certain, overt, manifest. And all the same, I surrendered myself to a dream. Your anguish pressurized me, it caused me deep pain. I thought: "He has been tainted by the impure; if only I were enough to purify him! I would be happy to be the holocaust of his purification." Your sadness attracted my sadness. It seemed to me that I would never be able to console you, but that perhaps you would feel some relief hearing a soul eternally answering *amen* to the volition of your pain.

She uttered these last words with such spiritual elevation in her entire body, that Andrea was invaded by a wave of almost mystical joy; and his only desire at that moment was to take both her hands and breathe his ineffable rapture onto those dear delicate immaculate hands.

—It's not possible! It's not possible! she continued, shaking her head in regret. —We must renounce any hopes forever. Life is implacable. Without wishing it, you would destroy an entire existence, and maybe not only one . . .

—Maria, Maria, don't say these things! the young man interrupted, once more leaning toward her, taking her hand, without impetuosity, but with a kind of beseeching trepidation as if before carrying out the act he were waiting for a sign of consent. —I will do what you wish; I will be humble and obedient; my only aspiration is to obey you; my only desire is to die in your name. To renounce you is to renounce salvation, to fall back into ruin forever, never to get up again. I love you more than any human word will ever be able to express. I need you. You alone are *true;* you are the Truth that my spirit is seeking. The rest is futile; the rest is nothing. To renounce you would be like entering into death. But if sacrificing me serves to keep peace for you, I owe you this sacrifice. Don't be afraid, Maria. I won't do you any harm.

He held her hand in his, but without placing any pressure on it. His words were not ardent, but were subdued, disheartened, sorrowful, filled with immense prostration. And his piteousness deceived Maria to such an extent that she did not withdraw her hand and she surrendered for a few minutes to the pure pleasure of that light contact. There was such a subtle sensual delight within her that it almost appeared not to have any organic effect; it was as if an essential fluid were flowing out of her innermost heart and down her arm, into her fingers and spreading beyond her fingers with a vaguely harmonious wave. When Andrea fell silent, certain words he had spoken in the park on that unforgettable morning returned to her memory, reawakened by the recent sound of his voice, driven by the new emotion: "Your visible presence alone was enough to intoxicate me. I felt it flow in my veins like blood, and invade my spirit, like a superhuman sentiment . . ."

An interval of silence followed. One heard, now and then, the wind shaking the windowpanes. A distant noise was carried to them by the wind, mingled with the rumbling of coaches. Light entered, as cold and clear as springwater; shadows were gathering in the corners and between the curtains made of fabrics from the Far East; here and there incrustations of jade, ivory, and mother-of-pearl glittered on the furniture; a large gilded Buddha could be seen in the background, beneath a *Musa paradisiaca* palm.[1] Those exotic forms lent the room some of their mystery.

—What are you thinking now? asked Andrea. —You aren't thinking of my demise?

She seemed to be engrossed in doubtful thought. She was, in appearance, irresolute, as if she were listening to two inner voices.

—I can't describe to you—she answered, passing her hand over her forehead with a light gesture—I can't describe to you the strange foreboding that has been weighing me down for a long time. I don't know why, but I *am afraid*.

She added, after a pause:

—To think that you are suffering, that you are ill, my poor friend, and that I cannot alleviate your pain, that I am absent in your moment of anguish, that I will not know if you are calling me . . . My God!

She had a tremor and a weakness in her voice, almost as if she were crying, as if her throat had closed up. Andrea kept his head lowered, in silence.

—To think that my soul will always follow you, always, and that it will never be able to mingle with yours, will never be able to be understood by you . . . Poor love!

Her voice was full of tears, her mouth twisted in pain.

—Don't abandon me! Don't abandon me! the young man burst out, taking both her hands, almost kneeling down, prey to a great exaltation. —I don't ask anything of you; I want nothing from you but compassion. The compassion that comes to me from you would be dearer than the passion of any other woman: you know that. Only your hands can heal me, can lead me back to life, lift me up from baseness, give me back my faith, free me from all the bad things that infect me and fill me with horror. Dear, dear hands . . .

He bent over to kiss them, and held his mouth pressed to them. He half closed his eyes, in an attitude of supreme bliss, while saying softly in an indefinable tone:

—I can feel you trembling.

She raised herself to her feet, trembling, bewildered, paler than when, on that memorable morning, they were walking beneath the flowers. The wind shook the windowpanes; a noise resembling a mutinous crowd could be heard. Those shouts carried in the wind coming from the Quirinal Palace[2] increased her agitation.

—Good-bye. Please, Andrea; don't stay here any longer; you will see me another time, when you like. But for now, good-bye. Please!

—Where will I see you?

—At the concert tomorrow. Good-bye.

She was completely distressed, as if she had committed a sin. She accompanied him to the door of the room. When she was alone, she hesitated, not knowing what to do, still gripped by dismay. She could feel her cheeks and temples and the area around her eyes burning with an intense heat, while the rest of her body was shivering; but on her hands the impression of the beloved mouth remained like a seal, and it was an exquisite impression, and she would have liked it to be indelible, like the Seal of God.

She looked around her. In the room the light was diminishing; forms were disappearing in the half-light; the large Buddha held a singular brightness in its gilding. Now and then the shouts could be heard. She went toward a window, opened it, and leaned out. A freezing wind blew over the street, on which the streetlamps were already beginning to be lit toward Piazza di Termini. Opposite, the trees of Villa Aldobrandini stretched skyward, barely tinged with a reddish reflection. A huge purple cloud hung over the Tower of the Milices, alone in the sky.

The evening seemed gloomy to her. She drew back and went to sit down in the same place as she had during the recent conversation. Why had Delfina not yet returned? She would have liked to avoid every reflection, every meditation; and yet some strange weakness kept her in that place where a few minutes before, Andrea had breathed, spoken, exhaled his love and his pain. All the efforts, the intentions, the compulsions, the prayers, the penitence of four months were dispersing, becoming undone, becoming useless, in a brief moment. She was lapsing, feeling perhaps more tired, more defeated, without volition and without power against the moral phenomena that were taking her by surprise, against the sensations that were upsetting her; and while she was surrendering to the anguish and the listlessness of a conscience in which all courage was failing, it seemed to her that something of *him* was floating in the shadow of the room and enveloping her entire body, with an infinitely gentle caress.

And the day after, she went up to Palazzo dei Sabini with her heart pounding beneath a bunch of violets.

Andrea was already waiting for her at the door of the hall. Pressing her hand, he said to her:

—Thank you.

He led her to a seat and sat down beside her. He said to her:

—I thought I would die waiting for you. I was afraid you would not come. How grateful I am to you!

He said to her:

—Late yesterday evening I passed by your house. I saw a light in a window, in the third window toward the Quirinal Palace. I don't know what I would have given, to know if you were there . . .

He also asked her:

—Who gave you those violets?

—Delfina, she answered.

—Did Delfina tell you about our encounter this morning in Piazza di Spagna?

—Yes, everything.

The concert began with a quartet by Mendelssohn. The hall was already almost completely full. The audience comprised mostly foreign women; and it was a blond audience, full of modesty in dress, full of concentration, silent and religious as in a place of piety. The wave of music passed over the immobile heads covered by dark hats, expanding into golden light, light that poured down from above, softened by the yellow curtains, made brighter by the blank white walls. And the old unadorned hall of the Philharmonic Society, in which faint traces of a frieze remained on the uniform whiteness and where the shabby blue door curtains were about to fall down, resembled a place that had been closed for a century and had been reopened just that day. But that color of old age, that air of poverty, that blankness of the walls, added some strange note to the exquisite delight of the audience; and the delight seemed more secret, more exalted, purer, in that place, because of the contrast. It was February 2, a Wednesday: in Montecitorio,[3] Parliament was debating the Dogali case;[4] the roads and nearby squares were swarming with populace and soldiers.

The musical memories of Schifanoja rose up in the minds of the two lovers; a reflection of that autumn illuminated their thoughts. The sound of Mendelssohn's minuet called forth visions of the seaside villa, the sitting room scented by the gardens below, from which one could see, between the columns of the vestibule and the pointed tips of the cypresses, flame-red sails atop a strip of calm sea.

Now and then Andrea, leaning toward the Sienese woman, asked her softly:

—What are you thinking about?

—She answered with such a faint smile that he could barely perceive it.

—Do you remember the twenty-third of September? she said.

Andrea did not distinctly recall that memory, but he nodded.

The calm and solemn andante, dominated by a distinct melody of pathos, was composed of extensive developments followed by a burst of sorrow. The finale was characterized by an insistent rhythmic monotony, full of tiredness.

She said:

—Now it's the turn of your Bach.

And both, when the music began, felt an instinctive need to draw closer to each other. Their elbows touched. At the end of every movement, Andrea leaned toward her to read the program that she held unfolded in her hands; and in the act, he pressed against her arm, smelling the scent of the violets, and transmitted a shiver of delight to her. The adagio had such a compelling elevation of melody, and rose with such soaring flight to the summits of ecstasy, and expanded into Infinity with such complete assurance, that it seemed to be the voice of a superhuman creature, pouring its rejoicing at an immortal conquest into the rhythm. All spirits present were swept along by the irresistible wave. When the music ended, the quivering of the instruments lasted for a few minutes in the auditorium. A whisper circulated from one end of the hall to the other. Applause broke out, after the delay, more intensely.

The two looked at each other with transfigured eyes, as if they were drawing apart after an unbearably pleasurable sexual embrace. The music was continuing; the light in the hall was becoming more unobtrusive; a pleasant warmth softened the air; in this warmth, Donna Maria's violets emanated a stronger scent. Andrea almost had the illusion of being *alone* with her, because he could not see anyone he knew in front of him.

But he was wrong. During an interval, turning around, he saw Elena Muti standing at the back of the hall, together with the Princess of Ferentino. His eyes immediately met hers. He greeted her, from afar. It seemed to him that he could discern a peculiar smile on Elena's lips.

—Who are you greeting? asked Donna Maria, also turning around. —Who are those ladies?

—Lady Heathfield and the Princess of Ferentino.

She thought she could hear a troubled note in his voice.

—Which is the Princess of Ferentino?

—The blonde.

—The other one is very beautiful.

Andrea remained silent.

—But is she English? she added.

—No, she is from Rome; she is the widow of the Duke of Scerni, and Lord Heathfield is her second husband.

—She is very beautiful.

Andrea asked, with concern:

—What are they going to play now?

—Brahms's Quartet in C minor.

—Do you know it?

—No.

—The second movement is wonderful.

He spoke in order to hide his uneasiness.

—When will I see you again?

—I don't know.

—Tomorrow?

She hesitated. A light shadow appeared to fall over her face. She replied:

—Tomorrow, if it is sunny, I will go with Delfina to Piazza di Spagna, toward noon.

—And if it isn't sunny?

—On Saturday evening I'm going to Countess Starnina's . . .

The music was starting up again. The first movement expressed a deep and virile struggle, full of vigor. The romanza expressed a yearning but very sad nostalgia, and hence a slow, uncertain, weak uplifting toward a very distant dawn. A clear melodic phrase was developing with deep modulations. It was a very different sentiment from the one that animated Bach's adagio; it was more human, more earthly, more elegiac. A breath of Ludwig van Beethoven ran through that music.

Andrea was possessed by such terrible anxiety that he feared he would betray himself. All the sweetness he had felt earlier was now converted to bitterness. He was not precisely conscious of this new suffering; he could neither pull himself together nor control himself; he wavered, disoriented, between the dual feminine attraction and the charm of the music, but was penetrated by none of the three forces; inside him he felt an indefinable impression, like a vacuum in which great blows constantly resounded with a painful echo; and his thoughts fragmented into a thousand pieces, became disconnected and undone; and the two feminine images superimposed themselves on each other, mingled together, and destroyed each other, so that he could not manage to separate them, and he could not manage to define his feelings for the one or his feelings for the other. And right on the surface of this troubled inner suffering there moved a restlessness generated by his immediate reality, by his practical worries. He did not miss even a slight change in Donna Maria's attitude toward him; and he believed he could feel Elena's assiduous and fixed gaze; and he could not manage to find a way to contain himself: he did not know whether he should accompany Donna Maria when leaving the hall, or whether he should approach Elena; nor did he know which instance would benefit or harm his prospects with the one and the other.

—I'm going, said Donna Maria, standing up, at the end of the romanza.

—Aren't you waiting for the end?

—No; I have to be home by five.

—Remember, tomorrow . . .

She held out her hand to him. Perhaps due to the heat in the stuffy room, a slight flame enlivened her paleness. Her whole body was covered by a velvet mantle in a dark leaden color, edged with a wide band of chinchilla; and amid the ashen fur the violets were dying gracefully. Walking out, she moved with sovereign elegance, and some of the ladies sitting there turned to watch her. And for the first time Andrea saw in her, in the spiritual woman, in the pure Sienese Madonna, the woman of the world.

The quartet was entering the third movement. As daylight was fading, the yellow curtains were raised, as in a church. Other ladies left the hall. Whispers could be heard here and there. In the auditorium, tiredness and inattention were setting in, which occurs at the end of every concert. With one of those peculiar phenomena of sudden elasticity and volubility, Andrea felt a sense of relief, almost cheerful. He suddenly lost every sentimental and passionate worry; and only the pleasurable adventure appeared, lucidly, to his vanity and his depravity. He thought that Donna Maria, in conceding to him those harmless meetings, had already placed her foot on the gentle slope at the bottom of which is sin, inevitable even for the most vigilant of souls; he thought that maybe a bit of jealousy could push Elena back into his arms, and hence, that perhaps one love affair would help the other along; he thought that perhaps a vague fear or a jealous foreboding had hastened Donna Maria's assent to their next meeting. He was therefore on his way toward a double conquest; and he smiled, noting that in both endeavors, difficulty presented itself in the same form. He had to convert two sisters—or rather, two women who wanted to play the role of sisters with him—into lovers. He noted other similarities between the two instances, smiling. That voice! How strange, Elena's tones in Donna Maria's voice! A crazy thought flashed into his head. That voice could be, for him, the element of an imaginative work: by virtue of such an affinity, he could fuse the two beauties in order to possess a third, imaginary one, more complex, more perfect, more *real* because she was ideal . . .

The third movement, executed with impeccable style, ended amid applause. Andrea stood up and approached Elena.

—Oh, Ugenta, where have you been until now? the Princess of Ferentino asked him. —*Au pays du Tendre?*[5]

—And that unknown woman, who's she? Elena said to him, lightly, smelling a bunch of violets she had pulled out of her marten-fur muff.

—She's a great friend of my cousin's: Donna Maria Ferres y Capdevila, wife of the new minister of Guatemala, Andrea answered, smoothly. —A lovely creature, very refined. She was at Francesca's, at Schifanoja, in September.

—And Francesca? Elena interrupted. —Don't you know when she'll be back?

—I've heard from her recently, from San Remo. Ferdinando is getting better. But I'm afraid she'll have to stay there for another month, maybe longer.

—What a pity!

The quartet was entering its last movement, which was very brief. Elena and the Princess of Ferentino had occupied two chairs at the back, along the wall, beneath the dim mirror that reflected the gloomy hall. Elena listened, her head bowed, running the ends of a shining marten-fur boa through her hands.

—Come with us, she said to Sperelli, when the concert had ended.

Climbing into the carriage after the Princess of Ferentino, she said:

—Come, get in. We'll drop Eva off at Palazzo Fiano. I'll let you off wherever you like.

—Thanks.

Sperelli accepted. Driving out onto the Corso, the carriage was forced to proceed very slowly because the entire road was cluttered with rioting people. Much noise came from Piazza di Montecitorio and from Piazza Colonna, and it spread like a din made by waves, growing, receding, rising again, mingled with the blaring of military trumpets. The sedition was growing, in the ashen, cold evening; the horror of the distant massacre was making the masses yell; men were running, waving great bundles of paper, cutting through the crowd; above the racket, the name "Africa" could distinctly be heard.

—All for four hundred brutes, who died brutally! Andrea murmured, drawing back after having looked out of the window.

—But what are you saying? exclaimed the Princess of Ferentino.

On the corner of Palazzo Chigi, the mayhem resembled a scuffle. The carriage was forced to come to a halt. Elena leaned to look out; her face, out of the shadow, was lit up in the reflection of the headlamp and in the twilight, she appeared to have an almost funereal pallor, a pallor that was frozen and slightly blue, which awoke in Andrea the vague memory of a head he had once seen—he could not say when or where—in a gallery, in a chapel.

—Here we are, said the princess, since the carriage had finally reached Palazzo Fiano. —Good-bye, then. See you tonight at the Angelieris'. Good-bye, Ugenta. Will you come and have lunch at my place tomorrow? Elena and the Viti woman and my cousin will be there, too.

—At what time?

—Half past twelve.

—All right. Thank you.

The princess dismounted from the carriage. The servant awaited an order.

—Where do you want me to take you? Elena asked Sperelli,

who had already sat down next to her, in the place her friend had vacated.

—*Far, far away . . .*[6]

—Come on, tell me: to your house?

And without waiting for an answer, she ordered:

—Trinità de' Monti, Palazzo Zuccari.

The servant closed the door. The carriage moved forward at a trot and turned into Via Frattina, leaving behind it the crowd, the shouts, the noise.

—Oh, Elena, after so long . . . Andrea burst out, leaning down to look at the desired woman, who had withdrawn into the shadows at the far end, as if avoiding any contact.

The brightness of a shopwindow crossed the shadow, in passing; and he saw that Elena was smiling, very pale, an alluring smile.

Still smiling in this way, she took the long marten-fur boa from her neck with an agile gesture and threw it around his neck like a lasso. It seemed that she was doing it as a game. But with that soft noose, scented with the same perfume that Andrea had smelled in the blue fox fur, she drew Andrea toward her; and offered him her lips, without speaking.

Both their mouths remembered the old mingling, those terrible and sweet conjunctions that lasted until they were short of breath and that gave their hearts an illusory sensation, as of a soft, dewy fruit dissolving. To make it last longer, they held their breaths. From Via dei Due Macelli,[7] the carriage rode up Via del Tritone,[8] turned into Via Sistina, and stopped in front of Palazzo Zuccari.

Rapidly, Elena pushed the young man away. She said to him, her voice a little husky:

—Go, Andrea.

—When will you come?

—Who knows!

The servant opened the door. Andrea descended. The carriage turned again, to drive back along Via Sistina. Andrea, still all aquiver, with his eyes still floating in a cloudy vapor, watched to see if Elena's face appeared from behind the glass; but he saw nothing. The carriage drove away.

Climbing the stairs again, he thought: *At last, she is coming around!* In his head, there was still something like a fog of euphoria; in his mouth, there was still the taste of the kiss; in his eyes, there was still the flash of the smile with which Elena had thrown that sort of shining, sweet-smelling snake around his neck. And Donna Maria? Most certainly, he owed this unexpected lust to the Sienese woman. Without any doubt, at the base of Elena's strange and fantastic act, there was the stirring of jealousy. Fearing, perhaps, that he would escape her, she had wanted to bind him, to entice him, to once again ignite the thirst in him. *Does she love me? Love me not?* And what did it matter to him, to know it? What good did it do him? By now the enchantment was broken. No miracle could ever resuscitate even a small part of the extinct happiness. It was better that he occupy himself with flesh that was still divine.

He considered the affair for a long time, with a sense of smugness. He was particularly satisfied with the elegant and unusual manner with which Elena had added spice to her whim. And the image of the boa aroused the image of Donna Maria's braid, and aroused a flurry of all the amorous dreams that he had dreamed about that vast virgin mass of hair, which once had made schoolgirls at the Florentine convent swoon with love. Again, he mingled the two desires; he cherished the duplicity of pleasure; he could faintly perceive the third ideal Lover.

He was entering into a reflective frame of mind. While dressing for dinner, he thought:—*Yesterday, there was a great scene of passion, almost with tears; today a small mute scene of sensuality. And yesterday it seemed to me that my feeling was sincere, just as my sensation before that was sincere. Moreover, on this very day, an hour before Elena's kiss, I had had another lyrical moment at the side of Donna Maria. Of all this, no trace remains. Tomorrow, certainly, I will begin again. I am chameleonic, chimeric, incoherent, inconsistent. Any effort I make to achieve unity will always be in vain. I must resign myself, by now. My law may be found in one word:* NUNC.[9] *May the will of the law be done.*

He laughed at himself. And from that moment, the new phase of his moral destitution began.

Without any regard, or any reserve, or any remorse, he threw himself completely into bringing his unwholesome imaginings into being. In order to induce Maria Ferres to surrender herself to him, he used the most subtle ploys, the most delicate entanglements, deceiving her in matters of the soul, in spirituality, in ideality, in the intimate life of the heart. In order to proceed with equal rapidity in the acquisition of his new lover, and the reacquisition of the old one, in order to benefit from every situation in each of his endeavors, he encountered a variety of setbacks, inconveniences, bizarre circumstances; and in order to extricate himself from these, he resorted to a variety of lies, contrivances, unkind expedients, degrading subterfuges, despicable tricks. Donna Maria's goodness, her faith, her candor, did not subdue him. He had placed the verse of a psalm at the basis of his seduction: *"Asperges me hyssopo et mundabor: lavabis me, et super nivem dealbabor."*[10] The poor creature believed she was saving a soul, redeeming an intelligence, purifying a tainted man with her purity; she still deeply believed the unforgettable words she had heard in the park, in that Epiphany of Love, in the presence of the sea, under those florid trees. And this faith of hers restored her and uplifted her in the midst of the Christian battles that constantly were being fought in her conscience; it freed her from suspicion and it intoxicated her with a kind of lustful mysticism in which she poured out rich quantities of tenderness, the whole wave of her concentrated languor, the sweetest flower of her life.

For the first time, perhaps, Andrea Sperelli found himself in the face of a *real* passion; for the first time, he found himself before one of those great, feminine, extremely rare sentiments that illuminate the gray and changeable sky of human loves with a beautiful, terrible flash. He himself was grooming it. He became the ruthless executioner of himself and of the poor creature.

Every day there was a deception, a base act.

On Thursday, February 3, according to the agreement they had made at the concert, he met her in Piazza di Spagna in front of an exhibition of antique gold jewelry, with Delfina. As soon as she heard his greeting, she turned around; and a flame tinged her paleness. Together they examined the eighteenth-century jewels, the buckles and tiaras made of rhinestone, the enameled brooches and watches, the snuffboxes made of gold, ivory, tortoiseshell; all those trifles from a bygone century, which in that clear morning light created a harmonious sumptuousness. All about, flower sellers were offering up for sale their baskets of yellow and white jonquils, double violets, long almond-tree branches. A breath of spring pervaded the air. The slender Column of the Immaculate Conception rose up to the sun, like a flower stalk, with the *Rosa mystica*[11] at its summit; the Barcaccia Fountain was laden with diamonds; the Trinità widened its flights of stairs in delight toward the church of Carlo VIII, rising up with its two towers into a blue sky ennobled by clouds, an ancient sky reminiscent of Piranesi.[12]

—How marvelous! Donna Maria exclaimed. —You are right to be so in love with Rome.

—Oh, you don't know it yet! Andrea said to her. —I would like to be your dux . . .[13]

She smiled.

—. . . to carry out beside you, this spring, a sentimental Virgilian expedition.[14]

She was smiling, her entire figure appearing less sad, less serious. Her morning apparel had a sober elegance, but revealed the stylish refinement of one whose tastes had been educated through art, through the delicacy of color. Her crossover jacket, in the form of a shawl, was of a gray fabric that tended slightly toward green; and a strip of otter fur decorated its edges; and the fur was embroidered with silken cord. And the jacket parted over an undercoat, also of otter fur. The outfit was cut superbly, and, together with the combination of the two tones, that indescribable gray and that opulent tawny shade, it was a delight to behold.

She asked:

—Where were you yesterday evening?

—I left the concert a few minutes after you. I went home; and I stayed there, because it seemed to me that your spirit was present. I reflected a lot. Did you not *feel* my thoughts?

—No, I did not feel them. My evening was gloomy, I don't know why. It seemed that I was so alone!

The Countess of Lùcoli passed by in a dogcart, driving a roan. Giulia Moceto walked by, accompanied by Giulio Musèllaro. Donna Isotta Cellesi went by.

Andrea greeted each of them. Donna Maria asked him the names of the ladies: Giulia Moceto's was not new to her. She remembered the day when it was spoken by Francesca, in front of the archangel Michael painted by Perugino,[15] when Andrea was paging through his drawings in the sitting room at Schifanoja; and she watched her beloved's ex-lover as she walked along. She was gripped by anxiety. Everything that tied Andrea to his previous life cast a shadow over her. She would have liked that life, unknown to her, never to have taken place; she would have liked to delete it completely from the memory of the one who had immersed himself in it with such avidness, and had emerged from it with so much fatigue, so much loss, so many ills. "To live uniquely in you and for you, without any tomorrow, without any yesterday, without any other bond, without any other preference, out of the world . . ." These were his words. Oh dream!

And Andrea was clutched by a different anxiety. Time was drawing near for the lunch to which he had been invited by the Princess of Ferentino.

—Where are you heading? he asked her.

—Delfina and I had tea and sandwiches at the Caffè Nazzarri,[16] with the intention of enjoying the sun. We're going up the Pincio and maybe we will visit Villa Medici. If you'd like to accompany us . . .

He wavered, painfully. The Pincio, Villa Medici, on a February afternoon, with her! But he could not miss the lunch invitation; and he was also tormented by the curiosity of encountering Elena after the episode of the evening before, since, although he had gone to the Angelieri house, she had not made an appearance. He said, with a desolate air:

—How unfortunate! I need to be at a luncheon, in a quarter of an hour. I accepted the invitation last week. But if I had known, I would have been able to free myself of any obligation. What a pity!

—Go; don't waste time. Don't keep them waiting . . .

He looked at his watch.

—I can still walk a little farther with you.

—Mommy—Delfina begged—let's go up the stairs. I went up them yesterday with Miss Dorothy. If you could only see!

As they were in the vicinity of Via del Babuino, they turned in order to cross the square. A boy followed them, persistently trying to sell them a large almond-tree branch, which Andrea bought and gave to Delfina. Blond ladies were emerging from hotels carrying red Baedeker books; heavy two-horsed carriages rode past each other, with metallic glints on their old-fashioned trimmings; flower sellers were lifting their full baskets toward foreign ladies and calling out to them, vying with one another for trade.

—Promise me—Andrea said to Donna Maria, placing his foot on the first step—promise me that you won't go to Villa Medici without me. Please don't go today; I beseech you.

She appeared preoccupied by a sad thought. She said:

—I won't go.

—Thank you.

The flight of stairs ahead of them rose up in triumph, emanating gentle warmth from the sun-heated stone; and the stone was the color of ancient silverware, similar to that of the fountains at Schifanoja. Delfina ran ahead of them, holding her flowered branch, and as she ran, some fragile rose-colored petals took off like butterflies in the breeze she generated.

Acute regret pierced the young man's heart. All the sweet pleasures of a sentimental walk along Medicean pathways appeared to him, beneath the mute boxwoods, in that early hour of the afternoon.

—Whose house are you going to?—Donna Maria asked him after a pause.

—To the old Princess Alberoni, answered Andrea. —A Catholic table.

He lied once more, because instinct warned him that perhaps the name of the Princess of Ferentino would arouse some suspicions in Donna Maria.

—Good-bye, then, she added, holding her hand out to him.

—No; I'll come as far as the square. My carriage is waiting for me there. Look: that is my house.

He pointed out Palazzo Zuccari, the *buen retiro,* drenched in sunlight and resembling a strange greenhouse that has become opaque and dark with time.

Donna Maria looked at it.

—Now that you know where it is, won't you—sometime . . . in spirit?

—In spirit, always.

—Won't I see you before Saturday evening?

—It will be difficult.

They said good-bye. With Delfina, she began walking up the tree-lined avenue. He mounted his carriage and drove away down Via Gregoriana.

He arrived at the Ferentino house a few minutes late. He apologized. Elena was there with her husband.

Lunch was served in a cheerful room decorated with tapestries from the Barberini factory,[17] which depicted Bambocciata[18] scenes in the style of Pieter van Laer. In the midst of that lovely grotesque seventeenth-century setting, a blaze of marvelous backbiting began to scintillate and crackle. All three women had a gay and ready wit. Barbarella Viti was laughing her strong masculine laugh, throwing back her lovely boyish head slightly; and her black eyes met and mingled too often with the green eyes of the princess. Elena was making witticisms with extraordinary vivacity; and she seemed so distant, so estranged, so indifferent to Andrea, that he almost feared: Was last night a dream? Ludovico Barbarisi and the Prince of Ferentino were indulging the ladies. The Marquis of Mount Edgcumbe was taking care to bore his *young friend* asking him for news about the impending auctions and talking to him about a very rare edition of Apuleius's novel, *Metamorphoses,* that he had acquired a few days earlier for 1,520 lire:—ROMA, 1469, in folio.—Every now and then he interrupted himself to follow one of Barbarella's gestures; and the look of a maniac came into his eyes, and a singular tremor began in his odious hands.

Andrea's irritation, vexation, intolerance, grew to such a level that he could no longer conceal them.

—Ugenta, are you in a bad mood? the Princess of Ferentino asked him.

—A little. Miching Mallecho is ill.

And then Barbarisi bored him with many questions about the horse's illness. And then Mount Edgcumbe began again with *Metamorphoses.* And the Princess of Ferentino said, laughing:

—You know, Ludovico, yesterday at the quintet concert, we caught him in a flirtation with an Unknown Woman.

—That's right, said Elena.

—An Unknown Woman? exclaimed Ludovico.

—Yes; but maybe you can give us some information about her. She is the wife of the new Guatemalan minister.

—Ah, I understand.

—Well?

—For now, I know only the minister. I see him playing cards at the club every night.

—Tell us, Ugenta: has she already been received by the queen?

—I don't know, Princess, Andrea answered, with a slight impatience in his voice.

That chatter was becoming unbearable to him; and Elena's gaiety was causing him horrible torment, and the proximity of her husband disgusted him as never before. He was angrier with himself than with the latter. At the base of his irritation, a sense of regret stirred at the happiness he had refused earlier on. His heart, disillusioned and offended by Elena's cruel attitude, turned to the other woman with acute repentance; and he saw her, thoughtful, in a solitary avenue, beautiful and noble as never before.

The princess stood up, and everyone stood up, to pass into the adjacent room. Barbarella ran to open the piano, which was hidden under a vast saddlecloth made of red velvet embroidered in dull gold; and she began to hum Georges Bizet's *Tarantelle,* dedicated to Christina Nilsson. Elena and Eva leaned over her to read the sheet of music. Ludovico stood behind them, smoking a cigarette. The prince had disappeared.

But Lord Heathfield did not leave Andrea alone. He had drawn him into a window alcove and was talking to him about certain "lover's cups" from Urbania that he had purchased at the sale of Cavalier Dàvila; and that strident voice, with those nauseating interrogative intonations, and those gestures indicating the dimensions of the cups, and that look in his eyes, alternating between dead and penetrating, beneath his enormous convex forehead, and in short, all those hateful features, caused Andrea such violent torture that he clenched his teeth together, convulsed like a man beneath a surgeon's instruments.

Only one desire occupied him: to leave. He thought of rushing to the Pincio; he hoped to find Donna Maria there, to take her to Villa Medici. It was possibly two o'clock. Through the window he saw the cornice of the house across the road, resplendent with sun in the blue sky. Turning around, he saw the group of women at the piano amid the vermilion glow cast by the saddlecloth. With this glow was mingled the light smoke of cigarettes; and the prattle and the laughter mixed with chords that Barbarella's fingers were trying out haphazardly on the keys. Ludovico spoke softly into his cousin's ear; and his cousin perhaps conveyed this information to her friends, because once again there was a clear and tinkling outburst, like a necklace that has spilled its beads onto a silver tray. Barbarella resumed with Bizet's allegretto, softly.

—*Tra la la . . . Le papillon s'est envolé . . .*[19] *Tra la la . . .*

Andrea was waiting for the right moment to interrupt Mount Edgcumbe's lecture and hence to take his leave. But the collector was emitting a string of sentences tied one to the other, without intervals, without pause. A pause would have saved the martyr, and it did not come; and his anxiety was growing with every second.

—*Oui ! Le papillon s'est envolé . . . Oui ! . . . Ah! ah! ah! ah! ah! . . .*

Andrea looked at his watch.

—It's already two o'clock! Forgive me, Marquis. I must go.

And approaching the group:

—Forgive me, Princess. At two I have a consultation at the stables with the veterinarians.

He greeted everyone in great haste. Elena gave him the tips of her fingers to press. Barbarella gave him a *fondant,* saying to him:

—Take this to poor Miching from me.

Ludovico wanted to accompany him.

—No, stay.

He bowed and went out. He ran down the stairs in an instant. He jumped into his carriage, shouting to the coachman:

—Fast, to the Pincio!

He was possessed by a mad desire to find Maria Ferres, to recover the happiness that he had earlier renounced. The rapid trot of the horses did not seem fast enough to him. He watched with anxiety, waiting to see the Trinità de' Monti finally appear, the wide tree-lined street, the gates.

The carriage passed through the gates. He ordered the coachman to slow down and to traverse all the avenues. His heart jumped each time he saw, from afar, amid the trees, the figure of a woman; but in vain. On the level he got out of the carriage and walked up the small roads that were closed to vehicles, exploring every corner: in vain. People watched him from benches, curiously, because his anxiety was evident.

As Villa Borghese was open, the Pincio was reposing in tranquillity beneath that languid February smile. Few coaches and few pedestrians interrupted the peace of the hill. The still-bare trees, whitish, some slightly violet, held their arms up to a delicate sky, scattered with fine spiderwebs that the wind was tearing and destroying with its gusts. The pine trees, the cypresses, the tall evergreen trees took on some of the common pallor, became indistinct, faded, fused in common accord. The diversity of tree trunks and the tracery of the branches lent greater solemnity to the uniformity of the herms.

Was there not something of Donna Maria's sadness still floating in that air? Leaning against the gate of Villa Medici, Andrea felt an enormous weight bear down on him for some minutes.

And the succession of events continued, in the coming days, with the same tortures, with worse tortures, with crueler lies. By some phenomenon not uncommon in the moral degradation of men of intellect, he now had a terrible lucidity of conscience, a continuous lucidity, without any more clouding, without any more eclipses. He knew what he was doing, and judged later whatever he had done. His contempt for himself was equal to the lassitude of his will.

But precisely these disparities of his, and his uncertainties and his strange silences and his strange effusions and, in short, all his peculiarities of expression, which brought about such a state of mind, increased and incited Donna Maria's passionate mercifulness. She saw him suffer and felt pain and tenderness because of it; and thought: *Little by little, I will heal him.* And little by little, without being aware of it, she was gradually losing her strength and submitting to the desire of the sick man.

She submitted gently.

In Countess Starnina's salon, she felt an indefinable shiver when she felt Andrea's gaze on her bare shoulders and arms. For the first time, Andrea was seeing her in an evening gown. He knew only her face and her hands: now her shoulders seemed to him of an exquisite form; her arms, too, albeit perhaps somewhat thin.

She was dressed in ivory-colored brocade mixed with sable. A narrow strip of sable ran along her neckline, lending an indescribable refinement to her skin; and the line that led from the base of her neck to the edge of her shoulder slanted downward somewhat, with that sloping grace that is a sign of physical aristocracy that by now has become extremely rare. On her abundant hair, arranged in that style that Verrocchio favored for his busts, there glittered neither a gem nor a flower.

In two or three opportune moments, Andrea murmured words of admiration and passion to her.

—It is the first time that we are seeing each other "in society," he said to her. —Will you give me a glove, as a memento?

—No.

—Why, Maria?

—No, no; be quiet.

—Oh, your hands! Do you remember when I drew them at Schifanoja? It seems that they belong to me by right; it seems that you should concede ownership of them to me, and that of your entire body, they are the things that are most intimately inspired by your soul, the most spiritualized, almost I could say the purest . . . Hands of goodness, hands of forgiveness . . . How happy I would be to own at least one glove: a shadow, a semblance of their form, a slough scented with their scent! . . . Will you give me a glove, before you leave?

She did not answer again. Their conversation was interrupted. After some time, since people were begging her to do so, she sat down at the piano; she took off her gloves and placed them on the music stand. Her fingers, out of those delicate sheaths, appeared extremely white, rather long, bejeweled. On her left ring finger a large opal sparkled with fiery brilliance.

She played Beethoven's two *Fantasia* sonatas (Op. 27).[20] The one, dedicated to Giulietta Guicciardi,[21] expressed a hopeless renunciation and narrated the reawakening after a dream dreamed for too long. The other, right from the first beats of the andante, in a gentle and soft rhythm, suggested the calm after the storm; then, passing through the restlessness of the second movement, it expanded into an adagio of luminous serenity and finished with an allegro vivace that contained an elevation of courage and almost passion.

Andrea felt that, in the midst of that engrossed audience, she was playing for him alone. Now and then, his eyes went from the pianist's fingers to the long gloves that hung from the stand, preserving the shape of those fingers, preserving an inexpressible grace in the small opening at the wrist where earlier, a little of her feminine skin just barely showed.

Donna Maria stood up, surrounded by praise. She did not pick up her gloves, and walked away. Andrea was overcome by the temptation to steal them.—Had she perhaps left them there for him?—But he wanted only one. As a refined lover refinedly said, a pair of gloves is entirely different from one single glove.

Led once more to the piano by the insistence of Countess Starnina, Donna Maria took the gloves from the music stand and placed them at one end of the keyboard, in the shadow of the corner. She then played Luigi Rameau's gavotte, the *Gavotte of the Yellow Ladies,* the unforgettable ancient dance of Tedium and Love. "Certain blond ladies, no longer young . . ."

Andrea gazed at her fixedly, with a little trepidation. When she stood up, she took only one glove. She left the other one in the shadow, on the keyboard, for him.

Three days later, with Rome lying stupefied under the snow, Andrea found this note at home: "*Tuesday, two p.m.*—This evening, from eleven to midnight, wait for me in a carriage in front of Palazzo Barberini, outside the gate. If I haven't yet arrived by midnight, you may go. —*A stranger.*" The note had an adventurous, mysterious tone. In truth, the Marchioness of Mount Edgcumbe overly abused the use of carriages in her amorous carryings-on. Was it perhaps as a memory of March 25, 1885? Did she perhaps want to recommence the affair in the same way with which she had interrupted it? And why that *stranger*? Andrea smiled at this. He was just then returning from a visit to Donna Maria, a very pleasant visit; and his spirit was inclining more toward the Sienese woman than toward the other one. He could still hear the vague and gentle words she had spoken while at the window watching the snow fall softly, like peach or apple blossoms, on the trees of Villa Aldobrandini, which had been deluded by the presage of spring. But, before leaving for lunch, he gave very precise orders to Stephen.

At eleven he was in front of the building; and was being devoured by anxiety and impatience. The oddness of the situation, the spectacle of the snowy night, the mystery, the uncertainty, all fired his imagination and lifted him up from reality.

A fabulous full moon, casting a light such as had never been seen before, shone on Rome that memorable February night. The air seemed to be impregnated by an ethereal milk; all things appeared to exist in a dream life, seemed to be impalpable images like those of a meteor, seemed to be visible from far away due to a chimeric illumination of their forms. Snow covered all the bars of the gates, hiding the iron, composing an embroidered work of art that was lighter and more delicate than filigree, borne by the white-mantled colossi the way oak trees bear spiderwebs. The frozen garden was flowering like an immobile forest of enormous, deformed lilies; it was a kitchen garden possessed by a lunar enchantment, a lifeless paradise presided over by Selene. Mute, solemn, profound, the Barberini house occupied the air: all its structural relief was accentuated, snow-white, casting a blue shadow as diaphanous as light; and that whiteness and those shadows superimposed onto the true architecture of the building the phantom of a prodigious Ariostean architecture.[22]

Leaning down and observing the scene, the waiting man felt that beneath the charm of that miracle, the longed-for ghosts of love were rising up again, and the lyrical summits of sentiment once again sparkled like the icy lances of the gates in the moonlight. But he did not know which of the two women he would have preferred in that fantastic scene: whether Elena Heathfield dressed in purple or Maria Ferres dressed in ermine. And as his mind took pleasure in lingering in the uncertainty of preference, it occurred that in the anxiety of the wait, two anxieties mixed and mingled together strangely; the real one for Elena, and the imaginary one for Maria.

A clock tolled nearby in the silence, with a clear and vibrating sound; and it seemed as if something made of glass in the air cracked with every toll. The clock of Trinità de' Monti replied to the call, as did that of the Quirinale; other clocks far away responded, faintly. It was a quarter past eleven.

Andrea looked toward the portico, watching carefully. Would she dare to walk across the garden? He thought about Elena's figure amid the great whiteness. The figure of the Sienese woman rose up spontaneously, obscured the other one, and outdid the whiteness: *candida super nivem.*[23] The night of moon and snow was hence under the dominion of Maria Ferres, as under an invincible astral influence. From the sovereign purity of things arose the image of the pure lover, symbolically. The force of the Symbol subjugated the poet's spirit.

Then, still watching to see if the other one was coming, he abandoned himself to the dream suggested to him by the appearance of things.

It was a poetic, almost mystical dream. He was waiting for Maria. Maria had chosen that night of supernatural whiteness in order to immolate her own whiteness to his desire. All the white things around him, conscious of the great immolation, were waiting to say *Hail* and *Amen* to the passage of the sister. The silence endured.

"Here, she's coming: *incedit per lilia et super nivem.*[24] She is enveloped in ermine; she is wearing her hair bound and hidden in a band; her step is lighter than her shadow; the moon and the snow are less pale than she. *Hail.*

"A shadow, cerulean like the light that colors a sapphire, accompanies her. The enormous, deformed lilies do not bow down, because the frost has petrified them, because the frost has made them similar to the asphodels that illuminated the pathways of Hades. However, like those of the Christian paradise, they have a voice; they say: *Amen.*

"So be it. The beloved goes to sacrifice herself. So be it. She is already near the waiting man; cold and mute, but with ardent and eloquent eyes. And first he kisses her hands, those dear hands that seal wounds and uncover dreams. So be it.

"Here and there, the churches vanish, from their places high up atop columns whose gables the snow illustrates with whorls and magic acanthi. The deep fora disappear, buried beneath the snow, immersed in an azure brightness, from which the ruins of the porticoes and arches rise up toward the moon, more incorporeal than their own shadows. The fountains disperse, sculpted in crystal rock, spilling not water but light.

"And then he kisses the lips, the dear lips that do not know false words. So be it. Her hair streams out of the loosened band, like a great dark wave, in which all the nocturnal shadows seem to be gathered, fleeing from the snow and the moon. *Comis suis obumbrabit tibi et sub comis peccabit.*[25] *Amen.*"

The other was not coming! Into the silence and the poetry the hours of men interceded once again, struck by the towers and belfries of Rome. A few carriages, making no noise, descended via the Four Fountains toward the square or ascended with difficulty to Santa Maria Maggiore; and their headlamps were yellow like topazes in the clarity. It seemed as if this clarity was growing and becoming more limpid, as night reached its highest point. The filigrees formed by the gates sparkled as if the silver embroidery were being adorned with gems. In the building, great circles of dazzling light shone at the windows, resembling diamond shields.

Andrea thought: *What if she does not come?*

That strange wave of lyricism that had passed through his spirit in the name of Maria had masked the anxiety of his wait, had assuaged his impatience and stilled his desire. For a moment, the thought that she was not coming appealed to him. Then, once more, the torment of uncertainty pierced him more strongly and he was disturbed by the image of pleasure that he would perhaps have enjoyed within that small warm alcove, where the roses exhaled such a soft scent. And as on New Year's Eve, his suffering was sharpened by vanity; since, after all, he regretted that such an exquisite setting for love should go wasted without being put to any use.

Inside there, the cold was moderated by the constant heat emitted by the metal tubes full of boiling water. A bunch of white roses, reminiscent of snow and the moon, lay on the small table in front of the seat. A white bear fur kept his knees warm. The quest for a kind of *Symphonie en blanc majeur*[26] was manifest in many other details. As King François I had done on the glass of his window, the Count of Ugenta had inscribed in his own hand on the carriage windowpane an erotic motto, which, in the clouded mist made by his breath, seemed to sparkle on an opal slab:

Pro amore curriculum
Pro amore cubiculum.[27]

And for the third time the hour tolled. It was a quarter to twelve. The wait had been too long: Andrea was becoming tired and irritated. In the apartment inhabited by Elena, in the windows of the left wing, no lights could be seen other than that of the moon outside. Was she going to come, then? And in what way? Secretly? Or with some pretext? Lord Heathfield was surely in Rome. How would she justify her nocturnal absence? Again, piercing curiosity sprung up in the ex-lover's soul regarding Elena's relationship with her husband, their conjugal ties, their mode of living together in the same house. Again, jealousy stung him and covetousness inflamed him. He remembered the cheerful words spoken by Giulio Musèllaro, one evening, regarding the husband; and he intended to gain possession of Elena at any cost, for delight and out of spite. Oh, if she only came!

A carriage arrived and entered the garden. He leaned down to see; he recognized Elena's horses; he glimpsed inside it the figure of a woman. The carriage disappeared under the portico. He was left feeling doubtful. Was she hence returning outside? Alone? He looked intently toward the portico. The carriage was going out through the garden, into the street, turning into Via Rasella: it was empty.

There were only two or three minutes left until the final hour; and she was not coming! The hour was struck. Terrible anguish gripped the disappointed man. She was not coming!

Unable to understand the reasons for her lack of punctuality, he turned against her; he had a sudden rush of anger; and he also had the idea that she had wished to inflict humiliation or punishment on him, or that she had wanted to satisfy a whim or accentuate her desire. He ordered the coachman, through the mouthpiece:

—Piazza del Quirinale.

He allowed himself to be allured by Maria Ferres; he once again surrendered to the vague feeling of tenderness that, after the afternoon visit, had left a scent in his soul, and had prompted thoughts and images of poetry. The recent disappointment, which for him was proof of Elena's indifference and malice, was driving him forcefully toward the love and goodness of the Sienese woman. His regret for the beautiful wasted night was increasing, but was subject to the reflection of the dream he had earlier dreamed. It was, in truth, one of the most beautiful nights that have ever passed through the Roman sky; it was one of those spectacles that oppress the human spirit with an immense sadness because they overwhelm all powers of admiration and elude the full comprehension of the intellect.

Piazza del Quirinale appeared completely white, amplified by the whiteness, solitary, as radiant as an Olympic acropolis above the silent city. Around it, buildings towered in the open sky; the tall papal door sculpted by Bernini, in the King's Palace, surmounted by the loggia, deceived the eye, standing free from the walls, set forward, isolated in its deformed magnificence, resembling a mausoleum sculpted in sidereal stone. The rich architraves by Fuga[28] in Palazzo della Consulta protruded above the door frames and over the columns, which were transfigured by the strange assemblage of snow. In the midst of the smooth white space, the Colossi stood, divine, seemingly towering above all things. The postures of the Dioscuri[29] and the horses were expanded in the light; their wide rumps shone as if they were adorned with jeweled caparisons; the shoulders and raised arm of each demigod sparkled. Above, between the horses, the obelisk could be seen soaring upward; below it was the cavity of the fountain basin; and the spurt and the spire rose up toward the moon like a stalk made of diamond and a stalk of granite.

An august solemnity emanated from the monument. In front of it, Rome was immersed in an almost deathly silence, immobile, void, like a city sleeping as a result of some fatal power. All the houses, the churches, the towers, all the melded and intermingled forests of pagan and Christian architecture shimmered white, like one sole unique unformed forest, between the Janiculum hills and Monte Mario, lost in a silvery vapor, very far away, of an inexpressible immateriality, similar perhaps to the horizons of a lunar landscape, which brought to mind the vision of some semi-extinguished star inhabited by the Mani.[30] The cupola of Saint Peter's Basilica, of a singular blue metallic luminosity in the blue air, loomed so near by that it seemed almost tangible. And the two young heroes, generated by a swan, beautiful in that immense brightness, as in an apotheosis of their origin, seemed to be the immortal Genii[31] of Rome, keeping vigil over the sacred city's sleep.

The carriage remained stationary in front of the palace for a long time. Once again, the poet followed his unreachable dream. Maria Ferres was close by; perhaps she, too, was awake, dreaming; perhaps she, too, felt all the greatness of the night weighing upon her heart, and was beset by anguish, fruitlessly.

The carriage passed slowly in front of Maria Ferres's door, which was closed, while above it, the windowpanes reflected the full moon, overlooking the hanging gardens of Villa Aldobrandini, where the trees rose up, prodigies of the air. And the poet threw the bunch of white roses onto the snow, as a homage, before Maria Ferres's door.

CHAPTER IV

—I saw: I guessed . . . I had been behind the windows, for a long time. I couldn't bring myself to leave. All that whiteness was attracting me . . . I saw the carriage pass by slowly in the snow. I felt that it was you, before I saw you throwing the roses. No words can ever explain to you the tenderness of my tears. I cried for you, out of love; and I cried for the roses, out of pity. Poor roses! It seemed that they must be living, and suffering and agonizing on the snow. It seemed, I don't know, that they called me, that they were lamenting, like abandoned creatures. When your carriage drove away, I looked out of the window to see. I was on the point of going down to the street to fetch them. But someone was still outside the house; and the servant was there in the entrance hall, waiting. I thought of a thousand ways, but I couldn't find one that was feasible. I was desperate . . . You're smiling? Really, I don't know what kind of madness gripped me. I stood there, keeping a watchful eye on the passersby, my eyes full of tears. If they had trampled the roses, they would have trampled my heart. And I was happy in that torment; I was happy for your love, for your delicate and passionate gesture, your kindness, your goodness . . . I was sad and happy when I fell asleep; and the roses must already have been dying. After a few hours of sleep I was awoken by the sound of shovels on the paving. They were clearing away the snow, right in front of our door. I stayed there listening; and the noise and the voices continued until after dawn, and were making me so sad . . . Poor roses! But they will always be alive in my memory. Certain memories are enough to scent a soul forever . . . Do you love me very much, Andrea?

And after a pause:

—Do you love only me? Have you forgotten the rest, entirely? Are all your thoughts of me?

She was shaking and trembling.

—I suffer . . . because of your earlier life, the one I don't know about; I suffer because of your memories, all the traces that perhaps still remain in your spirit, everything about you that I will never be able to understand and possess. Oh, if I could make you forget everything! I constantly hear your words, Andrea, the *very first* words. I think I will hear them at the instant of my death . . .

She shook and trembled beneath the force of overwhelming passion.

—I love you more each day, more each day!

Andrea intoxicated her with sweet and profound words, conquered her with ardor and recounted the dream of the snowy night and his desperate desire, and the entire convenient story of the roses and many other lyrical imaginings. It seemed to him that she was close to yielding; he could see her eyes swimming in a more bountiful wave of yearning; he could see on her suffering mouth the appearance of that inexpressible contraction which is like the concealment of an instinctive physical tendency to kiss; and he could see her hands, those delicate strong hands, archangel hands, quivering like the strings of a musical instrument, expressing all her internal agitation. *If I could steal even just one fleeting kiss from her today*—he thought—*I will have greatly speeded up the goal I'm aspiring to.*

But she, conscious of the danger, stood up suddenly, excusing herself; she rang the bell, ordered the servant to bring tea and to ask Miss Dorothy to bring Delfina into the sitting room. Then, turning to Andrea, somewhat convulsively, she said:

—It's better this way. Forgive me.

And from that day on she avoided receiving him on days that were not, like Tuesdays and Saturdays, common reception days.

She permitted him, however, to guide her on various peregrinations across Imperial Rome and the Rome of the popes. This Lenten Virgilian tour was carried out in the villas, the galleries, the churches, the ruins. Where Elena Muti had passed, now passed Maria Ferres. Not infrequently, things inspired the poet to utter the same effusions of words that Elena had already heard. Not infrequently, a memory took him away from present reality, or suddenly disturbed him.

—What are you thinking about now? Maria would ask him, looking deeply into his eyes with a shadow of suspicion.

And he answered:

—About you, always you. I'm gripped by a kind of curiosity to look inside myself to see if there is still some minimal part of my soul that is not in the possession of your soul, some minimal fold that has not been penetrated by your light. It is like an internal exploration, which I am doing for you, since you cannot do it. Well, Maria, I have nothing more to offer you. You have absolute control of my entire being. Never, I think, has a human creature been more intimately possessed by a human creature, in spirit. If my mouth could be joined to yours, the transfusion of my life into yours would take place. I think I would die.

She believed him, because his voice gave his words the flame of truth.

One day they were on the belvedere atop Villa Medici: they were watching the gold of the sun ebb away slowly from the ample, somber boxwood canopies, and Villa Borghese, still bare of foliage, gradually being submerged in a purplish vapor. Maria said, invaded by a sudden sadness:

—Who knows how many times you've come here, to feel loved!

Andrea answered in the tone of a man lost in thought:

—I don't know; I don't recall. Whatever are you saying?

She was silent. Then she stood up to read the inscriptions on the columns of the small temple. They were mostly inscriptions made by lovers, newlyweds, solitary contemplators.

One bore, below the date and the name of a woman, a fragment of *Pausias:*[1]

SIE

Immer allein sind Liebende sich in der grössten Versammlung;
Aber sind sie zu Zweien, stellt auch der Dritte sich ein.[2]

ER
Amor, ja![3]

Another one was the glorification of a sublime name:

A solis ortu usque ad occasum laudabile nomen Helles.[4]

Another was a plaintive quatrain by Petrarch:

I always loved and I still love intensely,
And I love more day by day,
That sweet place to which I return in tears
Many times when Love pierces my heart.[5]

Another seemed to be a loyal declaration, signed by two loyal lovers:

Ahora y no siempre.[6]

They all expressed an erotic, or sad, or cheerful sentiment; they sang the praises of a beautiful woman or mourned a remote happiness; they recounted an ardent kiss or a languid ecstasy; they thanked the old courteous boxwoods, indicated a secret hiding place to future happy couples, or noted the wonder of a sunset they had contemplated. Whoever they were, bridegroom or lover subject to feminine allure, they had been infused with lyrical enthusiasm on the small solitary belvedere, which is reached by a stone staircase carpeted with velvet. The walls spoke. Indefinable melancholy emanated from those unknown voices of dead loves, an almost sepulchral melancholy, such as from the epitaphs of a chapel.

Suddenly, Maria turned to Andrea, saying:

—You're here, too.

He answered, looking at her, in the same tone as before:

—I don't know; I don't remember. I don't remember anything. I love you.

She read it. It was, written in Andrea's hand, an epigram by Goethe, a distich, the one that begins: *"Sage, wie lebst du?"*—Tell me, how do you live?—*"Ich lebe!"*—I live! And, if I were given hundreds and hundreds of centuries, I would wish only that tomorrow were like today. Below there was a date: *Die ultima februarii 1885*,[7] and a name: *Helena Amyclaea*.[8]

She said:

—Let's go.

The boxwood canopy rained shadows over the velvet-covered staircase. He asked:

—Do you want to lean on me?

She answered:

—No, thank you.

They descended in silence, slowly. Both their hearts were heavy.

After a pause, she said:

—You were happy, two years ago.

And he, with considered obstinacy:

—I don't know; I don't remember.

The woods were mysterious in a green dusk. The trunks and branches rose up with serpentine tangles and snarls. A few leaves glittered like emerald eyes in the shade.

After a pause, she added:

—Who was that Elena?

—I don't know; I don't remember. I don't remember anything anymore. I love you. I love only you. I think only about you. I live only for you. I don't know anything else; I don't remember anything else; I don't desire anything else, besides your love. No string ties me to my past life any longer. I am outside of the world now, entirely lost in your being. I am in your blood and in your soul; I can *feel* myself in every beat of your arteries; I do not touch you, yet I am mingled with you as if I held you constantly in my arms, on my mouth, on my heart. I love you and you love me; and this has lasted for centuries, will last for centuries, forever. Near you, thinking about you, living for you, I am conscious of infinity, of eternity. I love you and you love me. I don't know anything else; I don't remember anything else.

He inundated her sadness and suspicion with a wave of burning and sweet eloquence. She listened, standing erect at the balustrades of the wide terrace that opened onto the edge of the woods.

—Is it true? Is it true? she repeated with a flat voice, which was like the faint echo of a cry coming from her inner soul. —Is it true?

—It's true, Maria; and only this is true. All the rest is a dream. I love you and you love me. And you possess me as I possess you. I know you to be so profoundly mine that I do not ask caresses of you; I do not ask you any proof of love. I wait. I prefer, more than any other thing, to obey you. I do not ask caresses of you; but I feel them in your voice, in your gaze, in your attitude, in your smallest gestures. Everything that comes from you intoxicates me like a kiss; and I don't know, when brushing against your hand, what is stronger: the pleasure of my senses or the upliftment of my spirit.

He placed his hand lightly on hers. Seduced, she trembled, feeling an insane desire to lean toward him, to offer him, finally, her lips, her kiss, her entire self. It seemed to her (because she had faith in Andrea's words) that with such an act she would tie him to her with the final knot, an indissoluble knot. She believed she was fainting, being consumed, dying. It was as if all the turmoils of passion that she had already suffered were swelling her heart, augmenting the turmoil of the present passion. It was as if she were reliving in that moment all the emotions she had passed through since she had met that man. Schifanoja's roses were flowering again among the bay trees and box trees of Villa Medici.

—I am waiting, Maria. I'm not asking anything of you. I'm keeping my promises. I'm waiting for the supreme hour. I can feel that it will come, because the power of love is invincible. And all fear, all terror will vanish from you; and the communion of bodies will seem as pure to you as the communion of souls, since all flames are equally pure . . .

He was pressing her gloved hand with his ungloved one. The garden seemed deserted. No noise, no voice reached them from the Academy building.[9] The gurgle of the fountain in the middle of the clearing could be heard distinctly; the avenues continued straight toward the Pincian Hill, as if they were enclosed between two bronze walls, on which the gilding of vespers had not yet faded; the immobility of all shapes gave the appearance of a petrified labyrinth: the tips of water reeds around the basin were immobile in the air, like statues.

—It seems—said the Sienese woman, half closing her eyes—as if I were on the terrace at Schifanoja, far, far away from Rome, alone . . . with you. If I close my eyes, I can see the sea.

She saw a great dream rising from her love and from the silence, and dispersing in the sunset. She fell silent, beneath Andrea's gaze, and smiled faintly. She had said "with you"![10] Uttering those two syllables, she had closed her eyes: and her mouth had appeared more luminous, almost as if the splendor hidden by her eyelids and eyelashes were also gathered there.

—It seems to me that all these things are not outside of me, but that you created them in my soul, for my own joy. I have this illusion in me, deep down, every time I am standing before some vision of beauty and you are near me.

She was speaking slowly, with pauses, as if her voice were the delayed echo of another inaudible voice. Her words had, therefore, a strange tone, taking on a mysterious sound, seeming to come from the most secret depths of her being; they were not the common imperfect symbol, they were an intense, more vibrant expression, transcendent, with a vaster significance.

"And from her lips, as from a hyacinth full / Of honeydew, a liquid murmur drops, / Killing the sense with passion; sweet as stops / Of planetary music heard in trance."[11] The poet was recalling the verses of Percy Shelley. He repeated them to Maria, feeling himself won over by her emotion, penetrated by the charm of the hour, exalted by the appearance of things. A shiver ran through him when he was about to address her with the mystical familiar "you."[12]

—I have never managed, in the wildest dreams of my spirit, to reach this height. You rise above all my idealities, you shine above all the splendors of my thoughts, you illuminate me with a light that is almost unbearable . . .

She was standing erect in front of the balustrades, with her hands resting on the stone, her head raised, paler than on that memorable morning when she was walking beneath the flowers. Tears filled her half-closed eyes and glinted between her lashes; and from below lowered lids, she saw the sky before her turn rose-pink through the veil of her weeping.

There was a rainfall of roses in the sky, as when on October evenings the sun sank behind the Rovigliano hill, lighting up the ponds throughout the pine forest in Vicomìle. "Everywhere, roses roses roses drifted down, slowly, densely, delicately, like snowfall at dawn." Villa Medici, eternally green and bare of flowers, caught the countless soft petals, fallen from celestial gardens, on the peaks of its rigid arboreal walls.

She turned to go down. Andrea followed her. They walked in silence toward the stairs; they observed the woods that extended between the terrace and the belvedere. It seemed as if the brightness stopped at the edge, where the two custodial herms rise up, and could not pierce the darkness; it seemed that those trees stretched their branches into a different atmosphere or into dark water, below the sea, like oceanic vegetation.

She was possessed by sudden fear; she hurried toward the stairs, went down five or six steps; stopped, lost, quivering, hearing the beating of her arteries in the silence expanding like an enormous din. The villa had vanished; the damp gray staircase was narrowly enclosed between two walls, invaded here and there by weeds, dismal as that of a subterranean prison. She saw Andrea bend toward her, with a sudden gesture, to kiss her on the mouth.

—No, no, Andrea . . . No!

He held out his hands to restrain her, to force her.

—No!

Lost, she took his hand and drew it to her lips; she kissed it two, three times, lost. Then she began to run down the stairs, toward the door, as if demented.

—Maria! Maria! Stop!

They met face-to-face in front of the closed door, pale, panting, shaken by a terrible tremor, looking at each other's altered eyes with the roaring of their blood in their ears, believing they would suffocate. And at the same time, with unanimous impulse, they drew close together and kissed.

She said, fearing that she would faint, leaning against the door with a gesture of supreme supplication:

—No more . . . I am dying.

They remained for a minute facing each other without touching. It seemed that all the silence of the villa weighed upon them in that narrow place surrounded by high walls, like an uncovered tomb. One could distinctly hear the low and fitful cawing of the crows that were gathering on the roofs of the building or traversing the sky. Again, a strange sense of fear occupied the woman's heart. She glanced upward in alarm, to the summit of the walls. With effort, she said:

—We can go out now . . . You can open the door.

And her hand encountered Andrea's on the banister, in the urgency of her haste.

As she passed the two granite columns beneath the jasmine, bare of flowers, Andrea said:

—Look! The jasmine is flowering.

She did not turn, but smiled; and her smile was very sad, full of the shadows that were cast over her soul by the sudden reappearance of the name written on the belvedere. And while she walked down the mysterious avenue feeling all her blood altered by the kiss, an implacable anguish engraved that name, that name, upon her heart!

FOURTH BOOK

CHAPTER I

The Marquis of Mount Edgcumbe, opening the great secret armoire, the arcane library, was saying to Sperelli:

—You should design the clasps for me. The volume is in quarto,[1] dated by Lampsaque[2] the same as *Les Aphrodites* by Nerciat: 1734.[3] These engravings seem very fine to me. You judge for yourself.

He handed Sperelli the rare book. It was titled GERVETII—*De Concubitu—libri tres,*[4] decorated with erotic vignettes.

—This image is very significant, he added, pointing to one of the vignettes, which depicted an indescribable coupling of bodies. —It's something new that I did not know about. None of my erotic writers makes any mention of it . . .

He continued to talk, discussing several details, following the lines of the drawing with that whitish finger sprinkled with hairs on the first phalanx and ending in a pointed, shiny, slightly bluish nail, like the nail of quadrumanous animals. His words penetrated into Andrea's ear with an atrocious stridency.

—This Dutch edition by Petronius is magnificent. And this is the *Erotopaegnion* printed in Paris in 1798. Do you know the poem attributed to John Wilkes, "An Essay on Woman"? Here is a 1763 edition.

The collection was exceptionally rich. It included all the Pantagruelic and rococo literature of France: the Priapeia, the scatological fantasies, the Monacologies, the burlesque elegies, the catechisms, the idylls, the novels, the poems from the *Pipe cassée* by Vadé to the *Dangerous Liaisons,* from the *Arétin* by Augustin Carrache to the *Tourterelles de Zelmis;* from the *Descouverture du style impudique* to the *Faublas*. It included everything that was most refined and most ignoble produced by the human mind over the centuries in exposition of the ancient sacred hymn to the god of Lampsacus:[5] *Salve, sancte pater.*[6]

The collector took the books from the rows in the armoire and showed them to his young friend, talking continuously. His obscene hands caressingly touched the obscene books bound in leather and precious fabrics. He smiled insidiously, constantly. And a flash of madness passed through his gray eyes, beneath his enormous convex forehead.

—I also possess the first edition of Martial's *Epigrams,* the Venetian one, made by Vindelino di Spira in folio. Here it is. And here is Beau, the translator of Martial, the commentator of the famous three hundred and eighty-two obscenities. What do you think of these bindings? The clasps are by a master hand. This composition of priapi is done with great style.

Sperelli listened and looked, with a kind of shock that little by little changed to horror and pain. At every moment his eyes were drawn to a portrait of Elena that hung on the red damask on the wall.

—It is the portrait of Elena painted by Sir Frederick Leighton. But look here, everything Sade wrote! *Le roman philosophique, La philosophie dans le boudoir, Les crimes de l'amour, Les malheurs de la vertu* . . . You, surely, do not know this edition. It was made especially for me by Hérissey, with eighteenth-century Elzivirian characters, on paper made by the imperial manufacturers in Japan, in only one hundred and twenty-five exemplars. The divine marquis deserved this glory. The frontispieces, the titles, the initials, all the decorations bring together all the most exquisite things we know of erotic iconography! Look at the clasps!

The bindings of the volumes were admirable. Sharkskin leather, rough and rugged like the kind that encases the hilt of Japanese sabers, covered the front, back, and spine; the clasps and studs were of a bronze very rich in silver, very elegantly engraved, recalling the most beautiful ironwork of the sixteenth century.

—The author, Francis Redgrave, died in a madhouse. He was a young genius. I own all his studies. I'll show them to you.

The collector was becoming excited. He left the room to fetch the album of drawings by Francis Redgrave in the adjacent room. He walked with an unsteady, skipping gait, like a man who has the beginnings of paralysis or an incipient spinal disease; his torso remained rigid, not coordinated with the movement of his legs, like the torso of an automaton.

Andrea Sperelli watched him as he walked to the doorway, disquieted. Left alone, he was gripped by a terrible sense of anxiety. The room, papered in dark red damask, like the room in which Elena had given herself to him two years earlier, now seemed to him tragic and dismal. Maybe those were the same hangings that had heard Elena's words: "I like it!" The open armoire displayed the rows of obscene books, their outlandish bindings engraved with phallic symbols. On the wall hung the portrait of Lady Heathfield, alongside a copy of Joshua Reynolds's *Nelly O'Brien*. Both of these creatures gazed out from the depths of the canvas with the same penetrating intensity, the same ardor of passion, the same flame of sensual desire, the same prodigious eloquence; both had an ambiguous, enigmatic, sibylline mouth, the mouth of indefatigable, inexorable drinkers of souls; and both had a marble, immaculate forehead shining with perpetual purity.

—Poor Redgrave! said Lord Heathfield, returning with the case of drawings in his hands. —Without a doubt, he was a genius. No erotic fantasy surpasses his. Look! . . . Look! . . . What style! No artist, I think, in the study of human physiognomy, has come close to the depth and acuteness Redgrave achieved in his study of the phallus. Look!

He walked away for a moment to go and close the door again. Then he returned to the table near the window; and began to leaf through the collection, with Sperelli looking on, talking constantly, indicating with his apelike nail, sharpened like a weapon, the details of every figure.

He was speaking in his own language,[7] starting every sentence with a questioning tone and ending each one in the same tiresome cadence. Certain words lacerated Andrea's ears like the harsh sound of iron being scraped, like the screeching of a steel blade against a crystal plate.

And the drawings of the late Francis Redgrave passed before him.

They were frightening: they seemed to be the dream of an undertaker tortured by satyriasis; they unfolded like a terrifying macabre and priapic dance; they represented a hundred variations of one single motif, a hundred episodes of one single drama. And there were two *dramatis personae:* a priapus and a skeleton, a phallus and a *rictus*.[8]

—This is the best page, exclaimed the Marquis of Mount Edgcumbe, pointing to the last drawing, upon which at that moment a pale gleam of sunlight fell, slanting through the windows.

It was, in fact, a composition of extraordinary imaginative power: female skeletons dancing, in a night sky, guided by a flagellating Death. Over the wanton face of the moon drifted a black, monstrous cloud, drawn with vigor and skill worthy of the pencil of Hokusai; the pose of the dark dancer, the expression of her skull with the empty eye sockets, were imprinted with an admirable vitality, with a breathing reality never achieved by any other artist in the representation of Death; and that entire grotesque Sicinnide dance[9] of dislocated skeletons in scanty skirts, threatened by the whip, revealed the fearsome fever that had gripped the hand of the artist, the fearsome madness that had gripped his brain.

—This is the book that inspired Francis Redgrave to create this masterpiece. A great book! . . . the rarest among the rare . . . Do you not know Daniel Maclisius?

Lord Heathfield held out to Sperelli the treatise *De verberatione amatoria*.[10] He became more and more aroused, reflecting on cruel pleasures. His bald temples reddened and the veins of his forehead swelled and his mouth wrinkled constantly, slightly convulsively. And his hands, those hateful hands, gesticulated with brief but excited gestures, while his elbows remained rigid, of a paralytic rigidity. The unclean, ugly, ferocious beast within him appeared, all veils stripped away. In Sperelli's imagination[11] all the horrors of English profligacy arose: the acts of the Black Army[12] on the pavements of London; the implacable hunt for the "green virgins"; the brothels of the West End and of Halfousn Street; the elegant houses of Anna Rosemberg[13] and of the Jefferies woman;[14] the secret hermetically sealed rooms, padded from floor to ceiling, which muffle the sharp cries of the victims being tortured . . .

—Mumps! Mumps! Are you alone?

It was Elena's voice. She was knocking softly on one of the doors.

—Mumps!

Andrea jumped: all his blood veiled his eyes, inflamed his forehead, roared in his ears, as if a sudden dizziness was about to come over him. An insurgency of brutality unsettled him; an obscene vision swept through his mind, lit by a flash of lightning; a criminal thought passed darkly through his brain; a bloodthirsty craving roused him for a moment. Amid the upheaval provoked in him by those books, those drawings, the words of that man, the same instinctive impulse was rising up again from the blind depths of his being, that he had already felt that day on the racecourse, after the victory over Rùtolo, amid the pungent exhalations of his steaming horse. The phantom of a crime of passion tempted him and dissipated, rapidly, in a flash of lightning: to kill that man, take that woman with violence, thus satisfying the terrible carnal covetousness, and then to kill himself.

—I'm not alone, said the husband, without opening the door. —In a few minutes I will be able to bring Count Sperelli, who is here with me, into the salon to you.

He replaced Daniel Maclisius's treatise in the armoire; closed the case of drawings by Francis Redgrave and carried it into the adjacent room.

Andrea would have paid any price to extract himself from the torment that was awaiting him, and he was drawn to that torment at the same time. Once more, his gaze went up to the red wall, toward the dark painting where Elena's bloodless face shone, with her eyes that followed one, and her sibylline mouth. An acute and constant fascination emanated from that imperious immobility. That unique pallor dominated the red dusk of the room in a somber way. And he felt, again, that his wretched passion was incurable.

A desperate anguish assailed him. Would he therefore never again be able to possess that flesh? Was she therefore determined not to surrender to him? And would he eternally harbor within him the flame of unfulfilled desire? The arousal provoked in him by Lord Heathfield's books intensified his suffering, stirred up the fever. There was, in his mind, a confused tumult of erotic images: Elena's naked body joined the vile groups in the vignettes engraved by Coiny, took up poses of pleasure he had already seen during their erstwhile affair, twisted itself into new positions and offered itself up to the bestial lasciviousness of her husband. Horror! Horror!

—Would you like to go into the salon? the husband asked, reappearing in the doorway, fully composed and tranquil. —Are you going to design those clasps for me, then, for my Gervetius?

Andrea answered:

—I will try.

He could not repress his inner tremor. In the salon, Elena looked at him curiously, with an irritating smile.

—What were you both doing there? she asked, still smiling in the same way.

—Your husband was showing me memorabilia.

—Ah!

Her mouth was sardonic and she had a certain derisive air and evident mockery in her voice. She made herself comfortable on a wide couch covered with an amaranth Bukhara rug, on which pale cushions languished, embroidered with dull gold palms. She lounged in a relaxed position, looking at Andrea from beneath her enticing lashes, with those eyes that seemed to be suffused with the purest and finest oil. And she began to talk about mundane things, but with a voice that penetrated right into the young man's deepest veins, like an invisible fire.

Two or three times Andrea caught a burning look from Lord Heathfield fixed on his wife: a look that seemed charged with all the impurities and infamies he had previously stirred up. Elena laughed at almost every sentence, a mocking laugh, with strange ease, undisturbed by the desire of those two men who together had become aroused at the figures in the obscene books. Once more, the criminal thought passed through Andrea's mind, in a flash of lightning. All his fibers trembled.

When Lord Heathfield got up and left the room, Andrea burst out in a hoarse voice, grabbing Elena's wrist, coming so close to her as to graze her with his vehement breath:

—I'm losing my mind . . . I am going insane . . . I need you, Elena . . . I want you . . .

She freed her wrist with a haughty gesture. Then she said, with terrible coldness:

—I will have my husband give you twenty francs. Once you leave here, you may go and satisfy your cravings.

Sperelli leaped to his feet, livid.

Reentering the room, Lord Heathfield asked:

—Are you already leaving? Whatever's wrong with you?

And he smiled at his young friend, because he knew the effects of his books.

Sperelli bowed. Elena held out her hand to him without losing composure. The marquis accompanied him to the door, saying to him softly:

—I urge you not to forget my Gervetius.

Once he reached the portico, Andrea saw a carriage approaching on the avenue. A man with a great blond beard looked out of the window, waving. It was Galeazzo Secìnaro.

Instantly, the memory of the May Fair returned to mind, with the episode of Galeazzo paying for Elena Muti to dry her beautiful fingers, dipped in champagne, on his beard. He walked faster and stepped out onto the street: his senses were numbed and confused as if a deafening noise were issuing from deep inside his brain.

It was a warm and humid afternoon toward the end of April. The sun appeared and disappeared between fleecy, idle clouds. The sluggishness of the sirocco held Rome in its grip.

On the sidewalk of Via Sistina, he glimpsed ahead of him a lady walking slowly toward the Trinità. He recognized Donna Maria Ferres. He looked at his watch: it was, in fact, around five; just a few minutes before their habitual meeting time. Maria was going, certainly, to Palazzo Zuccari. He speeded up to reach her. When he was near her, he called her by name:

—Maria!

She gave a start.

—What are you doing here? I was coming up to you. It's five o'clock.

—There's still a few minutes to go. I was running so that I could await you. Forgive me.

—What's wrong? You're very pale, all agitated . . . Where have you been?

She frowned, staring at him through her veil.

—From the stables, replied Andrea, holding her gaze without reddening, as if he had no more blood in his body. —A horse that is very dear to me has hurt its knee through the fault of the jockey. He won't be able to participate in the Derby on Sunday, therefore. It makes me upset and angry. Forgive me. I was delayed without realizing it. But there are still a few minutes to five . . .

—Fine. Good-bye. I'm going.

They were on Piazza della Trinità. She stopped to take her leave, holding out her hand. A crease still remained between her brows. In the midst of her great sweetness, sometimes she had bouts of intolerance that were almost harsh, and disdainful movements that transfigured her.

—No, Maria. Come. Be nice. I'm going up to await you. Go as far as the gates of the Pincian Hill and come back again. Will you?

The clock of Trinità de' Monti sounded five.

—Do you hear that? added Andrea.

She said, after a slight hesitation:

—I'll come.

—Thank you. I love you.

—I love you.

They parted.

Donna Maria continued her walk; she crossed the square and entered the tree-lined avenue. Above her head, at intervals, along the wall, the languid breeze of the sirocco stirred the green trees to a murmur. In the humid warmth of the air, waves of scent occasionally wafted by and vanished. The clouds appeared lower; flocks of birds almost grazed the ground. Yet, in that enervating heaviness, there was something mild that softened the tormented heart of the Sienese woman.

Since she had yielded to Andrea's desire, her heart pulsed in happiness furrowed with deep disquiet; all her Christian blood was becoming inflamed with the pleasure she had never experienced before, and chilled with the consternation of guilt. Her passion was supreme, overwhelming, immense; so fierce that often for long hours it deleted the memory of her daughter. She went so far as to forget Delfina sometimes; to neglect her! And then she had sudden recurrences of remorse, repentance, tenderness, in which she covered the head of her astonished daughter in kisses and tears, sobbing with a desperate grief, as if over the head of a dead person.

Her entire being was becoming refined by the flame, sharper, stimulated, was acquiring a prodigious sensitivity, a kind of clairvoyant lucidness, a faculty of divination that gave her strange tortures. Almost at each of Andrea's deceits, she felt a shadow pass over her soul and felt an undefined restlessness that sometimes became condensed, taking the form of suspicion. And suspicion ate at her, made kisses bitter and caresses sour for her, until it dissipated beneath the impulses and ardor of her uncomprehending lover.

She was jealous. Jealousy caused her an implacable spasm; jealousy not of the present but of the past. Due to that cruelty that jealous people inflict on themselves, she would have liked to read Andrea's mind, uncover all his memories, see all the traces left by ex-lovers; to know, to know. The question that most often came to her lips, when Andrea was silent, was this:—What are you thinking about?—And while she was uttering these words, inevitably the shadow was passing into her eyes and over her soul; inevitably a wave of sadness rose up from her heart.

That day, too, with Andrea's sudden arrival, had she not felt an instinctive stirring of suspicion deep inside her? Indeed, a lucid thought had flashed into her mind: the thought that Andrea had come from Lady Heathfield's house, from Palazzo Barberini.

She knew that Andrea had been that woman's lover; she knew that that woman's name was Elena, and lastly, she knew that she was the Elena of the inscription. "*Ich lebe! . . .*" Goethe's couplet blared loudly in her heart. That lyrical shout gave her the measure of Andrea's love for that beautiful woman. He must have loved her immensely!

Walking beneath the trees, she remembered Elena's appearance in the concert hall, at Palazzo dei Sabini, and the badly concealed agitation of her ex-lover. She remembered the terrible emotion that had overcome her one evening at a party at the Austrian Embassy, when Countess Starnina had said to her as Elena passed them: "How do you find the Heathfield woman? She was a great flame of our friend Sperelli's, and I think she still is."

"I think she still is." How much torment because of that phrase! She had watched her great rival, constantly, amid the elegant crowd; and more than once their eyes had met, and she had felt an indefinable shiver. Then, that same evening, having been introduced to each other by the Baroness of Boeckhorst, in the midst of the crowd, they had exchanged a simple bow of the head. And the tacit nod had been repeated subsequently, on the very rare occasions that Donna Maria Ferres y Capdevila had passed through a society salon.

Why were these fears, appeased or quelled beneath the wave of elation, rising up again with so much vehemence? Why could she not manage to repress them, expel them? Why did all those unknown forebodings agitate inside her at every small jolt of her imagination?

Walking beneath the trees, she felt her anxiety grow. Her heart was not satisfied; the dream that had risen in her heart—on that mystical morning, beneath the florid trees in the presence of the sea—had not come true. The purest and most precious part of that love had remained there, in the solitary wood, in the symbolic forest that flowers and bears fruit, perpetually contemplating the Infinite.

She stopped in front of the parapet that faces San Sebastianello. The ancient oaks, of a green so dark it seemed almost black, extended their branches over the fountain, creating an artificial, lifeless roof. The trunks bore numerous lesions, patched with lime and brick, like the openings in a wall.—Oh, young arbutuses radiant and breathing in the light! The water dripping from the upper granite basin into the lower basin emitted a burst of moans, at intervals, like a heart that fills up with anguish and then flows over in weeping. Oh, melody of the Hundred Fountains, on the bay-tree avenue! The city lay dead, as if covered by the ash of an invisible volcano, silent and funereal like a city undone by pestilence, enormous, formless, dominated by the cupola that rose up from its lap like a cloud. Oh, sea! Oh, calm sea!

She felt her anxiety grow. An obscure threat came to her from these things. She was invaded by that same sense of fear that she had already experienced more than once. The thought of punishment flashed into her Christian mind.

And yet she shivered deep within her being at the thought that her lover was waiting for her; at the thought of the kisses, the caresses, the crazy words, she felt her blood inflame, her soul become languid. The shiver of passion superseded the shiver of divine fear. And she set off toward her lover's house, anxious, upset, as if she were going to their first rendezvous.

—Oh, finally! exclaimed Andrea, gathering her into his arms, drinking in her breath from her breathless mouth.

Then, taking her hand and pressing it to his chest:

—Feel my heart. If you had delayed one more minute, it would have broken.

She placed her cheek where her hand had just been. He kissed the nape of her neck.

—Can you hear?

—Yes; it's speaking to me.

—What's it saying?

—That you don't love me.

—What's it saying to you? repeated the young man, biting her on the back of her neck, preventing her from straightening up.

She laughed.

—That you love me.

She took off her mantle, her hat, her gloves. She went to smell the white lilac flowers that filled the tall Florentine goblets; the ones in the Borghese tondo. On the carpets her steps were of an extraordinary lightness; and nothing was sweeter than the act with which she buried her face in the delicate blooms.

—Take it, she said, biting off a flower head and holding it in her mouth, outside her lips.

—No, I shall take another flower from your mouth, less white but more delicious . . .

They kissed, for a long, long time, amid the perfume.

He said, his voice slightly distorted, pulling her:

—Come, let's go there.

—No, Andrea, it's late. Not today. Let's stay here. I will make tea for you; you will give me lots of sweet caresses.

She took his hands and entwined her fingers with his.

—I don't know what's wrong with me. I feel my heart so full of tenderness I could almost cry.

Her words trembled; her eyes grew wet.

—If only I didn't have to leave you, if only I could stay all evening!

A deep sorrow in her was prompting tones of indefinable melancholy.

—To think that you will never know all of my love! To think that I will never know yours! Do you love me? Tell me, always tell me that you do, a hundred times, a thousand times, tirelessly! Do you love me?

—Don't you know, perhaps?

—I don't know.

She uttered these words in such a low voice that Andrea barely heard her.

—Maria!

She bent her head onto his chest, in silence; she rested her forehead on it, almost waiting for him to talk, to listen to him.

He looked at that poor head tilted under the burden of foreboding; he felt the light pressure of that noble and sad forehead on his breast, which was hardened by lies, bound in falseness. An anguished emotion constricted him; a sense of human mercy for that human suffering closed his throat. And that good sentiment of his soul converted itself into lying words, giving the tremor of sincerity to lying words.

—You *don't know*! . . . You spoke softly; the breath died on your lips; something inside you rose up against what you were saying; all those memories of our love rose up against what you were saying. You *don't know* that I love you! . . .

She remained bowed, listening, quivering intensely, recognizing, or believing that she recognized the real sound of passion in the young man's emotional voice, that intoxicating sound that she believed was inimitable. And he spoke to her almost in her ear, in the silence of the room, exhaling his warm breath onto her neck, with pauses softer than words.

—To have one single assiduous thought, at all times, at all moments; . . . not to conceive of any other happiness than the superhuman one irradiated by your sole presence onto my being; . . . to live all day in restless raging, terrible expectation, for the moment in which I will see you again; . . . to nurture the image of your caresses, once you have left, and again to possess you in a shadow I have almost created; . . . to feel you, when I sleep, to feel you on my heart, alive, real, palpable, mingled with my blood, mingled with my life; . . . and to believe *only* in you, to pledge myself *only* to you, to place my faith, my strength, my pride, my entire world, everything I dream, and everything I hope for, *only* in you . . .

She lifted her face streaked with tears. He fell silent, stopping the warm drops on her cheeks with his lips. She wept and smiled, placing her tremulous fingers in his hair, lost, sobbing:

—My soul, my soul!

He made her sit down and knelt at her feet, without ceasing to kiss her on the eyelids. Suddenly, he experienced a jolt. He had felt her long lashes palpitate rapidly on his lips, like a restless wing. It was a strange caress that gave him unbearable pleasure; it was a caress that Elena had once used to make, laughing, again and again, forcing her lover to feel the small nervous spasm caused by tickling; and Maria had learned it from him, and often, under the effects of that caress, he could evoke the image of the *other.*

At his jolt, Maria smiled. And as she still had one glittering tear remaining on her lashes, she said:

—Drink this one, too!

And as he drank, she laughed, unaware.

She was emerging from her weeping almost happy, reassured, full of charm.

—I will make tea for you, she said.

—No, stay here, seated, with me.

He was becoming aroused, seeing her on the sofa among the cushions. A sudden image of Elena superimposed itself on his mind.

—Let me get up! Maria begged, freeing her upper body from his embrace. —I want you to drink my tea. You'll see. The scent will go right into your soul.

She was talking about a precious tea that had arrived from Calcutta, which she had given to Andrea the day before.

She stood up and went to sit on a leather chair covered with Chimeras, where the saffron-pink color of the ancient dalmatic was still fading exquisitely. The fine Casteldurante majolica still shone on the small table.

In carrying out the task, she said many kind things, spreading her goodness and tenderness with complete abandon; she naively enjoyed that dear secret intimacy, in that tranquil room, amid that refined luxury. Behind her, as behind the Virgin in Sandro Botticelli's tondo, the crystal cups could be seen, crowned by bunches of white lilacs; and her archangel hands moved between Luzio Dolci's mythological scenes and Ovid's hexameters.

—What are you thinking about? she asked Andrea, who was near her, seated on the carpet, his head leaning against an arm of the chair.

—I'm listening to you. Speak some more!

—No more.

—Speak! Tell me lots of things, so many things . . .

—What things?

—Things that only you know.

He was allowing her voice to lull the anguish he felt, which came to him from the *other;* he was making her voice bring to life the figure of the *other.*

—Can you smell it? exclaimed Maria, pouring the boiling water over the aromatic leaves.

An intense scent pervaded the air with the steam. Andrea breathed it in. Then he said, closing his eyes and leaning his head back:

—Kiss me.

And as soon as he felt the contact of her lips, he started so violently that Maria was surprised.

She poured the drink into a cup and offered it to him with a mysterious smile.

—Be careful. There is a potion in it.

He refused the offer.

—I don't want to drink from that cup.

—Why?

—I want to drink—from you.

—But how?

—Like this. Take a sip and don't swallow.

—It's still too hot.

She laughed at this whim of her lover's. He was slightly convulsed, extremely pale, with a strange look in his eyes. They waited for the tea to cool down. Every so often, Maria brought the cup to her lips to try it; then she laughed, with a small fresh laugh that did not seem hers.

—Now we can drink it, she announced.

—Now, take a big sip. Like this.

She kept her lips closed, to keep the liquid in her mouth; but her large eyes, which the recent tears had made more splendid, were laughing.

—Now, let it out, bit by bit.

He drank from the kiss, sucking in the entire mouthful of tea. When she felt herself running out of breath, she hurried the slow drinker on by squeezing his temples.

—My God! You wanted to suffocate me.

She lay back on the cushions, almost as if to rest, languid and happy.

—How did it taste? You even drank my soul. I'm all empty.

He remained pensive, staring into space.

—What are you thinking about? Maria asked him again, raising herself up suddenly, placing one finger in the middle of his forehead as if to stop his invisible thought.

—Nothing, he replied. —I was not thinking. I was following inside myself the effects of the potion . . .

Then she also wanted to try. She drank from him with delight. Then she exclaimed, placing her hand on her heart and letting out a long sigh:

—How I like it!

Andrea trembled. Was that not the same tone as Elena's, the night she first gave herself to him? Were those not the same words? He looked at her mouth.

—Say it again.

—What?

—The thing you said.

—Why?

—It's such a sweet word, when you say it . . . You can't understand . . . Say it again.

She smiled, unaware, slightly agitated by her lover's strange, almost shy expression.

—Well, then, I like it!

—And me?

—What?

—Do you—me?

Perplexed, she looked at her lover, who was twisting at her feet, convulsed, waiting for the word he wanted to tear from her.

—And me?

—Ah! I . . . like you!

—Like that! Like that! Say it again! Again!

She did so, without knowing why. He felt an indefinable spasm and desire.

—Why are you closing your eyes? she asked, not suspiciously, but so that he would describe the sensations he was feeling to her.

—To die.

He leaned his head on her knees, remaining for a few minutes in that position, silent, obscure. She caressed his hair slowly, his temples, his forehead, where, below her caress, an evil thought was stirring. Around them the room was slowly being immersed in shadows; the intermingled scent of the flowers and the tea floated; forms were fusing into one single harmonious, rich appearance, without reality.

After a while, Maria said:

—Get up, love. I must leave you. It's late.

He stood up, begging her:

—Stay with me for another moment, until the Hail Mary.

And he pulled her down again onto the couch, where the cushions glittered in the shadows. In the shadows he laid her down with a sudden movement, holding her head tightly, covering her face with kisses. His ardor was almost irate. He imagined himself to be holding the *other's* head, and imagined that head tainted by her husband's lips; and he felt not revulsion at it but, on the contrary, an even more savage desire. From the basest depths of his instinct, all the turbid sensations aroused in the presence of that man rose up again in his heart; all the obscenities and depravities rose to his heart, like a wave of mud that has been stirred up; and all those vile things passed through his kisses onto Maria's cheeks, her forehead, her hair, her neck, her mouth.

—No, let me go! she shouted, freeing herself from his tight embrace with effort. And she ran toward the tea table to light the candles.

—Be good, she added, slightly out of breath, tidying herself with a gently vexatious air.

He had remained on the couch and was watching her, mute.

She went toward the wall, near the fireplace, where the small Mona Amorrosisca mirror hung. She put on her hat and veil in front of that clouded glass, which had the appearance of some murky, slightly greenish water.

—How sorry I am to leave you, this evening! . . . This evening more than other times . . . she murmured, oppressed by the melancholy of the hour.

In the room, the violet light of dusk grappled with the candlelight. The cup of tea was on the edge of the table, cold, diminished by two sips. Above the tall crystal vases the lilac flowers appeared whiter. The cushion of the armchair still retained the imprint of the body that had been pressed into it earlier.

The bell of Trinità de' Monti began to peal.

—My God, how late it is! Help me put on my mantle, said the poor creature, turning toward Andrea.

He grasped her once again in his arms, laid her down and covered her with furious kisses, blindly, lost, with a devouring ardor, without speaking, suffocating her moans on her mouth, suffocating on her mouth an impulse that came to him, almost invincible, to shout out Elena's name. And on the body of the unknowing woman, he consummated the horrible sacrilege.

They remained for a few minutes entwined together. She said, in an exhausted and elated voice:

—You are taking my very life!

That impassioned vehemence made her happy.

She said: —Soul, my soul, all, all mine!

She said, happy:

—I feel your heart beating . . . so strongly, so strongly!

Then she said, with a sigh:

—Let me get up. I must go.

Andrea was as white and agitated as a murderer.

—What is the matter? she asked him tenderly.

He forced himself to smile at her. He answered:

—I have never felt such a profound emotion. I thought I would die.

He turned to one of the vases, took out the bunch of flowers, and offered it to Maria, accompanying her to the door, almost urging her to leave, because every gesture, every look, every word of hers gave him an unbearable suffering.

—Good-bye, my love. Dream of me! said the poor creature from the doorway, with her supreme tenderness.

—

CHAPTER II

On the morning of May 20, Andrea Sperelli was walking up the Corso, inundated with sunlight, when he heard himself being called in front of the door of the club.

A cluster of his gentlemen friends stood on the sidewalk, enjoying the sight of ladies passing, and gossiping. Giulio Musèllaro was there, with Ludovico Barbarisi, the Duke of Grimiti, and Galeazzo Secìnaro; Gino Bommìnaco was there, too, with a few others.

—Don't you know about what happened last night? Barbarisi asked him.

—No. What happened?

—Don Manuel Ferres, the minister of Guatemala . . .

—Well?

—He was caught cheating while playing cards.

Sperelli controlled himself, although some of the gentlemen were watching him with a certain malicious curiosity.

—How?

—Galeazzo was there; in fact, he was playing at the same table.

Prince Secìnaro began to recount the details.

Andrea Sperelli did not affect indifference. He listened, rather, with an attentive and grave manner. Finally he said:

—I am very sorry about this.

He remained for a few more minutes in the group; then he greeted his friends, taking his leave.

—Which way are you walking? Secìnaro asked him.

—I'm going home.

—I'll walk with you for part of the way.

They walked down toward Via de' Condotti. The Corso was

a happy river of sunlight, from Piazza di Venezia to Piazza del Popolo. Ladies were walking alongside glittering shopwindows, dressed in light-colored spring outfits. The Princess of Ferentino walked past with Barbarella Viti, beneath a lace parasol. Bianca Dolcebuono walked by. Leonetto Lanza's young bride passed them.

—Did you know him, that Ferres? Galeazzo asked Sperelli, who was silent.

—Yes; I met him last year, in September, at Schifanoja, at my cousin Francesca Ateleta's. The wife is a great friend of Francesca's. I'm very sorry about this event, therefore. One should try to publicize this as little as possible. You would do me a service, by helping me . . .

Galeazzo offered to do so with cordial concern.

—I believe—he said—that the scandal could be avoided in part, if the minister presented his resignation to his government, but without delay, as the president of the club has enjoined him to do. The minister, however, is refusing. Last night he had the attitude of a person who has been offended; he was raising his voice. And the proof was there! It would be necessary to persuade him . . .

They continued talking about the fact as they walked along. Sperelli was grateful to Secìnaro for his cordial concern. Secìnaro was favorably inclined toward friendly confidences, by that intimacy.

On the corner of Via de' Condotti, they glimpsed Mount Edgcumbe's wife, who was walking along the sidewalk on the left, along the Japanese shopwindows, with that relaxed, rhythmic, fascinating gait of hers.

—Donna Elena, said Galeazzo.

Both looked at her; both felt the allure of that gait. But Andrea's gaze penetrated her clothing and saw the well-known form, her divine back.

When they caught up to her, they both greeted her; and overtook her. Now they could no longer observe her, and were instead observed. For Andrea it was a new torture, walking alongside a rival, beneath the gaze of the longed-for woman, thinking that the tormenting eyes were delighting in making a comparison. He compared himself mentally with Secìnaro.

The latter had the bovine structure of a blond, blue-eyed Lucius Verus;[1] and amid the magnificent golden abundance of his beard, there glistened a red mouth that was of no spiritual significance but that was beautiful. He was tall, square-shouldered, and vigorous, with an elegance that was not refined but self-assured.

—And so? Andrea inquired of him, pushed to boldness by an invincible frenzy. —Is the affair going well?

He knew he could speak that way to that man.

Galeazzo turned to him with an air that was half astonished, half questioning, because he did not expect such a question from him, and even less so in such a flippant, perfectly calm tone. Andrea was smiling.

—Ah, my siege has been going on for so long! replied the bearded prince. —Since time immemorial, with various resumptions, and always without any luck. I always got there too late: someone had already beaten me to the conquest. But I have never lost heart. I was convinced that, sooner or later, my turn would come. *Attendre pour atteindre.*[2] In fact . . .

—Well?

—Lady Heathfield is more benign to me than the Duchess of Scerni. I will have, I hope, the sought-after honor of being inscribed, after you, on the list . . .

He broke out in somewhat coarse laughter, showing his white teeth.

—I believe that my Indian feats, divulged by Giulio Musèllaro, have added a few heroic strands to my beard, of an irresistible virtue.

—Oh, but your beard, these days, must be quivering with memories . . .

—Which memories?

—Bacchic memories.

—I don't understand.

—What! You've forgotten the famous May Fair of '84?

—Oh, fancy! You've just reminded me of it. The third anniversary is due in the next few days . . . You weren't there, though. And who told you about it?

—You want to know too much, my dear fellow!

—Tell me, I beg of you.

—Rather think about making this anniversary worthwhile; and tell me about it soon.

—When will we see each other again?

—Whenever you like.

—Dine with me this evening, at the club, toward eight. This way we can take care of the other matter together.

—All right. Good-bye, Goldenbeard! Run!

They parted in Piazza di Spagna at the base of the stairs; and as Elena was crossing the square heading toward Via dei Due Macelli, to walk up toward the Four Fountains, Secìnaro caught up and walked together with her.

Andrea, after the effort of dissimulation, felt his heart weigh heavily, horribly, as he walked up the stairs. He felt he could not drag it to the summit. But he was sure, by now, that Secìnaro would confide everything to him, later on; and it almost seemed as if he had obtained some advantage! With a kind of drunkenness, a kind of madness caused him by the excess of suffering, he was going forth blindly toward new and ever crueler torments, ever more senseless, aggravating and complicating the condition of his spirit in a thousand ways, passing from perversion to perversion, from aberration to aberration, from atrocity to atrocity, without being able to stop, without having one moment of respite in the vertiginous fall. He was devoured by an unquenchable fever that with its heat released all the germs of human abjection within the obscure abysses of his being. Every thought, every feeling bore the blemish. He was one great wound.

And yet, deceit itself bound him strongly to the deceived woman. His spirit had adapted itself so strangely to the monstrous comedy that it almost could not conceive of other modes of pleasure, other modes of pain. That incarnation of one woman into another was no longer an act of exasperated passion, but a vice, and hence an urgent need, a necessity. And the unwitting instrument of that vice had therefore become as necessary to him as the vice itself. By some phenomenon of sensual depravity, he had almost gone so far as to believe that the actual possession of Elena would not have afforded him the intense, rare enjoyment afforded him by that imaginary possession. He had almost gone so far as not to be able to separate, in his imagining of pleasure, the two women. And as he thought that pleasure was diminished in the actual possession of one woman, so, too, did he feel all his nerves to be blunted when, through fatigue of the imagination, he found himself before the *immediate* real form of the other.

Therefore he could not tolerate the thought that Maria could be removed from him by the ruin of Don Manuel Ferres.

When Maria came to him toward evening, he immediately realized that the poor creature was still unaware of her misfortune. But the next day, she arrived panting, distressed, as pale as a corpse; and she sobbed in his arms, hiding her face:

—Do you know?

The news had spread. Scandal was inevitable; ruin was irremediable. Days of desperate torment followed, in which Maria, left alone after the hasty departure of the cheat, abandoned by her few friends, assailed by her husband's countless creditors, lost amid the legal formalities of the impoundment, amid the summoners and the usurers and other vile people, demonstrated heroic pride, but without managing to save herself from the final collapse that crushed all hope.

And she refused all help from her lover; she never spoke of her martyrdom to her lover, who reproached her for the brevity of her visits of love; she never complained; she could still muster a less sad smile for him; she could still obey his whims, concede her body passionately to the contaminations, and dispense the warmest tenderness of her soul onto the head of her executioner.

Everything was crumbling around her. Punishment had suddenly struck her. The forebodings had been true!

And she did not regret having yielded to her lover; she did not feel remorse for having given herself to him with so much abandon; she did not mourn her lost purity. She had only one sorrow, stronger than any remorse and any fear, stronger than any other pain: and it was the thought of having to go away, to leave, to have to part from the man who was, for her, the life of her life.

—I will die, my friend. I'm going to die far away from you, all alone. You will not close my eyes . . .

She spoke to him of her death with a sorrowful smile, full of resigned certainty. Andrea was still causing her to harbor some flashes of hope; was still sowing in her heart the seeds of a dream, the seed of future suffering!

—I will not allow you to die. You will still be mine, for a long time. Our love will still have happy days . . .

He spoke to her about an imminent future. He would move to Florence; from there he would travel often to Siena under the pretext of his studies; he would stay in Siena for months on end, copying ancient paintings, researching ancient chronicles. Their mysterious love affair would have its own hidden nest, in a deserted road, or outside the city walls, in the countryside, in a villa decorated with majolica made by the Della Robbias, surrounded by a kitchen garden. She would be able to find an hour here and there for him. Sometimes, she would also come to Florence for a week of happiness. She would transfer their idyll to the Fiesole hills, in a September that was as mild as April; and the cypresses of Montughi would be as clement as those of Schifanoja.

—If only it were true! If only it were true! sighed Maria.

—Don't you believe me?

—Yes, I believe you; but my heart tells me that all these things, these too-sweet things, will not be anything more than a dream.

She wanted Andrea to hold her for a long time in his arms; and she stayed there, leaning against his chest, without talking, huddling there as if to hide away, with the movement and the shivering of a sick person or one who has been threatened and needs protection. She asked Andrea for spiritual caresses, those that in her language of intimacy she called "good caresses," the ones that touched her and moved her to tears of yearning that were sweeter than any pleasure. She could not comprehend why, in those moments of supreme spirituality, in those last sorrowful hours of passion, in those hours of parting, her lover was not satisfied with kissing her hands.

She beseeched him, almost hurt by Andrea's crude desire:

—No, love! It seems that you are closer to me, more bound to me, more mingled with my being, when you sit next to me, when you take my hands, when you gaze deep into my eyes, when you tell me the things that only you know how to say. It seems that the other caresses distance us, that they place some kind of shadow between us . . . I can't explain my thoughts properly . . . The other caresses leave me so sad, so so sad . . . I don't know . . . and tired, with such a dreadful tiredness!

She beseeched him, humble, submissive, fearing that she would displease him. She did not cease to evoke memories, memories, memories, past ones, recent ones, in the minutest detail, remembering the slightest gestures, the most fleeting words, all the smallest, most insignificant facts that had had significance for her. Her heart returned with greatest frequency to the very first days at Schifanoja.

—Do you remember? Do you remember?

And suddenly tears would fill her despondent eyes.

One evening Andrea asked her, thinking of her husband:

—Since I met you, have you been *all* mine?

—Always.

—I'm not asking about your soul . . .

—Hush! Always *all* yours.

And he, who had never believed this of any of his adulterous lovers, believed her; he did not have even the shadow of a doubt regarding the truth of what she was stating.

He believed her; because, despite contaminating her and deceiving her without restraint, he knew that he was loved by an elevated and noble spirit; he knew by now that he was in the presence of a great and terrible passion; by now, he was as conscious of that greatness as he was of his own depravity. He knew, he knew he was immensely loved; and sometimes, in the frenzy of his imaginings, he went so far as to bite the mouth of the sweet creature to stop himself from shouting out a name that rose up in him with invincible force to his throat; and the good and sorrowful mouth bled in an unconscious smile, saying:

—Even like this, you don't hurt me.

Very few days were left until her departure. Miss Dorothy had taken Delfina to Siena and had returned to help the lady with the last, most onerous vexations and to accompany her on the journey. In Siena, in her mother's house, the truth was not known. Even Delfina knew nothing. Maria had restricted herself to sending the news that Manuel had suddenly been recalled by his government. She was preparing herself for the departure;

she was preparing herself to leave the rooms, full of beloved things, passing through the hands of public evaluators who had already written up the inventory and had established the day of the auction:— June 20, Monday, at ten in the morning.

On the evening of June 9, just about to leave Andrea, she was searching for a lost glove. While looking for it, she saw on a table the book by Percy Bysshe Shelley, the same volume that Andrea had lent her during the time at Schifanoja, the volume in which she had read the *Recollection* before the outing to Vicomìle, the dear, sad volume in which she had underlined two verses with her nail:

And forget me, for I can *never*
Be thine!

She picked it up with visible emotion; she leafed through it and found the page, the imprint of her nail, the two verses.

—*Never!* she murmured, shaking her head. —Do you remember? And barely eight months have passed!

She remained slightly pensive; she leafed through the book again; and read a few other verses.

—He is our poet, she added. —How many times you have promised to take me to the English cemetery! Do you remember? We were going to take flowers to the grave . . . Do you want to go? Take me before I leave. It will be our last outing.

He said:

—We'll go tomorrow.

They left when the sun was already sinking. In the open carriage, she held a bunch of roses on her lap. They passed below the tree-lined Aventino. In the port of Ripa Grande, they glimpsed ships at anchor, laden with Sicilian wine.

In the vicinity of the cemetery they alighted; they walked for a stretch, as far as the gate, in silence. Maria felt deep in her heart that she was not going only to take flowers to the grave of a poet, but that she was going to grieve, in that place of death, for something of herself that was irreparably lost. Percy's fragment, read in the night in her insomnia, resounded at the base of her soul, while she observed the cypresses reaching high into the sky, on the other side of the whitewashed wall.

Death is here and death is there,
Death is busy everywhere,
All around, within, beneath,
Above is death—and we are death.

Death has set his mark and seal
On all we are and all we feel
On all we know and all we fear,

First our pleasures die—and then
Our hopes, and then our fears—and when
These are dead, the debt is due,
Dust claims dust—and we die too.

All things that we love and cherish,
Like ourselves must fade and perish;
Such is our rude mortal lot—
Love itself would, did they not.[3]

Crossing over the threshold, she placed her arm beneath Andrea's, and a small shiver ran through her.

A sense of solitude pervaded the cemetery. Several gardeners were watering the plants against the wall, tilting the watering cans this way and that with constant and regular movements, in silence. The funereal cypresses rose up straight and immobile in the air: only their tips, tinted gold by the sun, had a slight tremor. Between the rigid, greenish trunks, like travertine stone, emerged white tombs, square gravestones, broken columns, urns, arches. A mysterious shadow, a sense of religious peace and almost human gentleness descended from the dark bulk of the cypresses, the way limpid, beneficent water trickles down from hard rock. That even regularity of the arboreal shapes and that modest candor of the sepulchral marble gave the soul a sense of grave and sweet repose. But in the midst of the trunks aligned like the pipes of an organ, and amid those gravestones, the oleanders undulated with grace, blushing red with fresh bunches of blooms; the roses were losing their petals at every gust of wind, shedding their scented snow on the grass; the eucalyptuses inclined their pale coiffures, which glinted silver here and there; the willows cascaded their soft tears over the crosses and the wreaths; cactuses here and there displayed their magnificent white clusters resembling sleeping flocks of butterflies or bunches of unusual feathers. The silence was interrupted now and then by the cry of some scattered bird.

Andrea said, pointing to the summit of the hill:

—The poet's tomb is up there, near the ruin, on the left, under the last tower.

Maria detached herself from him to walk up the narrow pathways, between the low myrtle hedges. She walked ahead and her lover followed. Her pace was somewhat tired; she stopped at frequent intervals; and at every interval she turned around to smile at her lover. She was wearing black; she wore a black veil over her face, which reached her top lip; and her faint smile trembled beneath the black edge, shaded as with a shadow of mourning. Her oval chin was whiter and purer than the roses she carried in her hand.

It happened that as she turned, a rose shed its petals. Andrea bent down to gather the petals from the path, before her feet. She looked at him. He knelt on the ground, saying:

—Beloved!

A memory rose up in her mind, as clear as a vision.

—Do you remember—she said—*that morning,* at Schifanoja, when I threw a fistful of petals at you from the penultimate terrace? You knelt on the step while I descended . . . Those days, I don't know, they seem so near and so distant! It seems as if I lived through them yesterday, that I lived through them a century ago. But did I dream them, perhaps?

Walking through the low myrtle hedges, they reached the last tower on the left, where the tomb of the poet and of Trelawny was to be found. The jasmine that climbs over the ancient ruin was in flower, but of the violets nothing remained except their dense foliage. The tips of the cypresses reached the line of vision and trembled, illuminated more intensely by the extreme flush of the sun, setting behind the black cross on Monte Testaccio. A violet cloud edged with burning gold navigated on high, toward the Aventine.

"These are two friends whose lives were undivided. / So let their memory be now they have glided / Under the grave: let

not their bones be parted / For their two hearts in life were single-hearted."[4]

Maria repeated the last verse. Then she said to Andrea, moved by a sensitive thought:

—Loosen my veil.

And she drew close to him, throwing her head back slightly so that he could untie the knot at the nape of her neck. His fingers touched her hair, that wonderful hair that, when it was loose, seemed to come alive like a forest, with a deep, sweet life of its own; in its shadow he had savored many times the voluptuousness of his deception, and many times he had evoked a perfidious image. She said:

—Thank you.

And she removed her veil from her face, looking at Andrea with eyes that were slightly dazzled. She appeared very beautiful. The circles around her eye sockets were darker and hollower, but her pupils shone with a fire that was more penetrating. The dense locks of her hair adhered to her temples, like clusters of dark, slightly violet hyacinths. The center of her forehead, uncovered and free, shone by contrast with a whiteness that was almost like that of the moon. All her features had become more refined, had lost something of their materiality in the assiduous flame of love and pain.

She wrapped her black veil around the rose stems and knotted the ends with great care; then she breathed in their scent, almost burying her face in the bunch. And then she deposited them on the simple stone where the name of the poet was inscribed. Her gesture contained an indefinable expression that Andrea could not comprehend.

They walked on, searching for the grave of John Keats, the poet of *Endymion*.

Andrea asked her, stopping to look back toward the tower:

—Where did you get those roses?

She smiled at him again, but with damp eyes.

—They're yours, the ones from the night it snowed; they flowered again last night. Don't you believe me?

The evening wind was picking up; and the entire sky behind the hill was diffused with the color of gold, in the midst of which the cloud was dissolving as if consumed by a pyre. The cypresses standing in order on that field of light were more grandiose and more mystical, completely penetrated by rays, their sharp peaks vibrating. The statue of Psyche at the top of the middle avenue had taken on the pallor of flesh. The oleanders rose up in the background like mobile purple cupolas. The crescent moon rose above the Pyramid of Cestius, in a deep glaucous sky like the water of a calm gulf.

They descended along the middle avenue until they reached the gate. The gardeners were still watering the plants at the base of the wall, moving the watering cans from side to side with a constant, regular movement, in silence. Two other men, holding a velvet-and-silver funeral pall by the corners, were shaking it hard; and the dust glittered as it dispersed. The sound of bells reached them from the Aventine.

Maria pressed herself against her lover's arm, no longer able to bear the anguish, feeling the ground cede under her feet at every step, believing that she would be drained of all her blood on the way. And as soon as she was in the carriage, she burst into desperate tears, sobbing on her lover's shoulder.

—I'm dying.

But she was not dying. And it would have been better for her if she had died.

Two days later, Andrea was lunching together with Galeazzo Secìnaro at a table in the Caffè di Roma. It was a warm morning. The caffè was almost deserted, immersed in shade and tedium. The waiters dozed amid the buzzing of flies.

—So—recounted the bearded prince—knowing that she likes to give herself in extraordinary, bizarre circumstances, I dared to . . .

He was crudely recounting the extremely audacious way in which he had managed to conquer Lady Heathfield; he recounted without scruples and without reticence, not leaving out any details, praising the attributes of his acquisition to the connoisseur. He interrupted himself, every now and then, to plunge his knife into a piece of steaming, succulent, rare meat, or to empty a glass of red wine. Health and strength emanated from all his gestures.

Andrea Sperelli lit a cigarette. He was feeling the impulse to retch, and hence could not manage to swallow any food, or to overcome the revulsion of his stomach, which was in utter turmoil, beset by a horrible tremor. When Secìnaro poured wine for him, he drank it together with poison.

Secìnaro, at a certain point, although he was not at all insightful, began to have some doubts. He looked at Elena's ex-lover. The latter was not showing, other than a lack of appetite, any outer sign of anxiety; he was calmly exhaling smoke into the air, and smiling his usual smile, slightly ironic, at the cheerful narrator.

The prince said:

—Today she is coming to me for the first time.

—Today? To your house?

—Yes.

—This is an excellent month, in Rome, for love. Between three and six in the afternoon, every *buen retiro* hides a couple . . .

—In fact—interrupted Galeazzo—she is coming at three.

Both looked at their watches. Andrea asked:

—Shall we go?

—Let's go, replied Galeazzo, rising. —We'll walk along Via Condotti together. I'm going to Via del Babuino for flowers. Tell me, you know these things: what flowers does she prefer?

Andrea began to laugh; and an atrocious witticism came to his lips. But he said, carelessly:

—Roses, once.

They separated in front of the Barcaccia Fountain.

Piazza di Spagna already had a deserted summer air to it, at that hour. Several workmen were restoring a water pipe; and a pile of earth, dried out by the sun, was being lifted in eddies of dust by the hot gusts of wind. The staircase of the Trinità shone white and deserted.

Andrea climbed the stairs, very slowly, pausing at every two or three steps as if he were dragging an enormous burden. He entered his house and remained in his room, on his bed, until a quarter to three. At a quarter to three, he went out. He took Via Sistina, continued past the Four Fountains, and went past Palazzo Barberini; he stopped just a little farther on, in front of the racks of a vendor of old books, waiting for three o'clock. The vendor, a tiny man all wrinkled and hairy, like a decrepit tortoise, offered him books. He was choosing his best volumes, one by one, and placing them in front of Andrea, talking with an unbearably monotonous nasal voice. It was only a few minutes to three. Andrea looked at the titles of the books and kept watch over the gates of the building, hearing the bookseller's voice vaguely in the midst of the din caused by his veins.

A woman went out through the gates, walked down the sidewalk toward the square, mounted a public carriage, and disappeared down Via del Tritone.

Andrea walked down in the direction she had taken, once again took Via Sistina, and entered his house once again. He waited for Maria to arrive. He threw himself onto the bed and lay there so still it seemed he was no longer suffering.

Maria arrived at five.

She said, panting:

—Do you know what? I can stay with you, for the whole evening, and the whole night, until tomorrow morning.

She said:

—This will be our first and last night of love! I am leaving on Tuesday.

She sobbed on his mouth, trembling violently, pressing herself hard against his body:

—Let me not see tomorrow! Let me die!

Looking at his troubled face, she asked him:

—Are you suffering? Do you also . . . think we will never see each other again?

He had immense difficulty talking to her, answering her. His tongue was sluggish; he could not find words. He felt an instinctive need to hide his face, to escape from her gaze, to evade questions. He could not console her; he could not delude her. He answered in a choked, unrecognizable voice:

—Hush.

He crouched down at her feet; he remained for a long time with his head on her lap, without talking. She held her hands on his temples, feeling the pulsing of his arteries, irregular and violent, feeling him suffer. And she herself was no longer suffering her own pain, but was suffering his, only his.

He rose to his feet; he took her hands; he drew her into the other room. She obeyed.

In bed, bewildered, frightened, in the presence of his dark demented ardor, she shouted:

—But what is wrong with you? What is wrong?

She wanted to look him in the eyes and understand that madness; and he hid his face, lost, in her breast, in her neck, in her hair, in the pillows.

Suddenly, she freed herself from his arms, with a terrible expression of horror manifest in her entire body, whiter than the pillows, more disfigured than if she had just leaped from the arms of Death.

That name! That name! She had heard that name!

Great silence emptied her soul. One of those abysses opened up inside her, into which the entire world seems to disappear under the blow of a single thought. She heard nothing else; she heard nothing more. Andrea shouted, begged, despaired in vain.

She did not hear. A kind of instinct guided her movements. She found her clothes and dressed.

Andrea sobbed on the bed, unhinged. He realized that she was leaving the room.

—Maria! Maria!

He listened.

—Maria!

He heard the sound of the door closing.

CHAPTER III

On the morning of June 20, Monday, at ten o'clock, the public sale began of the soft furnishings and movable fittings that had belonged to His Excellency the plenipotentiary minister of Guatemala.

It was a burning hot morning. Summer was already blazing in Rome. Trams ran up and down along Via Nazionale, constantly, drawn by horses that wore certain strange white hoods as protection against the sun. Long lines of laden carts cluttered the streetcar lines. In the stark light, between the walls plastered with multicolored notices, like leprosy, the blasts of horns mingled with the cracking of whips and the yells of the carters.

Before deciding to cross the threshold of that house, Andrea wandered along the sidewalks at random for a long time, feeling horrible tiredness, tiredness so void and desperate that it almost seemed like a physical need to die.

When he saw a porter come out of the door onto the street with a piece of furniture on his shoulder, he made up his mind. He entered the house and climbed the stairs rapidly. He heard, from the landing, the voice of the auctioneer.

—Do I hear . . . ?

The auction table was in the largest room, in the room containing the Buddha. All around, buyers were thronging. For the most part they were traders, secondhand furniture sellers, junk dealers: common people. As there were no connoisseurs around in summer, the dealers were rushing there, sure of acquiring precious objects at low prices. A bad odor spread through the warm air, emanating from those impure men.

—Do I hear . . . ?

Andrea was suffocating. He wandered through the other rooms, where only the wallpaper remained on the walls, and the curtains and the door curtains, since almost all the furnishings were gathered in the auction area. Although he was walking on a thick carpet, he heard his footsteps resound, distinctly, as if the vaulted ceilings were full of echoes.

He found a semicircular room. The walls were a deep red, scattered with sparkling flashes of gold. It resembled a temple or a sepulcher; it looked like a sad, mystical shelter, made for praying in and dying in. From the open windows the stark light entered, like a violation; the trees of Villa Aldobrandini could be seen.

He returned to the room where the auctioneer was. He again smelled the stench. Turning, he saw the Princess of Ferentino in a corner with Barbarella Viti. He approached them and said hello.

—Well, Ugenta, have you bought anything?

—Nothing.

—Nothing? I thought, rather, that you had bought everything.

—Whatever for?

—It was a . . . romantic idea I had.

The princess began to laugh. Barbarella imitated her.

—We're going. It's not possible to remain here, with this scent. Good-bye, Ugenta. Console yourself.

Andrea approached the table. The auctioneer recognized him.

—Would the Lord Count like something?

He answered:

—I'll see.

The sale was proceeding rapidly. He looked at the faces of the dealers around him; felt himself being touched by those elbows, those feet; he felt those breaths skimming him. Nausea choked his throat.

—Going once, twice, third and final call: SOLD!

The thud of the gavel resounded in his heart and gave him a painful jolt at his temples.

He bought the Buddha, a large armoire, some majolica, some fabrics. At a certain point he heard the sound of voices and feminine laughter, a rustle of feminine dresses, near the door. He turned. He saw Galeazzo Secìnaro entering with the Marchioness of Mount Edgcumbe, and then the Countess of Lùcoli, Gino Bommìnaco, Giovanella Daddi. Those gentlemen and ladies were talking and laughing loudly.

He tried to hide, to make himself smaller, amid the crowd that besieged the table. He trembled at the thought of being discovered. The voices and the laughter reached him above the sweating foreheads of the crowd in the suffocating heat. Luckily, after a few minutes, the cheerful visitors departed.

He opened up a passage for himself among the crowded bodies, overcoming his revulsion, making an enormous effort not to faint. In his mouth he had the sensation of an indescribably bitter and nauseating taste, which was surging up inside him from the dissolving of his heart. It seemed that he was leaving that place infected with obscure and immedicable ills, from the contact with all those strangers. Physical torture and moral anguish mingled in him.

Once he was in the street in the harsh light, he felt a slight dizziness. With an uncertain step he began to seek a carriage. He found one in Piazza del Quirinale and had himself taken to Palazzo Zuccari.

But toward evening, an invincible craving invaded him to see those uninhabited rooms once more. Once again, he climbed those stairs, and entered under the pretext of asking whether the porters had taken the furniture to his building.

A man replied:

—They're taking them right now. You must have seen them on your way here, Lord Count.

Almost nothing remained in the rooms. From the curtainless windows, the blushing splendor of sunset entered; all the clamor of the street below entered. Some men were still detaching some wall-hangings from the walls, uncovering the vulgar flowered wallpaper on which holes and tears were visible here and there. Others were removing the carpets and rolling them up, generating a dense cloud of dust that glinted in the rays of sunlight. One of them sang a lewd song under his breath. Dust mixed with pipe smoke floated up to the ceiling.

Andrea fled.

In Piazza del Quirinale, before the royal palace, a brass band was playing. The ample waves of that metallic music spread through the burning air. The obelisk, the fountain, the colossi, towered in the red glow and took on a purple tint as if penetrated by an impalpable flame. Immense Rome, dominated by a battle of clouds, seemed to illuminate the sky.

Andrea fled, almost out of his mind. He turned into Via del Quirinale, walked down past the Four Fountains, brushed past the gates of Palazzo Barberini, which cast glints of light from its windowpanes, and finally reached Palazzo Zuccari.

The porters were unloading the furniture from a cart, shouting. Some of them were already carrying the armoire up the stairs, with difficulty.

He entered the building. As the armoire took up the entire breadth of the staircase, he could not overtake it. Very slowly, he followed it, step by step, into his house.

FRANCAVILLA AL MARE: JULY–DECEMBER 1888.

Translator's Acknowledgments

With infinite thanks and appreciation to:

George C. Schoolfield, Yale University, for his advice, encouragement to undertake the endeavor of translating this novel in its entirety, and invaluable support.

John Siciliano, Taylor Sperry, and the production editors of Penguin Classics, for their enthusiasm, assistance, and dedication to ensuring the quality of this translation and its notes.

David Wardle, University of Cape Town, for his enormous patience and great help in providing translations, interpretations, and derivations of phrases in Latin and Greek.

Giuseppe (Pino) D'Errico, of the Biblioteca Nazionale Centrale di Roma, for his unflagging readiness to assist with bibliographical queries, information on Rome, and other matters.

John Woodhouse, Oxford University, for providing me with a copy of his invaluable article "La fortuna inglese del *Piacere* (1897–1920)."

Giuseppe Stellardi, Oxford University, for kindly contacting John Woodhouse and forwarding said article to me, as well as advice at the outset of this project.

Alexander d'Angelo, University of Cape Town Humanities Library, for kind assistance in tracing arcane terms.

The late Nelia Saxby, University of Cape Town, for unraveling some syntactical and other mysteries.

Matthew Shelton, University of Cape Town, for his hugely appreciated assistance with Latin and Greek.

Misha Galoukhin, University of Cape Town Fencing Club, for his kind assistance with fencing terminology.

Brigitte Selzer, Gunther Pakendorf, and Annette Behrensmeyer, University of Cape Town, for their kind assistance with German.

Jean-Louis Cornille, University of Cape Town, for his kind assistance with French.

Ainoa Polo, University of Cape Town, for her kind assistance with Spanish.

Davide Shamà for assistance with the complexities of Italian noble titles.

Michela Rizzieri of the Fondazione "Il Vittoriale degli Italiani," D'Annunzio's curators, for reassurance regarding copyright issues.

The "Eros from Sappho to Cyber" class of 2010, University of Cape Town, for their encouraging reaction to the first draft of this translation, which was used as the study text in the Decadent literature module of the course, and for their welcome and valuable feedback about aspects of the text.

My mother, Carole-Ann Gochin, for help with the English language, which sometimes eludes me.

My sister, Jeni Ruth Gochin, for her infinitely valued and invaluable assistance.

My daughter, Isabel Raffaelli, for her long-suffering patience with my absent mind and her fledgling yet commendable efforts at translation from Italian into English.

My husband, Sandro Raffaelli, for his bountiful assistance in reading aloud to me, for help in deciphering D'Annunzio's often cryptic meaning, and for his eternal loving support, my appreciation for which can never be expressed sufficiently.

Notes

FOREWORD

1. I must at the outset acknowledge my indebtedness to George Schoolfield and John Woodhouse, whose work on D'Annunzio's reception in Anglo-Saxon countries, particularly in connection with the effect of the bowdlerization of his novels, catalyzed and informed this project.
2. John Woodhouse, *Gabriele D'Annunzio: Defiant Archangel* (Oxford: Clarendon Press, 1998), p. 83.
3. George Schoolfield, *A Baedeker of Decadence: Charting a Literary Fashion 1884–1927* (New Haven and London: Yale University Press, 2003), p. 31.
4. Ibid., pp. 30–31.
5. Woodhouse, *Defiant Archangel,* p. 85.
6. Woodhouse, *"La fortuna inglese del Piacere," Il Piacere, Atti del XII Convegno,* a cura di Edoardo Tiboni (Pescara: Centro Studi Dannunziani, 1989), p. 231.
7. See, for instance, Clarence R. Decker, "Zola's Literary Reputation in England," *PMLA* 49, no. 4 (Dec. 1934), pp. 1140–53; Raymond S. Nelson, "Mrs. Warren's Profession and English Prostitution," *Journal of Modern Literature* 2, no. 3 (1971/1972), pp. 357–66. There is a good bibliography concerning this censorship in Anthony Cummins, "Émile Zola's Cheap English Dress: The Vizetelly Translations, Late-Victorian Print Culture, and the Crisis of Literary Value," *Review of English Studies* 60, no. 243 (2009), pp. 108–32.
8. Woodhouse, *"La fortuna inglese del Piacere,"* p. 233.

9. Woodhouse, *Defiant Archangel,* p. 85.
10. Ibid.
11. *Comstock:* Anthony Comstock was a much-feared anti-obscenity campaigner who suppressed many authors' works for decades in the United States in the early 1900s, both literary and other.
12. G. B. Rose, "Gabriele D'Annunzio," *The Sewanee Review* 5, no. 2 (Apr. 1897), p. 148.
13. Ibid., p. 150.
14. Woodhouse, *Defiant Archangel,* p. 86.
15. G. B. Rose, "Gabriele D'Annunzio," p. 152.

TO FRANCESCO PAOLO MICHETTI

1. *ex-voto:* An offering to show gratitude or dedication.
2. *Paolo Veronese:* Italian sixteenth-century artist.
3. *Ajax:* Mythological Greek hero; symbol of constancy and perseverance.
4. *pastorals:* Possible reference to musical compositions commonly played during the Christmas season, evoking rustic life.
5. *semihiante labello:* "With lips half open." From Catullus's *Carmina,* poem 61 (Latin).
6. *January 9, 1889:* In the original Italian, D'Annunzio signs with "*secondo Carmine 1889,*" which signifies "the second Wednesday" of 1889—namely, January 9, 1889. "Carmine" was the name given to Wednesday by Abruzzese peasants. Wednesday was the day dedicated to the Virgin Mary, and specifically to the Madonna del Carmine.

FIRST BOOK, CHAPTER I

1. *blue-black cobalt: Zàffara* in D'Annunzio's original text, or rather *zaffera,* also called Florentine blue, was an Asian blue-black cobalt pigment that came into use in Florence in the 1500s.
2. *buen retiro:* "Pleasant retreat" (Spanish).

3. *the Pincian Hill:* Monte Pincio, located in the northeast section of Rome.
4. *ever-moving light:* From Percy Bysshe Shelley's "The Witch of Atlas" (1820), stanza XXVII, lines 259–61: "Men scarcely know how beautiful fire is / Each flame of it is as a precious stone / Dissolved in ever-moving light."
5. *Carmelite fabric:* Likely to be brown wool used to make the habits of Carmelite monks.
6. *Chimeras:* In Greek mythology, the Chimera was a fire-breathing monster with the head of a lion, the body of a goat, and the tail of a serpent, slain by Bellerophon.
7. *Nelly O'Brien:* Portrait by Joshua Reynolds, c. 1763. Nelly O'Brien was a courtesan, the mistress of the third Viscount Bolingbroke.
8. *From Dreamland—A stranger hither:* From the poem "To a Dragon Fly" by A. Mary F. Robinson (1878): "You hail from Dream-land, Dragon-fly? / A stranger hither? so am I, / And (sooth to say) I wonder why / We either one of us came." In English in D'Annunzio's original text.
9. *Mona Amorrosisca or for a Laldomine:* Names of beautiful ladies found in Agnolo Firenzuola's *Dialogo delle bellezze delle donne* (Dialogue on the Beauties of Women, 1541) (Mona Amorrosisca); and in his *Ragionamenti,* "Novella terza," 1548 (Laldomine).
10. *rose:* The recurring references to roses in this novel are significant. Roses have many meanings, but with regard to this novel there are two that are most significant: that of symbolizing the female sex organs, and that of being associated with the Virgin Mary. In this novel, which frequently juxtaposes the sacred and the profane, the rose could be seen to be the most representative symbol of this juxtaposition.
11. *A stranger hither:* Words in italics here are in English in the original Italian text.

FIRST BOOK, CHAPTER II

1. *Simonetta:* Simonetta Cattaneo Vespucci (c. 1453–1476) was reputed to be the most beautiful woman in Florence.

e was the mistress of Giuliano de' Medici, and was possibly the model for Venus in Botticelli's *The Birth of Venus*.

2. *Beggar King:* The "Beggar King" (Re Lazzarone) was Ferdinand IV of Naples, later becoming Ferdinand I of the Two Sicilies.
3. *"Habere, non haberi":* "I possess, but I am not possessed" (Latin).
4. *springtime of the dead:* In Italy (and other Latinate cultures), November is considered the "month of the dead"—the *mese dei morti,* in which each family honors the memory of its dead relatives, especially on November 2 (the Commemoration of the Dead), when it is a tradition to visit the cemeteries where one's loved ones are buried. This day follows November 1, All Saints' Day.
5. *"I know you love me not":* In English in original text.
6. *daimyo:* Japanese feudal lord (Japanese).
7. *gibus:* Opera hat (French).
8. *Sanzio:* The surname of the artist Raphael (1483–1520) of Urbino.
9. *domus aurea:* "Golden house," i.e., Nero's palace in Rome (Latin).
10. *luigi:* Ancient French coin of gold, first minted in 1640 under Luigi (Louis) XIII. Also has generic sense of coins, money (Italian).
11. *All the perfumes:* In English in the original text.
12. *myrtle:* Latin poets who sang of love were crowned with leaves of myrtle; hence in Italian poetic language, the term "mirto" became a metaphor for love. The laurel, especially the laurel wreath or crown, is the symbol of the poet, of victory, of wisdom.
13. *Ut:* Ut was, in Italy until the 1600s, the name given to the musical note that in English is called C. It is now called Do (as in Do, Re, Me, Fa, So, La, Si). The names of the musical notes originate from the hymn *"Ut queant laxis,"* dedicated to Saint John the Baptist. Perhaps D'Annunzio derived his sense of the note C denoting love from Christian Schubart's *Ideen zu einer Aesthetik der Tonkunst* (1806), which ascribed characteristics and

emotions to each key: C minor, for instance, is associated with declarations of love, love-sickness and unhappy love.

14. *Je crains ce que j'espère:* "I fear that which I hope for" (French).

15. *La cote:* "The odds." Refers to the custom of bookmakers of shouting out the odds they are willing to offer for bets (French).

16. *Lucrezia Crivelli:* In a portrait by Leonardo called *La Belle Ferronnière,* Lucrezia Crivelli was a mistress of Ludovico Sforza and bore a son by him.

17. *netsuke:* In Japanese custom, a small, intricately carved toggle used to secure a tobacco pouch or other container to a sash (*obi*); often of great value.

18. *"Ich kann's nicht fassen, nicht glauben":* "I cannot grasp this, cannot believe it" (German).

FIRST BOOK, CHAPTER III

1. *"Maria Leczinska":* Marie Leszczyńska was a Polish princess who married King Louis XV of France during the 1700s.

2. *RUIT HORA:* Literally, "the hour has fled" (Latin).

3. *TIBI, HIPPOLYTA:* "To you, Hippolyta" (Latin; Ippolita is pronounced "IPPOLITA").

4. *Andrea del Verrocchio:* (1435–1488), Italian Renaissance sculptor and painter.

5. *pao rosa:* Rosewood oil used in perfumes, from the Amazonian Pao Rosa tree.

6. *corsage:* The bodice of a dress.

7. *Alma-Tadema:* "The paintings of Lawrence Alma-Tadema [1865–1940] had a real impact on the young D'Annunzio, stimulating his interest in English art, and Pre-Raphaelitism in particular. Above all, they provided him with a feminine type that he was later to develop, under the combined influence of D.G. Rossetti, into his own feminine icon." Giuliana Pieri, "D'Annunzio and Alma-Tadema: Between Pre-Raphaelitism and Aestheti-

cism," *Modern Language Review* 96, no. 2 (April 2001), pp. 361–69.

8. *She came forward:* The concordances with Dante's sonnets from *Vita nuova,* "Negli occhi porta la mia donna Amore" (In her eyes my lady bears Love) and "Tanto gentile e tanto onesta pare" (So gentle and so pure does my Lady appear) are notable in this description of Elena, which could be seen to be paralleled with the passage of Beatrice through crowds of people: the passage of the lady arousing intense interest in all those she passes; the description of the mouth, the eyes, the pallor, the thoughtfulness she inspires in men who see her pass; the effect on each person's heart. The greatest difference is that where Beatrice inspires uplifting and sanctifying feelings of humility and sweetness in those who observe her, Elena Muti arouses feelings of disquiet, regret, and sensual agitation, as each man longs for her to become his lover.
9. *"Ludovic, ne faites plus ça en dansant; je frissonne toute":* "Ludovico, don't do that while dancing; I quiver all over" (French).
10. *life of my life:* Yet another example of the mingling of sacred and profane, as "life of my life" is found commonly in various prayers to Jesus.

FIRST BOOK, CHAPTER IV

1. *velarium:* In ancient Rome, a large protective awning extended over an amphitheater against rain or sun.
2. *Bonne chance:* "Good luck" (French).
3. *the rose petal:* This expression, a variation of the Italian saying "the drop that made the pot overflow," is the equivalent of the English "the straw that broke the camel's back."
4. *that verb:* The verb "to like" in Italian is *piacere*—here D'Annunzio is referring to the seductiveness of the lips opening to say "*piace.*"
5. *Goethe:* Johann Wolfgang Goethe (1749–1832). Prolific German poet, playwright, novelist, and artist.

6. *"Laß dich":* Goethe's *"Laß dich, Geliebte,"* III, Erstes Buch, *Römische Elegien,* 1795.
7. *Faustina's divine elegiac poet:* Goethe, during his sojourn in Italy (1786–1788), had a lover by the name of Faustina, whom he described in his *Elegien.*
8. *a memory of love:* Here, D'Annunzio's association of Rome with love is a covert reference to Goethe's personal philosophy, expressed in the *Römische Elegien,* which embraced the palindrome "Roma-Amor" (amor = love).
9. *caryatids:* Sculpted female figures serving as columns.
10. *herms:* Four-cornered pillars topped by a head or bust, usually that of the god Hermes. Statues such as these were often found in ancient Athens, used as milestones, signposts, pillars, and so on.
11. *Juno, whom Wolfgang adored:* A very large sculpted head of Juno, once housed in Villa Ludovisi, so admired by Goethe that he had a copy of it made for his home.
12. *of the market and of death:* This cryptic description refers to the building speculation of those years, around 1889, which saw many green spaces and ancient constructions destroyed.
13. *"Of what use is blazing nature":* In the text is my translation of D'Annunzio's interpretation of Goethe's "Monolog des Liebhabers" (Monologue of a Lover), which I retain for the sake of authenticity.
14. *stil novo:* The *dolce stil nuovo,* or "sweet new style," in poetry inaugurated by Dante and his circle of literary friends; the term was first used in *Purgatory* in Dante's *Divine Comedy* (thirteenth-century Italian).
15. *Henri Taine:* Hyppolite-Adolphe Taine (1828–1893), historian and critic. D'Annunzio drew his knowledge of Elizabethan literature from Taine's *Histoire de la littérature anglaise.*
16. A. S. *calcographus aqua forti sibi tibi fecit:* "A.S. the Chalcographer (engraver/etcher on copper) made this copper etching/engraving for himself and for you." *Aqua forti*—nitric acid: a mixture of vitriolic and nitrous acids used in the engraving process (Latin).

17. *a tratti liberi:* "With free strokes." Rembrandt preferred a free, fluid style in his engraving technique (Italian).
18. *maniera nera:* Mezzotint, a printmaking method that produces half tones through scraping and burnishing of the metal plate, rather than through hatching or stippling (Italian).
19. *Green, Dixon, Earlom . . . Filippino Lippi:* These are, in chronological order and grouped by technique, the engravers Gérard Audran (1604–1703), Valentine Green (1739–1813), John Dixon (1740–1811), Richard Earlom (1743–1822), and Paolo Toschi (1788–1854); the painter/engraver Albrecht Dürer (1471–1528), the engraver/printmaker Marcantonio Raimondi (1480–1534), the etcher/engraver Jacques Callot (1592–1635); and the painters Sandro Botticelli (1445–1510), Domenico (Bigordi) Ghirlandaio (1449–1494), Filippino Lippi (c. 1457–1504), Hans Holbein the Younger (1497–1543), Francesco Mazzola, known as the Parmigianino (1503–1540), Annibale Carracci (1560–1609), and Guido Reni (1575–1642).
20. *Arcitenens, Caper, Amphora:* Sagittarius, Capricorn, Aquarius (Latin).
21. *Valentinois:* Cesare Borgia, son of Pope Alexander VI (c. 1475–1507), was made Duke of Valence (Valentinois in French, or Valentino in Italian) in 1498.
22. *Seigneur de Brântome:* Pierre de Bourdeille (c. 1540–1614), who wrote lengthy memoirs after his travels.

FIRST BOOK, CHAPTER V

1. *adieu au grand air:* "Farewell in the great outdoors" (French).
2. *"Remember the snuffed-out days":* I have translated in the text, for authenticity's sake, D'Annunzio's interpretation of Goethe's poem "Wechsel"—"*O ruf' sie zurücke, die vorigen Zeiten! / Es küßt sich so süße die Lippe der Zweiten, / Als kaum sich die Lippe der Ersten geküßt.*" However, I would more closely translate Goethe's text as "O, call them back, those earlier times! He kissed so sweetly the lips of the second one, the way he had just kissed the lips of the first."

3. *"With great pleasure and delight . . .":* Lorenzo the Magnificent, *Canzoni a ballo,* Canzone 1: *"E' si vede in ogni lato / Che 'l proverbio dice il vero, / Che ciascun muta pensiero / Come l'occhio è separato. / Vedesi cambiare amore: / Come l'occhio sta di lunge, / Così sta di lunge il core: / Perché appresso un altro il punge. / Col qual tosto e' si congiunge / Con piacere e con diletto . . ."*

4. *mascula:* A masculine woman (Latin).

5. *Giusto Suttermans:* Also known as Justus Sustermans, he was born in Antwerp in 1597 and traveled to Florence, where he became court painter to the Medicis. He died in 1681.

6. *semper:* "Always" (Latin).

7. *Miching Mallecho:* In Shakespeare, *Hamlet,* III, ii, 146: "Marry this is Miching Malicho, that means mischeefe." Other meanings to be found are veiled rebuke, misdeed, secret act.

8. *Ecce homo novus:* "Here is the new man" (Latin).

9. *No doubt:* In English in the original text.

10. *haute école dressage:* "High school" dressage, the highest form of classical horse-riding, entailing movements that the horse carries out above the ground, such as jumping, or up on its hind legs with forelegs raised in the air (French).

11. *Duke of Buckingham and De Lauzun:* The second Duke of Buckingham (George Villiers), (1628–1687), is notorious for having killed the Earl of Shrewsbury in a duel in 1668. Links between the Duke of Buckingham and Antoine Nompar de Caumont, duc de Lauzun (1632–1723) are complex. Lauzun was imprisoned at Pignerol in 1671. The Duke of Buckingham attempted to persuade Louis XIV to release him. There are fictional links, too, in Alexandre Dumas' *The Three Musketeers* (1844) and *The Vicomte de Bragelonne* (1848) in the section titled "The Man in the Iron Mask," both play a (fictional) role.

12. *Musée secret:* "Secret Museum"—poem by Théophile Gautier; the motif of "perfect absence" (of pubic hair) is taken up in greater depth later in this novel (French).

13. *Camillo Agrippa:* Renowned Renaissance fencer and theorist of fencing.
14. *a contre-tierce parry:* One of several types of counter-parry movements in fencing (French).
15. *coulé:* An attack action in fencing, where the sword slides against the opponent's blade (French).
16. *"inquartata":* A kind of counterattack in fencing.
17. *Barcaccia Fountain:* Famous fountain in Piazza di Spagna. It is shaped like a sinking barge; the name literally means "rotten old boat" in Italian.
18. *Ave, Roma, Moriturus te salutat:* Parody of a gladiator's salute to the magistrate at games: "Hail, Rome, a man about to die salutes you" (Latin).
19. *taffeta:* Used in bandaging.

SECOND BOOK, CHAPTER I

1. *Lethean bath:* Reference to the river Lethe, one of five rivers of the underworld. It is the river of forgetfulness and is associated with the afterlife and the belief in rebirth.
2. *Upanishad:* "One of four Vedas, sacred scriptures of most Hindu traditions.
3. *the Vedas:* The oldest known Indo-European religious and philosophical tracts.
4. *"Hae omnes creaturae in totum ego sum, et praeter me aliud ens non est":* "I am all this creation collectively and besides me there exists no other being"—from the Upanishad of the Veda, translated into Latin by the French historian and Orientalist Anquetil-Duperron and published as *Oupnek'hat* (Paris, 1801–1802) (Latin).
5. *"I am admitted by nature . . .":* Georges Maurice de Guérin, *Journal of Maurice de Guérin* (Paris, 1862).
6. *"The stars we never long to clasp . . .":* This verse is from Goethe's poem "Trost in Tränen" (Solace in Tears).
7. *"miro gurge":* From Dante, *Paradise,* canto XXX, 68, a double Latinism. Translated by Cary (1814), Sinclair (1939), and Singleton (1975) as "wondrous flood"; in

current Italian it is translated as *mirabile gorgo*—"wondrous whirlpool" (Latinism used in Italian).

8. *Titanomachia:* Battle of the Titans.

9. "ευλαβεια": *Eulabeia* is generally translated into English as "caution" or "concern," with older meanings of "religious scruple," "godly fear," "devotion," "dread." D'Annunzio has translated or interpreted it in Italian as in the text above (Ancient Greek).

10. *a contemporary poet:* Here D'Annunzio is self-inserting or self-inscribing himself into his work—this is his own poem and undoubtedly the "contemporary poet" is himself.

11. *Homer's liturgy:* For Goethe, Homer's writings were of greater spiritual significance and guidance than the Bible.

12. *Callimachus's capital:* Callimachus designed the Corinthian capital (column), decorating it with the acanthus leaf.

13. *"The Verse is everything": "Il Verso è tutto"*—verse from a sonnet from D'Annunzio's poetry collection *L'Isottèo,* 1886. *"O Poeta, divina è la Parola; / ne la pura Bellezza il ciel ripose / ogni nostra letizia; e il Verso è tutto"*—"O Poet, divine is the Word / in pure Beauty did heaven place / all of our joy; and the Verse is everything." Once again, D'Annunzio is inscribing himself.

14. *"Lightly and quickly depart":* Ballata 146 by Lorenzo de' Medici—*"Parton leggieri e pronti / del petto e miei pensieri."*

15. *the note La:* In Italy, as mentioned before, musical notation follows the scheme Do, Re, Mi, Fa, Sol, La, Si, as opposed to the English and German use of letters (A, B, C, D, E, F). *La* corresponds to *A.* Commonly, the diapason, or tuning fork, is set to *La* or *A,* and musicians take their pitch from this note.

16. *egipane:* Mythological. Deity of the woods; equivalent of the Greek god Pan, a satyr.

17. *"Pale, yes":* Original Italian *"Pallido sì"*—allusion to Petrarch's *Triumphi,* "Mortis I," v. 166: *"Pallida no, ma piú che neve bianca"* (Not pale, but whiter than snow).

18. *"hyacinth":* This flower, or the color of this flower, which recurs again later with reference to Maria, is as-

sociated with the Virgin Mary, and qualities of prudence, contemplation, constancy, and benevolence.

19. *"monsters":* As mentioned in the following line, these are the Sphinx, the Gorgon, and the Siren, all dual-natured monsters, a recurring motif in this novel. Of interest in this sonnet, which represents the attempt to move from perdition to redemption, is the symbolism of the monster. This represents the instinctual realm in human beings, which struggles against the realm of reason and control. This is representative of Andrea's struggle between carnal desire and higher, more spiritual artistic aspirations.
20. *"Plow with sad cries . . . songs of gladness":* From Psalms 126:5: "They that sow in tears shall reap in joy."
21. *DIE XII SEPTEMBRIS MDCCCLXXXVI:* On the day of September 12, 1886.

SECOND BOOK, CHAPTER II

1. *Schifanoja:* Pronounced "SKEEFANOYA"—meaning "escape from boredom," "avoiding boredom" (Italian).
2. *Vignola:* Jacopo Barozzi—fifteenth-century Italian architectural theorist; member of Vitruvian Academy.
3. *pour en tirer neuf ou dix muytz d'eaue rose:* "To derive from them nine or ten *muytz* of rose water." A *muytz* was a French measure of capacity used in the twelfth century, used for dry or wet substances (wine, grain, etc.), of varying capacity—some instances are cited of tonnes, some of 272 liters. The word more commonly found in Old English is *muid* (Old French).
4. *poet of the Vergier d'honneur:* André de la Vigne (born c. 1470), who wrote *Le Vergier d'honneur* (The Orchard of Honor).
5. *beauté sans traits:* "Beauty without features." Madame de Pompadour was noted for her unremarkable looks, which were, however, enlivened by her vibrant personality. (French.)
6. *Elissa and Tyre:* Elissa (also Alyssa) was a legendary Phoenician princess from Tyre, who established the city

of Carthage. Her story is recounted by Virgil in the *Aeneid,* where she is named Dido. Ancient Tyre was famed for its purple dye, extracted from the Murex snail; purple Tyrian fabrics were worn by royalty across Europe. It is situated in modern-day Lebanon.

7. *Rosa rosarum:* "Rose of roses" (Latin).
8. *"Thus he distributed the roses and the words":* From Petrarch's sonnet 245, "Così partìa le rose e le parole," *Il Canzoniere* (fourteenth-century Italian).
9. *"Story of Nastagio degli Onesti":* In Boccaccio's *Decameron,* Day 5, Story 8.
10. *turris eburnea:* "Ivory tower" (Latin).
11. *vas spirituale:* "Spiritual vessel." Reference to the Virgin Mary, who is the instrument and vessel of the Holy Spirit (Latin).
12. *"Ἰόπλοκ' ἄγνα μελλιχόμειδε": Ioploch' agnameilichomeide*—from Alcaeus, fragment 384—"violet-haired, holy, sweetly smiling." The original verse continues with the word "Sappho." (Ancient Greek.)

SECOND BOOK, CHAPTER III

1. *Adoremus:* "Let us adore/worship" (Latin).
2. *Termini:* Plural of Terminus, a boundary stone or post.
3. *genius loci:* In ancient Roman times, a genius loci was the guardian spirit of a place.
4. *quattrocento:* The fifteenth century (Italian).
5. *escutcheon:* A shield portraying a coat of arms.
6. *alerion:* An eagle, used as a symbol in heraldry.
7. *Obermann's words:* From *Selections from Letters to a Friend:* Novel by Étienne Pivert de Senancour (1770–1846), translated and republished in 1901. "Unhappy in the years of joy, what can I expect from future years? I am like those old men from whom all things have taken flight; but more unfortunate than they, I have lost everything long before I have myself reached the consummation of life."
8. *chryselephantine:* Made of gold and ivory.

SECOND BOOK, CHAPTER IV

1. *Luigi Rameau's gavotte:* Some critics believe this to refer to Jean-Philippe Rameau (1683–1764) and this gavotte to derive from his ballet *Naïs* (1749). Others believe that this gavotte and this composer are sheer invention on the part of D'Annunzio.
2. *punctum saliens:* The essential or most notable point (Latin).
3. *Memling:* The German-born painter, Hans Memling (c. 1430–August 1494).
4. *Be simple as a dove:* D'Annunzio has inverted the original quote from Matthew 10:16, which has been variously translated in different versions of the Bible; one of these, in its full extent, is "Behold I send you as sheep in the midst of wolves: therefore be shrewd as serpents and innocent as doves."
5. *Silver key of the fountain of tears:* Percy Bysshe Shelley, "A Fragment: To Music," 1817.
6. *such as dreams are made on:* In English in the original text. From William Shakespeare, *The Tempest,* act 4, scene 1, 148–58.
7. *This allegory:* The passage in the text I translated from D'Annunzio's interpretation of Percy Bysshe Shelley's poem "An Allegory" (1824), which reads as follows: "I. A portal as of shadowy adamant / Stands yawning on the highway of the life / Which we all tread, a cavern huge and gaunt; / Around it rages an unceasing strife / Of shadows, like the restless clouds that haunt / The gap of some cleft mountain, lifted high / Into the whirlwinds of the upper sky. / II. And many pass it by with careless tread, / Not knowing that a shadowy . . . / Tracks every traveller even to where the dead / Wait peacefully for their companion new; / But others, by more curious humour led, / Pause to examine;—these are very few, / And they learn little there, except to know / That shadows follow them where'er they go."
8. *"Who ever lov'd, that lov'd not at first sight?":* In English in the original.

9. *Monte Cassino:* Montecassino Abbey is a Benedictine monastery founded in approximately A.D. 529 by Saint Benedict, on the mountain Monte Cassino, about eighty miles south of Rome. It has had a turbulent history, having been destroyed and rebuilt several times, and is now a national monument. It houses a five-thousand-reed organ.
10. *ostensorium:* The ostensorium, also called ostensory or monstrance, is a vessel used to display the host (Blessed Sacrament), made of gold, silver, brass, or copper. It usually takes the form of a sun emitting rays.
11. *each pond seemed . . . undulating there:* From Percy Bysshe Shelley's poem "To Jane: The Recollection" (1822), stanza 5: "We paused beside the pools that lie / Under the forest bough,— / Each seemed as 'twere a little sky / Gulfed in a world below; / A firmament of purple light / Which in the dark earth lay, / More boundless than the depth of night, / And purer than the day— / In which the lovely forests grew, / As in the upper air, / More perfect both in shape and hue / Than any spreading there."
12. *And delicate views . . . gentler than the one above:* The rest of this paragraph also echoes Shelley's poem, as it continues in the same stanza.
13. *And forget me, for I can* never *Be thine!:* In English in the original. From a poem by Percy Bysshe Shelley, "The Magnetic Lady to Her Patient" (1822).

THIRD BOOK, CHAPTER I

1. *Amie avec les hanches:* "Female friend with hips" (French).
2. *Claudio Lorenese:* Claude Lorrain (Gellée) (c. 1600–1682), also called le Lorrain, Claudio Lorenese, or Claude. A French painter who lived mostly in Italy and was noted for his landscapes full of harmony and light.
3. *demi-mondaines:* Literally, "half-world"; referring to women in the late nineteenth century who were generally divorced or single, and led an active social life supported by rich lovers (French).

4. *Gratulor tibi!:* "I congratulate you" (Latin).
5. *O douce barbe feminine:* "O sweet feminine beard" (French).
6. *le drap de la blonde qui dort:* "The sheet of the sleeping blonde" (French).
7. *Philippe de Bourgogne:* Philippe III de Bourgogne, Duke of Burgundy (1396–1467), founded the Order of the Golden Fleece.
8. *sans plume et sans duvet:* "Without feathers and without down" (French).
9. *Anabasis:* Term stemming from the retreat of Greek mercenaries in Asia Minor, described in the *Anabasis* of Xenophon; a difficult, perilous military retreat.
10. *speculum voluptatis:* "Mirror of pleasure" (Latin).
11. *voluptatis ocellus:* "The little eye of pleasure" (Latin).
12. *Breviarium Arcanum:* "Secret/mysterious breviary" (Latin).
13. *cabinets particuliers:* A private room where a man could meet his lover (French).
14. *we will not have to resign ourselves:* "As for women, there is no indication that women of any class were admitted to the Caffe Greco." Margaret Farrand Thorp, "Literary Sculptors in the Caffe Greco," *American Quarterly* 12, no. 2, pt. 1 (Summer 1960), p. 172.
15. *Caffè di Roma:* D'Annunzio is undoubtedly referring to the Caffè Greco in Via de' Condotti, a gathering place of intellectuals and artists, which he often frequented (and which still exists). As women were not encouraged to visit the caffè, Andrea Sperelli would have to "resign" himself to the erotic stimulation of a painting. Many artworks did not survive after the 1890s, so it is unclear whether the two paintings (*Judith* and the *Bather*) actually exist. However, one painting portrays a woman in scanty garments sitting next to a waterfall.
16. *I love you more . . . :* In English in the original.
17. *keepsake:* In English in the original.
18. *Adolphus Jeckyll:* It is commonly accepted by critics that this figure is based on Dante Gabriel Rossetti.

19. *Sibylla palmifera:* "Palm-bearing sibyl" (prophetess). Dante Gabriel Rossetti painted a picture by this name. (Latin.)
20. *Madonna of the Lily:* This could represent Rossetti's painting *Ecce Ancilla Domini,* in which the handmaiden of the Lord is shown with a lily stalk in her hand.
21. *in Boccaccio's story: Decameron,* Day 4, Story 5.
22. *Who would have thought:* In the original, this sentence is in English, but in an English so distorted I deemed it better to correct it, since an Englishwoman, such as Clara Green is, would not speak in such stilted, incorrect language. The original text reads: "Who would have thought we should stand again together, Andrew."
23. *white rose:* In English in the original.
24. *Love me this evening, Andrew!:* In English in the original.
25. *Ecce:* "Behold!"; "Here is" (Latin).
26. *Ancilla Domini, Sibylla palmifera, candida puella:* "Handmaiden of the Lord, Palm-bearing sibyl, pure girl." Could once again be a reference to Dante Gabriel Rossetti's painting *Sibylla palmifera* and his sonnet by the same title, and his painting *Ecce Ancilla Domini.* (Latin.)
27. *Ora pro nobis:* "Pray for us." Response during the litany in church, directed at the Virgin Mary. (Latin.)
28. *chica pero guapa:* Small but pretty (Spanish).
29. *Pinturicchio:* The fifteenth-century painter Bernardo di Betto, who painted Giulia Farnese, the mistress of Pope Alexander VI, above a door in the pope's apartments in the Vatican City. This fresco was considered scandalous and blasphemous, as it depicted Giulia as the Madonna holding the baby Jesus, and the pope holding the baby's foot.
30. *Sala Quinta:* The Fifth Hall, most likely of the Appartamenti Borgia in the Vatican. See http://www.1911encyclopedia.org/Pinturicchio, accessed March 1, 2010.
31. *olla podrida:* A Spanish stew made with various meats, legumes, and vegetables (Spanish).
32. *Sal y pimiento:* "Salt and pepper" (Spanish).

33. *Madame de Parabère:* Marie Madeleine de la Vieuville (1693–1750), wife of the Marquis de Parabère, was the mistress of Philippe II, Regent of France, from 1715 to 1723.

34. *Julia:* This is the Latin form of the name Giulia (deriving from the name of the ancient patrician family "gens Iulia" at Rome, the family of Julius Caesar). "Julia" is pronounced "Yulia," whereas "Giulia" is pronounced as the English name Julia, with a hard *J*.

35. *San Bernardino:* Saint Bernardino of Siena (1380–1444) was a Franciscan priest and theologian who preached all over Italy, seeking to combat lawlessness, strife, and immorality. The play on words that Andrea proceeds to make is a reference to one of the saint's famous sermons against sins of the tongue (e.g., gossip, gluttony, lying, etc.), but Andrea is obviously distorting the saint's pure intent for his own profane ends.

36. *linguatica:* "Tongued" (Latin).

37. *"Rosa linguatica, glube nos":* "Tongued rose, unpeel us" (*glubere* = "peel, strip" in Latin). *Glube* also has more obscene connotations, possibly referring to the foreskin or stimulation of male genitals.

38. *a Violante and an Imperia:* Names of courtesans.

39. *À ma chimère:* "About my chimera" (French).

40. *hetaerae:* Courtesans or concubines in ancient Greece, but distinguished from ordinary prostitutes by their sophistication and the respect they generally garnered from men for their education and influence (Ancient Greek).

41. *Peek Frean:* A brand of biscuits produced by Peek, Frean and Co., established in Britain in 1857.

42. *"Quia nominor Bébé":* "Because my name is Bébé" (Latin).

43. *"Semper parata":* "Always ready," "always prepared" (Latin).

44. *"Diu saepe fortiter":* "For a long time, always bravely/ strongly" (Latin).

45. *"Non timeo dona ferentes":* "I do not fear the bearers of gifts." Play on *"Timeo Danaos et dona ferentes"*— "Beware of Greeks bearing gifts"—from Virgil, *Aeneid*, II; referring to the Trojan Horse. (Latin.)

46. *"Rarae nates cum gurgite vasto":* Were this phrase spelled *Rari nantes in gurgite vasto,* it would mean "only the few swim in whirlpools/the rough sea"; found in Virgil, *Aeneid,* I, 118. However, the way D'Annunzio has spelled this phrase signifies "Between two widely spread buttocks there is a vast whirlpool." (Latin.)
47. *Love me tonight, Andrew!:* Clara Green is speaking in English in the original text.

THIRD BOOK, CHAPTER II

1. *Cui bono?:* "To whose benefit?" (Latin).
2. *Comprends et prends:* "Understand and take" (French).
3. *been familiar with him:* In the original, the text says "he had called him *tu*"—namely, he had addressed the servant with the familiar *tu,* as opposed to the more formal *voi.* This is termed the "T-V Distinction" in sociolinguistics.
4. *Ciociaria:* Area of Italy between Rome and Naples, in the province of Frosinone.
5. *Capuchins:* The Church of Santa Maria della Concezione dei Cappuccini, or Our Lady of the Conception of the Capuchins, is situated on Via Veneto, hence close to where Andrea was walking through Piazza Barberini.
6. *liqueur hawkers: Acquavitari* in Italian. Vendors would go around selling small glasses of various types of liqueur.
7. *Centocelle:* The name derives from Centum Cellae, literally "one hundred rooms," dating back to ancient Rome. In the nineteenth century it was still wild and well stocked with foxes, favored by D'Annunzio himself for his foxhunts. It is a suburb of Rome.
8. *Not at the Four Fountains:* The joke here plays on the fact that Elena's home in Palazzo Barberini is found in Via delle Quattro Fontane (Four Fountains Road), where Andrea attempted vainly to go "hunting," whereas his friends went foxhunting in the area south of Rome called Tre Fontane (Three Fountains).
9. *Menelaus:* Menelaus, husband of Helen (of Sparta, later

of Troy), was cuckolded when Paris lured Helen away from him.

THIRD BOOK, CHAPTER III

1. *Musa paradisiaca palm:* Banana plant.
2. *Quirinal Palace:* Palazzo Quirinale—originally the papal residence, then the residence of Italian kings, now the official residence and workplace of presidents of the Italian Republic.
3. *Montecitorio:* Building that houses the Italian Chamber of Deputies.
4. *Dogali case:* Battle that had taken place the week before, on January 26, 1887, at Dogali in Eritrea, which Italy had colonized in 1879. More than four hundred Italian soldiers died, as well as several hundred Eritreans.
5. *Au pays du Tendre?:* A reference to the 1660 novel *Clélie, Histoire romaine,* by Madeleine de Scudéry, which describes an imaginary country, Tendre. (French.)
6. *Far, far away:* In English in the original.
7. *Via dei Due Macelli:* Literally, "Street of the Two Butcheries" (Italian).
8. *Via del Tritone:* Literally, "Street of the Triton" (Italian).
9. *Nunc:* "Now" (Latin).
10. *"Asperges me":* From Psalms 51:7: "Purify me with hyssop, and I shall be clean: Wash me, and I shall be whiter than snow" (Latin).
11. *Rosa mystica:* "Mystical Rose." At the summit of the Column of the Immaculate Conception in Piazza di Spagna there is a bronze statue of the Madonna, also known as Mystical Rose. The rose is associated with the Virgin Mary, as it is with the rosary. (Latin.)
12. *Piranesi:* Giovanni Battista Piranesi (1720–1778), an Italian artist.
13. *dux:* In the original Italian, *duca,* with the common meaning of "duke." One of the meanings of *duca,* however, is "guide," referring to its ancient derivation from the Latin *dux* (from the verb *ducere,* which in Italian is

condurre, meaning "to lead, guide, conduct"). The words *duce* and *doge* also derive from this. Other ancient meanings of *duca* are spiritual guide, and ruler or leader.

14. *Virgilian excursion:* In the original Italian *vergiliato,* a term coined by D'Annunzio to signify a route followed by two people, as in the case of Dante, who was accompanied or guided by Virgil through Hell and Purgatory in the *Divine Comedy.*

15. *Perugino:* Pietro Perugino (1446–1524), Umbrian artist.

16. *Caffè Nazzarri:* A coffeehouse in Piazza di Spagna that had a pastry shop and confectioner's attached to it.

17. *Barberini factory:* Cardinal Barberini founded a tapestry factory at Palazzo Barberini in Rome in about 1630.

18. *Pieter van Laer:* Pieter van Laer (1592–1642), nicknamed "Il Bamboccio," lived in Rome. His style of humorous/grotesque paintings were called "Bambocciate."

19. *Le papillon s'est envolé:* "The butterfly has flown away" (Bizet's *Tarantelle*) (French).

20. *Fantasia sonatas:* Piano Sonata no. 13 in E-flat major, op. 27, no. 1. *Quasi una fantasia* (In the Manner of a Fantasy); Piano Sonata no. 14 in C-sharp minor, op. 27, no. 2. *Moonlight Sonata.*

21. *Giulietta Guicciardi:* Beethoven's student, with whom he fell in love. He proposed to her but her parents forbade the marriage.

22. *Ariostean architecture:* A reference to Ludovico Ariosto's *Orlando furioso,* in which he creates an enchanted castle that represents illusion, ambiguity, the falsity of ephemeral things, and above all the elusiveness of the objects of men's desires, which, as soon as they are satisfied, make way for new ones.

23. *candida super nivem:* "Whiter than snow." Could be a reference to a poem, "The Nativity of the Blessed Virgin," by Adam of Saint Victor, a twelfth-century French poet who composed liturgical hymns. In the poem, the phrase is *super nivem candida* (white beyond snow).

24. *"incedit per lilia et super nivem":* "Advances through lilies and over snow" (Latin).

25. *"Comis suis obumbrabit tibi et sub comis peccabit":* "He will cover you up with his fleece and he will commit sin under the covers." Possible distortion of Psalms 91:4: "*Scapulis sui obumbrabit tibi, et sub pennies ejus sperabis*": "He will overshadow thee with his shoulders: and under his wings thou shalt trust." (Latin.)
26. *Symphonie en blanc majeur:* "Symphony in White Major," poem by Théophile Gautier (French).
27. *"Pro amore curriculum / Pro amore cubiculum":* "The vehicle or small carriage for love / the bedchamber for love" (Latin).
28. *Fuga:* Ferdinando Fuga, who designed the Palazzo della Consulta between 1732 and 1737.
29. *Dioscuri:* Twin brothers Castor and Polydeuces/Pollux, depicted in great marble statues in Piazza del Quirinale. Mythologically, they are the brothers of Helen of Troy and Clytemnestra, all born to Leda, wife of Tyndareus, seduced by Zeus in the guise of a swan.
30. *the Mani:* Spirits of the dead, revered by the ancient Romans as gods.
31. *Genii:* Plural of Genius. See Second Book, Chapter III, note 3 (Latin).

THIRD BOOK, CHAPTER IV

1. *Pausias:* Reference to poem by Goethe: "Der neue Pausias und sein Blumenmädchen" (The New Pausias and His Flower Maiden) (1797).
2. *"Immer allein sind . . .":* "Lovers are always alone unto themselves in the largest gathering / but when they are a twosome, a third one joins them" (German).
3. *"Amor, ja!":* "Love, yes!"
4. *"A solis ortu usque ad occasum laudabile nomen Helles":* "From the rising up of the sun unto the going down of the same: the name of Helen is to be praised." (The name Helen is to be linked to that of Elena, its Italian equivalent.) The origin of this phrase is liturgical, from Psalms 112:3: *A solis ortu usque ad occasum laudabile nomen Domini:* "From the rising up of the sun unto the going

down of the same: the name of the Lord is to be praised" (Latin).

5. *"I always loved . . .":* Petrarch, *Il Canzoniere,* Sonnet 85, "Io amai sempre ed amo forte ancora."
6. *"Ahora y no siempre":* "Now and not forever" (Spanish).
7. *Die ultima februarii 1885:* "Last day of February 1885" (Latin).
8. *Helena Amyclaea:* Literally, "the Spartan Helen." Reference to Helen of Troy, who was from Sparta. (Latin.)
9. *Academy building:* Villa Medici has housed the French Academy for the arts since 1803.
10. *"with you":* Until this point in the novel, in every exchange between Andrea and Donna Maria, they have used the formal *voi,* which creates social and psychological distance between interlocutors, instead of the familiar (informal) *tu,* which breaks down this barrier and allows for intimacy; "with you" in the original Italian is expressed as *"con te"*—using the familiar *tu* form for the first time.
11. *"And from her lips":* Percy Bysshe Shelley, from the poem "Epipsychidion" (1821).
12. *mystical familiar "you":* Here, Andrea is about to use the familiar form *tu* rather than the formal *voi* with Donna Maria, and it is a significant moment, because it symbolizes a new, unprecedented intimacy.

FOURTH BOOK, CHAPTER I

1. *in quarto:* Reference to format of printed book, namely how the paper on which a volume is printed has been folded, and the size of the original paper. "In folio" means that the paper has been folded once; "in quarto" means that it has been folded twice, producing eight pages. It is also written as "in-4°."
2. *Lampsaque:* Lampsaque was a fictitious publishing house in Paris in the 1700s and 1800s, specializing in erotic material: bibliographical references cite "A Lampsaque [Paris]" followed by the year. It published all libertine material that otherwise would have been subject to

censorship, such as Nerciat's *Les Aphrodites*. This name is that of the town Lampsacus in ancient Greece, home to the god Priapus, and associated with erotica.

3. *Nerciat: 1734:* This reference by D'Annunzio to Andrea (André-Robert) de Nerciat's *Les Aphrodites* is incorrect; all bibliographical references to Nerciat show that he lived from 1739 to 1800, and various sources show the work as dated at 1793 or 1794.
4. *De Concubitu—libri tres:* "On sleeping together—book three" (Latin).
5. *god of Lampsacus:* Here the reference is to the ancient Greek town, origin of the cult of the fertility god Priapus, son of Aphrodite and possibly of Dionysus.
6. *Salve, sancte pater:* Reference to Tibullus's *Elegiae,* I, 4, which begins *"Salve, sancte pater Priape rerum, salve"* (Hail, Priapus, primal father).
7. *his own language:* English.
8. *rictus:* Gaping grimace, open mouth (Latin).
9. *Sicinnide dance:* A dance carried out by satyrs and menads in honor of Dionysus and the goddess Cybele.
10. *De verberatione amatoria:* "On love beating" (Latin).
11. *In Sperelli's imagination:* In this paragraph, D'Annunzio's "borrowings" from other authors become evident. D'Annunzio's knowledge of de Sade's work is derived from the Goncourts' *Journal* and from French translations of the English journalist William T. Stead's articles "The Maiden Tribute of Modern Babylon," serialized in the *Pall Mall Gazette* in 1885. Transcription errors in the French versions are worsened by D'Annunzio: Halfmoon Street (Halfsoon Street in French) becomes Halfousn Street in *Il piacere*. The paragraph refers to shocking practices uncovered by Stead, of pedophilia and child prostitution in London.
12. *Black Army*: This reference is from Stead's "The Maiden Tribute of Modern Babylon," referring to the large numbers of young women recruited to become prostitutes; they are referred to therein as the "Black Army."
13. *Anna Rosemberg*: Anna Rosenberg is referred to in Stead's "Maiden Tribute," with regard to the practice of

strapping down women in order to violate them, in her brothel in Liverpool. Text of novel shows the author's misspelling.

14. *Jefferies woman*: Mary Jeffries (1854–1907) was engaged in running brothels in London, in abducting girls and young women and selling them to foreign countries. Text of novel shows the author's misspelling.

FOURTH BOOK, CHAPTER II

1. *Lucius Verus:* A Roman emperor.
2. *attendre pour atteindre:* "Wait in order to achieve" (French).
3. *"Death is here":* "Death" by Percy Bysshe Shelley, 1824.
4. *"These are two friends":* Shelley's "Epitaph," also inscribed on his grave. The last phrase in the original text is given in English.

MORE DECADENCE FROM PENGUIN CLASSICS

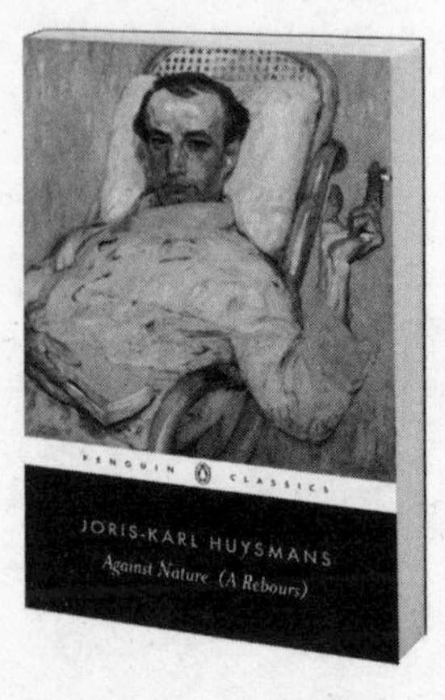

Against Nature (A Rebours)
Joris-Karl Huysmans
ISBN 978-0-14-044763-7

The Damned (Là-Bas)
Joris-Karl Huysmans
ISBN 978-0-14-044767-5

Decadent Poetry
ISBN 978-0-14-042413-3

The Picture of Dorian Gray
Oscar Wilde
ISBN 978-0-14-310614-2

MORE ITALIAN LITERATURE FROM PENGUIN CLASSICS

The Betrothed
Alessandro Manzoni
ISBN 978-0-14-044274-8

Cavalleria Rusticana and Other Stories
Giovanni Verga
ISBN 978-0-14-044741-5

If Not Now, When?
Primo Levi
ISBN 978-0-14-018893-6

Moments of Reprieve
Primo Levi
ISBN 978-0-14-018895-0

MORE ITALIAN LITERATURE FROM PENGUIN CLASSICS

The Monkey's Wrench
Primo Levi
ISBN 978-0-14-018892-9

Six Characters in Search of an Author and Other Plays
Luigi Pirandello
ISBN 978-0-14-018922-3

The Story of My Life
Giacomo Casanova
ISBN 978-0-14-043915-1

THE STORY OF PENGUIN CLASSICS

Before 1946 . . . "Classics" are mainly the domain of academics and students; readable editions for everyone else are almost unheard of. This all changes when a little-known classicist, E. V. Rieu, presents Penguin founder Allen Lane with the translation of Homer's *Odyssey* that he has been working on in his spare time.

1946 Penguin Classics debuts with *The Odyssey,* which promptly sells three million copies. Suddenly, classics are no longer for the privileged few.

1950s Rieu, now series editor, turns to professional writers for the best modern, readable translations, including Dorothy L. Sayers's *Inferno* and Robert Graves's unexpurgated *Twelve Caesars*.

1960s The Classics are given the distinctive black covers that have remained a constant throughout the life of the series. Rieu retires in 1964, hailing the Penguin Classics list as "the greatest educative force of the twentieth century."

1970s A new generation of translators swells the Penguin Classics ranks, introducing readers of English to classics of world literature from more than twenty languages. The list grows to encompass more history, philosophy, science, religion, and politics.

1980s The Penguin American Library launches with titles such as *Uncle Tom's Cabin* and joins forces with Penguin Classics to provide the most comprehensive library of world literature available from any paperback publisher.

1990s The launch of Penguin Audiobooks brings the classics to a listening audience for the first time, and in 1999 the worldwide launch of the Penguin Classics Web site extends their reach to the global online community.

The 21st Century Penguin Classics are completely redesigned for the first time in nearly twenty years. This world-famous series now consists of more than 1,300 titles, making the widest range of the best books ever written available to millions—and constantly redefining what makes a "classic."

The Odyssey continues . . .

The best books ever written

SINCE 1946

CLICK ON A CLASSIC

www.penguinclassics.com

The world's greatest literature at your fingertips

Constantly updated information on more than a thousand titles, from Icelandic sagas to ancient Indian epics, Russian drama to Italian romance, American greats to African masterpieces

•

The latest news on recent additions to the list, updated editions, and specially commissioned translations

•

Original essays by leading writers

•

A wealth of background material, including biographies of every classic author from Aristotle to Zamyatin, plot synopses, readers' and teachers' guides, useful Web links

•

Online desk and examination copy assistance for academics

•

Trivia quizzes, competitions, giveaways, news on forthcoming screen adaptations